THE
ROCK
CRIED
OUT

OTHER BOOKS BY

ELLEN DOUGLAS

A Family's Affairs

Black Cloud White Cloud

Where the Dreams Cross

Apostles of Light

THE ROCK CRIED OUT

BY ELLEN DOUGLAS

Harcourt Brace Jovanovich

New York and London

Requests for permission to make copies
of any part of the work should be mailed to:
Permissions, Harcourt Brace Jovanovich, Inc.
757 Third Avenue, New York, N.Y. 10017

Printed in the United States of America

Library of Congress Cataloging in Publication Data
Douglas, Ellen, pseud.
The rock cried out.
I. Title.
PZ4.D7345Ro [PS3554.0825]   813'.5'4   79-87474
ISBN 0-15-178322-5

First edition

B C D E

For Emma and Bert

ACKNOWLEDGMENT

The author wishes to express her gratitude for support during the writing of this book from the National Endowment for the Arts.

*"I went to the rock to hide my face.
The rock cried out, 'No hiding place.'
No hiding place down there."*

THE
ROCK
CRIED
OUT

I GOT OFF the bus at the intersection, wearing my old army surplus trench coat, carrying my backpack, my portable typewriter, and a suitcase full of books and papers, and walked two blocks to the overpass through which the road ran out toward Chickasaw Ridge. I figured it would be easy to thumb a ride as far as the front gate. I had stood there only a minute or two watching the sun go down, dull red behind heavy clouds, before a car stopped, a white VW with a young girl in it. Her dark hair was long and shining and on both hands she wore silver rings set with turquoise, and, around her neck, a silver chain. With my hand on the door handle, I bent down and looked in at her.

"I thought you were my brother thumbing a ride home," she said. "You look like my brother."

"I *am* thumbing a ride home," I said.

"Where do you live?"

"Chickasaw Ridge."

"You're thumbing the wrong way," she said. "They've finished the new ramp now and blocked off the old entrance to the road. This way you'll end up back on the bypass, headed west."

"Thanks," I said, picking up my bag.

"Get in," she said. "I'll take you around to the new ramp." In the car she looked me over with an opaque, spaced-out smile. "I didn't know any freaks lived at Chickasaw Ridge," she said.

"Come *on*," I said.

We whipped under the overpass, down the frontage road a block, up a ramp on the other side, and a quarter of a mile down the bypass to the next exit. She pulled off on the shoulder and smiled at me again. "You might get where you're going from here," she said. "Good luck."

I got out and reached into the backseat for my suitcase and typewriter.

"How long since you've been out to Chickasaw Ridge?" she said.

"A good while."

"They're square out there, man."

"Yeah, I know," I said.

"Take care of yourself." With a vague wave of her hand, she smiled and drove away and left me standing there.

The sun was still above the horizon. As I stood on the ramp looking around me, a cold wind came up and blew dust and leaves scratching and spinning along the aggregate shoulder. Below me to the west and south the scrambled edges of Homochitto bordered the access road: black slums, a huge new hospital set in an expanse of frost-grayed grass, Gulf and Texaco stations, and a Sheraton Motor Inn sign towering up into the streaky sky; while to the east, beyond the end of the ramp, the Chickasaw road passed between a welding supply warehouse and the concrete desert surrounding an unfinished mall; then it narrowed, curved, and disappeared into a blind opening between shale banks overhung by dark, squat live-oak trees. I walked down the ramp to the Chickasaw road and stood waiting.

A green Mercury passed and I raised my thumb. I saw black faces: kids, college age, and then something—a Coke bottle—flew past my head, hit the road sign beside me, and shattered. I was standing a little behind the sign, fortunately, and the fragments ricocheted away from me.

Shit! What the fuck is this?

They drove on. Someone—a woman—leaned out the window

4

and shouted back at me. I couldn't make out what she said.

I shook the folds of my trench coat, the sleeves, to make sure there was no glass in them. My heart was pounding.

Cars passed. No one picked me up. Then I heard wheels and the hum of an engine on the ramp behind me and turned to put up my thumb again, to put on my "I'm harmless and lovable" smile. It was the same carful of black students: they had circled around and come back. The driver, braking, going no more than fifteen, passed me (I had stepped behind the sign to protect myself), pulled over onto the shoulder, and backed. I glanced around. Anybody near who might give me a hand? Only the cars above and behind us on the bypass, nobody traveling under forty-five or fifty.

The driver got out, walked toward me, crunching glass underfoot, looked me over. He was light-skinned, handsome, in his middle twenties. "Hey, man, we're sorry," he said. "She didn't see you standing there. OK?"

"Sure," I said.

"You want a ride?"

I looked at him, looked at the car. There were two young girls in the back and in the front another man, a kid in his late teens.

The driver reached out, offered the black power grip, and I accepted it. "We didn't mean to hassle you," he said. "She's a little bit stoned."

"Sure. OK." I picked up my suitcase and he took the typewriter, and we loaded the gear in his trunk.

The guy sitting in the front climbed out and got in the back. I got in by the driver and turned. "My name's Alan," I said. The girl sitting behind me giggled. The other said, "Hi." The boy said nothing. We pulled out on the road, the driver talking, conciliatory. He didn't hate honkies.

They were on their way back to Jackson, he said, from a week in New Orleans. The others were students at Jackson State; he was a graduate instructor. They were all sorry about the Coke bottle. It was an accident. Where was I headed?

I felt a feathery touch on my hair. Or did I?

"I lived in Jackson a couple of years," I said. "Worked at Whitfield."

"The loony bin," one of the girls said.

"Yeah? What did you do?" the driver said.

"Orderly."

5

I felt the touch on my hair again. Jackson State. I had not been there in the spring when the students were murdered. I could not bring myself to speak of that time.

Again.

I turned slowly. For all I knew, she might have a snake in her pocket which she intended to put down my neck.

But she was staring at my hair, reaching out, empty-handed. Beside her, the other guy had put his arms around the second girl and they were turned away, murmuring into each other's ears.

"Do you want to feel it?" I said.

She nodded and giggled again and I laughed, too, all the while glancing at the driver out of the corner of my eye to see how he would take this exchange. He said nothing, kept his eye on the road, while she stroked my hair, took a curl between thumb and finger, pulled it out and let it go, touched my reddish beard. "I like it," she said.

"I like yours." Her hair was cut in a perfect short natural. It was that deep black that glitters with light like crystals of coal.

"Where are you going?" the driver said again.

I turned back. "Just down the road about ten miles."

"You *live* in this town?" he asked incredulously.

"Sometimes," I said. "Out from it." And then, "You're bound to know I'm from *around* here. You must've known that as soon as I opened my mouth."

"This town is the worst," he said. "Worse than Yazoo City. Or Jackson." He looked again at the beard, the trench coat. "What do they think about you?"

"I stay in the country," I said. "Out near Chickasaw Ridge. There aren't very many white people out there."

The girl with the sparkling hair had stopped touching me and leaned back. I looked again at her. Her eyes had lost the stoned, inward look. She stared at me, sullen.

"They burned Mercy Seat Church out there the summer of 'sixty-four," the driver said.

"I know." It did not occur to me to ask how he happened to know. I took it for granted that people like him would know the name of every church in Mississippi that got burned the summer of '64—all twenty-seven of them.

"Were you living around here then?"

"I was living in the Delta," I said. "Besides, I was only fifteen. I didn't know what was going on." In a sense that was true.

There was silence in the car. The lovers in the backseat had disentangled themselves and were staring at me.

We had been whirling along the winding two-lane black-topped road deep between sheer loess bluffs, traveling as fast as the car would take the curves; and now we were climbing toward Chickasaw Ridge, narrow backbone of the hills, where straggling bands of Chickasaw Indians had made their camps before they crossed the river on the way westward, after the Treaty of Pontotoc Creek robbed them of their lands.

"The other side of this hill we're going up," I said; "that's where I get off."

The driver began to brake the car. At the top of the ridge, we passed the road on the left that led back to Mercy Seat Church; you could just make out its ruined, dissolving shape in the dusk. The fire-blackened joists and studs leaned inward under the collapsed roof and a tangle of bare vines (maypop, probably, and trumpet and poison ivy) that looked as if they might have been planted to conceal the location of the new church deep in the grove of pine trees behind the old one.

"That's Mercy Seat," I said. I had not meant to point it out.

"Yeah."

By the time we reached the bottom of the hill, we were crawling along at twenty.

"Here to the left," I said. "Here's where I get out. There's room to pull off the road by the gate."

He pulled off and stopped with his headlights trained on the Chickasaw gate: the cedar posts, twice as thick as telephone poles, that my Great-uncle Dennison had turned on his wood lathe (I had been here when he rigged the lathe to the flywheel of the tractor and shaped them, after he, Sam Daniels, and Noah, Jr., had cut the trees and let them season a year in the barn) and the gate of poplar slats painted the color of dried blood.

DENNISON MCLAURIN—TREE FARM, a small faded sign by the gate read; and another nailed to a fence post: POSTED. KEEP OUT. NO HUNTING. NO FISHING.

"You *own* this place?" the driver of the car asked.

"No," I said. "I just stay here sometimes." This was not what I had meant my arrival to be like, not at all. I opened the door of the car and got out. He gave me the key and I unloaded my gear from the trunk and handed the key back to him. "Thanks for the lift," I said. "Good luck." *Right on* stuck decently in my throat.

7

"Same to you, brother," the driver said.

The girl leaned out. "I *meant* to hit you," she said.

"I'm sorry," I said.

The driver started the car, backed, turned, bore down once on his horn, and pulled out onto the road, flooring the accelerator so abruptly that he spattered me with dirt and gravel as he went. But I had already turned away and was lifting down the chain from the nail in the top of the gate to let myself in; at least the gravel didn't hit me in the face. I shrugged, gave my trench coat a shake, and brushed a few bits of dirt out of my hair.

That's the way things are and I already know it, I said to myself. Forget it.

I slammed the gate and started up the road to the house. Far off I heard a whippoorwill mourn and suddenly the piercing shriek of a screech owl, a brief rustling flurry in the leaves that choked the ditch on the left-hand side of the road, and the scream of a caught mouse. I stopped short, listening, the hairs rising on my arms. No more birdcalls. It was dark now: not yet six o'clock, but in January it gets dark early. The night was quiet except for the distant steady tocking of an oil well pump. I walked on more slowly, a quarter of a mile up the winding, graveled road, rutted by winter rains and walled in on both sides by deep woods, through a second gate that opened out on the moon-washed lawn, the dark scattered shapes of trees, and the house beyond.

I had never arrived here alone, after dark, with the house empty —always before had thought of it as a place crowded with people: with my own family—my sister and brother, our parents, my cousins Lester and Dennison Chipman and, before she died, their sister Phoebe (my cousins were the children of my father's sister Denny and her husband), my Aunt Leila, and my grandmother and grand- father; and with the black people who came and went—Sam Daniels, his father Noah, and all their kin and connections. The place then had belonged to my grandfather and my Great-uncle Dennison, and during my childhood all the family used it for summer vacations.

In those days, when one came in at dusk from an afternoon's fishing on the lake, the windows would be streaming yellow light onto the long porch across the front of the house; and on the lawn children with Mason jars would be chasing fireflies (there were still fireflies here in this place, far from cotton poison) or unsaddling horses and rubbing them down on the horse lot out back; and on the porch the adults would be gathering for drinks, stepping out again in their lifelong complex dance of conjunction and parting.

But the house was dark now, and silent. I stopped inside the second gate, put down my suitcase and typewriter, and looked into the sky, orienting myself to the wheeling stars. I was facing north and could see, directly above the black bulk of the house, Cepheus and Cassiopeia, "that starred aethiop queen that strove to see her beauty's praise above the sea nymphs. . . ." I tended at that time in my life to quote Milton and Blake and, if I were writing a letter and knew no quotations appropriate to my context, to look up a few in Bartlett. To the east of Cassiopeia I could see Andromeda (curious, one never thought of Andromeda as "aethiop"—as *black*) and, lower down, Perseus, the hero, carrying the bloody Gorgon's head. Cozy family gathering. Higher up and to the west of Cepheus was the Northern Cross. What planets were in what constellations tonight? I looked around to the southeast for Saturn, which should be rising, but then picked up my bags and walked on. There would be time enough this winter to watch the stars.

I'd been living all summer and fall that year in Boston with a woman named Miriam and working in a sugar refinery. In December I'd decided to go home. I thought I'd had enough for a while of cities and factories and punching a time clock. I wanted a vacation in the country, wanted to be alone. At the time I believed I was a poet and was sure my brain was teeming with poems my ears couldn't catch for the traffic noises outside my window in Roxbury and the roar of machinery at the Israel Putnam Sugar Company, Inc. I spent Christmas in the Delta with my parents and on the day after New Year's rode the bus down Highway 61; past the national cemetery at Vicksburg, the Yankee dead lying under grids of gravestones like so many sheets of graph paper; and up into the dissolving hills, bones of the oldest mountains in the Western world.

Winter in Homochitto County might sound to a man from Boston as if it would be pleasant; but south Mississippi is not Florida. In December rain begins to fall; sleet blows in on a raw north wind;

9

in the crawl spaces under old-fashioned country houses water pipes freeze and burst. No one in the family goes to Chickasaw in January and February except my Aunt Leila and me. We like it then, or for that matter, any time. But especially in winter, perhaps *because* it's forbidding then, no place for a vacation. The days and nights are a long, peaceful, and (it still seems to me) purifying battle against cold and damp: bringing in wood, laying the fire, building it up, keeping it fed, banking it at night, and, next morning, raking away the ashes from the buried coals and blowing them to life.

Besides, that winter I was fleeing the city and dreaming of solitude and inviting my soul; dreaming, too, of wintry woods— of the pervasive smell, not of boiling syrup and automobile exhaust fumes, but of cedar and pine; of smilax and jasmine twisting dark green up into the bare dogwood and walnut and cherry trees; of oaks under shawls of gray moss that turn out when you look closely to be throbbing with pale green life; of the winter silence, above all, broken only by the voices of birds that stay with us all year: the towhee, the crow, the mourning goatsucker. I knew the house would be empty—dove and quail seasons over, the dry bronze days of November and early December past, and winter lowering from a heavy sky.

January 1971: seven years ago. Our high school biology teacher once told us that all the molecules in the human body are replaced every seven years; so I am not the same man I was then—not just seven years older, but wholly different. Maybe now this new man can make sense of all the tangled events of that winter, can make peace with his younger self. (And make peace, too, with a still earlier time, an earlier self. For, like Jacob waiting twice seven years for Rachel, I have another seven-year term to lay to rest. All that I want to think about, to write about, began for me when I was fifteen—the summer of 1964.)

By then I was already used to living in a world where terrible things happened every day: I recall the mornings of my childhood, my father at the breakfast table opening the morning paper; the very air, the coffee-and-bacon-fragrant air, had the smell of violence in it. He opened the paper to see what new terrible thing had happened yesterday, not in Hungary or Russia, or even in Dallas or Birmingham, but down the road, in Greenwood maybe, or Itta Bena, or Chickasaw Ridge. That was the way things were.

Once I asked my friend Sam Daniels how he managed to stay clear of the Klan during those years, if they'd ever given him any trouble. Sam is black and some people would say he is quarrelsome. He isn't humble, anyhow, and never has been.

He thought a minute (editing out, I realized later, what he didn't want to talk about) and then he said, "Not much, Alan." He was silent again. Then he grinned. "I remember one time," he said, "I came home from town, turned in out there at the gate, got down to open it, and found two white crosses painted on the gateposts. That was the sign, you know, you're supposed to do right or else. I went on up to my house, sat down, and thought about it a little while; and then I called Old Man Selman Boykin. He was Supervisor for our beat then. Told him I had something I wanted to show him.

" 'All right, Sam,' he says. 'I'll be coming out to Chickasaw Ridge tomorrow morning. You going to be home?'

" 'Sure,' I said.

" 'I'll stop by,' he says, and he did.

"He was an old man by then, white-headed, but still spry. Always wanted to know what was going on. 'Well, Sam,' he says, 'how you doing?'

" 'Doing fine, Mr. Boykin,' I said. 'Doing *fine*. I got something I want to show you that you might be interested in.' Climbed up in his pickup with him and we drove down to the gate and I got out and he got out and we stood there and looked at them crosses and he didn't say a word.

" 'Now, what you reckon those are?' I say, and I smiled at him as sweet as cream.

" 'Well, Sam,' he says, 'looks like they put their mark on you, don't it?'

" 'Ain't it lucky,' I said, 'they didn't come in the gate onto my land and put their mark on my house? I mean, considering what a good shot I am and all.'

" 'You right about that,' he says. He'd been squirrel hunting with me more than once.

"I suppose he spread the word. I never had any more trouble after that."

Sam was *ready,* you might say.

And people like the Boykins and the Levitts. They've always been ready—to take risks, to stand on *their own feet,* as Henry Levitt said to me the day he knocked me down at Calloway's store.

A quarrelsome lot, all of us, white and black.

11

But I was very young in 1971—only twenty-two—and I thought that I could stay clear of other people's quarrels, even thought I could set an example. I would have no part of *anybody's* violence.

Now—now, as I said, I am not the same man. But I would like to imagine myself back into his shoes, his skin (shoes size thirteen-E lace-up work boots bought for six ninety-five at Harry's Discount Shoe Store, the soles half eaten away by the syrup on the floor of Israel Putnam's sugar refinery; skin made pallid by a Boston winter); and I suppose the reason is that, molecules or no molecules, he is still important to me. I'm stuck with him, have to make myself over every day out of memories he hands me.

He was tall and skinny, that young man—six-two and maybe a hundred and sixty-five pounds—and his feet in their lace-up boots didn't look quite so large as you might think they would, seen in relation to the body, but of a size to keep him upright and reasonably steady in a strong wind. His face was long and hungry-looking, the nose straight, the eyes that shade of light, almost silvery blue that novelists like to assign to murderers, the brow wide and bony, the hair very curly, very blond, and already beginning to recede at the temples, the beard reddish. (He was too vain to seek the advice of a dermatologist about his premature baldness and too vain to try to conceal it, but not too vain to examine his hairline with sad attention whenever he looked in the mirror.)

We thought of ourselves in those days as more grown-up than most American generations had been at their majority. We had taken part, after all, in the so-called sexual revolution—had screwed around whenever we had the opportunity; or, if we'd been choosy or timid or unlucky, we'd had plenty of chances to hear the stories (and in the next room the moans and whispers and thrashing about) of our friends and acquaintances. We'd won the battle for parietal rights (those having to do with the walls of our dorms, not our craniums). Not only that. We were special. We'd taken part in the anti-war movement and, some of us (not me, except in the most marginal way), in the civil rights movement. About most things we knew we were right.

Being right has turned out to be less useful to me than I thought it would be. It was "being right" (or blindness, or self-absorption— take your choice) that made me fail that winter to try to fit what was going on around me into the pattern it cried out for—a pattern I hadn't put my attention on. In the same way our parents,

I suppose, were right about the Second World War—and look what they did with themselves and the patterns they overlooked in the world.

But never mind my shortcomings. I have a story to tell, to make my peace with, about the young man who went home to Mississippi, to Chickasaw Ridge, to the deep woods, and invited his soul; about what happened to him and what he learned that year; and about what had happened in the past to people he knew and cared for.

TWO

I LET MYSELF into the house, turned on a light, and put my typewriter on the dining-room table, breathing the familiar air: the smell of age, emptiness, damp plaster, and ashes. The chill struck through my trench coat as through paper. In winter an old house like this, empty, untended, gets colder than the outdoors; the log walls under their clapboard sheathing are like thick slabs of ice, and the plaster is clammy with icy sweat. It takes days of roaring fires to make it dry and warm.

I got my flashlight from the backpack and stepped out onto the back porch into the overwhelming fragrance of cedar. Standing at the edge of the porch, I flashed my light around the yard. To the west of the corncrib one of the cedar trees was gone—the one where Sam had treed the bobcat when I was seven. It had been dying for years. I flashed my light across the corncrib and the old outdoor kitchen (now the tack room) and saw that someone had sawed it up and split it and piled it against the kitchen wall for kindling. Next to the cedar was a stack of oak and pecan sheltered from rain under sheets of corrugated tin, and on the porch of the kitchen was a keg that would, if I was lucky, be full of fat pine chips.

I began to bring in wood and kept at it until I had enough on the porch for a couple of days and enough against the wall in the dining room to last out tonight and start tomorrow. Then I laid and lit a fire with pine chips (so fat you could start them with a match) on the bottom, a few pieces of cedar above (thinking, as I laid it, that I must remember how dangerous cedar was, how it popped), and oak and pecan on top.

Afterwards I looked around me, deciding how I would arrange things for myself. I would live here in the dining room; no point in keeping more than one fire going and this fireplace had the best draft. The tiny indoor kitchen that had been, at some dim time in the past, a pantry, I could warm with the electric cook stove. There was a long rough dining table made by Uncle Dennison of cherry planks sawn from a tree cut in his own woods and screwed onto a trestle frame with flat-headed iron screws put in from the top side—every beautiful board ruined. Uncle D. would have said (after he said, "Eh? Eh? What's that?") that cherry is a good close-grained wood for a table, that screws make a strong join, and that the top side is more accessible than the bottom for putting them in.

Anyhow, the table was sturdy. I could use one end for spreading out my work, the other for eating. But the room was crowded: a monstrous sideboard with scrolled and mirror-backed shelves attached to its marble top stood against one wall and three collapsing overstuffed armchairs, their guts spilling out of tattered upholstery, against another; the table was surrounded by a dozen cane-bottomed dining-room chairs. I stacked all but one of the caned chairs out of my way in what my grandmother—my father's mother—called the "parlor," dragged one of the armchairs into the nearest bedroom, and brought back a floor lamp and a roll-away bed, which I opened and made up with sheets, blankets, and the heaviest wool comforter I could find.

By this time Sam Daniels, whose house was a hundred yards from ours, had seen the light in the dining-room window; as I straightened up from making the bed, I heard his heavy halting step on the back porch. Without knocking, he opened the door and looked in. He had a worn hickory stick held in his hand like a weapon and at his heels a feisty-looking mongrel. It was only a month since he'd been released from the state penitentiary at Parchman.

"Alan! I couldn't think who'd be out here," he said. "Minute there, I was afraid somebody had busted in. Especially when I didn't see no car. But I might've known it would be you—this time of year." Then, "Out!" He gave the dog a shove through the door with his stick and closed it.

"Yeah," I said. "It's me."

I crossed the room and we shook hands, grinning at each other. Glad as I was to see him (and even though my father had prepared me for the change in him), I could scarcely keep the shock from my face. He was a different man—looked inches shorter than when I had seen him more than three years earlier, and walked with a rolling, listing gait like a sailor on the slanting deck of a ship. He *was* shorter, of course; the left leg had been so badly shattered they had had to take out an inch of bone and the right hip socket had been damaged. His hair was different, too—he was wearing it in a short Afro now. It had been shaved at Parchman, I suppose, and was beginning to grow. He had used to wear it pulled back and plaited into a kind of short pigtail almost like a scalp lock. I never saw another black man wear his hair that way. His face was worn and drawn with pain; one eyelid drooped over his blind eye.

Even so, he was still strong—and handsome (although I was young enough to think him almost too old to be called "handsome"—he was, after all, in his forties). His arms and shoulders were heavy and muscular. He'd always had the strongest arms in Homochitto County; a year hauling his crippled legs along, at first on crutches and then with a walker, had made them even stronger. He still had that hawkish Indian look: the high-bridged thin nose, the cheekbones wide apart, the lips almost uncontrolledly sensual, the one good eye brilliant and alert. All with skin so black you could scarcely believe he had a drop of Indian blood.

But his father, Noah, had always said that *his* grandmother (a woman who had been "brought down from West Virginia and sold on the block like a piece of horse meat," as Noah never failed to tell me, always in the same words, as if he might be singing a song) had been a black Indian and his other grandmother a white Indian. The Indian blood was there, then, and, evidently, a tinge of white. To me, though, the Indian had always seemed even more evident in his walk than in his face. I once read how the men of the Six

Nations put one foot before the other so precisely that they step in their own moccasin prints; and that nowadays they are mostly high steel men, walking along steel girders a hundred feet up in the air as confidently as I would cross a yard-wide footbridge. That was how Sam had walked.

Looking at him now, towering over him, I remembered all of a sudden seeing him a summer day years ago looming up over *me* like a giant, as he stepped out along a slimy fallen log that lay across a ravine at the back of the place; while I, terrified, hitched myself along behind him, sitting with a leg hanging down on either side of the log, wondering if I would lose my balance. I saw myself gazing up at his impossibly strong and easy figure and then, in a panic (was the ravine six feet deep or sixty?), clutching the log with both arms and, in the still, ferny pool below me, seeing my own thin white face and tight cap of blond curls and my huge foreshortened feet reflected for a moment in the brown water.

Sam would never walk a log again.

But here he was and I was glad to see him. We kept shaking hands and grinning at each other; then he came into the room, took off his worn army field jacket, sat down in the armchair that I had pulled up to the fire for him, and immediately warned me about how dangerous the cedar was, how it might pop out and set the house on fire.

"I was thinking that, myself, when I laid the fire."

But he went on talking, repeating himself in a deep strong voice with a trace of hoarseness in it. "You got to be careful how you use it. For kindling only. And don't leave the house with no cedar fire burning. Don't never leave it. You stay right here and watch it." He has a tendency to repeat himself—a habit that may come partly from the notion that you are not listening to him, not paying attention (as he himself doesn't always pay attention), and partly from the repetitive rhythm, the diurnal, seasonal movement of his life in the country—a kind of ebb and flow, a rising and setting that invites, requires, a repetitive cast of mind.

I went out to the refrigerator in the back hall, found a six-pack (you'll usually find someone has left at least a couple of beers the last time he was here), opened two cans, and brought them back. Then I pulled the other armchair up to the fire, sat down, and we began to talk.

It wasn't so difficult as it might have been. I had written to him every three or four months while he was at Parchman and I north in school and, later, doing my C.O. at the state mental hospital at Whitfield, and I'd heard from him a few times, once, shortly after he got out of the prison hospital where he spent the first four months he was at Parchman (he'd been shot trying to escape when he was being transferred from the Homochitto County jail to the state prison—both his legs broken and one eye shot out). This is what he wrote: *God visited me in there, Alan. Hadn't come, I'd be dead. I never would've made it on my own.* I had not known what to answer. God had never visited me. I sent Sam a package— food, cards, cigarettes, magazines—and said I was thinking about him, we all were.

Later he wrote: *I'm still here, Alan, sweating it out, and it seems a long time, a long time dead and buried; but I reckon I'll make it through. Your daddy's already started working on a parole for me, so he says, and I know he'll do the best he can.*

Everybody in the family kept in touch in a desultory way, sending a package now and then, feeling, I suppose, some vague, half-resentful guilt. They would have had to have skins like crocodiles not to feel guilty, I thought, "although it wasn't our fault, God knows," my father said.

My father and his sisters, my Aunts Leila and Denny, pulled what strings they could (we have about as much political power in this state as any other anonymous, reasonably honest, white, middle-class family—which is to say, very little) to get him out early. It was easier than it might have been because his body was so broken he was no threat to anybody. Then, for the same reason, the federal government did not bring him to trial.

There was never any doubt that he would come back to Chickasaw. Denny's husband, Lester Chipman, opposed it; but with the rest of the family (my father, Leila, Denny, and my grandmother) in favor, he mostly kept his opinion to himself. I don't suppose it crossed their minds (my father's and my aunts') to be afraid of Sam, even considering all that had happened. They all had their private convictions, though none of them might say so, about *why* it had happened. But the occasion had been freakish and "that was all over now," long past. Sam had "learned his lesson." They still needed him—no one they had hired to fill his place as caretaker, forester, and guardian had "worked out."

As for Sam, he would never have thought of going anyplace else.

Now he looked at me with a sideways pursed-up grin, the good eye merry and squinting, the lid on the other drooping like a wink, and said, "You here all by yourself, Alan? No girl friend?"

"Yeah, I'm by myself," I said. "I'm going to stay out here awhile. Two or three months, maybe. Or longer."

He looked puzzled. "What for?" he said.

"What do *you* stay out in the country for, Sam?"

"Oh, you know. . . . I never cared about town. You know that. Too cramped up. I got to have room to swing free. And here . . ." He hesitated. Then, "In spite of everything that happened, I feel like Chickasaw's mine. I got to keep roaming over it and I got to have room to swing free. That's why it come over me to run off on the way to Parchman, and they shot me. It just come over me to roam. But that ain't the case with you."

I shrugged. "Chickasaw is mine and isn't mine, too. And you're not the only one who needs room to roam."

He gave me a look and said no more about the place. But I knew he thought I was just talking—that I knew nothing of what he meant. "What about a girl?" he said. "That's what I'm asking you. You got a girl?"

"She's up North teaching. She can't come down."

"More than one girl in the world."

"I like this one a lot," I said. "I've got my mind on *her.*"

"When I was your age . . ." He sighed and broke off. Then, "I could fuck all night and work all day and never know I'd been working. Come home, round up the cows, and eat, and then off again looking for more. Lie down in the field or in the back of a car with the first girl I could find. Stars shining up there and girls shining down here." He smiled. "It don't do to stick to one, young as you are. Time enough for that."

"You think I could get a girl to come out here in the middle of winter?" I said.

He considered. "It might seem spooky to a city girl," he said, "with the moss and all and the house so old and empty. To somebody not used to it. It ain't *Chicago*, I can see that. I had plenty of trouble in my time trying to *keep* one out here, but . . ." He looked me over. "You ought to be able to get one to come once," he said, "and then you could move on to another." We both laughed and then he added, "I'll be glad to give you the loan of my car. You ain't good-looking enough to get one to *walk* out here."

"OK," I said. "I might take you up on it." I thought of the dark-haired girl and her turquoise and silver rings. Sex—the lack of it —was going to be a problem. We were silent awhile, watching the fire, breathing the pervasive fragrance of cedar. He got up and put on a couple of oak logs. Showers of sparks flew up from the popping cedar, caught on the corrugations of the iron reflectors at the back of the fireplace, and pulsed like tiny red signal lights.

"We got plenty cedar since I cut that tree," he said, "but you see what I mean about how it pops. Now, don't go to sleep with it like that. Bank it before you go to sleep."

"Sam, I was thinking awhile ago, when I first came in and saw that that old tree was down . . . Do you remember the day the dogs treed the bobcat? And you climbed up and caught him?"

"Yeah." He stared into the fire for a time. "I give the skin to Timmie," he said.

"Phoebe cried," I said. "She wanted it for a pet."

"I don't remember Phoebe crying. I remember I give the skin to Timmie."

The bottom log collapsed into glowing coals and the heat on my face made me move my chair back from the fire.

Phoebe . . .

It had been a spring day, the thicket by the lake, of blackberry briars and mock orange covered with fragile white bloom, the smell of cut grass and fresh manure in the air. Had we been fishing? I heard the dogs bark. Without warning, a bobcat loped across the dam. The dogs, yapping and yowling, burst out of the ravine after the cat; and we ran after the dogs; then we were all in the back-yard—dogs, children, and grown people—yelling and milling around the cedar tree.

"You were a hero to me then," I said. "Up there, shinnying along a limb, and the bobcat on the limb below you. I *couldn't* remember all of it, could I? It must partly be hearing people talk about it. But I see the cat reaching up, hanging on with three legs, and raking at you with the fourth."

"I was a hero to myself," he said. "One reason I never could stay out of trouble."

We had told each other this story before, hadn't we? More than once? But each of us went on with his part of it, as it if were new— or perhaps more as if the retelling would knot up those frail strands that tied us to our lives, to our pasts, to Chickasaw. One day in the telling, I thought, some new thing would be revealed and we would gaze at each other, amazed, brothers reunited or enemies revealed.

"Why didn't you stay on the ground and shoot him?" I said.

"Didn't want to ruin the skin, probably," he said. "And then, it didn't look to me like it would be no problem to get him. He was a young cat, not even full grown, and the dogs scared him up, and he didn't have no experience, and he come up out of the ravine when he should've gone the other way and run up here in the yard and then he panicked and run up that tree. You remember that tree had a hive of bees in it?"

"Yeah."

"Bees commenced buzzing and raising a ruckus and the cat got a couple of stings. Climbing around up there, scared and hurting. I figured I could take him. Then, too, I might've been scared he'd get away if I went to get my gun. I wanted that skin for Timmie. I was courting her then. Nailed it to the side of her house." He cocked his good eye at me. "Grabbed a pair of gloves and a croker sack and a rope out of the tack room," he said. "Shinnied up that tree. I wasn't scared of no bees. They never would sting me. Or, if they did, it didn't hurt no more than a mosquito bite. Flung the sack over him and tied him up and threw him down before he knew what hit him. Got some honey, too, same time. Leila pitched me a bucket and I cut off all that was hanging on the outside of the tree."

He shook his head. "I wasn't thinking about Phoebe," he said gloomily. "Nobody but Timmie. I was still a crazy kid. Cared for nothing but women—and maybe seeing to my cows and horses." Then, heavily, "No more tree-climbing and such foolishness for me," he said. "They took my strength. My sight. My spirit. I'm not the same man, it seems to me sometimes."

"Sam, what was it like at Parchman?" I said, and when he didn't answer, "I don't want to make you talk about it, if you don't want to."

"The worst of it was in the beginning, after they shot me, laying there so long with the block and tackle and the sandbags to my legs and my eyes bandaged up. Couldn't see at all because at first they had both of 'em bandaged. And couldn't move a tap. I lay up there . . . Like I wrote you afterwards, I had time to do some thinking. I *prayed*. And it's true, God come to me, brought me through. Later . . ." He shrugged. "Far as the work was concerned, I been farming all my life. They put me on a tractor. I couldn't have done nothing required me to stand up all day. The nights . . ." Again he moved his massive shoulders. "I could still take care of myself. But what about you, Alan? What you going to *do* out here? I mean, in the middle of winter and all."

"Well," I said, "you know that house over there where Leona Carter used to live?"

He nodded.

"Nobody's been living in it for three years. Not since . . ." I hesitated. "Since they leased the land to the government."

"Yeah. Leona's rented some land on Duck Pond now. Moved her cows over there and she's living in town. That house ain't fit to live in, nohow. Hasn't been since the old man died and your people quit keeping up the houses on the place."

"Well, Daddy and Leila said it would be OK for me to tear down the abandoned house by the SPASURSTA" (this was the navy's satellite tracking station, built on land leased from us) "and use the boards to patch up Leona's house. I want a place of my own to stay, where, if I'm here, I'll be out of everybody's way. I'm going to keep on spending some time here off and on."

"You're like the old man," he said. "Your Uncle Dennison, I mean, not your granddaddy. You don't watch out, you'll end up a loner like him."

"That wouldn't be so bad," I said.

"What does Lester Chipman think about you fixing up that house?" Sam said. He never called my uncle-in-law "Mr. Chipman" or "Mr. Lester," but always, as if it were a Russian given name and patronymic, "Lester Chipman." I had never heard him say "sir," nor had I ever heard him seem to be discourteous. He could arrange a conversation to suit himself—one way, if he chose, he could either dazzle you or put you to sleep with repetitions.

"We didn't exactly ask him," I said. "Denny seemed to think it would be OK."

Silence again. I got up and went into the back hall and brought us each another beer. "I was thinking about planting a garden in the spring," I said. "I might stay all summer."

"*You?* What do you know about gardening?"

"Well, I was thinking I could ask your advice," I said.

"Won't be long now before you could put in greens. Onions. Cabbage sets. They go in early. Beets, too."

"Where would be the best place to put it?" I said.

He sat there looking grim, thinking, I supposed, of what the place had been in the past, when Uncle Dennison had been alive and there had been five hundred acres or more to work, besides the four hundred in woods: room enough for our cattle and his and Noah's, for cornfields and pasture and garden strips. Now, except for the oil well sites, the fire lanes, and the hundred acres of the Space Surveillance Station, the fields were planted with close-set rows of pine trees.

"The only cleared land left on the place is my garden," he said. "The horse lot and pasture. That fifteen-acre strip on the other side of the SPASURSTA where Daddy's got a garden and pasture for his mule and milk cows. Aside from the fire lanes. We graze the mule and cows some on the fire lanes."

"Are you going to put in a garden this year?" I asked.

"I've got an acre or more fenced in back there," he said, "but it's grown up in brambles since I been gone. Need to get a bush hog in there before you could do anything with it." He stretched his legs, moved stiffly in the chair, and grimaced. Then he gestured abruptly to himself. "I'm not much good," he said. "I'll put in what I need and can take care of. Six or eight rows. After all, I'm by myself."

"Would you care if I used a piece of it? I could take the tractor in there and bush-hog it for you, turn as much as we need, and cultivate yours in exchange for a quarter of it for me—and some advice."

"If we can get the tractor to working," he said. "It's been sitting up two years. Not only that, the frame on the bush hog is busted. I've got a cracker box in the barn—old welding outfit that belonged to your Uncle Dennison. I ought to be able to fix it. You can help me." Then, again, the mischievous smile. "Let's see," he said, "me and Daddy got plenty seed—mustards, field peas, yellow squash, cushaw, okra. . . . Also, in the barn for fertilizer, plenty old cow flops and horse shit. You want us to *furnish* you, Alan? On shares? Quarter shares?"

I laughed. "That's about it. Would you furnish me?"

"Sure," he said. "That suits me fine. You go in town tomorrow and get some welding rods and we'll get to work on the tractor." He got up, picked up the poker leaning against the wall by the fireplace, and carefully rearranged the logs on the fire.

"What about you?" I said idly, more to speak than because I

expected an answer. "You been asking me about girls. You're not thinking about getting married again, are you?"

He shook his head. "Women!" he said. "I've been a fool about women in my day." He did not sit down, but stood leaning one arm on the mantel, watching the fire.

"You talk like you're an old man," I said. "You're not even forty-five yet."

"After all," he said, "it's not like I'm as good as another man. I'm beginning to get my strength back. Beginning to feel like I can respect myself. But it's been a long dark time for me, Alan. *Dark*. I don't feel like it's over yet. I won't be out looking for no wife no time soon." He hunched his shoulders and moved them restlessly, as if testing invisible bonds. Then he sat down and held out his arms to me, palms down, wrists close together. "I feel the chains on me," he said. "The cuffs on my wrists. The weights on my legs. I'm not good for anything yet."

I said nothing in reply, but I was filled with a restless, sick impatience and would have liked to tell him to put all that behind him and forget it.

"Dallas Boykin's around," Sam said abruptly.

"Yeah?"

"You might have heard, after his family moved to Texas, Dallas went in the service. He come back while I was gone, so Daddy told me. Cutting pulpwood over on Duck Pond."

"I haven't seen Dallas since I was fifteen," I said.

"I thought you be looking for somebody to go fishing and hang out with."

"I'm not going to do much fishing in January," I said. "Besides, Dallas and I might not get along as well as we did when we were kids. Leila told me the whole family is mixed up in the Klan."

"Lindsay Lee's been here, too," Sam said. "Visiting. Daddy seen him in town. He don't look like no Ku Kluxer. Hair a good bit longer than yours." He gestured at my cap of blond curls. "Not so curly, though. You've about got you a white Afro there."

I wondered vaguely why Sam had brought up the Boykins and thought there was probably some purpose in it that would come out when he was ready. There is always a purpose in what he says, but I sometimes find it hard—sometimes impossible—to get at.

"Talking about hair," he said (so that was it), "you don't mind if I give you a piece of advice, do you?"

24

I shook my head.

He looked me over. "You're big," he said. "I see you're big. Tall as I used to be. I know you're able to take care of yourself in a fight—I mean, man to man."

"I'm not much on fighting," I said.

He paid no attention. "Even big as you are and all," he said, "I can't help thinking about you like you're still a kid. A *kid*. You know?"

"Sure," I said.

"I was your age, I was careless," he said. "I run through Homochitto County like a grass fire, didn't care who I burned. But times are different now. It ain't always man to man. I mean, things might be dangerous for you, now. *Dangerous*. You ought not to be careless."

"What do you mean, Sam?"

"Shave off your beard. Get your hair cut shorter. Or get you a cap. One them knitted caps to keep your ears warm. You going to be working outside a lot, you'll need one, anyhow."

"I've got one of those."

"Well, stick your hair up in it. Wear it all the time. I mean, when you go to Calloway's or to town. You been up North, you don't know how they hate hippies around here. Hippies and niggerlovers, it's all the same thing to them."

"OK," I said. "I'll wear a cap. I don't want any trouble. The beard, I don't know about. I don't want to fool with shaving."

"We're out in the country," he said. "You get in trouble, there's nobody around but me, and God knows I'm no good."

"You're growing an Afro yourself," I said. "Seems as if being a black hippie would be even more dangerous than being a white one."

"Everybody knows me," he said. "And besides, I'm crippled. *Harmless*. They're sorry for me." He clasped his powerful huge hands between his knees and under the sleeves of his faded knit shirt I could see the swelling muscles of his upper arms.

"Maybe Dallas Boykin hates hippies," I said. "What you putting me up to going fishing with him for?"

"Maybe he does," Sam said. "I don't know. I'm just telling you he's hanging around. Best to know who's in the neighborhood. The other one—Lindsay Lee—you ought to watch out for him, too, if he comes back. From his appearance, looks like he's done become a hippie for sure. Also, I hear he's got a black girl friend in New Orleans. That's where he lives now. You reckon that could be true?" Again he gave me that sly sideways grin, the blind eye veiled under its drooping lid, the good eye sharp and merry. Then he answered himself. "Not if his daddy knows about it," he said. "And not if the girl knows anything about his daddy."

But I was more interested in advice about my projects than I was in the Boykins. "What do you think about Leona's house, Sam?" I said. "Think I can fix it up enough to live in?"

"Sure. It was as good as my house five years ago."

"I looked around when I was here last summer, and I can see I'm going to need a truck to haul the lumber. Is the pickup running?"

Sam shook his head. "Wasn't the last time I checked it. Somebody lost the cap off the gas tank and the gas got water in it. I'll see if I can help you get it started tomorrow. I might could find a cap for the tank around here somewhere."

"That would be great," I said. "Another thing, look the tractor over and see what else it needs—parts and all. Daddy and Leila ought to be willing to buy the parts, if we fix it, don't you think?"

"Yeah, they got to keep a tractor working out here. Trees fall across the road, how're you going to get 'em out of the way? How're you going to keep the briars down in the fire lanes? Things done fell apart while I been gone."

After Sam left, I built up the fire and went back to the kitchen to fix some supper. Found a can of pork and beans and, in the freezer, a battered loaf of bread. I was hungry and they tasted good. I could put in supplies tomorrow, after we got the truck running.

I got my books out of the suitcase and stacked them on the table. Shoved the table toward the kitchen to make more room around the bed. Then I pulled off my boots and jeans and lay down under the blankets and comforter to read. I didn't read long, though. I lay there awhile, watching the fire and sniffing the musty smell of the house and the blankets and going over in my mind what I would do tomorrow; then I got up. The fire was low and the room already beginning to get chilly. I stood in front of the fire a few minutes and then took the shovel, drew the ashes away from the sides and back, scattered them on the flaming logs, and banked it as well as I could. There weren't enough ashes yet to do a good job. I looked at my watch: ten o'clock. I put on my trench coat and stepped out on the porch for a last look at the stars.

Saturn was high in Taurus, shining so brilliantly it dimmed everything in the western sky, but I could make out the Pleiades and see Aldebaran close by. While I watched, a meteor drifted down and vanished behind the line of pine trees. I walked to the east end of the porch and, leaning out over the banister there, saw to the northward, looming above the house, the dark bulk of the earthen dam that contained the lake. Above it, the Lynx followed Perseus around the sky. I heard the trees moving in the wind.

Too cold and lazy to go back to the bathroom, I pissed off the end of the porch, still gazing absently into the darkness, thinking now of Miriam and my empty bed.

Inside, I crawled shivering under the covers and lay watching the fire die down until I fell asleep.

THREE

EARLY THE next morning, chirp-
ing like a cricket, excited as a kid on Christmas Eve, I went to look
at the abandoned house my father had told me I could tear down
—circled northward around the horse lot and through the woods,
climbed the steeply sloping grassy side of the dam, and ran across
its broad wheel-rutted top. The sun, just risen behind the dead
pecan tree at the southeast corner of the lake, unhooked itself from
a snag and shed a feeble light on the blackish water; a few wisps
of fog drifted southward across the lake (a light north wind was
blowing); and in the pine trees the crows called out warnings to
each other. The oil well beyond the SPASURSTA tocked steadily on,
like the works of a giant clock. On the other side of the dam, I
climbed a barbed-wire fence and walked on more slowly through
the close-set rows of pines that covered fifty or so acres of land
on the east side of the lake. Then I came out abruptly on what
had once been garden land, pasture, and cornfields and was now
the SPASURSTA.

A barbed-wire fence marked off the clipped and manicured area that contained the SPASURSTA. I stood, breathing hard and looking at it. The hairs rose on my arms and I felt a flood of acid burning in the back of my throat and all the way down to my gut. Without thinking, I half reached out to rest my hand on the top wire of the fence and then snatched it back as if I had been burned—not that there was the least chance the fence might be electrified: even after what Sam had done, the possibility of anyone's wanting to break in was so slight that the government had not troubled to take any new precautions. Here and there along the fence small signs were posted reading:

SPASURSTA
Naval Space Surveillance Station
Keep Out
No entry to unauthorized personnel

But you could climb under or over the fence or, for that matter, walk across the cattle gap in the road connecting the station with the highway.

The SPASURSTA land stretched east and west—a long narrow strip very like (except for what was on it) an old-fashioned country landing field. That was what it had been for a while. Originally cultivated land and pasture, it was the only long level strip of ground for several miles around and, shortly after the Second World War, Uncle Dennison, together with the owners of a couple of adjacent farms, had graded and leveled it to use for landing crop-dusting planes. It was three hundred feet wide now (widened and lengthened when it was leased to the government) and nearly a mile long, with a small gray asbestos-shingled building set roughly in the middle. Three or four outbuildings hardly larger than privies were scattered here and there around the central building; from a pole beside the cattle gap ran the station's umbilical cord—the electric power and telephone cables connecting it to its mother station and the outside world.

On either side of the main building were the monstrous electronic contraptions that were its purpose for being here. The long one, the sending device, on the side of the building nearer to me (supported four feet above the ground on a system of steel trestles), stretched four thousand feet toward the eastern horizon: it might have been a web spun around and over the trestles by a huge ambitious spider bent on spinning her way around the world—a

29

spider that climbed up again and again to throw out above the girders a trap—a fragile wire antenna in the shape of a truncated cone, very like the cone-shaped web of a garden spider—and then crawled on, extruding twisted ropes of black silk, shiny and slick as patent leather and thicker than a man's arm. (And, above the trees, above the clouds, I thought, she continued to spin that other invisible web of soundless signals to net the moon, the falling stars, the sun itself.) The ground beneath the web was bare, as if the spinning creature's body, as she crawled, had exuded some poison which killed everything it touched.

On the far side of the building, six less complex and shorter systems of webs, spun by smaller creatures (offspring of the mother monster?), each only a few hundred feet long, received, bounced back by airplanes and satellites (and by angels and demons?), the signals their mother unceasingly sent out.

Nothing in this great apparatus made a sound. Dead stillness lay around me as thick as if I wore a foam-lined helmet. Even the crows were silent.

Inside the building, I knew, row after row of coffin-gray metal cabinets, lined up like the stacks in a library and filled with more mazes of cable, were pulsing with power; row after row of pens untouched by human hands wrote their messages on silently re-volving, endlessly unwinding reels of paper—messages (unintel-ligible to the men who tended the station) to be transmitted across the country to some inconceivably complex monster in Virginia that deciphered them.

These were the creatures that had stolen Sam's pastures and his garden.

Sometime in the middle sixties (as I had pieced it together from what I heard and what my father told me), Lester Chipman had persuaded his wife Denny and my father and Leila to lease a hun-dred acres (the airstrip and surrounding fields and pastures) to the government to build its SPASURSTA. It had been a reasonable de-cision. The herd of cattle that my Great-uncle Dennison put to-gether during his last years had slowly deteriorated after his death. Chickasaw, in part because of the way my grandfather and Uncle Dennison had left it, was no longer a working farm. A child's share each had gone to my grandmother, my father, Leila, and Denny. My grandmother was old. Neither my father nor Leila had the time or the skill for farming or the inclination to move back to

30

the land or back to Homochitto. (We lived in the Delta, Leila in Memphis.) Denny knew nothing of cattle, and Lester, who had come to Homochitto as an employee of the local J. C. Penney store and was now its manager, knew less (although my father could be heard to mutter sometimes that Lester *thought* he knew everything about everything). Besides, no one was in charge. No one owned a controlling interest.

In any case, affairs on Chickasaw had gone from bad to worse. True, the oil wells still produced modest royalties; but the royalties, making possible, as they did, the upkeep of the house and roads, contributed to everyone's neglect of the farm and forestland. The pulpwood cutters, Lester said (with the connivance of Sam Daniels's father, Noah, who marked the trees to be cut and was supposed to keep an eye on the cutting), were raping our woods and stealing us blind. Sam rented a hundred acres of land for his cattle and was in charge of ours on a wholly unworkable shares basis: it always seemed that our calves died and his thrived. No one was sure what to do and conference after conference held over drinks on the front porch at Chickasaw brought decisions that were not carried out or no decisions at all.

I remember one day in particular when I lay in the hammock (I must have been eleven or twelve at the time) idly listening while they went over and over the same old ground, with everyone agreeing that something had to be done and no one knowing what or caring to do it himself.

Lester and Denny had brought my grandmother out from town and they were all three dressed, not for Chickasaw, but for a wedding in the neighborhood: Lester, with his short straight nose, thin mouth, and every hair in place, looking, in his gleaming summer tux, like an extra in a 1930s movie ball scene; Denny, still young and almost as pretty as the wide-eyed smiling blond picture in her college annual; my grandmother, who had broken her hip at seventy and walked with a slight limp, erect and slender, her curly dark hair streaked with gray, alert to every nuance of conversation and always ready to cast herself in the role of family peacemaker, whether it required that she pretend to be a fool or allow us to catch a glimpse of the clear, practical intelligence that everyone knew she had, but that she usually considered it her duty as a woman to conceal.

She came up the steps briskly, waving her cane like a fencer's épée at my father and mother and Leila, who had been fishing all afternoon at the graveyard pond and looked it. "Don't touch us," she cried. "We're all prepared for the festivities."

And so they sat and talked and had their drinks, and dusk came on, and once Lester shouted, "Sell it! You'd be better off to sell the whole damn place and forget it. Better do that than sit here and watch it go down the drain."

"Down the drain!" Leila said. "What drain? It's land, isn't it? It'll always be land and land will always be valuable."

My father always takes his time answering. Solid and stocky like Leila, he has clear gray eyes and a surface calm that I've seldom seen ruffled, although he's charged with nervous energy, ready to act.

"Lester," he said slowly, "you know we've had the place a long time. I don't believe any of us . . ."

"Noah!" Lester said. "Sam! Those good-for-nothing, treacherous . . . !" He ground his teeth and I shivered.

"Now, Lester," Denny said, "you know how fond we are of . . ."

"Fond!" Lester glared at his wife. He had disliked Sam and Noah the first time he had seen them. To Leila and my father (as I had heard them say more than once), his dislike seemed mysterious—irrational. Sam was Sam—a fact of Chickasaw life. One couldn't dislike him; one had to deal with him. But soon after Uncle Dennison's death, even before the contest over the cattle began, Lester had told all the family that Sam and Noah and the whole Daniels tribe should be "gotten rid of." They were unreliable, he said, and they were arrogant and they drank too much. I suppose everything he said was true—in a way. I don't think my father and Leila even tried to answer him. My father, who usually pursues his ends by indirection, probably said, "Hmmmm," or perhaps, "You've got something there, Lester. We'll have to think about it."

Later, after the wreck in which Sam's wife, Timmie, and Lester's daughter, Phoebe, were killed, his dislike had seemed to turn to a kind of permanent silent rage: looking at his rigid back, his frozen face, I thought that he would have punished not only Sam, who had driven the car, but the world for Phoebe's death. But this particular evening was at least three years before the wreck. Remembering it now, I can almost believe that he was practicing for his own future misery, his long, dry sorrow. And I, watching him,

32

listening, embedded in the certainties of childhood, might have been practicing for the future, too.

"Sam reminds me of Jacob," my grandmother said thoughtfully. "Dividing the cattle, you know: that he should get the spotted and speckled ones and Laban the rest. And he used the ring-straked and the spotted and speckled rods."

"Jacob?" my father said.

"In the Bible," she said. She hated to see everyone against Lester, or for that matter everyone against anyone, and would say the first thing that came into her head to avert a quarrel.

"Well, he doesn't remind me of anyone in the Bible," Lester said, "unless it's the Devil."

My father looked at my grandmother, tilted back in his chair, and laughed aloud.

". . . all very well for you two to make fun of me, but it's a perfect parallel." She got up and went into the house and brought back a dog-eared old Bible. "Right here: '. . . and it came to pass, whensoever the strong cattle did conceive, that Jacob laid the rods before the eyes of the cattle in the gutters that they might conceive among the rods. And when the cattle were feeble he put them not in: so the feebler were Laban's and the stronger Jacob's. And the man increased exceedingly, and had much cattle and . . .'"

My father got up and kissed my grandmother on the top of her head and took the Bible from her. "All right, Mama," he said. "Sam's got much cattle. But what can we do about it? With nobody living here. Nobody in charge."

"Well, you know how it ended," my grandmother said. "Jacob went off with everything Laban had. So I say Lester's got a point." She looked at her watch. "It's twenty minutes to eight, darling," she said to Denny. "If we're going to the wedding, we'd better get started."

That was how such conversations almost always ended.

But within a few years (long years to me, encompassing Phoebe's death and the end of my childhood), it appeared to me that, either through the indifference of my father and Leila or through his own superior capacity for persistence, Lester had won. A lease for the SPASURSTA land was drawn up and everybody was persuaded to consent to it. Sam was informed that there was no longer any pasture available for rent and our cattle were sold at auction. Sam

33

sold some of his. The rest he pastured on the fire lanes between the stands of pine trees and around the ponds and on the dam, and, when he could get away with it, among the seedling pines on the back of the place. Construction of the SPASURSTA began and by 1967 the station was in operation.

Very little of what I had known of Sam as a boy would have prepared me for what followed. To me he had been a powerful, beneficent presence, a man never too busy to stop and help me saddle a horse or mend a bridle, a wanderer (always looking after the cattle and sheep, seeking the newborn calf or the lost lamb) whom one could follow all day over the hills and across the bayous that wound through Chickasaw, learning where the scuppernong and muscadine vines grew, where the bobwhites built their nests, and where the springs that fed the lake were hidden. He took me up before him on the saddle when I was three, taught me to ride bareback when I was five and how to break a colt when I was ten.

True, I'd seen him drunk, had seen him lose his temper and knock his son halfway across the room; but I had also seen him weep when he spoke of his wife's and Phoebe's deaths. All grown people lost their tempers and took out their inexplicable rages on children. Very few showed you muscadine vines or taught you to tame a colt or trusted you to see their grief.

Soon after the SPASURSTA was built, Sam lost his temper.

It was July, a summer of drought, corn dry and yellowing under a sun that seemed never to set, pastures eaten to the bare ground. The state forester discovered that Sam was pasturing his cows among the pine seedlings and called Lester to say that if we didn't put a stop to it, the state would not contribute anymore (as they had in the past under some reforestation program or other) to the planting and supervision of the forestland.

Early the following Saturday morning Lester drove out to Chickasaw and delivered the ultimatum. The cows must go. Not next month or next year, but next Wednesday at the weekly stock auction. At the time (for I saw what happened), I was sure it gave Lester pleasure to be able to wield this power, to give Sam an order that would make him angry and cause him pain. Maybe he even thought he could drive the Daniels family off Chickasaw.

He stood beside his sleek gray Oldsmobile, dressed for the day in a Penney's gray polyester suit and a narrow navy blue tie (Penney's had not yet at that time begun to follow the revolution in men's clothing styles), a trim balding man (he did calisthenics every day and played golf on the weekends) in his early fifties. His skin, since his daughter's death, had acquired the curious dry parchment look of a eunuch's; his face, a fixed expression, as if he were not wholly alive.

Does it seem from everything I put down that I hate Lester? I did then. But now? Now he is getting older and it is hard to hate people who are getting older. Besides, too many things have happened. . . . None, it's true, particularly designed to raise my estimation of Lester, but . . . But anyhow, I don't hate him anymore.

We were vacationing at Chickasaw with Leila, and I saw him drive up, his car raising a heavy cloud of dust above the dry road, saw him talking briefly to Sam, heard him raise his voice as Sam turned away. "You hear me? You understand? They've got to go."

Sam walked off toward the horse lot without answering.

"Next week," Lester shouted after him. "That's all there is to it." He got into his Oldsmobile and drove off, dust boiling up behind him. Leila was in the attic working at her loom and took no part in any of it.

Sam saddled his stallion, Bald Eagle, and rode the seven miles to Homochitto at a gallop. He did not drive his pickup, as he ordinarily would have, but flailed the tall bay horse with a piece of rope and pounded down the middle of the narrow winding road —trucks and cars swerving with screeching tires to get out of his way. He stayed in town all morning and then, under the pulsing noon heat, drunk with rage and gin, rode out again.

We knew nothing of any of this until late afternoon. Leila worked all day at her loom and I spent the day on the lake fishing with one of Sam's nephews; it was not until the sheriff arrived that we learned what had happened.

Sam went to the back of the place, still on horseback, rounded up the few cattle that were grazing among the pine seedlings, and drove them over to the woods by the SPASURSTA. Then he went to the fire lanes and along the open land at the edges of the ponds and got together the rest. Gently he coaxed them, too, across the dam and into the woods by the SPASURSTA fence—so gently that the cattle egrets flying and lighting and flying and lighting beside them drifted along and lit in the trees above their heads and in the open space of the SPASURSTA itself.

Then, from all anyone could make out about it afterwards, Sam went back to the barn and got his wire cutters and a pair of insulated cable cutters from the jumble of tools there. He cut a wide gap in the fence and quietly started the cattle through (they glad enough to leave the needle-carpeted ground under the pine trees for the grassy SPASURSTA). Inside the building, the two men on duty, busy at their work of changing reels of paper and inventorying supplies and watching the jiggling needles thread their zigzags across the unwinding reels, did not even look out a window while this was happening. Sam took his hand ax and cable cutters, climbed the power pole, cut the cables that powered the station, and climbed down.

After a few minutes one of the two men came out of the station and headed for the little outbuilding that housed the auxiliary generator. When he did, he must have stopped, astonished, to see the herd of cattle grazing his neat field. Then a wild, reeling, shouting black man on a huge stallion materialized out of the glare of afternoon sun to the west, driving the cattle before him, riding back and forth over the SPASURSTA at a gallop, hallooing and whirling a rope.

The cattle started up and plunged this way and that, stumbling into the cables that wound in and out of the framework that supported them. The cattle egrets, with guttural squawks of fear and outrage, flew in every direction, crashing into the antennae that raised their webs skyward above the cables.

The station operator was courageous enough in defense of his post—a more prudent man would have gone inside the SPASURSTA and locked the door. Instead, this fellow, a thin sandy-haired man of thirty-five or so, with the slack muscles and small round paunch of a file clerk by day and a television watcher by night, ran toward Sam—who towered above him on Bald Eagle—and shouted at him to get his cattle out, damn it. (He must surely have believed this stampede out of a Deep South Western to be either a mistake or a nightmare.) Sam, intent on his business of destruction, paid no more attention than if the man had not been there, but went on herding his cows and egrets from one complex of equipment to another.

An egret with a broken wing dragged itself along the ground under a sender. Another, dead, its neck broken when it flew into an antenna, lay on the grass near the door of the neat gray building, its beautiful white wings outspread in the warm dust. Three or four of the cows were huddled against the fence, terrified now, refusing to move. One, entangled in the cables that looped between the metal trestles, bellowed and lunged. The others Sam rounded up with a few deft passes and urged toward the other side of the enclosure.

"Get em *out!*" the man shouted again.

"Whooo-ee-eee!" Sam roared.

The station operator ran toward the auxiliary generator, but before he reached it, a terrified bull charged and ran him down. The bull stood over him, quietly gazing down at him and nudging him. The man lay still.

Now the second man on duty in the station heard the noise and looked out. The break in the fence was directly opposite his window. He saw the body of his colleague on the ground, the clipped wires, the melee of birds and cattle, and the huge roaring black man; grabbed a .22 pistol (the only weapon in the station) out of one of his gray steel filing cabinets, and rushed out. By the time he reached the gap, Sam had herded the cattle all the way around the station and through the maze of receivers on the other side, breaking antennae and jerking cables loose, and was driving them back toward the gap. Cows and calves lowed and moaned, veered off on either side of the man, and scrambled through the gap, as he stood waving his pistol and shouting at Sam to stop.

Sam, riding Bald Eagle, galloped toward him with an awful yell. The station operator fired his pistol (hardly more than a toy) into the air. Bald Eagle's hooves beat the dry ground and it vibrated under his feet as in an earthquake. Again the station operator fired his pistol into the air. Bald Eagle bore down on him standing in the gap in the fence. He fired off one shot point-blank at Sam. If it struck either man or horse, he could see no effect.

He panicked then, as he told it in court afterwards, and ran through the gap and across the narrow open space between the fence and the woods. He had gone scarcely ten yards before they overtook him and ran him down as casually as if they had not seen him. One of Bald Eagle's hooves struck his head. Sam rode on, not looking back. The man lay on the ground and did not move.

Sam's behavior afterwards was mysterious. He had hours of grace —neither man at the SPASURSTA recovered consciousness for twenty minutes or more; and then the less badly injured one, the one inside the enclosure, had to start up the auxiliary generator and use the teletype to call his home station in Virginia (Sam had cut the phone lines and he was afraid he might black out again if he used his car to go for help). When the sheriff and an ambulance and the FBI (alerted by telephone from Virginia) arrived, he did not know who his attacker had been. Still in shock, confused by the blow to his head from the bull's horns, he remembered only that a black man had been there on a horse. The sheriff ended by tracing Sam through the brands on his cows. (One, with a broken leg, was still entangled in the cable and others were wandering in the woods.) But Sam had not run away or hidden or done any of the things one might have expected. Instead, he took Bald Eagle home and rubbed him down and turned him out. Then he got into the pickup and went out on the back of the place to mend a fence that he had seen was down when he was rounding up his cows at noon. Late in the afternoon he came home. I remember seeing him standing in the backyard talking to Leila when we got in from fishing. Shortly afterwards, toward dusk, the sheriff came to get him. That was when I found out what had happened. By night he was in the Homochitto County jail.

He didn't stay long. He looked his cell over, found a loose bar, and that same night bent it, pulled it out of its socket, and came home. I was down by the pond with a flashlight grabbing frogs when I saw the lights of a car flashing on the trees overhanging the winding road. A door slammed and I heard voices, Sam's and his brother-in-law's. I took my dripping sack of frogs and waited by the fence in the hot darkness until I saw the brother-in-law drive away, and then I walked over to Sam's house to find out what was going on. He was sitting on his front porch in the dark, smoking a cigarette.

"Hey," I said, "they let you out?"

"Nope."

I was seventeen years old, shy and self-absorbed, obsessed with my looming battle with the draft board, but I loved Sam.

"What happened?" I said.

"I come home. I wasn't going to stay in there."

"Sam!" I knew what he meant, but I said hopefully, "You got out on bond?"

He shook his head. "Ain't the first time I broke out of that jail. Come to think of it . . ." He laughed. "One time, Alan, I broke into it first and *then* out of it. It was simple to get in, but then they locked up and went off and I had to bust the back door off the hinges to get out. That was about a girl they had shut up in there. Nobody ever found out who done it."

I said nothing.

"I got my cows to tend to," he said, "among other things."

I couldn't think what to say or do next. "I got a bunch of frogs tonight," I said. "I'll skin 'em and bring you some legs."

"I hated it about them birds," he said, "and Easter Bell." Easter Bell was the cow that had broken her leg.

I had walked over to the SPASURSTA early in the evening before dark and had seen the damage, the cow, and the bodies of three dead birds, one, claws delicately curved, a trickle of dried blood at the corner of its eye, lying by the SPASURSTA door, one under the sender, and the third hanging, like a dragonfly in a spiderweb, in the tangled wire of a broken antenna.

"Noah shot Easter Bell," I said.

"Freddie told me." Freddie was Sam's brother-in-law.

We sat there awhile, neither of us saying anything. I was in a belly-gripping misery of uncertainty and anguish and fear for Sam's future, and I did not want to have to think about any of it.

At last he said, "Go on back up to the house, Alan. Tell your Aunt Leila I'm home, will you?"

I was glad to go.

Leila got up without a word and went back to Sam's house and was gone for a long time.

In the early morning of the following day, the dry grass in one of the fire lanes caught fire. Lovers who had come in the SPASURSTA road to park in the seclusion of our deserted woods? Or had Sam set it? I didn't know. The fire ran leaping and crackling along the lane under a dry August breeze and, by the time we got up and saw the smoke, had burned its way over the parched grass around the deserted SPASURSTA, scorching the asbestos-shingled buildings and melting the rubber cable insulation. The Homochitto fire department came out and the forestry service sent fire fighters from the post in the next county, and it took all day to put it out. We lost twenty acres of young trees, but they managed to save the buildings of the SPASURSTA.

Smoke hung in the air, and the smell of wet, burned-over land. I spent all day with the fire fighters, beating the smoldering grass with wet towsacks and ditching with the tractor between the fire and the next stand of trees. Soot blew in my eyes and settled in my hair and on my face, and the heat parched my skin and blistered my hands, and I did not have to think about anything.

Sam sat on his front porch all day. But the man Bald Eagle had kicked was in the hospital with a fractured skull, and the sheriff came in the late afternoon and Sam went back to jail. Did Leila call the sheriff? I didn't know. Sam let them keep him awhile, almost contemptuously, it seemed, not ready yet to leave; let them indict him for assault with intent to murder before he broke out again.

Again he did not try to run away. Came back to Chickasaw (we were gone home to the Delta by then), sat on his front porch and watched the sun go down, wandered over the place on Bald Eagle, as he had always done (no cows now, no sheep, no lost calves or ewes in labor to look for), stopped in to see his father and mother, and went to bed.

Next morning, Denny told us afterwards, they went out to get him as if they knew they'd find him there.

He was convicted of assault, got five years in the state penitentiary at Parchman, and they took him away.

FOUR

I KNEW IN my teens that our life at Chickasaw had been different for a long time before Sam attacked the SPASURSTA. The change had come when Phoebe and Timmie were killed: the wrecking of the SPASURSTA was the crackling up of a fire smoldering since that year—1964; a dark slow fire without air to fan it, under the mat of pine needles, as it were, consuming the earth, hollowing out underground caves, as a fire smoldering in the refuse piles around a sawmill will burn out caves in the mounds of sawdust before anyone sees even a wisp of smoke, and then, one day, someone will step on what looks like solid ground and fall screaming into the inferno that bursts through the broken crust at the first touch of air.

Neither Sam nor Lester was ever the same again. Nor was I. Those deaths, not the deaths of civil rights workers nor the burning of churches, were for us the tragedies of Freedom Summer. As I had told the students who picked me up and drove me past the ruins of Mercy Seat Church, I was only fifteen years old when it burned. I didn't add that Mercy Seat burned the week after Phoebe's death or that she was seventeen and that I had been in love with her for as long as I could remember.

At the time it seemed to me that Sam and Lester blamed each other for the accident, Sam for reasons even more obscure than Lester's. It seemed obvious that the wreck was neither Sam's nor Phoebe's (and certainly not Lester's) fault; and even if there had been some fault to be found, if Sam had been driving too fast (as he often did), if Phoebe had grabbed the wheel when the car began to swerve by Mercy Seat Road (possible, if she lost her head), what good would it have done to place the blame?

Afterwards, it was as if some almost undetectable physical change had taken place in Sam. His black skin looked blacker, duller, rougher, poreless, like the surface of a stone; for a long time he seemed, with expressionless eyes, scarcely to see what passed under his gaze, and when he did, there would be in his face a kind of bewilderment, uncertainty, as if he still doubted the reality of what had happened.

Lester and Denny stayed mostly in town (I suppose they couldn't bear to see that we were alive and healthy), and the Chipman boys, although they came out occasionally to fish or ride, no longer spent their vacations with us at Chickasaw. And I—I knew that I would never be whole or happy again. It was as if then, at the tail end of childhood, the world was still an extension of myself, as if Phoebe had been a part of me, a leg or an arm hacked off with a dull jagged knife, or half of a hermaphroditic whole, carrying with her into the earth half my heart and liver and lights.

For months, I thought of nothing else. No, I didn't think. (Could I think at fifteen?) I *felt* myself shrivel and grow dry and cold, as if the springs of my body closed up. My fingernails began to split, I had an attack of fever blisters, my lips cracked, and I could scarcely eat. My mother looked at me with worried eyes and said to my father things like, "He's growing too fast," and "No resistance —he must have a vitamin deficiency," and to me, "You stay up entirely too late," and "You shouldn't drink so many Coca-Colas," but she knew it was Phoebe's death that made me sick.

As I think about that time, it occurs to me that I scarcely missed Timmie—even though she and Sam had been married so long (since 1956, I believe) that she had been at Chickasaw since my early childhood. Nor did I notice when Lindsay Lee and Dallas vanished from our lives at almost the same time Phoebe did.

As for Lester and Denny! I remember, as vividly as my own pain, my hatred of their grief. What right had *they* to mourn Phoebe? They were only her parents. Lester in his sharp Penney's suit, driving his new Oldsmobile (he bought a new car every other year and, having an aversion to allowing anyone else at the wheel, drove his own car—even to his daughter's funeral), and Denny, her face as swollen and battered as if she had been in a fight and her hair in an immovable lacquered puff. What had they to do with Phoebe? Phoebe, who had spent long hours telling me how little they understood her, how impossible they made her life.

While I . . . ! At the funeral I stared at the dry, cracked August ground, the iron clods scattered at the edge of the flower-masked mound of dirt, and saw: a June morning, and Phoebe riding bareback on Bald Eagle (wheedled out of Sam because she preferred him to her own gentle mare), bent low against his out-stretched neck, her long tan legs and bare feet digging into his sides, as they jumped the fence by the dam; a July noon, and Phoebe opposite me in the water, shouting, as we wrestled with the overturned canoe, "This way, stupid! Lift. *Lift!*" A still, hot August afternoon, and Phoebe dancing alone on the long front porch to the songs of the Beatles blaring from the radio in the car pulled up by the steps ("I should have known better . . ."). She had taken ballet lessons since she was six and carried her small classic head under its coil of fair braids so high she might have been hanging, like a puppet dancing girl, from a string in the sky, and used her hands and arms with disciplined grace ("Can't buy me love . . ."). She shook her hips and shoulders as if her bones were made of music, while I lay in the hammock watching, filled with yearning— not just for her, but for joy, adventure, beauty: for the world.

I held my sister's sweaty hand in mine, felt her tears on my wrist, and could not weep.

I remember, too, after the funerals, the questions and explanations. Sam went over and over the story of the wreck—with Leila, with my father and mother, with Noah, with Timmie's family, with everyone concerned except Lester and Denny. They would not talk to him about it, and Lester would not talk to anyone. He listened to the sheriff's report, he went in his Oldsmobile to the funeral, and he would hear no more. Phoebe's brother, Dennison, told me that for a long time his father would not allow her name to be mentioned in his presence. "Mama would want to talk about her," he said, "and she did, to us. Still does. She says it's like if we don't talk about her, she was never alive, like we're taking away the life she had. . . . But Daddy couldn't. Maybe he couldn't bear even to think of her. It was three years, at least, before . . . and even now, if Mama forces him—asks him questions like, 'Do you remember when Phoebe . . . ?' and so forth—he'll put his hands behind him so you can't see him clench his fists while he answers."

But I thought of her, I talked about her, I wrote terrible poems and songs about her—she was the star of all my fantasies. Like Denny, I meant her to live, to be as alive as she was to me that last summer afternoon lying on the raft, the wind lifting her fair hair from her forehead—more alive, if I could make her so. I would draw a translucent veil over her life (I thought of the veil the sun makes of fog on a Delta winter morning—a shimmering silver mist through which the icy fields glitter as in a dream) and through it she would be more visible, more real, more beautiful than the moon.

That was how I felt then. The truth is—*a* truth, anyhow—I was fifteen. Like most fifteen-year-olds, I had my hand in my pocket half the day to conceal a hard-on. Watching her dance, I had felt a yearning that was much more specifically for her than it was for joy and beauty. But at the same time she was *my own,* as no other girl ever has been. And she was, it's true, the embodiment of my dreams. I'd been in love with her all my life—still am. Some nights I wake from a dream of her so real I weep. No matter who lies beside me, she dances through my sleep, as lively as if I'd seen her yesterday.

But *of course* Lester's grief, so acute a pain that he dared not touch the wound, was more and mine less. And Lester's grief, too, contained something else—knowledge that I did not have, that he did not want.

I knew nothing then, in my teens, of all those tangled circumstances. I knew only my memories of Phoebe—I had a high and noble purpose in my soul. Later, and not much later, all those adolescent poems and fantasies sickened me. I stopped thinking about Phoebe. I put her out of my mind until the day I saw Miriam for the first time.

I was in the student center at school and she was standing by her post office box, half turned away from me clutching an armload of books with one hand and tearing open a letter with her teeth and the other. A heavy blond pigtail hung down her back. The set of her shoulders, one carried forward and a fraction of an inch higher than the other, as if she might be preparing to ride into battle or to ward off a blow, and the tall, spare, graceful body: it was Phoebe. My heart turned over and I was inside my dream. I got up from the table where I had sat down to read my mail and drink a cup of tea and started toward her, unconscious as a sleep-walker. She turned and I saw, not Phoebe's but Miriam's face: the round forehead, the blue-green eyes under straight dark brows looking at me with austere appraisal, followed by a quizzical smile, as if she said, *Can I help it if I'm smarter than you? Forgive me.*

No, she was never like Phoebe: Phoebe's eyes were defiant and her intelligence without hesitation. She flung herself into her short life as if she knew how soon it would end, and I followed her—over ravines too deep to bear looking into, through beds of quick-sand where she shrieked with mock terror while muck dragged at our knees and ankles, on horseback at a gallop under the low-hanging branches of the live-oak trees and along the narrow deep-cut trails, at the back of the place where the muscadines grow. Always in my memories we seem to have been laughing or shout-ing. Except for her occasional diatribes against her parents and her wild schemes for leading a free life, we scarcely talked to each other during those years. When I think of her now, when I consider that the only things she said to me were things that all adolescents say when they are unhappy or when their plans are thwarted, I realize that I never knew her. To the last, for me, she was all possibility.

❧

She had been all weekend with us at Chickasaw and it was Mon-day. We spent the day on the lake—took our lunch and paddled up the creek in the morning to a point so far back the canoe scraped the sandy bottom. We saw the bass fingerlings and min-nows dart through green pools or hold themselves still against the current, and, ahead of us in the shallow water, under the over-hanging bluffs festooned with wild hydrangea bloom and grown up thickly with wax myrtle and Virginia creeper, the great blue herons wade and fish. We lay down in the bottom of the canoe

45

and pushed ourselves closer and closer to them, until we could have reached out and touched their long dusky legs, could look straight into their round chrome-yellow eyes. In the still, hot air raincrows called, and pine siskins and cicadas. A black and yellow butterfly sat on the brown sand and fanned its veiny wings. By the time we got back to the cove, fringed around with willows and cottonwoods, where the creek opens out into the lake, it was mid-afternoon. Phoebe jumped out of the canoe and turned it over with me in it; and then together we turned it over and over in the water and ducked each other, and swam down into the cold darkness and up, bursting out of the water, gasping for air. We righted the canoe and tied it to the raft and sat in dripping cutoffs and T-shirts while she combed out her yellow hair and dried it in the sun. That is the picture of her that stays in my mind: her back bent, her face half hidden, and her hair, spread out on her shoulders, slowly lightening and beginning to glint as the sun warmed it and the dry air lifted it from her forehead. A water spider ran across her thigh and she took him up and dropped him on the surface of the lake and he skittered away. Grains of sand stuck to the smooth brown skin of her calf when she lay down and rolled over on her stomach. There was a tiny scrape on her cheek with a drop of blood drying on it, where I had scratched her when we were wrestling in the water.

In the late afternoon we came in and she wandered over to Sam and Timmie's house while I went to sleep in the hammock on the back porch. I awakened at dusk to the sound of a car starting up and tires grinding the dry gravel and saw them drive away in Sam's car. I wondered why she was going to town. She had said she would stay on until the following day. Besides, I was fifteen now. I had a driver's license and could have taken her in myself, if she'd told me she wanted to go.

Ten minutes later she and Timmie were dead.

After you close the Chickasaw gate behind you and get back into the car and pull out on the road to Homochitto, there is a long, gently sloping climb—half a mile or more—past the high meadow on the right where old Mercy Seat Church stood. The road is narrow—two lanes. At that time it had not yet been black-topped.

If you pulled out from Chickasaw gate in a hurry, spurts of loose gravel flew every which way and the car slewed. Directly ahead, as you drive up the slope, is a knob of Chickasaw Ridge around which the road seems to divide like the current of a creek around a jutting clay bank. The right-hand branch climbs steeply up to the church, the left-hand veers off around the knob and continues on to Homochitto. Both roads are worn deep into the loess land; crumbling bluffs rear up on either side—on the right so close to the road that there is no shoulder; on the left a few yards back, leaving room (or so it appears) for another car to pull off in an emergency into thickets of ironweed, French mulberry, and black-berry briars. But appearance is illusion. A deep wash runs along between the road and the rearing bluff. The briars will serve for a warbler to light on but nothing much heavier. Just beyond Mercy Seat, at the foot of the knob that divides the road, the wash passes through a culvert under the road, veers northward, and continues along by the side of Mercy Seat Road. The oil companies keep up the roads on Chickasaw that give access to well locations, but Mercy Seat Road leads to a dry hole. Every now and then the county dumps a load of gravel where the road climbs toward the church, but other than that, nobody keeps it up. It tends to crumble off into the wash.

Afterwards, when Sam was telling us over and over what happened, he said a car coming from the direction of Homochitto passed him traveling fast, just before he got to the point at the foot of the knob where the road divides. "Driving along, thinking about nothing," he said. "Car passed me, went on down the hill, I reckon, *traveling*. My windshield exploded. No other way to say it. Blew up. Right before we come to the spot where you turn off toward Mercy Seat. Why? What happened? It was a rock thrown up by that car, I reckon, and they never even knew it. No other explanation. But I didn't see it. All I knew was glass everywhere. Hailstones of glass. I must've jerked the wheel to the right. I couldn't see what I was doing for the glass in my face, but I must've jerked to the right, because I give my head a shake and found us heading up Mercy Seat Road, car slewing its back end one way and then the other. Slammed against the bluff. Must've blown out the back tire—I heard it pop, I think. Flung itself to the left. God knows, I knew the gully was there. I been up that road too many times. It all happened without me. Skidded across the road, over the edge, and we was gone, turning side over side down the gully. Two whole turns, must be—that gully is deep—and ended up against a big old pignut growing out of the bottom.

"The gully," he said. "I could've handled it all, but for the gully. Spite of my knowing it was there. . . .

"I felt us thrown around like dice in a cup and then I was outside the car, lying on the ground. I could hear the people singing up over my head: 'Oh, I feel like going on. On my way to Zion and I feel like going on. . . .' I thought I must be dead. But I smelled the gasoline and knew I was still in Homochitto County, blood running down my face. I stood up. Cut bad here over my eye." He touched his bandaged forehead. "How did I get thrown out? Did I jump out? How did it happen? I don't know. I was outside. The car lying up against the tree on its side, driver side down. Doors bent in. Timmie and Phoebe inside, neither one of them moving. Fire started some way. I begun to see little flames. That jagged windshield, I couldn't drag 'em through that. Climbed on top of the car, top of the *side* of the car, and tried to open a door. Both jammed. I got aholt of the back door and tried to rip it off. Couldn't. Tried the front door. Yelling all the time. They couldn't hear me in the church for the singing. And I said, *Lord, give me strength,* and grabbed the front door and bent to it with all I had and pulled it off. I did that," he said to my father and Leila, while I listened, silent, in the background. "The sheriff can tell you it was ripped off. Neither one of 'em moving. Phoebe was in the front seat, so I grabbed her first and drug her out and then I started back for Timmie. Too late. Car was burning good by then." He rubbed his singed eyebrows and showed us his burned and bandaged hands again and again. "Practically blown up in my face."

Timmie burned to death. She was probably unconscious from a blow on the head. Sam said she never moved. Maybe she didn't even feel it. Phoebe's throat was cut. She was already dead when Sam pulled her out of the car.

The preacher and all the people in Mercy Seat were outside by then. The explosion brought them out.

There was no telephone at the church; someone ran up the road to the preacher's house and called Lester. I suppose Lester must have called the doctor and the doctor called the highway patrol. It was Noah who thought of us at Chickasaw. He had been at the church meeting and had gone to tell Timmie's family.

I was still sulking in the hammock when I heard a curious strangling sound like nothing I had heard before. I got up and ran to the front of the house, thinking somebody must be choking to death. By then Leila was saying "You're *sure?* They're both dead?" And then, "Phoebe's dead?" The moon was high and brilliant that night, a light breeze blowing tree shadows across the porch floor and across Leila's white face. A pair of Phoebe's tennies, damp and mud-encrusted, lay on the cistern cover waiting to be washed. Our wet cutoffs were hanging on the porch banister.

Noah stood with one foot on the bottom step and tore at the lapels of his dark Sunday suit as if it might be on fire. Yes, he said, he was sure. Out on the driveway, Freddie and his wife waited in the car and said nothing. I heard Freddie give a humming moan.

When I stepped out on the porch, Leila stared at me as if I weren't there; then she seemed to see me and said, "A wreck, Alan. On the way to town. Phoebe . . ."

I shook my head.

"I'd better go," she said. "They've already called Lester. You stay here with the children. OK?"

My brother and sister were asleep.

I shook my head again. "No."

"All right," she said. "Come on."

The car was still smoldering. The smell of Timmie's burning flesh was everywhere and the strangling smoke of burning tires. An ambulance and a highway patrol car had pulled in just ahead of us. Lester sat on the ground, his legs straight out in front of him, his feet in Penney's neat dark bedroom slippers pointing rigidly at the sky. Phoebe's head was in his lap, her chin tucked down, so that you could just see the end of the long clean cut across her throat. Her shirt was bloody, but there was no blood left in her body. Her hand and wrist, lying palm up on her lap, were white as bleached bone. The ground was bloody, the smell in the air like hot rusty iron. I crouched in the grass and retched and heard Leila's soft voice above me saying coldly, "Get hold of yourself, Alan. Be a man."

Lester sat on the ground and said nothing. They put Phoebe on a stretcher and covered her and put her in the ambulance and slammed the door.

Lester stood up all bloody and looked at Leila and said, "I have to tell Denny."

"You can't go like that," Leila said.

I said, "Where is Timmie?"

"Can't get her out of there yet, son," one of the patrolmen said. Someone was directing a foam fire extinguisher toward the car and the small flames were sizzling and dying. Sam stood at the edge of the ravine with his back to all of us. Somebody—a white man— stood beside him with a notebook in his hands and asked soft-voiced questions and he shook his head and stamped his foot like a horse shooing off flies.

"I'll go with Phoebe," I said.

"No," the patrolman said, and the ambulance started up and pulled away without me.

Leila put Lester in the car and took us back to Chickasaw and found him a pair of clean khaki pants and a shirt and washed the blood off his hands while he stood holding them over the basin, staring into the mirror. "I have to tell Denny," he said to the mirror.

Leila led him out of the house and put him in the car.

"I'll drive," he said.

"Not tonight. Not my car." She left me there in the quiet house with the sleeping children and took him to town. That was the way it happened.

FIVE

I WOULD NOT cross the SPA-SURSTA. Instead, I detoured around the northern end—no more than a quarter of a mile out of my way—and tramped down the dry bed of a ravine, bare now, except where the open network of unleaved branches was broken by the winter green of cedar, live oak, holly, or magnolia; or where the evergreen smilax twined among the bare limbs. A foot-deep carpet of leaves lay on the ground, live and springy to the step. In March yellow jasmine and dogwood bloom here; trillium springs up everywhere, thousands of fragile three-pointed stars; and wood ferns unfurl their pale green scrolls. I would be here for spring this year, I thought.

Another quarter of a mile down the ravine, surrounded by a waist-high thicket of young pine trees, I found the house. It looked as if you could tie a rope to the post at one corner of the porch and use the truck to pull it down. Indeed, if I leaned on it, I thought, it would probably collapse.

I stood there for a while looking at it, thinking about all those beautiful boards being mine, figuring the best way to start taking it apart and the tools I would need to find. Then I walked home again, got Sam, and together we drained the tank of the pickup that belongs to the place, cleaned the carburetor, found in the clutter of the barn a cap for the tank, and siphoned in some gas from Sam's car. He jumped me off with his cables and I drove cautiously up the winding hilly road to Calloway's store (I would have to do some work on the brakes), put a quick charge on the battery, filled the gas tank, bought a week's supply of groceries, and renewed my acquaintance with Mr. and Mrs. Calloway. Then I drove in to the welding supply warehouse on the edge of town and got some rods and Sam and I fixed the bush hog. I was serious about a garden.

Next day I took the truck around by a back road and a fire lane to the abandoned house and set to work.

Day followed day, every day's work a pleasure. I ripped off the weathered poplar and cypress boards and the thin age-silvered cedar shakes and exposed joists and studs and rafters hewn out by hand, marked by broadax and adze stroke, so clean and dry they might have been shaped yesterday. As I hammered straight the square-headed hand-forged nails and scavenged the trash heap behind the house, bringing up whiskey bottles, rusted washboards, broken chamber pots, and rotting rags, I imagined myself Schliemann, digging through the ruins of Troy.

I spent three days tearing the house apart, loading lumber onto the pickup, and taking it around by one of the fire lanes (the weather was dry) to the road, and so to Leona's house. There I spent another three days brushing down the cobwebs from the walls and ceiling, sweeping and scrubbing the floors, shoveling debris out of the basement and attic, loading it onto the truck, and carrying it three miles to the Chickasaw dump. I kept a few things: a cracked churn; a chain contraption for weighing cotton; a child's school desk without a back and a broken church pew (where had they come from?); a three-legged iron kettle with a rimmed lid for coals; two or three bottles, the translucent green of the Gulf Stream, with tiny bubbles floating in the glass. Nothing except the kettle that anyone could have used for any purpose: the detritus of utter poverty.

Somewhere far away, Charles Manson and his "family" were being tried for the murder of Sharon Tate. The My Lai court-martials were still going on. Jerry Rubin was being paid fifteen hundred a throw for telling huge crowds of college students to "do it." Angela Davis was being extradited to California.

Exactly ten years had elapsed since the first American military dead were logged in Vietnam.

But I never saw a newspaper or a television set or heard a radio. As I worked, I felt myself drifting beyond the time of clocks and calendars, suspended like the bubbles in my glass bottles, in a liquid so viscid it might take tens of centuries to pour itself out. When the sun rose, I got up and went to work; when it set, I walked the quarter mile to the gate and checked the mailbox; then I closed myself into the dining room of the big house, built up the fire, cooked my supper, and ate and read—or wrote.

I have said that I intend to imagine myself back into that younger Alan McLaurin's shoes, to try to recall, for the purposes of the story, what he was like in 1971. And I know very well what he "had in mind" when he went to Chickasaw that winter: the experience of solitude—days and nights that would bring on the wings of February storms the poems he knew must be waiting to surface, if only he were quiet and patient enough to invite them; and the romance of life in the country—building, sowing, gathering, observing. (At the time I would have said, the *reality* of country life, rather than the *romance,* I suppose.) What I now believe, though, when I think of him working so single-mindedly at his eccentric tasks, is that he thought himself pure, that he believed purity to be possible. He thought he could pay his dues from time to time and live, by the light of his convictions, an untroubled, perhaps even a heroic, life—a not uncommon belief among young men of twenty-two with deep-set silver-blue eyes and wide bony foreheads.

He took his sea-green bottles to the kitchen sink and scrubbed them inside and out with an old gnawed bottle brush and soaked them in ammonia and filled them with number eight shot and shook them furiously up and down and rinsed them out. Then he held them to the light and before his eyes the captive bubbles seemed to drift visibly upward (as a poem might that very moment be drifting upward through the pure clear layers of his mind).

Uncle Dennison once told me that when his grandfather came

back to Chickasaw at the end of the Civil War, a neighboring farmer stopped by to see him—ruined, like everybody else, come down from high cotton to nothing—and said, standing out by the cistern in a ragged piece of uniform, toes showing through the broken uppers of his boots, "Mr. McLaurin, I still can't pay you that ten thousand dollars been owing you five years." Took out a handful of paper Confederate money and threw it down on the iron cistern cover. "That's all the money I got." "What have you got besides no-'count money?" my great-great-grandfather said. "Well, I got two cows." "Gimme one of your cows and we'll call it quits," the old man said. He lived in a desperate present enterprise.

And I—I am not now the boy who gathered churns and empty medicine bottles and broken desks and thought of himself as an archaeologist of the spirit; the boy who thought he knew the questions and had acted out the answers; who made the error of supposing he had earned a holiday and this was it. I would *like* to be more like that old man—hopeful enough, practical enough, ruthless enough to take one of the cows and call it quits.

⟋

The sequence of events that led to my "holiday" had begun when I was fourteen, the week Oswald killed JFK—that smiling young man with the tousled hair and the beautiful wife and children, who, so my parents had assured each other and us, was going to make a start at solving all our problems. JFK sang to people like them, in Mississippi, at that time, a siren song. Surely, they said (and I listened), *surely* things couldn't continue to go badly if Casals was invited to play his cello in the White House.

My ninth-grade classmates and, yes, even a teacher greeted the assassination with cheers: *Somebody got the bastard!* I left school and went home to sit with my parents in silence in front of the television set, watching the tears roll down my mother's face, hearing the moans of our black cook, who would not watch with us, but went to the kitchen and doubled up over the table and clutched her belly. I saw the bier roll through the streets of Washington, heard the interminable sad drums, saw Ruby kill Oswald. Sometime in that week the conviction began to form in my head that I was not going to kill anybody.

Then, a year later, Phoebe and Timmie were killed. I smelled

Phoebe's blood and Timmie's burning flesh. *I was never going to kill anybody*.

My senior year in high school, my best friend, who had graduated the preceding June and gone, as I thought, brainlessly, crazily, into the Marines, sent his Christmas card to me from Vietnam. It was a slick white card with a color photograph on it (he had taken the picture himself) of the bodies of two Viet Cong soldiers lying side by side. You can see that the hands of one are tied in front of him. The hands of the other are not visible, but his arms are bent at an angle toward each other, so that you know they are tied, too. The bodies are spattered with blood. One man's face is shot half away. My friend had printed in neat letters below the picture, CHRISTMAS GREETINGS FROM VIETNAM and signed his name. I was *not* going to kill anybody and I decided to say so.

I bore my father's wounded silence (never a soldier out of preference, he was a believer in the performance of the duties of citizenship) and my mother's reasonable arguments, and I carried it through. I was lucky: I had a draft board that would take a religious conviction outside the structure of a church—take it, that is, if you had some plausible substitute. I was middle-class and articulate, I cut my hair before the hearing, filled in the forms properly (mentioning my loathing of contact sports, my study of existential responsibility, and the meaning of the territorial instinct), and got the necessary reassuring letters from teachers and lawyers and even a banker, who looked at me distastefully but who had, after all, gone to school with my father. I didn't research the luck of people who were black and inarticulate, didn't know any bankers, hadn't read Camus and Lorenz, and maybe didn't even know it was possible to tell the draft board you wouldn't kill anybody.

I had a low draft number and I had forfeited my student deferment when I applied for C.O. status. In February of my sophomore year in college they sent me to the state mental hospital at Whitfield to do two years of alternate service. I was an aide, herding the patients (mostly as docile as sleepwalkers) in and out, shoving food at their gray, slack faces, cleaning up their shit from the floor when they didn't bother to use the bathroom, dragging them into and out of bed when they didn't want to get up or lie down. All day every day I lived with men so damaged by the world or else so drugged they neither moved nor spoke, but stood in their gray prison pajamas, leaning against the gray, sweat- and grease-stained walls; with men who drifted from room to room like silent ghosts. Once, late at night during bed check, a sixteen-year-old boy who had not spoken since he had come to us lunged out of his cot, still silent, wrapped his arm around my leg, and fastened his teeth in my thigh. I heard them click when they met. It took three of us to pry open his jaws and pull him loose. In the infirmary they swabbed my leg and gave me tetanus and penicillin. None of us asked any questions—not of each other or of the boy. We already knew what the consequences would be. Next day they took him up to Receiving for shock.

In the evenings and on weekends I left Whitfield behind. I had paid my dues all week, eight hours a day in the loony bin. Outside, I took part in the demonstrations, went to the meetings, did what I was supposed to do about the war.

Not long ago I saw a friend of mine from those days who said to me sadly, "Jesus, but we were happy then! That was the best time of our lives. We were brave and we were doing the right thing and it was going to work. And we had all the dope we could smoke and girls. . . . The girls were beautiful. Do you remember how it was?" He reminded me of an aging jock talking about the big season.

But for me it was as if I were on a bad trip, drifting like my loonies through an unreal world, with an occasional therapeutic jolt of shock to keep me humble. I was bored at the endless meetings and I hated the demonstrations—the involvement with people I vaguely knew in projects that seemed either to threaten disaster or to be doomed to failure. I wasn't happy—I felt like hell. I wanted to be at home reading, or out in the country fishing (I had decided it was OK to kill cold-blooded creatures if I ate them), or looking at birds, or even chopping wood.

I was still scarcely more than a child and I was angry with my parents because they hadn't supported me as I believed they should have; weren't marching and protesting with us; and I was angry with myself because I kept thinking that really I should be doing *more*—doing things I hadn't done because I was a coward. I knew I hadn't burned my draft card because I didn't want to go to prison —I was *afraid,* aware of my innocence and vulnerability, afraid of rape. As for the girls—all the girls I met in the Movement (well, not all, but a lot of them) looked to me like girls who were there because they hadn't got a bid to a sorority. Not beautiful, but like sad, or wistful, or angry discards. Shit. It was a mess.

In 1969 when it was over I went back to college and met Miriam.

I had done my time. I was twenty. It was the first time I had lived with a woman. Christ, I forgot that two years in two weeks—the meetings and demonstrations, the men in their silent apathy and filth, the guy who cried and beat the floor, the one who stood all day long in the middle of the dayroom and rubbed his hands together, so that they had calluses on them as thick as the pads on a dog's paws. I forgot them.

Some cold nights in that northern city, snow a foot deep, the sky heavy with mauve-colored smoke that smothered all the stars, we felt so good, Miriam and I, we'd run outside and roll in the snow. And in the spring, before they lit the floodlights on the tennis courts, we invented a game called blind tennis and played it when we were stoned, running around the court barefoot, trying to hit balls in the dark. We were so alert, we thought, we could *hear* them coming.

In June of 1970 I abandoned college. Miriam was graduating and going to Boston to teach and I wanted to go with her. Again there were quiet and reasonable and fruitless discussions with my parents. But I did as I pleased, and I was pleased to go to Boston and work for Israel Putnam. There were better schools for poets than college, and better poets than I had attended them.

That summer and fall I shoveled sugar and wrote poems by the score. One or two of them, after I had rewritten them so many times they were like recalcitrant children to me, I fondly thought of as good. No one at any of the magazines I sent them to agreed with me, but that wasn't what started me wanting to go home. Editors would eventually recognize my worth, or, if not, I would continue doing what I was going to do, anyhow. But by November I had begun to feel a pull—like gravity, maybe, whatever it is that makes one sure the world is the best planet we have and that one's own part of it is a necessary spiritual terrain, as much one's own as a cast in the eye—that drew me southward again.

That, at any rate, was what the poet said to himself at the time. But the other thing that drove him out of Boston he did not speak of to himself. He wanted a vacation from Miriam.

How could he have wanted to leave her? That thick fair hair, those eyes as blue as Wedgwood teacups, as green as summer light, the lovely long spare body that responded so delightfully to his desire? The blond and furry mons? And if he did, why not say so to himself?

Perhaps because he knew that wanting a vacation from his first great passion was not worthy of the poet. It was not that he lusted after other women. Oh, yes, he saw a woman now and then whom he lusted after for ten minutes or an hour. But that was not what made him uneasy. He and Miriam had made the usual solemn commitment to personal freedom that one made in those days and he vaguely intended to live by it.

But there was something else. Perhaps she was too much for him. Could that have been it? Or was it that, just as he tried to forget the sad sorority rejects he had worked with in the Movement, he wanted to forget in her some minute human imperfection that made her unworthy of the poet; and that therefore there were times when he found it unpleasant to think about her.

Some evenings he saw her looking at him with a detached and ironic eye; and some mornings he heard her brushing her teeth and spitting as she bent over the basin in the bathroom. Both these events tended to make his foot itch. In short, sometimes he felt and acted like a son of a bitch.

But working at Chickasaw, I didn't think about politics or the war or human imperfections—not often. I dug up my bottles and thought poetic thoughts about them. I lay in bed and thought of Miriam's long legs and went step by step through my favorite fucking routines (with her and with the girl with the turquoise rings and with a couple of other girls of whom I had tender memories). I fucked them all—right-side-up, upside-down, frontwards, backwards, and sideways; and then I took the necessary measures to ensure a night's sleep. In the daytime I went on knocking planks off joists and sills and knocking nails out of the planks and laying the nails on a board and hammering them straight and dropping them into paper bags, assorted by size, and loading and unloading my truck. I even wrote some poems about planks and nails and one about welding the bush hog, but I could see that they were no good. It was not a time to write poetry, I decided. And so, as a substitute, I began to account to myself occasionally at the typewriter for this holiday time that was passing and what happened in it: to jot down the notes and observations that have turned into this record.

SIX

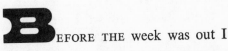EFORE THE week was out I
had visitors.

The sixth day Noah Daniels, Sam's father, came by. It was mid-
afternoon and I had just come from emptying the last load of debris
at Chickasaw dump. Surrounded by leafless briars that in May and
June would be loaded with dewberries and blackberries, I was standing in the abandoned garden, admiring my house. A four-room
cabin with a long porch across the south side, it grew out of the
south slope of Chickasaw Ridge like a plant, gray as lichen on the
clay-colored brick of its high foundation. What distinguished it from
the other tenant houses on the place was, first, that it was high on
the ridge, so that from its porch and windows one could see in every
direction across the ravines and briary abandoned fields; and, second, that it was set up on a lower half-story of brick, buried in the
sloping hillside. The porch on the south side jutted out above the
ground, high enough for me to walk under. The cellar had the floor
and joists of the rooms above for a ceiling. Small barred windows
looked out onto the area under the porch and a trap door opened

into one of the rooms above. When I had cleared out the debris,
discovered that the floor was made of ancient bricks, laid as if b
a drunken man in lines that were straight to begin with but curve
gradually into an involuted serpentine pattern. Here it would b
cool in summer and snug in winter—if I could rig some way to hea
it. There was no fireplace, only the brick foundation rising throug
the middle of the room for the hearths and chimney above.

Northwest of the house, mounded over with the earth that ha
been excavated from it, was a huge brick-lined cistern; rusting gut
ters (I would have to patch them somehow) ran along the edges o
the eaves and porch and drained through a system of downspout
and buried tiles into the cistern.

Beyond the cistern and lower down the slope was a privy, still
weather-tight. I could sweep out the spiderwebs, knock down the
dirt dauber nests, throw in some lime, and use it. Across the ravine,
still lower down the slope and a quarter of a mile to the southeast,
I could see the big house among its oak trees, green-shuttered and
white, freshly painted and well-cared-for, its tin roof sprayed against
rust with red metal primer, and to the northeast of the big house (I
could look down on everything around me from this point) the steely
glint of the lake.

A bumblebee, roused from winter dreams by the unseasonably
warm day, buzzed heavily around my head. The low sun warmed
my back as I stood planning and wool-gathering. Far off, I could
hear the muffled cardiac thump of an oil well pump, and even farther off, the diesel engine of a work-over rig, and like the labored
wheeze of an asthmatic monster, the repeated sound of pipe being
drawn from a well. Then, coming rapidly nearer, the beat of a
horse's hooves on the old half-obliterated wagon track that led to
my house from Chickasaw road. Noah, on Bald Eagle, rode up at a
canter, reining in the great bay horse, and prancing him sideways,
as if for effect. He swung down from the creaking saddle in one
long-limbed easy movement, swept off his hat, and made an exag-
gerated mocking bow. "Alan!"

I looked at him in amazement—an amazement renewed every
time I saw him. He was two years older than my father's father—
dead now some years—and that made him eighty-six. He and my
grandfather and Uncle Dennison had been boys together—had
hunted and fished and grown up together—Noah's father the gar-
dener and his mother the cook. He looked indestructible and was

as agile as a boy. Tall, like Sam, or even taller, his body worn down to an ultimate economy of flesh, the long black face and high forehead deeply seamed, he was all bone and stringy muscle. His eyeballs were as yellow as bile and his gaze, alternately moving and intently still, added you to your surroundings and refigured the results every time he saw you.

Sam was Noah's youngest child, born to his third wife, Sarah, when she was over forty—the child of their middle age. His other children (how many? twelve? eighteen? twenty? I did not know, for he changed the count whenever he chose, having, it appeared, the conviction that a statement should be *truth*, not fact, and a fondness for multiples of six and ten) were scattered across the county and the country. He had, he said, altogether, sixty grandchildren, a hundred great-grandchildren, and twenty-four great-great-grandchildren. (Enough had stayed in Homochitto County, enough on Chickasaw Ridge, for him to be the patriarch of the neighborhood.) Twelve of his grands and great-grands, he told me that winter, had been baptized in Chickasaw Pond last June.

One reason my family had been glad to take Sam back after Parchman—had asked no questions and suppressed whatever doubts they may have had—was that Sam was Noah's son. We were an island of McLaurins in a sea of Danielses. Who could say what the untraceable retaliation might be if we were to turn our backs on Sam? Someone might even set fire to the house one winter night when it was empty. That, at any rate, was what Denny had said; my father and Leila said nothing. At the time I believed they didn't want to think about unpleasant possibilities.

Noah and I walked over the place together, he pointing out here and there what he thought would be useful to me and telling me about it in his rusty bardic voice: there was a fig tree yonder by the privy. Cows had eaten it and tramped it to the ground, but the root was good and I could fertilize it and put a wire enclosure around it for protection. It would bear in a few years. " 'And they shall sit, every man under his vine and under his fig tree; and won't nobody make them afraid, for the mouth of the Lord of hosts said it,' " he said. He looked at me.

"OK, I will," I said.

And there (pointing the long, thin, scuffed and grayish hand at the edge of the field in front of the house) was a plum thicket. He would teach me to make plum brandy in June, if I was still here, brandy like Sarah used to make. Here (he kicked the brick pillar that held up a corner of the front porch and the mortar sifted out), here, I could see, the mortar was rotten. Did I know how to mix mortar? He would come and help me with it. I took him into the basement for an opinion of the state of the bricks there. He told me I should take a wire brush and clean the walls down and scrape out the joints and then plaster the whole room. He would show me how.

"The old man" (he meant my Great-uncle Dennison) "and me, we plastered the dairy—hadn't been twenty years ago. It was in bad a shape as this. We'll see to it," he said. " 'For if the foundations is destroyed, what can the righteous do?' Yeah. When you go back over there, take a look at the dairy. See what a good job we did. The old man was like me: could turn his hand to anything."

"But I like the bricks," I said. "I don't want to cover them up."

He opened his eyes wide and bugged his yellow eyeballs at me in disbelief. "Plaster it, Alan," he said. "You don't want no brick walls. Not if you going to use this place. You be steady sweeping out dust. And put some concrete on this yere floor. Ain't nothing but bricks laid on dirt."

"Look here, Noah," I said. "There's a funny thing about the chimney. Seems like if they were going to make a room down here, they would have brought the flue all the way down. No way to heat this part of the house."

"When my granddaddy lived here, he used it for a root cellar," Noah said, "but I heard since I was a child . . ." He looked sideways at me—one of his earnest looks, the kind that always made me think he was lying, and . . .

Lying is not what I mean. More a way of talking about the world —like his use of those numbers: eighteen children, sixty grandchildren, a hundred great-grandchildren; like the "song" of his grandmother, "brought down from West Virginia and sold on the block like a piece of horse meat." He dropped into his past, into the pasts of his parents and grandparents and even into mine, and appropriated them, as if his mission was to keep us all alive—not only alive, but interesting, larger than life, all our acts performed with symmetry and charged with meaning.

"I remember" (he'd say) "that was when Mercy Seat Church was over on the creek, right on the Duck Pond Line, before your grandpa was born, and the peoples on Duck Pond wasn't let come to church and they would sneak off and come and they would sing real soft, *quiet,* so the patterrollers wouldn't hear." He is only two years older than my grandfather and there hasn't been a *patterroller* since Reconstruction.

"That was the year the stars fell. All the peoples had visions and they thought the world would end. I told you about the year the stars fell?" The stars fell in 1822.

Or: "Right there, that's where my grandmama and grandpa lived. Right there. Not the grandma come down from West Virginia, the other one. She was a white Indian and he was Guinea. You never seen a Guinea to know it, have you? Little bit of a man. He could talk their language and all. And he could *dance*—dance on his belly like a toadfrog. Both my granddaddies could dance. I taken my talent from them. Sam, too. In our day we both had a reputation for dancing. Ain't no sin. 'Dance before the Lord'—that's what David done.

"But that ain't what I aim to tell you. This is what I aim to tell you, Alan, and you remember it. Put it down and remember it. I'm the last one. Your granddaddy dead. The old man dead. My mama and daddy. All those old peoples. I'm the onliest one left can tell you all that happened. Yeah. All you got to do is ask. Yeah. Well, like I was saying, I'm going to tell you this story about my grandmama, the one was a white Indian. She was mammy to your great-grandpa, see? From the time he was born, and that was during of the Civil War when the soldiers come. You know all that? Yeah. And they was killing all the boy babies, see? Not colored, *white.* So they can't grow up and fight 'em, see? And my granny, she took and hid your great-grandpa in her bosom and flung her shawl over him and set down in her rocking chair—right *there,* yonder, in that house (used to be the cook's house when I was a little boy), and she rock and sing and set and rock and sing and set, and they pass on by and go their way and never see him. She save his life."

He looks at me and I look at him.

"Come on, Noah! Is that true?"

"That's *right.* As I stand here, that's the God's truth."

Now he walked over to one of the windows in my basement. "You see these yere little bitty windows?" he said. "Cat couldn't hardly get through 'em. But they barred. Now, ain't that strange? No glass in 'em and never has been. Yeah, this yere was the slave jail. Overseer lived upstairs. And the slaves, when they got obstreperous, they stuck 'em down here. No fire. Cold. No bed to lay on.

A bucket to pee and shit in. And that there"—he pointed overhead —"that used to be a trap door. Nailed shut now. Overseer upstairs. He lift up the trap door and stick his head down here. 'Y'all ready to do right?' he say. 'Y'all not going to run off no more?' And after a couple of days they say, 'Yas, Massa.' " He mimicked the servile voice and looked at me, his yellow eyes cold. "Yeah," he said. "That's what my granddaddy told me. He was a slave."

"Hmm," I said. I had an instant's irreconcilable vision of my own grandfather ordering any such thing done to Noah.

As if he read my thought, "No doubt, your peoples didn't know about it," he said. And then, "Ain't we lucky we didn't live then?"

"I can glaze the windows," I said, "but what do you think would be the best way to heat the place?"

"Get one them old potbelly stoves and put it down here," he said. "Heat it better than butane."

"But where would the flue go? Got to go higher than the ridge pole or it'll set the place on fire."

"That's a problem, ain't it? We got to figure on that."

"Do you think I could knock some bricks out of the foundation here and run the flue up into the chimney?"

"Looks to me like this yere foundation is solid all the way up," he said. "You'd have to run your flue up through the ceiling to get to the chimley. That ain't going to do." He picked up a piece of baling wire from the floor, reached up, and scratched at the rotten mortar. "We talk it over with Sam," he said. "He's a better brick man than me any day. He can help us with the plastering, too," he added. "Getting stronger every day. Soon be his old self."

"Noah," I said (I had been thinking about saying it to him or to Sam or to both of them ever since I had seen Sam), "what about Sam's leg? Isn't there anything else they can do for it? And his hip. They do these operations now where they replace the whole ball and socket. Has he seen a bone man?"

"Bone man!" Noah gave me a sly look, the yellow eyeballs shining in the long black face. "What you talking about, *bone man?* We don't fool with none of that. We good Christians. You suppose to be the same."

"A bone *doctor,* I mean."

"Hmmph." He shook his head. "He done had enough of doctors. He be better off leaving them doctors alone. Anyways, he's getting stronger every day."

"If he hadn't run off like that, it never would have happened," I said. "Why did he have to do that?"

"It come over him, that's why." He shrugged. "Sam always did think he could do what he want to—nobody could stop him."

"There's a good bone doctor in Jackson," I said. "I'd take him up there, if he would go. Do you think he would?"

"No," Noah said. "He ain't going to do that." He shook the baling wire at me. "Let me tell you this about Sam," he said. "He's *willful*. Always has been. From the beginning. And there's a reason why." He was silent for a moment, then, "Strange, strange," he said. "The ways of the Lord is past understanding." He had lapsed into his bardic, storytelling voice. "Yeah," he said. "Listen to this, Alan: It come to pass in the year before he was born, Sarah was through with all that. You understand? And she tells me one night, 'Noah, it's done come on me again. Ain't that strange? Here, it's been most a year, and it's done come on me again.'

"Well, I didn't think nothing of it, and I says, 'Well,' or something like that.

"But she worries about it. She thinks it must be a sickness. Two, three days pass and, lo, son, she has a dream. She dreams she's setting by the fire worrying about her sickness, saying, 'Lord, is this cancer I got inside of me, eating on me, making me bleed?'

"And a voice say, 'Hold on there, Sarah, ain't nothing to worry about.' Say, 'You going to have another son, Sarah.'

"And in her dream she's laughing because she says, 'How come you to say I'm going to find me another child, old as I is?' But just as she says that, the log in the fireplace breaks, sends up, *whoosh,* a shower of sparks up the chimley, roll right off the dogs and out onto the hearth and wakes her up."

"Hmmm," I said.

"Oh, you can have a true dream, Alan! You can have a false dream, or you can have a true dream, and you can learn to tell the difference.

"Well, anyhow," he went on, "you can see by that, when Sam come, he would be welcome. Like the fountains of her blood was renewed by him and she was a young woman again. And so he was always special to her. He was a beautiful child—*fine*. She loved him like she never did no other of her children. She gave him the wishbone every time. And in my judgment, that's how come he's so willful. He's *willful*.

"Like, take women. When I was a young man I learn to look on a woman and say to myself, 'Whoa, boy, she's dangerous.' And on another and say, 'Here I come!' But Sam, he looks on the same woman and says both. She's dangerous. Here I come." He laughed. "Ain't nobody going to direct him to do this or that. *Now* he calls it the will of God he's crippled. Says *God* come to him when he was up there in the hospital in Parchman."

"Damn, Noah!" I followed him out. "It might be the will of God for him to get well, if he went to the right doctor."

"I never said *I* thought it was the will of God. It was the Devil, if you ask me. The Devil tempt him. And it was the Devil got after him the night Phoebe and Timmie got killed, too. And the Devil tempt your daddy and your aunts, both of 'em, and Lester Chipman, to sell the land for that contraption they got over there. The Devil done the whole thing from start to finish. 'Going to and fro in the earth, and walking up and down in it.' Oh, he's a smart rascal!"

"What do you mean, when Phoebe and Timmie got killed? That was an *accident*. Are you trying to put the blame for that on Sam?"

"Yeah, it was an accident. But how do we know the Devil didn't lay his hand on the steering wheel? Devil lay his hand on the steering wheel and look what he gets out of it. Lester Chipman eating up his soul with meanness. Sam give down to rage and running over peoples with old Eagle here like they was dogs!"

He walked, with me still following, around the house and climbed up the slope past the cistern to the highest point of the ridge, where he stopped and looked around him. Below us to the south lay the weed-choked garden, where leafless briars moved stiffly in the rising wind. At the foot of the north side of the ridge, a couple of hundred yards away, we could see an abandoned well site, scattered stumps of concrete where the drilling rig had stood, a few lengths of rusting pipe, oil-stained gravel grown up with cockleburs, and, off to one side, the gleaming black sludge of the waste pit. The sun was dropping rapidly and lead-colored clouds had gathered in the north.

I turned away and looked at my house.

"Leona Carter's family—cousins to us—lived in that house from time my granddaddy died until the old man died," Noah said. "Fifty years. Farmed all this land y'all done let go back to woods."

"I know," I said. "If *you* would talk to Sam, Noah . . ."

"The Devil everywhere in this world," Noah said. "Going to and fro. Walking up and down. You think you can come out here in the country, live a peaceful life, like nothing ever happens when you're away from cities and peoples and have everything according to your lights. You can take Sam up to Jackson and feel fine about helping him out. Maybe even do him some good. But it ain't so. More to it than that." He turned back toward the cistern, and again I followed him. As we walked I became aware that the sound of drilling had stopped while we talked—only because I heard it start up again, the far-off asthmatic wheeze.

"Drilling over on Duck Pond," Noah said. "Done brought one in. Starting another." By the cistern he stopped.

"Getting ready to drill an offset on Chickasaw," he said. "I seen 'em back in there. Duck Pond well ain't no more than fifty yards from the line." He looked at me with a calculating eye.

Now what?

"Y'all made plenty money out of them wells," he said. "Hadn't you?"

"I reckon they did. Some."

"First well come in in 'fifty-three. Down there back of my house. Pumped ten years. Is that right?"

"I don't know," I said. "I was too little to pay any attention and the money didn't belong to me."

"Me neither," he said. "I never seen a nickel of it."

Shit. "Why do you want to make me feel bad?" I said. "I didn't have anything to do with any of it. Still don't."

He did not answer, but instead walked around the house, untied Bald Eagle, flung the reins over his head, and swung himself up. "You know Dallas Boykin's back to Chickasaw Ridge?" he said.

"Sam told me. Have you seen him?" I was glad to get off the subject of the Devil and the oil wells.

"I seen his old pickup yestiddy, parked down yonder by the double-gate pond." He said *yawnder* and *pawnd,* as my grandfather had, in a way that seemed to fill the distance with blue air, to give the water a heavy rippling clarity.

"Probably hunting squirrel."

"Ain't none of his to hunt. Our'n. I ain't told him he could hunt."

"What do you care?" I said.

"I'm suppose to be in charge of this place. He suppose to ask *me*." He illustrated his control with a jerk on Bald Eagle's rein, and the horse danced sideways and walled his eyes around at Noah's skinny leg, as if he'd like to take a bite out of it.

"What's he doing back here?" I said.

said. He slacked the reins. "People say both them boys fell out with they daddy. They mamma died, let's see, sometime in 'sixty-four, I believe 'twas. Yeah. After they burnt the church. And they daddy married again. Moved out to Texas, so I heard. Some way he got aholt of some money." He paused and looked at me as if I might be able to tell him how Mr. Boykin got his money. Then he went on. "Bought him some machines and now he done turnt hisself into one of these yere tree peoples."

"What?"

"These yere peoples contract with the light company to trim up the trees around the light wires and clear the right-of-ways. And they clear lots and all—in town. Travel all over the country doing that. One of my grandbabies—Jawn (the one graduated last year from Tougaloo)—he works for 'em when they come to Homochitto. Lot of money in it, he says—if you own the machines. But the boys —Dallas and Lindsay Lee—they hadn't got nothing to do with it, fur as I know. Least Jawn never sees 'em when he's working for they daddy. So I don't know what they hanging around here for."

"Don't worry about it, Noah," I said. "Dallas is used to hunting on Chickasaw. Maybe he asked Lester and Denny if it was OK."

"He suppose to ask *me*."

"I'll tell him you're the one to check it out with, if I see him," I said. "OK?" And then, "What have you and Sam got against Dallas, Noah?" I asked. "Sam acted like I ought to look out for him."

"Nothing personal," Noah said. "Some people of a dangerous type, that's all, and that's them. I'm going to tell you this, Alan, and you listen. You can't trust 'em. Like, who do you think told your uncle 'twas my fault they cut the wrong trees that time he got so mad at me? Mac Boykin, that's who. The kind of man finds it natural to blame anything happens on a nigger. He don't even know he done wrong. He can talk himself into believing I'm cheating y'all, when in actual fact . . ."

"But that wasn't Dallas. He was a kid then."

"Just the same I want to know when him and his brother come on this place and what they're doing."

"I'll tell Dallas you're the one to check it out with, if I see him," I said again.

Feeling a vague impatient irritation (*Let me alone, for Christ's sake*), I watched him ride away. Ask him about Sam and he gives me a lot of shit about Sarah's dreams and about the Devil. Ask him about Dallas and he wants to talk about Mr. Boykin. Ask him about the bricks and he wants to cover them up with plaster. Well, quit asking, then.

I got a hammer and crowbar out of the toolbox in the pickup and set to work jerking off the boards that had been nailed on to enclose the back porch.

It was the middle of the morning of the next day and I was still ripping off boards, knocking out nails, and straightening them when I had my second visitor: Dallas Boykin. I knew him right away, even though we hadn't seen each other since we were both fifteen.

SEVEN

CARRYING A thirty-aught-six rifle balanced muzzle down in his right hand, Dallas came quietly out of the woods. Silence—that's the quality in him that has always struck me first. As a child I felt called upon to chatter, to entertain, to ingratiate myself, and his silence must have seemed to me then to be a statement of his confidence in his own worth.

Small (as tall at fifteen as he would ever be), compact, dark-haired, and pale-skinned, the thin firm mouth always closed, not as if it were natural to keep it closed, but in a straight line, slightly compressed, as if he guarded himself against frivolous speech, he listened and watched us. In his brown eyes, intelligent and appraising, I saw, when I was a child, what I believed to be contempt, and I believed his contempt for me to be justified. He was poised where I was awkward, a master of himself in the woods; and, although he was only a few months older, I sensed in him a precocious sexual maturity that filled me with envy. But he liked me, I suppose, in spite of my shortcomings, since he came by every summer and allowed me to take to the woods with him.

I had wanted to learn his skills and had had sense enough, even as a talkative child, to keep my mouth shut and take in what he had to teach me. We spent long days together fishing the lakes and creeks and ponds on the place. He knew every shade of wind and weather and time of day that a fisherman needed to know, and I believe he knew where every bass in every pond on Chickasaw had its headquarters. He was a hunter, too, and I had hunted with him and practiced target-shooting until I was fifteen—until I decided to stop killing for sport. But Dallas knew nothing of that decision or of the roots or consequences of it in my life. He and his family had left Homochitto County sometime during the winter of 1965 and I had not seen him since.

He came along by the side of the fence without the sound of a footfall, but I sensed—already, in the silence and loneliness of the country, I had got more alert to human presence—his coming, saw a change in the light behind my left shoulder and, when I turned, the movement of his body among the trees. A Walker hound trotted lightly out of the woods and Dallas followed.

I laid aside the crowbar with which I had been prizing boards off the porch, jumped to the ground, and stood waiting for him. He came up to the house and nodded as if we had parted yesterday.

"Alan."

"Hello," I said. "How you been, Dallas?" He had not offered to shake hands and, after I half raised mine, I dropped it and said, "Sam told me you were around."

"Yeah." He turned away and walked around the house slowly, looking it over. His dog did not follow, but sniffed at my leg, growled softly, and sat down maybe ten feet off, keeping his eyes fixed steadily on me, as if Dallas had given him a command to watch me. "What you trying to do with this nigger shack?" he said, when he got back to where I was standing.

"I'm going to live in it when I get it fixed up," I said.

"It's a damn rag," he said.

"You should've seen it before I got started. I've ripped off the worst of it."

He left me and walked around the house again, this time more slowly. He knocked at a beam here and there, laid his gun against a post and vaulted up onto the high front porch (I had torn off the rotten steps), walked around inside, and then came back. "Sounder than it looks," he said. "The roof don't leak but in one

71

place." Then, "What you going to do with these?" He tapped the two creosoted telephone poles that I had dragged in from the back of the place.

I showed him how the roof sagged on one side and how rotten the old posts were. "I've got to prop up the roof while I rebuild the bases; then I'll cut the telephone posts in half and mount them on the new bases and I'll have supports for my porch roof."

He looked me over. "You done growed," he said, his voice exaggeratedly nasal, twangy. (Later I would observe that he used his country voice for strangers and enemies and another, less nasal, with a slightly different set of inflections, when he began to feel kindly toward you.) "Last time I seen you, you wasn't five-three, and now you look to be six-two. But you probably ain't big enough to do all that by yourself. Besides, I don't remember you was much of a carpenter."

"I've improved," I said. "I spent one summer as a carpenter's helper—framing up, mostly."

He said nothing.

"I reckon I'll do as much as I can by myself," I said, "and then see if I can get hold of somebody to give me a hand. One of Sam's kids, maybe. He's got a couple of sons, high school age, that live in town with their aunt."

"I've seen them. They fish out here." He continued to stare at me and I saw in his eyes an opaque, almost blank look that I took for hostility. The day was warm and I had taken off my knit cap. My hair was wooly and dusty. I brushed a cobweb out of my beard and returned his stare.

"You gonna get you one of these *communes* going or something?" he said. "One of these live-in-sex-for-everybody outfits like Lindsay Lee told me about when he come up here from New Or*leans?* Plant a garden and say heathen prayers over it like I seen on the TV?"

"No," I said. "Mostly I expect I'm going to stay by myself."

"Well, I'll see you around." He picked up his gun and walked off toward the ravine that ran along the west side of Leona's house, his dog trotting behind him. Once, he turned as if about to say something more, but then he shrugged and went his way, slipping into the shadows of the deep woods.

Later on that morning I heard a shot far away in the direction of the SPASURSTA, and toward noon another close by. He came out of the woods afterwards with a couple of squirrels hanging from his belt. I was still working. Again he stopped.

"Roof's gonna fall in on you, you damn fool," he said. "Can't you see that stud's load-bearing? Why don't you brace the joist with a couple of them two-by-sixes you got under the porch there?"

"It'll take two to brace the roof," I said. "I want to do as much as I can by myself before I hire somebody to help me. I haven't got any money to waste on help."

He smiled and, reaching down, scratched his dog's head. "All these hippies say they so goddamn poor," he said, "but they always got the money for grass and cocaine and acid and like that. Their daddies send 'em money to stay away from home, I reckon. Or they're good-looking like you and some woman takes care of them."

"Come on, Dallas," I said, "you're a damn fool yourself. I'm not a hippie—whatever a hippie is."

"How do I know what you are?" he said. "I hadn't seen you in seven years."

"How do I know what *you* are?" I said.

We looked at each other, him expressionless as usual, balancing the gun lightly, the dog sitting close to his left heel, me irritable, nervous, but with my mind already made up that I wasn't going to fight.

"I'll give you a hand with a couple of these two-by-sixes," he said. "We can nail 'em together, toenail 'em in, and then use your truck jack to jack 'em up and take the load off the stud."

"Thanks," I said.

"Those beams you got under there are blue poplar," he said. "Where'd you get 'em?"

I told him that I had torn down another abandoned house for the wood in it and showed him my boards, cypress and poplar, gray as moss with wind and weather, worn in the grain, some of them twelve or more inches wide. "Beautiful, aren't they?" I said.

He looked at me and shook his head. "Anyway, they're not rotten."

"Main thing I'm lacking is doors and windows," I said. "I've either got to make some or get some second-hand."

After that conversation, Dallas came by almost every day. He never said it was to see if I needed help—rather, that it was more or less on his way home from the next place down the road where he was cutting pulpwood. The second time he came I told him I'd like to swap out with him if he needed any work done at his place, but he shook his head.

"Tell Sam I'm hunting over here," he said. "That's a better swap for me. And let me know any time your uncle or his friends are coming out here, so I can keep out of their way."

"OK," I said. "And you mention it to Noah, will you? He likes to think he's in charge out here."

"I might even get a deer or two," he said.

I hesitated. "Out of season?"

He didn't even bother to answer.

"Well. But no does. And be careful. The state forester is out here sometimes checking on the trees. He might report you to the game warden."

"I see him when he comes out. He does some poaching himself. I can keep out of his way."

"I can't guarantee I'll always know when my uncle-in-law might be coming," I said, "but he doesn't hunt and he doesn't ride over the place very often."

"Somebody needs to hunt this place," he said. "It's already over-populated—you'll be having an epidemic in a year or two." He smiled. "I'm doing your uncle a favor."

"I know," I said. "I just hate to kill 'em."

"You grieve over cows when you're eating steak?"

"OK. OK."

"The wild turkeys are coming back," he said. "A flock jumped up in front of me the other day—thirty or forty birds. I hadn't killed any yet. Let 'em alone another year or two."

"If you were to tell anybody where they were, they'd all be dead in a month."

Again he allowed himself a smile. "Don't you know I don't tell *nobody nothing?*"

Next time he came we talked over what had to be done, and afterwards he would usually drop by late in the afternoon, sometimes driving an old piece of pickup truck—a blue '62 Chevy with a gun rack on the back of the cab and a CB radio muttering messages from under the dashboard—sometimes walking, gun in hand, dog trotting ahead. We planned the work so that he could help me do what required two people; the rest of the day I would work alone. Or he would show me how to do something alone that I thought would take two people.

He never said much, but I learned from a chance remark one

day, an answer to a direct question another, first that he was working with a pulpwood cutter from Buchanan County (after he got out of the army, he had gone in on shares with another man to buy the flatbed truck and winch and a pickup to get started with); then that his mother had died the winter of '65 and that his father had remarried within six months. He never saw his father anymore. He had quit school when he was seventeen, he said, and joined the army. Two years in the infantry, one in Vietnam. He hated the gooks. "When I got out," he said, "I liked to kill people. I thought I might want to be a cop. Or a narc, maybe. But I'm over all that now." He had his own place—a trailer in a park half a mile south of Chickasaw.

We worked together off and on for three weeks before he told me that he was married and had a child. It had never crossed my mind that he might be.

"I'd like to meet your wife and kid," I said.

"Yeah? Sometime." We were standing in the basement where I had been at work all day scouring the bricks with a wire brush to clear away the rotten mortar. "You need to get you some Bondex for these walls," he said. "Keep the damp out."

I was always careful what I said to him, had felt it was possible to ask about his father and say I was sorry his mother had died, only because it seemed proper. I *had* known them, after all, had sat down to more than one meal in their house. But except for that sort of ceremonious question, I was careful. I wanted to ask him about Vietnam, what he had seen and done, but I didn't. Even after three weeks of seeing each other almost daily, we knew scarcely anything about each other. He knew—what? That I could drive a nail and was willing to take advice. I did say to him that I had worked in the sugar refinery and described to him what it had been like. I did not mention writing or women or college or the war or what I had done instead of getting drafted. I wanted to get to know him again, and I sensed the need for caution, had a feeling that he was in some way like a wounded or threatened animal, not to be drawn out by trampling the undergrowth or setting the dogs to dig at his burrow. Long ago he had gone to ground, lay quiet behind a curtain of vines—master of who knew how many alternate tunnels and entrances?—lay there, looking out, brown eyes alert, intelligent, stoic, at the turmoil of dogs and men crashing through his home woods.

And so I talked about the refinery and about how I had lived in Roxbury, in a black slum, feeling safe because my landlord (the foreman of my shift) was a giant of a Jamaican black man who had owned his own house in the neighborhood for fifteen years, whose friend or tenant no man dared touch; how he and I went to work together every afternoon on the subway, riding underground in cars crowded with children who were coming home from school just as we were going to work. That was the best part of the day, riding with the children. Almost everything else was bad.

"I wouldn't work in no factory," he said. "I wouldn't have no man tell me what to do and me have to do it. The army—OK. But never again."

"It was one huge room," I said, "big as the inside of the high school I went to; concrete floors running with spilled syrup, sugar dust in the air like a sandstorm; and all the time a scream so loud I wore earplugs, from the vacuum machine that pulled the sugar out of the air for reprocessing. The syrup ran down the walls from the floors above, where they had refining vats as big as swimming pools, and turned into sugar icicles. The syrup would eat through the soles of your shoes and everything you had on; and your hands and face and hair were stiff with it, and your sweat turned to syrup and your arms stuck together and your balls stuck to your legs."

"What did you do?" he said.

"Sometimes I swept sugar into a hole. Sometimes I was in the bins. Half a day I held the bags under the spout that the finished sugar came out of. You hold up the bag until the gauge says sixty pounds, then you step on a treadle to cut off the flow, hand the bag to the next guy, and pick up another. Do that four hours a day and you keep fit—if you don't die of candied lungs."

"I see you're not the weak kid you used to be," he said. And then, again, "I wouldn't work for no man."

"It wasn't exactly like I was working for any *man*—foreman or superintendent," I said. "More like we were all working for some kind of gigantic roaring *nothing*. Everybody hated it . . . if you can hate *nothing*. I've seen a man more than once shit or piss in a pile of sugar and kick sugar over it like a cat. Nobody cared."

I was sitting on the ridgepole of the roof while we talked. I had spent the morning stacking the thin, weather-silvered cedar shakes, carrying the stacks up to the roof, and ripping away one long section that leaked; then I had begun to patch the roof. He had come at noon and, after watching me a few minutes: "Here," he said, "I can do it quicker than you. Gimme the hatchet." Now I watched him and talked as he moved up the roof laying and nailing the shingles with a rhythm as exact as a metronome: Tap, TAP; tap, TAP, his hands flashing from shingle to nail, nail to shingle, with the grace and precision of a ballet dancer.

He stopped and looked thoughtfully at me. "The Devil's probably in on it," he said. "Sometimes the Devil may call himself *Nothing.*"

"Noah says the Devil made Sam . . ." I hesitated. ". . . made Sam wreck the SPASURSTA."

He looked at me steadily, his brown eyes squinting in the pale winter sunshine, his mouth a straight neutral line. "Could be," he said.

"Hmmm," I said.

Immediately I saw him withdraw into his burrow.

"All that money your daddy's got," he said, "what you doing working in a sugar factory?"

"My daddy hasn't got all that much money, Dallas," I said irritably. "That's the truth. He never has put his mind on money, and so he hasn't made it. He makes a living. And we make enough off the trees and the oil to keep this place like it is. But he's got two more kids to raise. Besides, I'm grown. He's not supposed to be taking care of me."

Dallas did not answer, but reversed the hatchet, split a shingle in half to finish off the last row, and nailed it in place. "I'm through," he said. "So long." He climbed down off the roof and drove away.

And so we stumbled along, side by side, working together, trying to talk or keeping a queer companionable silence; and I grew fond of him again, for the reasons I had always been fond of him: the economy of movement, the skill at everything he undertook, the control and concentration, and the generosity with which, during the time he was with me, he gave me everything he had to give.

And, of course, I needed him.

EIGHT

SOME DAYS I might be sorry when he came, because he broke into the solitude that for the first time in my life I had imposed on myself. But I could always walk away from the house. If I wanted to be alone all day, I would knock off and take a walk in the woods (telling him the day before, if he came by, that I wasn't going to be working the following afternoon). Sometimes on my walks I had an eerie feeling that he was watching me. I would pass through the close-set ranks of pine trees, hearing, a moment too soon, as it seemed, the voices of the crows that always announced the approach of a human being; come out on the edge of a deep ravine and scramble down to its bed where the ferns were still green under a blanket of leaves and, as I walked along, my feet noiseless on the sand, hear the snap of a twig above my head; I would look up expecting to see a goat or a cow peering down at me from the embankment and see nothing.

But I was both watched and watcher. Early in February I began to listen and watch for the coming of the first spring migrants: magnolia warblers and juncos. Or I would sit in one spot for an hour watching a chipmunk at his work. One night I took my sleeping bag and flashlight and star maps and paddled out to the raft that we kept anchored for swimming in the middle of the lake. There I could see the whole sweep of the heavens unblocked by trees or hills. The mist rose off the lake, and the pages of my atlas and my sleeping bag and my hair were icy with dew that turned to frost in the early morning. I was tough enough for only one night of that.

Any place, any time, you can tell yourself romantic stories and try to live in them. One day when I walked over to the house to begin work I found a starving kitten—black as Noah, with green-flecked bronze eyes—lying by my back steps. I fattened him up and de-fleaed him and he would ride on my shoulder like Robinson Crusoe's parrot. I taught him to sit beside me in the truck like a dog and ride back and forth to the lake and to Calloway's store.

There's a painting someplace that I would have liked at that time to think of as myself: a trapper is paddling a canoe through misty air across a wide lake. A tongue of land juts toward him out of mist. He has just finished a long stroke and his canoe seems to be emerging toward land and the promise of a night's campfire. The canoe rides low in the water, a pile of skins mounded amidships. His cat, alert and peaceful, big and black, sits high above the water on the skins.

One day I took my cat, named to begin with Lucifer, on the strength of Noah's and Dallas's remarks, but afterwards (for spirits, when they please, can either sex assume) Lucy, out with me in the canoe. The pickup had suited Lucy well enough, but she drew the line at water transport. She moaned and mewed, while I held her with one hand and paddled with the other until we were well out in the lake—fifty yards or so. The instant I let her go, she jumped overboard and struck out. I picked her up and she scratched hell out of me and jumped overboard again. That time she swam straight in and took off through the woods. She was sitting on the porch sunning herself and waiting for lunch when I got home.

So much for the romance of the lonely trapper and his cat.

Another day I followed a ravine that twisted down the north side of Chickasaw Ridge and sloped off through deep woods toward the back of the place, and found a spring I'd never seen before. It had been enclosed with cedar boards, mostly rotted away now, and a path led down to it from an overgrown wagon track.

The water was clear and icy, welling up under the noon sun and roiling the glittering bronze sand. I remembered my grandfather telling me that when he was a boy only winter rain was stored in the cisterns. Summer rain was thought to carry fever. If the winter was dry, the cisterns would run low in August, and he and Noah would take a wagon back each week to a spring and draw barrels of pure drinking water. A battered dipper still hung by a rusty chain from a ring in one of the locust posts. I drank and walked homeward in deep silence through the woods, imagining myself a traveler who found that spring in a country he had never walked through before, who drank and walked on, alert for smoke from the chimney of a wilderness home and the sight of the man who had chained the dipper there.

Half lost, I passed through an almost impenetrable pine plantation, and came out on the east side of the horse lot. This is what my traveler, whom I had imagined coming out abruptly on the wide oak-shaded lawn, the snug white house, and, across the way, the gray cabin, would have seen: an abandoned tractor with rusted disks and harrows scattered around it; the fallen-down tin shed that had once housed it; a gully choked with garbage—tin cans, broken bottles, a broken washing machine; a 1953 Ford pickup parked out in the weather; a new shed (Sam's with his 1969 green Oldsmobile under it); beyond the lot to the south, the tip of a tower that housed part of the SPASURSTA sending equipment; and to the north, an old oil well site with its scattered concrete slabs and black sludge pit.

I remembered, too, that Uncle Dennison had died of typhoid fever.

So much for the romance of the wilderness home.

As the days passed, my work went well: the carpentering (I even built my own crude doors and put together and framed in and glazed some windows that I bought from a house being demolished in Homochitto); the work of solitude and watching; and early in the morning every day, after I had built up the fire and dressed and drunk my coffee and fed the cat and brought in the wood, the beginning of *this*—the work of taking notes and jotting down observations. Sometimes I wrote at night, too, but usually I would be tired. Once in a while Sam might come down to the house and drink a beer with me and talk about specific problems: a fence that needed repairing—would I help him cut some locust posts on the back of the place? a washout in the road that I must be careful to avoid until it had dried out enough so that we could fill it; the beginnings of our garden. But mostly I came in tired, cooked my supper, read awhile, and went to bed.

Day after day, waking every morning alone, I began to think less about birds and stars and heroic lonely men and more about women. I had then, as I have said, an ideal of sexual freedom, a vague Blakean conviction (the lust of the goat is the glory of God) that the joys of the flesh are pure, that at the heart of love lies *freedom*. (Miriam and I had talked it over.) I kept remembering the girl with the long black hair and the silver and turquoise rings and the white VW. One day, in town for a call on my grandmother, I saw her again at a stoplight and flagged her down.

"Hello," I said, standing in the middle of the street and bending down at the car window. "Remember me? I'm the freak you picked up last month on the road to Chickasaw Ridge."

"Hey, man," she said, "what's happening?" She smiled happily up at me.

"At Chickasaw Ridge, not much," I said. "I'm lonesome." The light would change in a minute and there was no time to waste. "What are you doing tonight?" I said.

"Man, it's a school night. My parents are square."

"Couldn't you go to the library?" The light was green and she began to pull away while my hand was still on the door. I trotted along beside her for a few steps. "Seven o'clock," I said. "I'll wait for you there."

Well, I borrowed Sam's car and we met at the library and behind the "Hey, man, what's happening?" I found on guard a vigilant sixteen-year-old southern virgin who would probably take her maidenhead to her marriage with the promising young executive whose daddy had just bought him a McDonald's franchise.

So much for the romance of sexual freedom.

The year moved on toward spring and Miriam finished her semester of practice teaching and went home to Ohio for a few weeks with her parents. Neither of us was sure what to do next. She had to get a job and wrote of looking for something temporary through the spring and summer—teaching jobs being nonexistent at this time of year. I had the empty bed blues, I told her, and I wanted her to come first to Mississippi and spend some time with me. She was broke, but she talked her father into lending her plane fare and agreed to come.

At my end of the line there were problems—problems that

would never have occurred to Miriam, whose father was a professor of psychology with deep convictions about everybody's freedom to "choose his own life-style."

Chickasaw Ridge and Homochitto are small, Chickasaw Ridge a hamlet and Homochitto a town of twenty thousand or so people, most of whom know each other and many of whom are cousins. The McLaurins and their friends and cousins persist in a "life-style" that includes respectability, monogamy, and sin; or so my father's and mother's behavior, the behavior of all that generation except for my Aunt Leila (not to mention the feeble remnants of the generation above), had led me to believe. I didn't want to bother anybody; I thought of Stephen Dedalus refusing to pray by his mother's deathbed and said to myself that that sort of pride was not for me. Casting about, therefore, for a way to bring Miriam down and at the same time satisfy my relatives' notions of propriety, I decided to write Leila.

NINE

LEILA IS divorced. At the time she came down to chaperon Miriam and me at Chickasaw she had already led a celibate—that is to say, unmarried, but not abstemious—life for years. She has told me that she married too young. (I'll get to the details of that later.) I suppose a great many girls like her used to marry too young. (I should use some qualifier here: small-town girls, southern, God-fearing girls.) Their mothers and fathers filled them with ideals of chastity and monogamy, and at seventeen or eighteen, when they had been soul-kissing and petting to climax in the backseats of cars for a couple of years, they decided that, as St. Paul said, it is better to marry than burn. It would be hard to convince me that they *really* believed all their mothers said, but they must have thought they did. Most of them never drive up to any alternative sexual arrangements except divorce and remarriage. Women's lib came too late for them and they can't bear to admit they may have been wrong for twenty or thirty years.

But Leila didn't stay trapped in her early marriage. Nor did she escape from it to another like it. Once free, she stayed single. She is a "law unto herself," as I remember overhearing my grandmother say.

What is she like? For one thing, she's a night person—she probably wore out her husband and her marriage, staying up until three and four o'clock in the morning drinking whiskey and settling moral and philosophical questions. It's interesting to watch her strength increase as the evening advances and the level in the whiskey bottle gets lower. I've spent a dozen marathon night sessions with her since I've been old enough to stay up with the grown folks and talk about love and life; and by two A.M., lecturing on politics or religion or her craft, she glows with energy and charges up and down the room like . . . like what? I hesitate to use the word *bull,* because I don't mean to suggest that she is dikey. But *bullish* is the word to describe her charges in the middle of the night, the (as it begins to seem at four A.M.) inexhaustible power of her attack and the solidity of her person.

Nor is she alcoholic. But she likes to drink, and, because she's heavy, has the capacity of a man. Alcohol vanishes into her tissues like water. She's a typical endomorph—solid and stocky, with legs still smooth heavy columns, and arms strong and young-looking. (She was in her early forties the year she came down to Chickasaw to chaperon Miriam and me.) Ten or fifteen pounds overweight for her body type—five-six, say, and a hundred and forty-five; but she needs weight and strength for her work, and unless you're one of those strange guys who like the spooks they pass off for women in *Vogue* magazine, you wouldn't say she was fat. You *would* say she was attractive—long-lashed, loving green eyes, short dark curly hair, a thin mouth with a smile that curls up at the corners like a medieval angel's, and a face as round and pale and lovely as the moon.

I like her. I have an accumulation of good memories of her: helping us to catch fireflies for our lantern jars; joining us in finger-painting sessions or touch football games; teaching us to weave at her huge heavy loom. And we have in common that, although we're supposed to be grown people, we still like to play games. Or rather that, like her, I spend my life working at what seems to some people no better than playing—unless, of course, you're lucky enough to earn a lot of money at it.

She was able, more readily than any other member of my

father's generation, to bridge with us nieces and nephews the gap between childhood and adulthood, the years when family hostilities crystallize or dissolve. She never treated us like children; there was, therefore, never any time when she had to stop treating us like children or lose us.

This minute I can see her barreling down the living room at home (long after my mother and father have given up and gone to bed), arm outstretched, finger pointed at me, dark hair springing in damp curls (she's worked herself into a sweat over, say, the venality—not to mention the invincible stupidity—of the state political machine), saying, "Wait! Wait! Listen to *me,* Alan. I *know* what happened."

Or, if I have been telling her about my difficulties with some girl or other (or even with the draft board), "Let *me* talk to them, I can straighten everything out."

I had a helluva time convincing her that all I wanted from her for the draft board was a statement that she knew what my convictions were and how long I had held them. She wanted to send her banker, who had a hold over two of the board members, just to sit outside the door of the conference room during the hearing.

But one tends to forgive her errors in judgment, the times when, out of that same excess of enthusiasm and energy and affection, she interferes outrageously in your life, even her occasional treacheries (there are, after all, other people for whom she pours out the same flood of energy and affection and sometimes their interests may conflict with yours), because, no matter how things may turn out, you know she *means* to cherish you.

What more should I put down about her? As I began by saying, she married young—at nineteen. Stayed married maybe ten years, maybe only eight, I can't remember. I remember only that over the years, when she came to the Delta or to Chickasaw to visit, when we children were beginning to know and love her, the husband seldom came along.

I seem to remember lying in bed at night more than once during my childhood and hearing my parents talk in the living room about Leila's life: my father might have been reading aloud to my mother—they often took turns reading aloud in the evenings and I would have been listening to his strong expressive voice and the flow of language, whether or not I understood what he read. My mother, tall and slender and fragile (he had married the physical likeness of his own mother), would be bent over some work or other—knitting, hooking a rug, shelling peas. She never does *nothing*. And abruptly, instead of *Dr. Faustus* or *Henderson, the Rain King*, I would hear my mother, as if she had been thinking all the while he read and now could not help interrupting him: "If they would just have a child, it would stabilize the marriage."

He must have been thinking, too, while he read, for he would immediately take her up. "No, darling. She's right. That's the worst possible reason to have children. Disastrous."

"Plenty of good marriages have been made out of the necessity to stay married—for whatever reason." My mother has more than a touch of the puritan in her, and reading modern novels hasn't much influenced her views on sex and marriage.

They would talk on and I would listen from my bed, feeling their powerful presence all around me, my mother's character revealing itself in her voice, expressive and flexible, making drama of the least incident in our lives, and always shaping, shaping: whether it was the sweater she was knitting, the curve of the flower bed she was outlining with bricks, or *us*—my sister and brother and me, even my father—on the basis of her image of our best environment and our best selves.

As for my father, he survived it. Made, I suppose, of a material so unmalleable that it adapted itself only minimally to her attacks upon its shape. He stayed himself.

But he, too, worried about Leila. I recall hearing him say, some time after the divorce, "All this sleeping around is immoral—*inhuman*."

Now my mother was on the other side. She flew up, angry. "You wouldn't say that if she were a man."

"I don't sleep around."

"Oh, you!" My mother was amused. "You're not like anybody else. Besides," she added, "I don't believe Leila sleeps around. She has *a* lover."

"Hmmm," my father said.

"People have to have somebody to sleep with," my mother said. "It's not her morals I worry about. It's the consequences. The world always takes its revenge. . . ."

Recalling those conversations that I eavesdropped on with the absorption of the child gathering data on its world, I am amazed, *amazed*, at their naiveté. Did my mother really think there was a "world" that gave a damn who Leila slept with? Did my father really think it immoral to "sleep around"? That *God* cared if she slept around? Shades of Henry James and Tolstoi!

Fortunately for their peace of mind, Leila doesn't live in the Delta. They aren't confronted with her "arrangements" every day. (Fiftyish now, she still likes men.) She travels (to sell her work and for pleasure) and, when she is working, she lives in a small house high on the bluff above the river outside Memphis. She is a fabric designer—started out in a small way with her own loom. But she doesn't have those loving green eyes and all that energy for nothing. She can sell herself and her work, and she did, first to a couple of interior decorators in Memphis, then to Neiman Marcus and a few other prestigious stores. Now she designs fabrics to order and has a connection with a small factory in west Tennessee that makes them. She uses the attic at Chickasaw as a kind of extra studio—has a loom and worktables there—and comes down two or three times a year to be alone and dream up her designs.

She is more or less her own woman—always ready to take a few days off for a trip to Chickasaw—and it was inevitable when I began to plan for Miriam's visit that I call on her to chaperon.

To my parents (as I told Miriam at the time) "Living Together" was like shooting up cocaine, using marijuana, or being a homosexual—OK for Sherlock Holmes, Gene Krupa, and Proust, but productive, in one's own home territory, of a terrible unease.

They knew about Miriam and me. At the beginning they let out a few moans and screams of anguish: Mama talked about "mutual responsibility" and "the deep reality of the structures a society lives by," and Daddy said, "I believe that if people are ready to live together, they should commit their lives to each other before God. I'm sorry, but I do, and that's all there is to it." But, having practiced on Leila—practiced, that is, not judging or rejecting her, having to some degree worn out their capacity for anxiety about irregular sexual arrangements, it didn't take them long to give up on us. The thought of our life together must have given my mother her chronic case of gastritis, must have lain like a stone at the pit of my father's stomach, but it couldn't be helped. Everyone has to go his own way.

So it was not my parents, but the elderly cousins and great-aunts, my ancient grandmother, and Lester and Denny Chipman, who had to be protected from the knowledge of my depravity—from whom I, equally, had to be protected, for all of us would have been unhappy if they had been compelled to strike me off their list.

It was absurd that I could get away with using Leila as a sop to respectability, but since they believed, or pretended to believe, that she was the soul of sexual virtue ("Why doesn't she *marry* that nice beau?" my grandmother used to say from time to time), they would have to accept her as a proper chaperon for us.

To give us some time alone together, I arranged for Miriam to arrive the day before Leila did. There was scarcely a chance anyone would find out she was there: February at Chickasaw Ridge, and I didn't have a stream of visitors from town. As it turned out, it had been raining and sleeting for two days before she came and I had been doing inside work on my house and spending the rest of the time holed up in my dining-room lair with the fire crackling and Lucy dozing and purring on my worktable; I didn't give my town relatives a thought and they, I suppose, gathered around their own fires, if they thought of me at all, thought that I would soon be coming to town for an evening in a warm house and some human companionship.

Miriam came on the noon plane from Memphis, down the flight stairs, carrying her guitar case and a shoulder bag, with the awkward grace of the girl who has always thought herself too tall and has discovered late that she is beautiful; crossed the runway toward me, looking so much herself that I felt my heart stop. Her hair, long and thick and blond, blew across her face in the wind that swept the runway, and she put it aside to kiss me and then looked me over in the capable, motherly way she puts on to hide emotion, and said, "Well, Alan . . ." as if we were no more than acquaintances. I gave her a hug that made her gasp.

As we drove up the winding road toward the house, the sun struck through a break in the heavy clouds and the wind began to turn around to the south. Water dripped and sparkled in the gray-green mats of Spanish moss. We could hear the water rushing in the bed of the ravine that carried the runoff from the lake, and the water in the pond on the west side of the house sparkled blue under a patch of pale blue sky.

Inside I built up the fire in the bedroom and we brought in stacks of wood. Then we threw off our clothes and fell into bed and stayed there most of the next twenty-four hours. We brought drinks and supper in on a tray and ate and drank in bed with blankets around our shoulders. She got out her guitar and sat cross-legged on the bed and sang to me: "Western wind, when wilt thou blow? The small rain down can rain. Christ, that my love were in my arms and I in my bed again." And the small rain rained down in little droplets from the Spanish moss and the wind blew and the skin on her belly was as white and soft as I remembered it, with a faint haze of golden hair running down to the mons, and the fire crackled in the cedar and the mole in the hollow above her clavicle was still exactly where it was supposed to be.

The next afternoon was sunny; the south wind had blown away the cold snap. We got up, cleared my gear out of the dining room, cleaned house, made beds, and got ready for Leila.

She came in the middle of the afternoon, bringing, as she always does, all sorts of good things to eat and drink. Together we unloaded the car and unpacked bottles of wine and whiskey, loaves of homemade bread and pound cake, bouquets of fresh romaine and Bibb, a gallon of shrimp gumbo, chickens and a pork roast to cook on the barbecue grill, and cheeses and honey and pickles and fruit.

Leila, inspecting my larder, kept up a running commentary as she worked: "No wonder you're so thin! What have you been living on? Beans and wieners? Is that what he fed you last night, Miriam? Here, let's make a list of what we need and you children can go to Calloway's and I'll go back and see Sam and . . . Are the hens laying? I want to make corn bread to go with the gumbo. Let's see. . . . We need meal and milk and bacon. *Butter,* not margarine. . . ."

"Noah has collards," I interrupted, "and sweet potatoes and onions in his root cellar. And he has some ground artichokes he's been saving for you."

"Good," Leila said. "Add salad oil to your list. We don't want to starve you to death, Miriam, the first time you're here."

I caught her hand in mine. "That's Leila's mission in life, Miriam," I said, "to keep feckless people like us from starving to death or dying of a surfeit of beans and wieners. She always gets here barely in time to save me."

"Fool," Leila said. And then, "One more thing. Bring in those brown paper sacks full of yarn and all those weeds from the trunk."

When I had piled them at her direction on the parlor table, she began immediately to lay out seedpods and twigs and rummage through the yarn. "Look," she said, "look! I got this great idea on the way down, looking at the bearded sumac and the old dock in the ditches . . ." and then, interrupting herself, "How is Sam? Is he able to do any work? What about him?"

"He's been working a little every day on the fences," I said. "He says he's getting stronger. But he's not good for much." I didn't say more. She would see for herself.

TEN

IT WAS at Calloway's store that Miriam and I met Lindsay Lee Boykin.

We left Leila surrounded by skeins of yarn and drove off to the store, Miriam, who had never been in the Deep South before, hanging out the window of the pickup and gazing at the moss-dripping live oaks and twisted dark cedars that rose from mats of sodden leaves and hung across the road from the tops of crumbling shale bluffs. Bare tangled vines dragged at the trees and reached down to reroot themselves, and clumps of wood fern clung, limp and frost-blackened, to the bluff sides.

"What is this, anyhow, Alan? Could be the set for a bad movie. Faulkner? Tennessee Williams?"

I wanted praise for my woods. "Never mind Tennessee Williams," I said. "Look—there's a red-tailed hawk."

"You could set up the camera on top of the truck cab, ride down the road, doing the trees like in that old Japanese movie—what was it—*Rashomon?*—only stark, not leafy, get a shot of the house from the gate, pan around to the rusty tractor parts and falling-down sheds and back to the front porch, put your aunt in a hammock with a box of chocolates. . . ."

I laughed. "In the hammock in February?"

She shrugged.

"Hey, Miriam, it's the *country*. It's beautiful."

"I wish you weren't down here," she said. "What are you *doing* down here? I miss you. I'm lonesome."

"I miss you, too."

"Maybe it's beautiful in the spring," she said. Then, "If you miss me, why are you down here?"

I didn't know. I didn't want to ask myself. "I'm writing," I said, but I knew that was no answer. I reached over and touched her cheek, felt a surge of tenderness, tried to be honest. "I don't know," I said.

"I worry about you." She looked at me and shivered and rolled up the window of the pickup. "Where *are* you?" she said. Then, without waiting for an answer, "Are you coming back?"

"Of course I'm coming back." We had reached the gate now and I stopped the truck and kissed her. I suppose she sensed in me the reservation I concealed from myself. She broke away.

"There's Noah." I said.

"Who's Noah?"

"You'll see."

He was riding toward us at a smart canter, sitting the giant stallion as easily as if he were in a rocking chair, holding the reins in one hand and a sack of artichokes in the other. I called to him that we would open and close the gate, but he pulled up and swung down anyhow, sweeping off his hat with a grandiose gesture and bowing deeply to Miriam when I introduced her. Then he went into his standard Act for Strangers: old retainer, patriarch, court jester, philosopher, bard, and knave—while Miriam gazed at him, speechless. I was conscious of trying to be myself, whatever that was, and of feeling uncomfortable.

"Unreal!" Miriam said, as we drove away. "Do you *like* that?"

"Christ, Miriam, lay off. I'm not in charge of Noah."

She opened her eyes wide, tucked her chin down, tilted her head, smiled sweetly, and said, "Now, Alan, honey, don't *be* like that, you heah! Why y'all bein' mean to me?"

I laughed. "Where'd you get the phony southern accent?"

"At the movies, honey. I learned just about evahthin' I know at the movies."

"Southerners don't say *y'all* to one person," I said. "And they never say *evahthin'* for *evahthing.*"

Outside the front gate we had turned left and headed downhill toward the Palestine Creek Bridge. We crossed it now, pulled up in front of Calloway's, and went in.

Calloway's is the neighborhood gathering place for the Chickasaw Ridge community. It is clean and warm and smells like salami and lettuce. The checkout counter is at one side and a clear space with three or four split-bottom chairs around a butane heater at the other. The neighborhood women bring fresh eggs here to sell, and vegetables in season. The only beer and soft drinks for three or four miles around are in the cooler and the only gas pump outside the front door. In the spring and summer, Mrs. Calloway sells worms and crickets and, in the fall and winter, shells. Mr. Calloway is usually busy elsewhere—he farms a hundred acres behind the store along the east side of the creek.

You'll see almost everyone from Chickasaw Ridge here at one time or another, and it was no surprise on a February afternoon to see two elderly men standing by the fire drinking beer. They were drunk, I saw at once (while I was in the act of introducing Miriam to Mrs. Calloway), or one of them was, waving his can of beer and saying something about a dog in a blurry drunken voice.

I was struck immediately by their appearance: heavily muscled shoulders and big hard-looking bellies, grizzled hair and swarthy faces full of the self-reliance and subtle arrogance of men who have known adversity all their lives and dealt with it. They looked to be brothers, perhaps even twins. Looking at them, I remembered what Sam had said the night I arrived: "Hippies or nigger-lovers. It's all the same thing to them. . . ."

I glanced outside and, as I had expected, saw a pickup truck fitted with a gun rack holding a rifle and a shotgun; a dog lay on a pile of croker sacks in the truck bed. At that time the signal in our part of the world for quick recognition of dangerous red-necks was a pickup with a gun rack and guns, a dog or two, and a citizens' band radio. The only thing missing was the antenna for the CB radio.

All these details I took in while Miriam exchanged greetings with Mrs. Calloway. Miriam began immediately to make friends: saw behind the counter a workbasket with a crochet hook, a skein of thread, and a half-finished table mat in it and asked a question about crocheting. As I started toward the row of carts by the front window, the front door banged open and a young man came in. Short, stocky, and square-faced, he had a heavy brown beard and, hanging to his shoulders, thick brown-streaked blond hair, held in place with a beaded headband. He wore a fringed leather jacket, old jeans with flowered gussets let into the legs, and harness boots. He had a camera—a Leica, I observed, with a twinge of envy— slung from a strap around his neck. But the envy was smothered, almost before I felt it, under a rush of brotherly affection. Fringe and headband, hair and beard and boots and gussets all spoke to me in accents of brotherhood: *Here I am,* they said, *a friend, vulnerable, courageous, open-hearted. I may even be able to direct you to a trustworthy source of dope.* That's the way things were in those days.

The Leica, though—that was not quite in character. And another thing—curious—he had come through the door with the alert, brisk, heads-up walk of the born salesman, and he greeted Mrs. Calloway as if he knew her.

I had got my cart, headed toward the back of the store, and was picking up salad oil and meal and bacon when one of the old men by the fire hollered out, "Hey! Looky yawnder, Calhoun! Where you reckon *that* come in from?"

I felt the involuntary tightening of my stomach muscles, the warmth of a flush in my ears inside my knit cap. *Shit! Are we going to have trouble?* I glanced at Miriam, still exchanging pleasantries with Mrs. Calloway, and then leaned against a case full of Campbell's Soup and waited to see what would happen next.

The other old man muttered something I didn't catch, took a swig from his beer can, and frowned at his brother, who paid no attention to him, but yelled again, "Hey there, *you!* You over there by the milk. Boy!"

The young man in the fringed jacket glanced around and then crossed the store to the fire. "Did you say something to me, sir?" he asked politely. He had detached his camera from its strap as he crossed the store and now carried it low and half-concealed in one hand, his finger on the shutter release.

"Yeah, *you!*" The old man's beer can wavered and beer slopped over onto his sleeve and dripped on the floor. He rocked back unsteadily, held his beer at arm's length, and squinted down his arm, as if it were a rifle barrel. "Lemme ax you something, boy," he said. "Why you hippies wear your hair like gulls, huh? Why is that?"

94

I was looking at the camera, and I saw the young man shift its angle rapidly and unobtrusively with as much skill as if he had an eye in the back of his thumb. He grinned eagerly and confidently. He might have been a car salesman meeting a difficult prospect. "It's the style," he said. "You know, lots of men wear their hair like this nowadays. You like it?"

I cringed. As I had noted when he came through the door, we were brothers (uncongenial brothers, it now occurred to me), and he, with an insouciance that could come only from ignorance or stupidity, was baiting the enemy.

The old man's manner changed. He smiled the benevolent smile of a father about to give his son some man-to-man advice. "But you look like a *gull*," he said in a kindly, puzzled voice. "Or a gobbler."

Shit!

"It's all in your point of view, I reckon. My girl friend doesn't think I look like a girl." With his free hand he stroked his beard.

The old man turned and looked at his brother. "You hear that, Calhoun? He say he got a *gull* friend. You believe they's a woman alive would take to that ribbon he got on his haid and them flowered pants legs?"

Something in his voice, in the pitch and rhythm of his speech, something I could not quite isolate, sounded different from the speech of the country people I knew around Chickasaw Ridge. Face and voice somehow didn't go together. I began to look more closely at both of them. Who were they, anyhow? Had I ever seen them before?

"Come on, Henry." The other man's face was unamused. "We got to git on home."

Henry put his beer can down on a case of antifreeze beside the butane heater, leaned forward, hands on thighs and bleary eyes hostile. "I ain't ready," he said. "I wanta talk to this yere . . . this yere . . ."

The camera clicked. "You dress like you want to, sir, and wear your hair like you want to, don't you? And I dress like I want to and wear my hair like I want to. It's a free country. Or supposed to be."

"*Suppose* to be. Now what does that mean, *suppose to be?* You one of these yere radicals, too? Along with . . ."

"No more radical than anybody ought to be that . . ." He hesitated and began again. "I'm interested in everybody getting a fair shake, if that's radical."

On the other side of the store Mrs. Calloway was checking out a young black girl with a basketful of groceries. Miriam had begun to watch and listen to the scene by the fire and to look worried. I beckoned and she joined me.

"Do you hear this nitwit," I said in a low voice. "What the hell does he think he's doing?"

"He doesn't sound so stupid to me," she said.

"If he wants to stay healthy, he'd better shut up and get out of here," I said.

Miriam gave me a cold look. "They're just two old men," she said; and then I heard from the other side of the store, ". . . poor man's son. Raised in the country, and . . . Plenty of times I've been out of a job. Even hungry. Looks to me like you might've been in the same boat in your day, one way or another. Like we're supposed to be friends. *For* the same things." All the time he talked, the Leica moved infinitesimally this way and that, and occasionally clicked.

"Jesus," I said to Miriam, "what does he think he's doing?"

"Betrayed . . ." he was saying. "Unions. . . . *And* the government. Business. If you stop and think about it, all us poor people . . . Who's gonna be for us, if we're not for each other?"

"What you talking about, *betrayed,* and *us poor people,* and *I look to be like you?* Ain't nothing about me like you. And I ain't *poor.* That right, Calhoun?" He blinked and swayed. "Eh?"

"You're not like anybody I know," Calhoun said. "Except maybe me."

"Come on, sir," the young man said. "You keep trying to insult me, but I don't insult easy. All I'm talking about, you know, is politics. Our interests. Making the system work for us." He hesitated and for a moment I thought he might extricate himself, but then, "You're bound to know nobody gets heard these days," he said, "unless he gets with other people and organizes. I mean, people with the same *interests.* Now look here, for example. My daddy was a pulpwood cutter. He never got a fair shake in his life. But *now—* right now—the pulpwood cutters are beginning to organize. Right here in Homochitto County. Either they're going to get good contracts or the I.P. and the Georgia Pacific aren't going to get the wood. See? Black and white. They're getting together. And the companies will get together and try to keep 'em stirred up against each other, but *this* time . . ."

"Pulpwood," the old man muttered in a ruminative way. "Pulpwood?"

". . . this time it's not going to work. Cooperation. Rights. Organization. Democracy. In fact, that's one of the things I'm doing here. Getting the truth about it, you know, the story. So the whole country . . ."

"I knew it. He's one of these yere agitators. *Black and white together.* You hear that, Calhoun? Lemme tell you, boy, I ain't interested in no black and white together. Understand? And there ain't a agitator in the state of Mississippi big enough to organize me. My own mama couldn't organize me. Tried thirty, forty years before she give me up. I stood on my own feet all my life, gonna keep on standing on 'em. My own feet!" He stamped the floor with a heavy mud-crusted boot, picked up his beer can off the case of antifreeze, threw back his head, and drank the rest of the beer.

The Leica clicked.

Damn, that was a good shot, I thought.

". . . might have been OK when you were young, sir, but . . ."

"What you doing there, anyhow?" Henry said. "What you got there? You takin' our pitchers? Calhoun, he got a *Kodak* there. You know it?"

"You have such fine faces, sir—typical . . . uh, typical of the best in the South. And I . . ." The young man's face shone with intense seraphic sincerity.

"Pinch me. I'm dreaming," I muttered to Miriam.

"Well, he's right, you know," she said. "If this was any place but Mississippi, they would've already . . ."

We were still standing near the Campbell's Soup case and no one was paying any attention to us. "We're in the country, Miriam," I said in a stern voice. "People get killed out here for messing in other people's business. And that didn't just start in 1964."

She gave me a look. "Why don't you leave, if you're scared," she said.

"Shit," I said again. As I recall, I felt pretty gloomy at this point. "Come on," I said.

"I'm not leaving him here to face those . . . those people by himself," she said, but she followed me across the store to where Mrs. Calloway was still standing behind the counter in her fresh yellow print housedress and white butcher's apron. Her short gray hair was combed in tiny waves against her head and she was as neat and perky as a small white and yellow bird. I asked her if she knew the two old men.

"Sure, honey," she said. "That's the Levitt brothers—Henry Clay and Calhoun. Peculiar folks, that whole family. Keep to themselves. They own about two hundred acres of good land down on the edge of Homochitto Bottom. Don't come into Chickasaw Ridge very much except when they're drunk—not since . . . well, I guess not since your great-uncle died. They used to go over and work for him sometimes by the day years ago."

"And the young guy? Have you ever seen him before?"

"You don't know who *that* is? You used to hang around with him when you was a kid, him and his brother. It's Lindsay Lee Boykin. Used to live over on the Shields place."

"Jesus!" I looked again and under the disguise of beard and beads recognized the stocky, brash, sharp-eyed, clever boy I had last seen seven years ago. He was bound to know better than to come in here dressed up like that. "Jesus," I said again.

"Alan," Mrs. Calloway said, "you know I don't like to hear nobody taking the Lord's name in vain in my store."

"Gimme damn Kodak. No damn hippie agitator gonna take my pitcher!" Henry shouted.

"I'm sorry. I didn't mean . . . Excuse me," I said to Mrs. Calloway; and to Miriam without looking at her, "Hang on a minute, OK?"

I walked back across the store and eased in between Lindsay Lee and the Levitts as if I were reaching for a can of antifreeze out of the case against the wall, gave an exclamation of surprise, nudged Lindsay Lee out of my way, and, sticking out my hand, began to talk in as slow and deep a voice as I could bring out. "Mr. Levitt! Thought I recognized you, sir. I'm Alan McLaurin. You know, *McLaurin.* You remember my Uncle Dennison, don't you—from Chickasaw? And this . . ." I didn't move aside, but continued to keep myself between him and Lindsay Lee. ". . . this is Lindsay Lee Boykin, used to live around here. *Boykin."* There had been Boykins as well as McLaurins in the county for a hundred and fifty years, and I counted on his recognizing the name.

The old man looked at my hand, blinked, stared at me, and hiccupped. "You hear that, Calhoun?" he said. "Times sho' done changed."

"Alan!" Lindsay Lee said. "I . . ."

I turned toward him for a moment and spoke in a low rapid voice. "Shut up, you damn jackass. And get that camera out of sight. You want to get yourself killed?"

"I'm telling him the *truth*," Lindsay Lee said. "I believe in talking to a man straight."

While I spoke over my shoulder to Lindsay Lee, I had kept my hand stuck out, and now Henry, blear-eyed and dazed-looking, rubbed his own hand in his khaki shirt front, took mine, and shook it. "Kodak," he said firmly. "Don't nobody take my pitcher without asking me."

Calhoun stared at us as if we were some strange animals come in out of the February woods. "Boykin?" he said. *"Boykin? That's* a Boykin? Now I heard everything." He stood up. "Come on, Henry."

"I, uh, certainly am glad to have met you, sir," I said. "I've, uh, heard my Uncle Dennison talk about you."

"McLaurin. Ole Man McLaurin," Henry said.

"Hah!" Calhoun said. He took his brother's sleeve. "He was crazy, too," I heard him mutter. He began to pull Henry toward the door.

But Henry reached out, snatched at the camera strap hanging loose around Lindsay Lee's neck, and gave it a jerk. "Kodak?" he said.

"Wait a minute. Wait a minute," Lindsay Lee said.

Calhoun continued on his way, dragging Henry by the sleeve, Henry dragging Lindsay Lee by the strap, and me caught in between.

Lindsay Lee reached back and put the Leica on top of the nearest display case as we bumped along toward the front of the store. "I'm on your *side,* sir," he said. "I told you I . . . Y'all just don't understand the *issues,* sir. If you would . . ."

"Shut up," I said again through clenched teeth.

"My side! Ain't got no side. *I'm* my side. Gimme damn Kodak. Where'd it go to?" He jerked loose from Calhoun and, still hanging onto the strap, flailed out at Lindsay Lee. Broke the strap and hit me instead, with all the force of that heavy shoulder and solid body behind the blow, stumbled over my big feet, and fell toward me at the same time, as Calhoun let go of his shirt-sleeve. Then he grabbed at a rack full of brooms and mops and steadied himself.

Right in the solar plexus. *Oooof!* I felt the wind go out of me and heard the wheezing sound of my own lungs as I gasped for air. Brooms and mops clattered down around me. I felt one rolling under my feet and flailed my arms for balance. Falling, I doubled up and rolled away from the heavy booted foot that I saw next to my nose. Remembering predemonstration survival lessons, I protected my head with my arms, drew up my knees, and squirmed around with my back against the wall to shield my kidneys. But he swung again at Lindsay Lee and missed. Lindsay Lee caught him and helped him recover his balance.

"Sir!" he said again, raising his forefinger like a preacher ticking off points. "Just a minute. First . . ."

"My goodness," Mrs. Calloway called. 'What are you folks doing over there? Calhoun? What's Henry up to?"

That was when Scarlett O'Hara joined us. Her soft voice slid over the confusion like suntan oil. "My Lord, Alan, what in the *wuld*" (her thickest movie-southern accent) "y'all doing doubled up on the floah like a roly-poly bug?" She did not wait for an answer. "And what in the *wuld* all y'all talkin' about so long? We got to get on back to the house. Leila's waitin' on this cawn meal. Why . . ." She gazed wide-eyed first at Calhoun, who was tugging at Henry's sleeve again, then at Henry, standing spraddle-legged, hanging onto the camera strap, staring at it and blinking and muttering. Then she appeared to see Lindsay Lee for the first time. "And you're Lindsay Lee!" she said. "Alan's told me all about you." Ducked her head and I was ready to swear she curtsied.

I had crawled to my knees and was beginning to get my breath back. "Yeah, Lindsay Lee," I said. "I hadn't seen you in a coon's age. Where you been keeping yourself?"

"Coon!" Henry said. "Who talking about *coon?* Calhoun, you hear somebody say *coon?*"

"Now, listen to me, y'all," Miriam said. "(Get up, Alan.) You folks are neighbors. *Neighbors.* What's your brother so mad about, anyhow, Mr. Calhoun?" She had opened her eyes until they looked as big and blue as Wedgwood teacups.

I pulled myself to my feet.

"Henry!" Mrs. Calloway called again from behind the checkout counter. "You and Calhoun let those boys alone, you hear me? They're Chickasaw Ridge boys."

"Don't nobody call me *coon,* Mrs. Calloway. *Nobody!*"

"Why, who would do such a thing as that?" Miriam said.

"*Mr.* Calhoun!" Calhoun said. "*Mr.* Levitt! We're niggers, lady, *Niggers.*"

I heard a click in my head: the swarthy skin, the intonation of the voices, the faintly Indian look. And no citizens' band radio on the truck.

"I'm leaving, Henry," Calhoun said. "You can do what you want to."

"Niggers!" Lindsay Lee said. "Hey, wait a minute. I mean, if y'all are niggers, I'm *really* on your side. I mean, why in New Orleans, I . . ."

I stepped back, grabbed the Leica off the top of the display case, pushed it into Miriam's hand, and gave her and Lindsay Lee a shove toward the front of the store. "Get him out of here," I said, "before they get sure enough mad at him."

"Come on, Lindsay Lee," Miriam said.

She took his hand in hers and he looked at her for the first time, saw her slender figure, the small beautiful breasts, nipples bumped up like pebbles under her T-shirt, the pale translucent skin, and gazed into those blue-green eyes that a man could swim in. "I'm coming," he said. "I'm coming," and he followed her as quietly as a well-trained hound. I heard him as they went through the door. "Call me *Lee*," he said. "That's my name now. Nobody calls me Lindsay Lee anymore."

ELEVEN

HE CELLS die and slough off, the body changes, but events stay intractable. There they are, stored in my memory, seeming gradually to become detached from the living dying body, but *there* still. My life flows over the past like water over a rocky, sandy creek bed, and the changing light on the surface strikes off now this distortion, now another. In 1970, again in 1975, it may be in 1985, Sam, his back and shoulders looming against the branches, steps out ahead of the boy sitting on the log across the ravine. The child balances precariously, admiring Sam, feeling the spongy cold moss under his hands. At Phoebe's funeral another boy stares at the dry ground, yellow grass sifted over with a haze of dust, cracks gaping wide and deep enough to lose a golf ball in, his sister's sweaty hand in his. Easter Bell lies dead in the tangled cables of the SPASURSTA and the dead cattle egret hangs like a captured insect in the web of broken antennae.

Or I recall every detail of a dream dreamed—how many years ago?

In the dream I have been swimming in the lake on a day so

green and light it seems as if gravity has been suspended and I and the day and the scene are floating weightless in sunshine. Trees on the bluff behind me flame like green torches under the sky; I am sitting on the ground eating a peach and watching a pair of dragonflies mate in the air. I see the delicate segmented body of the male pulse and flex as he impregnates the female. Then the day clouds over, a shadow darkens the bluff behind me, and I see a bear, heavy-footed and black-furred, ambling toward me along the narrow shore between water and bluff, swinging her head. *I can fly away,* I think, but as I try to get up, I find that I am chained to a stake driven into the ground. I pull at it, but I cannot uproot it. I see that it is not a stake at all, but a peach tree, its roots spreading in every direction like barky tentacles. Peaches litter the ground. The bear comes on, not hurrying. The darkness behind me is the mouth of a cave opening into the bluff. *She lives here, and I am in her way.* The bear stops in front of me, picks up my foot in huge clumsy paws, and unties my shoe, hooking a claw under the lace, while I stare at her and say, "Wait, wait." She throws aside my shoe and holds my foot between her paws and begins to gnaw it off. I see splintered bone and shreds of bloody flesh and hold out a peach to her, hoping to distract her attention, and she says, "No, I don't want it, it's rotten," and knocks it aside and keeps on eating my foot.

I remember that we had a party the night of the day we met Lee. All that's left of my journal entry, made the next day, reads: *Dallas and Lorene and Lee came for supper last night. Talked to Leila for a long time afterwards.* At the time I wrote pages of deep thoughts about the Pain of Love, the Sexual Basis of Religious Feeling, Leila's Oedipus Complex, etc. But when I read the pages over a few months later, most of what I had put down seemed callow and sentimental. I couldn't bear then to think of myself as having been callow and sentimental enough to have written it, and so I tore it up. I tried to think of something new to say, but all I felt was bewilderment—and pain. I wrote no more. Now, though, I remember it all.

I remember the sounds: the sizzle and explosion of fat pine and cedar burning and subsiding under a layer of oak logs; the tentative plucked notes of Miriam's guitar as she picked out a tune to fill the gaps of silence in our conversation, and later the driving beat of the hymn we sang. And the smells: the pervasive odor of cedar and smoke, the smell of Leila's seafood gumbo simmering on the kitchen stove and of corn bread cooking in the oven, the sweet smell of bourbon and later the stronger sweeter smell of Lee's marijuana.

And I see us there, a curious, ill-assorted group in that houseful of curious, ill-assorted things. How could anyone have thought we would make a successful "party"?

It had been Miriam's idea. She had driven to the house with Lee in his trim Volkswagen station wagon, leaving me to gather the groceries and follow, had taken an instant liking to him and invited him to supper. Then she'd persuaded me to go over to the trailer park to invite Dallas and Lorene. I hadn't wanted to go. All these weeks Dallas had still not invited me to come and meet his wife. But Miriam, perpetually optimistic, is sure once people get to know each other they will be able to have some kind of good time.

Dallas was not at home. Lorene met us at the door of the trailer with a joyful smile, as if she'd been expecting us, and immediately seemed to me to be the girl Dallas would have married. Thin and pale and sexless at first glance—but then I had second thoughts. She spoke with a hill-country twangy drawl and an eager, almost patronizing poise. I imagined her background: she was the daughter of a teacher in the Copiah County school system and a small truck farmer who lived out from Hazlehurst and took vegetables in to the Jackson Farmers' Market every Saturday during the spring and summer. She said that Dallas had mentioned me and my house and that they would be glad to come to supper.

I have said that I remember everything that happened that night, but of course I couldn't; just as I may have forgotten the most significant detail of the bear dream, or have made up part of it to make it more interesting to myself, and then forgotten I made it up. But the first thing I remember, anyhow (or have made up), is the three of them arriving, one car behind the other, Dallas and Lorene in their pickup and Lee in the VW; and the men coming through the door ahead of Lorene, Dallas stopping inside the door, almost blocking it, staring, his brown eyes narrowed, as if he might be sighting down a gun barrel; Lorene had to sidle past him with the child in her arms, pushing him out of the way to get in.

The house has two front doors, one opening into the dining room and the other into the parlor, and the Boykins had come in through the dining-room door. Miriam, her back turned to us, was at the sink in the kitchen, washing salad greens. Leila was standing by the fire. I went through introductions; and the mechanics of acknowledgment, the usual exclamations over the child, covered Dallas's rigid silence, as he continued to stand, acknowledging nothing and not introducing his wife.

"This is Lorene, Leila, and you remember Dallas and Lee . . ." As I spoke, I followed the line of his stare and saw that there was nothing for him to look at except Miriam's back framed by the doorway to the kitchen. Then Leila was talking. Lorene got a pad from the diaper bag which she had taken out of Dallas's hand and set the baby down on it. Everyone except Dallas moved toward the fire. But I kept glancing at him, even though I was talking, too.

It was as if he watched a squirrel flirt his tail high in a pecan tree and waited for a clear shot. Miriam turned, dried her hands on a dish towel hanging by the door, and came forward.

"Dallas—my friend Miriam. . . ."

Dallas breathed and moved into the room, as if the squirrel had slipped into a hole and he had lost his shot. Miriam nodded to him and joined the others by the fireplace.

He looked directly at me, crossed the room to my side, and said, "I thought it was Phoebe."

I stared. *Phoebe!* "Phoebe is dead," I said in a low voice. "You were *here*. You knew she was dead, didn't you?"

"Yes," he said, "but for a minute . . ."

"Yeah." It had not crossed my mind that he, too, might see her as Phoebe. I had never thought of him in connection with Phoebe, would have assumed that he had forgotten her. Girls were not included, not even Phoebe, in his and my adolescent wanderings.

"Dallas, darlin'," Lorene said, "did you hear Miss Leila speaking to you?"

"Not *Miss*," Leila said. "Just Leila."

Then, a little later, we had poured drinks or wine for everybody who wanted them, the baby was asleep in Miriam's and my bedroom, Leila was in the kitchen, and the rest of us were sitting in the parlor (we had built a fire there, too), Dallas in a straight-backed chair against the wall, not ill-at-ease—he never seems ill-at-ease—but withdrawn, hands in his pockets, chair tilted back; Lee in a battered old Sears wing chair in front of the fire; Miriam on the floor and me with my head in her lap. She was talking about cooking to Lorene, who was sitting against the wall beside Dallas. Narrow-faced and childish-looking, with fine sandy hair in a tight braid around her head and a thin virginal body (seventeen when Dallas married her, she was only nineteen now), Lorene did not look as if she could have borne a child. She sat up straight, her hands folded together in her lap, her feet side by side, as if she might be at Sunday school, and spoke when she was spoken to.

Miriam, perhaps I should say parenthetically here, didn't ordinarily talk much about cooking—or crocheting, either, for that matter. But she is always courteous to strangers, and it began to seem that day that she had decided these were subjects that southern women talked about—when in truth, most of the ones I know, like men, talk about sex and money and politics and movies and television and books and vice and crime and drugs and the vagaries of human nature and tragedies of human fate.

Anyhow, Lorene looked at us, timidly, as I thought at first (she had refused a drink), but at the same time happy, answering Miriam and smiling at the room and everybody and everything in it in an impersonal, almost trancelike way.

Lee, in his flower-child outfit, drank wine and bent down to me and talked cautiously in a low voice about marijuana. He asked what Leila would think about our smoking and I shrugged and said that I didn't know whether or not she had ever smoked, but I didn't think she'd turn us over to the narcs. "What about Dallas and Lorene?" I said. "I don't think . . ."

"Dallas!" he said. "Dallas is a fucking maniac. You can't pay any attention to him."

"And Lorene?"

"She needs to find out more about the world than she can learn shut up in that trailer all day with the kid. It'll be good for her." But he said no more for the time and turned from me to Miriam.

I watched him go into his salesman act. He meant to charm her and to my outraged surprise he succeeded.

Oh, I could see that there was something *about* him. He was good-looking in a squarish chunky way. He had a kind of openness, a sweetness, I suppose you might call it, if you can imagine such a thing as a sweet salesman. And after his performance at Calloway's a girl might think him brave—even heroic. Then, too (the only quality that made him seem brother to Dallas), he had a coiled-spring intensity that to a woman could have been sex appeal.

To me, in Lee, it was more like the intensity of the Ford salesman getting ready to close a deal.

I sat up and stared glumly into the fire. Blake on love was OK for me when I was feeling horny, OK in theory for anybody who recognized the holy joy of the flesh. But the spectacle of the salesman working so hard to sell himself to my girl didn't seem to me to have any connection with holy joy.

Dallas asked me a question about my house and with an effort I began to talk to him. Lorene sat with her hands folded, like a child ready to say the blessing at a table surrounded by strange cousins. She did not say much but, when she did, spoke rapidly in a high clear passionate voice, as if afraid you might interrupt before you understood what she was trying to tell you. She made me think of the way you might look (if you were suddenly transported there) at a houseful of creatures on another planet: you would be more conscious than you had thought possible of your humanity— your differentness; you would be afraid but, even so, resolved to convince them, whatever they were, that they should not harm you; further, that you would not harm them and that you might even have something to tell them—a message, perhaps, about the existence of the human world, what it would mean to them if they were to establish communication with it.

It *is* a strange house. No one had lived there for fifty years when the oil derricks began to sprout and drop their green fruit on the family in the fifties—no one except Uncle Dennison, who had his quarters in the outside kitchen and had never bothered to put electric lights or an inside bath in the big house. A privy and a few kerosene lamps suited him fine. He did run a power line into the tractor shed for the practical purpose of using power tools, and he drilled a deep well a couple of years before he died, but he always preferred to drink cistern water. I believe I've said that he died of typhoid fever—probably the last white person in the history of Homochitto County to die of typhoid. Screens? One of the advantages of Chickasaw was that you could sit on the front gallery in the evening and never feel a bite. And what was the matter with a mosquito net over your bed? That was what he'd had when he was a boy and that was what he continued to use. True, he had cleared the north pasture for the dusting planes to land. But you couldn't see it from the house; and, besides (to his immense satisfaction, no doubt), dusting hadn't worked on this hilly wooded land. He'd lost money raising cotton the newfangled way.

Now, of course, we have screens and a bath and electric lights. But the ceilings and fireplaces still bear the marks of Uncle Dennison's and Noah's handiwork: unsanded spackling meanders along the cracks in the plaster and a couple of trowelfuls of concrete cover the rusty spots in the cast-iron reflectors at the back of the fireplace.

Mama's and Denny's notion of making things homey was to hang cheap ruffled curtains and a few pictures: a "grouping" of family photographs above the parlor mantel, a peeling landscape at the opposite end of the room, and, on a side wall, a portrait of one of our female ancestors, one of those bad paintings that look as if the artist brought the body along already done and stuck on the head—in this case the head of a blond, crinkly-haired middle-aged lady with high cheekbones, a wide bony forehead, a large straight nose, and an ascetic (or perhaps the word is *fanatic*) look about the thin mouth and deep-set blue eyes. She looks, my mother says, like a preacher with a wig on. My father says she looks like Galahad in drag. Leila says she looks like me.

The furniture and ornaments are a conglomeration of the discarded possessions of six generations of moderately prosperous country people (Scotsmen torn from ancient lands and settled at last, after who knows what stormy crossings, what wanderings through Pennsylvania and North Carolina and Tennessee, in a forest of live oaks and rolling hills that curiously resembles the hills and dark beech woods of their starting place in Morayshire), who cultivated a romantic attachment to their raw new land and hoarded the talismans that would give their children's past a material reality. The "good" things—a few pieces of Hepplewhite or Sheraton furniture, the old silver, and such—are scattered in the town residences of various descendants of those old Scots. From what's left at Chickasaw, it's plain some of my ancestors had at best uncertain and at worst execrable taste in talismans: a knobby Victorian étagère, its shelves littered with seashells engraved with sentimental or pious mottoes, arrowheads and shards of broken pottery turned up at one time or another in the plowing (it was as if they had tried to appropriate the Indians' past, too), a coy nude alabaster Venus, standing under a glass cloche as if it were a plastic umbrella and she were shielding her breasts and pubes from a cold rain.

In the middle of the room is a square Grand Rapids oak dining table, circa 1925, surrounded by queer old folding circuit rider's chairs with carpet seats. There, on rainy days when we were small, we used to play fan-tan and Monopoly and Parcheesi. On either side of the fireplace are two Sears wing chairs and against the wall the cane-bottomed dining chairs where Lorene and Dallas were sitting.

In the windows hang the same venetian blinds that have hung there for—how long? Since sometime around 1800, I suppose, the dark red tapes replaced every forty or fifty years; the wooden cornices above are carved with the egg and dart design and backed with tattered dark red linen. Weird bird's-eye maple graining decorates the doors and window frames, and the mantelpiece is marbleized red and black in the style of the 1930s.

After Mama and Denny had made the place comfortable with wing chairs and curtains and so on, Leila must have come along, taken one look, and begun to drag things down from the attic to make it campy. A calendar on the wall over the étagère is dated 1905 and features a bevy of beauties in the style of the period, surrounded by "beaus," all of whom look like the Arrow Shirt Man. On the étagère she sneaked in an old false tooth in a gold wire frame and a tooled leather album entitled *Mother, Home and Heaven.*

The baby cried out and Lorene got up and went to quiet him. I lay back again with my head in Miriam's lap and pulled her long loose hair over my face like a veil, so that I could watch its pale shine in the firelight. She stopped talking to Lee about *The Bird* or the Weathermen or whatever it was he thought was so important and bent over me and smiled and I looked into her eyes—deep blue now with flecks of green in them—and thought of creek water running over green rocks under a blue sky. I didn't care whether anybody was congenial with anybody else or not—what anybody thought about us or our house or what Lee had on his mind—was aware only of her, of her warm thighs under my head, of the clean smell of her hair and the touch of her finger tracing a feathery path along my cheekbone. I felt the throb of lust and stood up abruptly, muttering "Later, man, later" to myself.

"What I was telling Miriam," Lee said, "the lower-middle-class whites in the South, nobody's even *looked* at those folks except at Klan meetings—not since Walker Evans. And I'm in a position . . ."

I put a fresh log on the fire.

". . . for example, logging—pulpwood cutting. That's where they are beginning to see their problems in common with the blacks. And so, if I could get next to these guys we met this morning—the Levitts—I might . . ."

"Might what?" I said.

"Dallas says they log off and on. They can get me in with the blacks. And I know a couple of Daddy's old buddies on the white side. I want to work up a couple of specs. A picture story, first. I know I could sell that without any trouble. I've done the pictures for a couple of pieces on the Movement for the *New York Times Sunday Magazine,* and . . ."

"You *have?*"

"Yeah," he said. "I have. I know the Movement people in New Orleans and Atlanta. I've been in the right place at the right time. And then, if I can sell the idea and get a writer, we could put together a book. . . . This guy who writes for *The Bird* might . . . But it would have to be worth my while."

"I don't know," I said. "The Levitts didn't seem like the kind of folks who would want to have their pictures taken for the *New York Times.*"

"Everybody wants his picture in the paper," Lee said. "Without exception."

"I don't," Dallas said. "I hate your goddamn publicity."

Lorene had returned to the room. *"Dallas,"* she said.

He looked at her and shut up.

"Here's another angle," Lee said. "Look at our daddy, at the success he's made. Up from pulpwood cutter to bonded tree surgeon. What goes into that? Why him and not some other guy?"

Leila had come in from the kitchen. "Where is your daddy now?" she said.

"He's out in Houston," Lee said. "We don't see much of him, but . . ."

Dallas looked at Leila. "I haven't seen him since I went into the service," he said. "Don't care if I don't ever seen him." He looked at Lee. "There's been a lot of loose government money floating around Mississippi the last four or five years," he said.

"Exactly," Lee said. "Still is, if you could get hold of some and put it to work for you. I might get a grant for the book, if . . ."

"What I'm talking about is where Daddy got his money," Dallas said.

"Well, I haven't heard about any grants from the government for cutting pulpwood," Lee said.

Dallas shrugged and subsided again into silence.

"Supper's ready," Leila said.

TWELVE

CHAIRS WERE scraping into place and I was gazing, transfixed with joy, on my bowl of gumbo, when Lorene, still standing behind her chair, slight and shy and hesitant, said, "May I say a blessing, Miss Leila?" and Leila said, "Of course."

" 'The people asked and he brought quails and satisfied them with the bread of heaven,' " Lorene said. " 'He opened the rock and the waters gushed out; they ran in the dry places like a river. And he brought forth his people with joy and his chosen with gladness. Praise ye the Lord. Amen.' " She sat down, smiled at us all, picked up her spoon, and touched it to the soup in the manner of someone pretending to eat. "My Bible opened to that psalm today," she said, "and it came to me that it was a blessing."

We made it through the meal talking about old times, telling Miriam and Lorene about the exploits of our childhood. Or Lee and I talked and Dallas contributed an occasional "Yeah." After supper Leila brought out brandy and bourbon and she and Miriam and I began drinking bourbon on the rocks. Lee took a glass of brandy, which he tasted now and then, and the others drank coffee. Leila began to talk to Dallas about her work and he relaxed as he had not all evening, absorbed in listening to someone explain a craft: the way the loom works, the way she plans a design on graph paper after she has experimented with colors and textures on the loom, the transfer to the factory looms—and so forth.

At the first pause in the conversation, Lee stroked his handsome square beard and said that he had some dope, if anybody wanted to smoke, some very good Colombian stuff that he had bought off a sailor in New Orleans. "And you don't want to drink too much, if you're going to smoke," he said to Leila (initiate to neophyte). "It masks the effect."

Recall, friends, that at this time in history people were still being sentenced to life imprisonment (in Texas, for example) for possession. Bravado and/or anxiety were the inevitable accompaniments of smoking dope.

"Bring it out," Miriam said. She pushed back from the table, reached behind her, picked up the guitar that she had left on a chair against the wall, and began to pluck it softly.

"You don't mind, do you, Leila?" Lee said. "Alan said he didn't think you'd mind. Have you ever tried it?"

"I don't mind, if you're careful," Leila said, "if you don't leave any roaches lying around. Other people besides us come out here. OK? And yes, I've tried it a couple of times, but I didn't like it." She grinned at Lee. "Maybe I'm too old to take on new habits. I've been drinking bourbon for twenty-five years and I've gotten used to being a *serious* drunk—philosophical. Marijuana—I don't know —I can't seem to get silly. It makes me self-conscious."

"You've got to practice," Lee said earnestly. "You ought not to give up after just two tries."

"Maybe it was three," Leila said. "Anyhow, it hurts my throat, so don't waste your good Colombian stuff on me. I'll stick to whiskey."

Miriam struck a few tentative chords and began to hum "Greensleeves." Lorene sat with her hands folded on the table in front of her, her cup of coffee untouched, and stared at the opposite wall.

Lee pulled a plastic bag, papers, and a dollar bill from his jacket pocket, spread a piece of newspaper on the table to catch the spill, and began to roll a joint. "I won't let a crumb fall on your table," he said, "although I don't think the narcs are cruising rural Homochitto County these days."

"Might be, if they seen you and Alan wandering around loose," Dallas said.

Lee did not look up or answer, but laid the first joint to one side and began to roll another. After he finished the second, he said with studied carelessness, "Y'all ought to try it, Dallas. Nothing to be uptight about."

"I know more about marijuana than you'll find out in thirty years—if you're lucky," Dallas said. "And I found it out without smoking any."

"Man, that's not possible," Lee said.

I got up and poked the fire, thinking, Why does Dallas have to be such a shit? What goes on between him and Lee, anyhow? Thinking, too, of what Dallas had said soon after he began to help me with the house: *I liked to kill people.* And *I thought about being a narc.*

He tilted back in his chair, arms folded across his chest. "You gonna poke that far to death, Alan," he said in his twangiest country voice. "Whyn't you put on a log?"

Putting on his red-neck voice to irritate Lee, I thought.

Miriam laid aside her guitar. "Leila, you fixed," she said. "We'll clean up. Let's do it now, Alan, if we're going to smoke. We might forget later."

I laid aside the poker. "Keep on playing," I said. "We'd rather listen to you sing than rattle dishes. We'll clean up."

She began to play again and to hum softly and then to sing, "The Answer Is Blowing in the Wind." Lee laid a second joint on the table and began to roll a third. "Wait a second," he said. "I'll help."

Dallas, I thought, probably considered table-clearing women's work. As for Lorene, she had evidently not even heard what Miriam had said. She sat and gazed at the wall and at Lee and then around at the rest of us, smiling that ecstatic trancelike smile. I began to stack the dishes and take them to the kitchen. Who *are* these people? I was thinking in an irritated way. And: I like to smoke with my *friends.*

Lorene drew a deep breath, reached across the table, and laid a hand affectionately on Lee's arm. "Come on, Lee, darlin'," she said. "I know you *think* you want to smoke that stuff. I know your life is hard in lots of ways. You think marijuana is going to make it easier for you. I know how temptation besets you, how hard it is to resist. 'For every man is tempted when he is drawn away of his own lust and is enticed.' "

I felt my eyes crossing as if they were checking on each other to be sure they were both present at the same scene. Miriam got up and wandered over to the window, still singing softly.

"You're in the middle of a dark wood," Lorene said. "You've lost your way." She gestured toward the window beyond which the trees soughed in the wind. "Dark as the woods out there," she said. "Miriam says the answer is blowing in the wind, and it's true. Listen to this: 'The wind bloweth where it listeth, and thou hearest the sound thereof, but canst not tell whence it cometh and whither it goeth: so is everyone that is born of the Spirit.' "

"*Lorene*," Dallas said in a low voice, "don't you start that, you hear me? What he does is his business." He put his arm around the back of the chair, laid his hand on her shoulder, and drew her closer to him.

Lee laid aside the third joint, tilted his chair back, braced his knees under the table, stroked his brown beard, and said nothing.

She went on, " 'Verily, verily, I say unto thee, we speak that we do know, and testify that we have seen; and ye receive not our witness.' "

"That's not the way it is, Lorene," Lee said. "You've got the wrong idea altogether. I'm *receiving* your witness. I just don't agree with it." He shook back the locks of hair that had fallen over his face as he worked at rolling the joints. "I'm not in any dark wood. I don't need saving. I'm *saved*—so to speak. I'm happy. Just as happy as you would be at a family reunion down at Liberty, Miss. All the cousins there, tables in the yard, preacher to say the blessing, plenty of fried chicken and potato salad. I'm not saying, understand, that nothing's wrong. But I'm *working* on the things that are wrong."

She was shaking her head slowly back and forth.

"I've got my obligations and I take them seriously," Lee said. "I'm for the *people,* see? Born again into the people. Just like you're for God. I live my life on principle, like you. Why, I even smoke dope on principle."

"*Principle?*" Lorene said. "I didn't say anything about principle. I'm talking about letting the Spirit have His way with you."

Lee went on as if she hadn't spoken. "Smoking dope ought to be just like a family reunion," he said. "Won't hurt you a bit more than a slice of apple pie with homemade ice cream on it. It'll give you a good feeling, just like eating apple pie and seeing all your friends and cousins gives you a good feeling. It would come natural to Jesus. I swear to God that's the truth. Give it a try. All I want you to do is give it a try and see if I'm telling the truth."

Lorene opened her eyes wide and gazed at him and smiled; and the way she looked at him made my chest feel tight, as if the room were too full of air, like a balloon, and the air were too thick to breathe. "I already feel good," she said. "I feel so good I could shout for joy right this minute. And I could give *you* some dope— only you couldn't call it dope unless you call the real truth dope— to make you feel so good, you'll never give that stuff another thought. Nor whiskey, either." She spoke rapidly, as if to prevent interruption, and would have gone on, but Dallas said again, "Lorene! Lee don't want to hear the truth. About that or nothing else."

She turned on him. "And you listen to me, too, Dallas Boykin. You know if I got to *witness,* I'm going to witness."

Lee said to me in an offhand way, as if to speak directly to Dallas and Lorene were to give what they said more importance than it deserved, "She's a Jesus freak."

Dallas brought his chair down hard on all four legs and looked across the table at Lee. "Lorene ain't *no* kind of freak," he said. "You understand? Any freaks around here, it's you."

I had turned on the water in the sink and was putting in a stack of dishes and now Leila got up and joined me. While she washed (with a good deal of noisy splashing and turning on and off of the faucet), I continued to come and go, clearing off and stacking, and then drying and putting away, trying halfheartedly not to look miserable. Now, thinking back on that conversation, I believe it took place under those circumstances, with all of us present, because it was so loaded it could not safely take place anywhere the three of them might be alone together. Or maybe each one thought we would serve the purpose of keeping the other from getting up and leaving. But I didn't think any of that then. I just wished they would let each other alone and talk about something else—or go home and let Miriam and me go to bed.

"Sure, I'm a freak," Lee said. "One kind of freak. And I have a lot of friends who are Jesus freaks. That's their bag. It's OK with me. But what I'm talking about is my bag." He shook his plastic sack of dope. "Now, don't turn me off—just listen a minute." And on he went, and on and on. The old alcohol versus dope routine; statistics on the good health of marijuana smokers that he probably got out of *Rolling Stone;* dope cures asthma and high blood pressure, kidney stones, cavities in your teeth, and glaucoma. He even got onto the "rush" with speed and heroin, the mind-blowing experience of LSD—"if you *really* want to see God." Etc., etc.

"You don't need whiskey or marijuana or LSD to see God, Lee," Lorene said. " 'Blessed are the pure in heart, for *they* shall see God.' " She turned to me. "You excuse me, please, Alan," she said in her high, clear, rapid voice. "I don't want you folks to think I'm so rude I'll come to your house and eat your food and accept your hospitality and then tell you you ought not to drink whiskey. I know Jesus turned the water into wine at the wedding at Cana (although I *will* say there was no mention of His turning any of it into whiskey and I never saw where He turned *one thing* into marijuana or LSD or cocaine or *reds* or any of that stuff Lee fools around with)." She turned back to Lee. "You're going to burn up the precious brain God gave you, fooling with that terrible stuff. But if you listen to me, if you let me *show* you—how to open your ears and your soul—and your *body* to the joy of the presence of the Holy Spirit . . ."

My eyes consulted each other again across the bridge of my nose. I decided to continue silent.

"Marijuana never burned up anybody's brain," Lee said, and again he stroked his beard in a calm thoughtful way. He reminded me of a square-faced serious young schoolmaster of the 1870s. "And I don't use heroin—or speed either. I have tried them, understand. I am *open* to human experience. I don't close my mind. But I am not an addictive personality." He picked up a joint, lit it, inhaled deeply with both hands cupped to conserve every wisp of smoke, and raised his voice. "Miriam? If you're going to smoke, come on."

Miriam brought her guitar to the table and sat down and at the same time Leila, a tall amber drink in one hand, slipped quietly out of the kitchen and vanished into the parlor.

Lorene was talking again. "Please! You *are* addictive. Everybody is addicted—either to this world or to heaven. And *you* can be addicted to heaven. You can be drunk with the Spirit. Lee, darlin', I've *prayed* about you and I've *fasted* about you and the Spirit has come down to me and told me, and I *know*." Again she reached across the table and laid her hand on Lee's arm. "I'm giving you God's strength through my hand," she said. "I'm breathing in, *receiving* the Spirit, and the Spirit is coming to you through me. The light of the Spirit is coming to flood your soul with God's glorious day." She inhaled deeply and opened her eyes so wide it made my eyeballs ache.

Lee lifted her hand off his arm, laid it on the table, took another hit, and handed the joint to Miriam who held it in her hand and let it smolder. "Lee," she said in a quiet sensible voice, "if it worries Lorene and Dallas for us to smoke, let's don't. What difference does it make?"

"Oh, it makes a difference," Lorene said. "Everything in your life makes a difference, Miriam. 'For His eye is on the sparrow, and I know He watches me'—and *you*."

Dallas stood up. "That's right," he said. "Everything you do. Everything. Even if it's an accident." He clamped his mouth shut, as if he had spoken against his will. I could see the tensed muscle moving in his jaw. Then he said, "Come on, Lorene. We got to get the baby and go on home. Hear?"

"Jesus!" Lee said. "All this smoke is going up in *smoke*." He laughed in a forced way, took the joint back from Miriam, inhaled, and held his breath.

I put away the last stack of dishes and came back into the room, feeling sad. It wasn't often I got the chance to smoke Colombian dope. In Boston that year it had run twenty dollars a lid, and you were never sure you wouldn't get cheated.

Lorene had not gotten up, but Dallas was still standing, glowering.

"Look," I said, "let's forget it. Like Miriam says, why make an issue of it? Put it out, Lee, OK? We're supposed to be having a good time. Why don't we . . . ?"

"Come on, Lee," Miriam said. "Where's your spirit of compromise?"

"I'm not much on compromise," Lee said. "That's what's wrong with . . ."

I thought he was going to deliver another lecture, but he broke off and said nothing more for a minute, frowning and looking seriously at Miriam. Then he carefully put out his joint and said,

"Hey, here's a compromise. Why don't you and me, Miriam, go up and take a look at Alan's lake? Did you know he's got a big beautiful lake up yonder behind his house, built and paid for entirely by the U.S. government? When we were kids we used to go back there frog-grabbing. Did you know when you're shining a flashlight around looking for frogs, you sometimes can't tell a frog's eye from a spider's? Who would think you'd have that kind of problem? Come on. We can smoke our dope up there, won't bother a soul, watch the stars float off like fireflies. OK, Alan?"

"Sure," I said, not meaning a word of it. "Y'all do what you want to." I waited to see what Miriam would say to this interesting proposal.

She shook her head. "Another night, maybe. But thanks."

Lee stood up, wrapped his three joints in a twist of newspaper, put them in the plastic bag with the rest of his dope, balled up the newspaper he had spread out on the table, and threw it in the fire. "The evidence is destroyed," he said. Again he looked at Miriam. "I'm going to be around for a couple of weeks, probably," he said. "I hope I'll see y'all again." This *y'all* was directed to one person and it wasn't me. I answered anyhow, in what sounded in my own ears like an unnaturally loud voice: "Yeah, come back. Come back to see us."

Miriam struck a series of chords on the guitar and smiled at him. "Please!" she said.

Lee touched Lorene on the shoulder on his way out and said, "No hard feelings, OK? You got to go your way and I got to go mine."

"I'm praying for you, Lee," she said. "Right this minute I'm praying for you."

Miriam continued to sit by the fire with a fuzzy dreamy smile on her face, the guitar on her lap, her fingers moving over the strings. The front door banged shut. The sound of the guitar softly, insistently filled the space that followed. A log broke apart and fell in on itself in a shower of sparks. Miriam began to hum. A whispering, murmuring gaseous sound came from the dying fire.

I cleared my throat and cast around for the next thing to say. I would call Leila, if she wasn't asleep, I decided, and get her to take us up to the attic and show us her studio and demonstrate the loom to Dallas. Then I began to be conscious of a rapid monotonous *tap-tap-tap-tap* like the sound of a loud clock ticking. For a moment I thought of the familiar movie or TV scene where the ticking gets louder and louder as the hour draws nearer for the time bomb to go off. Then Miriam began to play a rapid sequence of chord progressions that she must have unconsciously adapted to the time of the taps—taps, I suddenly realized, that came from Lorene's heel, clicking against the floor like a metronome, only twice as fast as the fastest time a metronome can beat. Her knee and leg were vibrating, her hands still clasped in front of her.

While I was wondering if she might be getting ready to go into grand mal (I'd seen that at Whitfield more than once), she gave a low singing cry and, raising both arms above her head, reached upward, turned her face upward, and held her palms outspread, as if she might receive through them signals from some distant source, or perhaps, like Danaë, a shower of impregnating gold. Her lips moved and she began to speak—a continuous murmur of unintelligible syllables whispered in time to the flow of music from Miriam's guitar. I stared and listened, trying to understand what she was saying, but I could not make out a word. Abruptly, she stood up, overturning her chair.

Miriam stopped playing.

"Play!" Dallas said. *"Play!"*

Lorene began to move around the table backwards, her arms still raised, in a kind of slow undulating dance, and Miriam began to play again, now slower, now faster, adjusting her rhythm to Lorene's dance. Dallas reached down, picked up the overturned chair, and set it straight.

Lorene brought her palms together above her head again and again, clap-clap, clap-clap, throwing her head back and bringing it forward and moving her feet in a graceful little backwards jump-step as she clapped, until, seeming to receive the power she invoked, *"Ahhhhh,"* she breathed out, and began to whisper again rapidly and brokenly.

I realized that Leila was standing in the doorway between the dining room and the parlor. "Dallas," she said, "is Lorene all right?"

"She's been fasting three days," he said. "Worrying and praying over *him*—for one thing." He jerked his head toward the door. "And me," he added. Then he began to beat on the table with both palms open, a complex drumlike tattoo in counterrhythm to Lorene's *clap-clap! clap-clap!* and the accompanying guitar. "Sing," he commanded. "Ain't nothing wrong with praising the Lord. If you can't speak with tongues and you can't dance and you can't prophesy and you can't interpret, then *sing!*"

To Miriam it appeared the most natural thing in the world. "What shall we sing?" she said.

He continued to beat on the table with the flat of his hand, altering the rhythm from square time to a driving six-eight. "Let's sing, 'I Was Sinking Deep in Sin,' " he said.

Leila looked on from the doorway and took a sip of bourbon on the rocks. She's always ready to sing.

He didn't ask if we knew the hymn, and I suppose it's true most people in our part of the country take in those old hymns with their mother's milk—whether they want to or not. He led out and set a rapid, ecstatic pace unlike any hymn-singing I had heard outside a black church. Miriam picked up the tune and the pace after the first verse and she played and we sang, half drunk, bewildered, swept up in Lorene's rapturous dance:

"I was sinking deep in sin, far from the peaceful shore,
Very deeply stained within, sinking to rise no more.
But the Master of the sea heard my despairing cry.
From the waters lifted me. Now safe am I.

Love lifted me. Love lifted me.
When nothing else could help, love lifted me!"

Lorene sank on her knees now, beside the table, and, leaning on a chair, lapsed into the rhythmic whispered unintelligible speech again, but we sang on.

"Souls in danger, look above. Jesus completely saves.
He will lift you by his love out of the angry waves.
He's the Master of the sea. Billows His will obey.
He your saviour wants to be. Be saved today.

Love lifted me. Love lifted me. . . ."

Halfway through the third chorus, the baby began to cry and Lorene stopped praying (or whatever it was she was doing) and looked at Dallas with soft bewildered eyes.

"Was that the baby?"

He nodded and helped her to her feet, but went right on singing and we finished with a triumphant "When no-o-thing else—would—help / Love—lifted—*me!*"

Then, "The Spirit was on you, Lorene," Dallas said, "and we been singing with you. Looks like we sung and hollered so loud we woke him up. We better get on home."

She smiled and came back to us, poised and courteous, her braided hair neat, her narrow face clear and childish. "We've had *such* a good time," she said. She picked up the diaper bag and put on her coat. "Dallas, honey, are you going to get the baby?" She held out her hand to Leila. "Now, y'all will all have to come and have supper with *us*. Real soon, now, you hear. Will you?"

THIRTEEN

SINCE Lorene had achieved such success dancing around the table and speaking in tongues, Leila may have thought she should try out her version of the same thing. And although Lorene's act was a hard one to follow, Leila was up to it. Some of us are reckless enough to follow any act. Besides, Leila, under the influence of the moon or of whiskey, or both, goes naturally into her own kind of trance. She gets the Spirit. The tongue she speaks in (unfortunately, I thought at the time, since I had no desire to hear what she said) is not unknown.

Before I write down all that she told us that night, I want to say more about what she is like—and about Miriam, too. I've said that I intend to tell the truth. Perhaps I have put off writing about them because I know that telling the truth about anybody you think you love or hate, especially a woman you have lived with, is impossible. But impossible or not, I'm going to give it a try. Maybe I can tell *a* truth.

Leila thrives on revelation. The day after she has told me (or somebody else) all about whatever is going on in her head (or the world) at the time, she sings like a bird—usually her favorite mountain song—"Love, Oh, Love, Oh, Careless Love"—in the authentic bluegrass style, hitting the *u* sound in love and pronouncing *careless* "cär-less." Explanations, reasons, light shed in dim corners, have brought the world temporarily under her control.

But explanations—of Leila's affair with Sam or of any of the things that happened the winter I lived at Chickasaw or that had happened there in the past and that I found out about that year— have their own foolishness.

You might expect, from what I have said about myself, that I, too, would have had faith in cause and effect. I *had* taken the effects of my own actions seriously enough to go and do the C.O. But the center of that part of my life had been that *I was not going to kill anybody*. I just was not. The effect on anybody else—other than the person I didn't kill—I hadn't given much thought to.

Now, thinking about Leila's explanations, I feel mostly wonder at how our lives move, by twists and turns, as a creek moves, rippling in its bed, doubling around and shaping itself against the contours of rock and silt and fallen log, eating out a bank and appearing one day, after a rainstorm, flowing down a ravine that yesterday was half a mile from its course. But then logs and mudbanks are, after all, *causes*.

It's as if cause and chance, fate and fortuitousness, are a nest of Chinese boxes opening infinitely inward (or outward, depending on the point from which one is looking at them).

The feeling I had at the time was shock. A very real sensation of movement—as if the house and everybody and everything in it shifted along a fault. It was almost impossible for me to admit that I had grown up with Sam and Leila staring at each other across my head, so to speak, and had not noticed them. And *that*, I suppose, is what I mean about trying to tell the truth about someone you think you know. What you know may turn out to be no more than the end of your own nose, which you have been contemplating with loving attention, while other people have been acting out tragedies and idylls at a point only slightly beyond the blackhead you're focusing on.

Anyhow, one thing Leila said that night (she talked a lot about her marriage) was that as a young girl she had had all kinds of dreams of what she wanted her life to be like, but that the most urgent had been a dream of sex—to lie, peacefully, legally, religiously, respectably, passionately, lustily, *nightly* in bed with the lover she chose.

"I couldn't bear to be a virgin for another year," she said. "Eighteen years is long enough to stay chaste.

"But," she added, "my brains kept getting in the way. I couldn't bear, either, to think of living with a man who didn't have as much sense as I did. What kind of life could you have if (as Mama had explained to me, all women had to do) you were always protecting a man from the threat of your intelligence? And also (something she did not bother to tell me, but that she and I both knew well enough) I had to find a man who was aware that women were human beings. It was a difficult search.

"I was in school in Washington at the time—one of those fine schools for turning out Southern Ladies. It was early in 1945, the war still going on. I'd met a couple of men who would have filled my requirements: I might have fallen in love with either of them, if they'd given me the least encouragement, but they did not. The three or four who made signals to me weren't up to my standards.

"And then I met Bill. He overheard me talking to a friend on a bus, recognized the Mississippi accent, poor homesick sailor, and introduced himself with 'You're from Vicksburg, aren't you? Or is it Port Gibson? Do you know . . . ?' Of course we had mutual friends. It didn't take more than a couple of evenings with him for me to decide he had sense enough to suit me (I mistook drive for what I mean by sense). And he treated me—like a friend. That was the most reassuring thing about him. He hardly seemed aware at the beginning that I was a woman. We were friends three months before he began to court me.

"I couldn't make up my mind," she said, "even frantic as I was to shed my virginity. Did I love him? I had to love him a lot. Mama had never intimated that marriage might be less than final—and I had taken her word for it. I must have had a great many deep thoughts about our future together. What were they? I don't remember. And I don't know what his were, either. Finally, one night at the end of a forty-eight-hour leave (New York was his home port and I had gone up to meet him), he said, 'Well, I haven't any more time to waste. I'm not going to ask you again. OK? If you decide you want to, let me know. Maybe I'll still be interested.' And off he went into the North Atlantic on his destroyer."

She was nineteen by then, ten years younger than I am now.

"Sometimes," she said, "I would have sense enough to know that I didn't even know anything about *myself,* much less about him. But what difference did that make? If I were to meet a new man tomorrow, I'd be more reckless than I was then. I have less time now, and sex—*love*—has always been—still is—everything to me—more reason than any other reason. The only difference in me now is that I wouldn't expect sex to solve my extra-sexual problems. Although, hmm . . . sometimes . . .

"Well, anyhow, while I was travailing over all this and while he was at sea, I went one night to a concert. Somebody, I forget who, played the Sibelius Violin Concerto. You know it. . . .

"My whole nature soared out on the music," she told us, "and I said to myself, 'He's my fate.' After that night I never had a moment's doubt. Next time he came into port, I told him not only that I wanted to marry him, but that I wanted to go to bed with him *that night*. He declined. He didn't think it would be right. We were married the following week."

Imagine deciding to the strains of the Sibelius Violin Concerto that you will spend your life with a sailor who picked you up on a bus in Washington, D.C.! That's what I meant about creeks.

Enough about Leila for now. As for Miriam, at the beginning I took her presence so entirely for granted that I realize now I have put down scarcely a word about her—what she thought, what she did, what she wanted. I *have* written about what she looks like: her hair, her body, her smile—and my lust. Looking back, I see that so far she is scarcely more than a ghost in these pages—a ghost of the look and smell and taste of flesh to a randy young man, and the ghost, too, of my cousin Phoebe. I even forgot to write that she plays the guitar like an angel—or that she plays at all—until I remembered that it was her music that brought on Lorene's fit, and went back over this record to put in the guitar.

She is the daughter of a college professor, a moderately successful Ph.D. who has taught psychology in various small colleges for most of his life. He, too, was a C.O. (maybe that's what made Miriam begin to think seriously about me) and a C.O. during the Second World War, when pacifism was more difficult and less fashionable among intellectual young people than it was in the sixties.

Her family seems to me to be cut loose from all that I grew up thinking of as natural. They live an uprooted life in one college town after another, moving up and down and sideways in the academic world. They are political, of course: in the forties they were conscientious objectors, in the fifties they resisted McCarthyism, in the sixties it was the Movement. And now . . . Now they're getting old. The last I heard, her father was writing articles on Death with Dignity. But I doubt they've ever had a cousin on the Board of Supervisors, or had to find out who you persuade to dump a load of gravel on your road, or been personally acquainted with a sheriff's deputy. Such a phenomenon as a place in the United States to which a real American citizen is attached, which holds his past and considerable of the past of his parents and grandparents, and even his great-grandparents, the landscape of his nightmares and of all those dreams so sweet they make your teeth ache —the existence of such a place was unimaginable to Miriam until she began to know me.

I may have been a curiosity to her to begin with. Was there really such a person as a white Mississippian who was a C.O.? What did I think of George Wallace? Were any of my friends in the Klan? Did my father belong to the Citizens' Council? No? Then what was he *doing* in 1964? Or, for that matter, in 1954, when the court ruled on *Brown* versus *the Board of Education?* (In 1964, 1954, too, he was saying what he thought and writing letters to the paper, but he was never much on marching.)

Principles. Ideas. Disciplines. Plans of action. That's what they cared about. But Chickasaw? Cousins? *Black tenants?* Send for the anthropologists!

Still, there are ideas and ideas. I remember once talking to her about religion—this was when we first began to be friends. I asked what her family believed and she said they were Friends. That her mother and father had joined during the war when he had been a C.O.

"What do they believe about God?" I said. (I didn't know any more about the Quakers than what you read in high school history books about George Fox and William Penn. And, of course, that now, in the sixties, the American Friends Service Committee was active in the anti-war and civil rights movements.)

She hesitated, looked puzzled. "About *God?* I . . . I'm not sure. I don't think they joined because of anything about God. Maybe they don't even believe in God. They never mention Him. It's more . . . Well, they lead a lonely kind of life. My mother is . . . shy. And my father is wrapped up in his work. He teaches a few years, takes a sabbatical year, maybe moves on to another school. They don't like to drink or party and they're not—you know—middle-class. No country club or Rotary Club. The Meeting, the Friends—anywhere you go you can find a . . . a social context. A place where you meet people who share your interests —your convictions. The Friends become your friends. You go to covered-dish suppers and take part in lecture series and marches. They joined for all those things, not because of anything about God. Or, anyhow, God was secondary."

At the time, I didn't pay much attention to what she said. I was too busy watching her—her green-flecked blue eyes, the wide expressive mouth, the spare beautiful body, thin white skin gleaming along her shoulder, a mole set in the hollow of her throat where clavicle and tendon meet. I do remember thinking briefly, *Imagine that!* and trying to figure out how you would explain to anybody in my family that some people join a church without considering what it teaches about God—that "God is secondary," that "they never mention Him." They—my family—are all either passionate atheists, passionate believers, or engaged in some lifelong quest for truth— agonized at times, I suppose they would say it was, although it never keeps them (us) from eating well, drinking well, or (when we have the money) taking expensive trips and buying expensive toys. Puritan in our dreams, Catholic in our flesh, my father might say.

But I've forgotten Miriam and gone back to contemplating the blackhead on my nose.

What else? What is she like? Direct. Reasonable. Unused to violence. Unused even to people who shout at each other and rush up and down the room when they argue, as we are all prone to do. Competent. Sexy. Most important at the time, she loved me. Since she loved me, she must have been intelligent, discriminating, and sensitive. Right? And, as I've written, she was beautiful, with a severe, big-boned, wide-hipped, pioneer beauty; and she looked like Phoebe—one of those pieces of reality that lie like logs in the current of our lives. But she wasn't like Phoebe in her ways—or like any of the other women in my family. She had an openness— an expectation of justice, perhaps—that would have been foreign to any of them. Oh, she could be devious—witness the Scarlett O'Hara act at Calloway's store. But, unlike the women in my family, she would never be seriously devious. They—Leila and my mother and grandmother—whether for practical reasons or kicks or, like the chameleon, to avoid being eaten could, and (it seemed to me) often did, put on at will a new appearance and character. The possibility of being eaten is one they have taken into account from birth; and the expectation of justice in this world for themselves or anyone else would be to them a piece of excess baggage for which they have no room—a toy for young men (like me) and perhaps for Yankee girls, the children of professors of psychology.

We built up the fire and pulled our chairs close to it and Leila continued to drink. But I wasn't interested in whiskey. The big bed beyond the wall tilted invitingly through my head. Miriam lay on it. . . . Too chilly tonight for my favorite vision of exposed spread-legged nakedness, so I put her under the down comforter and crawled in beside her. No confessions, no politics tonight, please, Leila. Just a brief postmortem on Lorene and then good night.

I heard Sam's uneven steps on the porch. Coming home from a visit to his daddy, he told us, he'd seen the lights on and stopped in to speak. He was not drunk.

He had told me weeks earlier that he was not drinking. "Oh, I'll have a beer or two with you or Freddie, but I give up all that foolishness along with women," he said. "You do without women in Parchman and you come to find yourself in a new world. Your desires are elsewhere. And as for drinking—the stuff you can smuggle in or make to drink liable to kill you, so I give that up, too. I said to God after they shot me, 'Lord, give me the strength to live it through and I'll lay off all that.' " He had looked at me thoughtfully. Then, "You seen that old sorghum mill your Uncle Dennison used to grind cane with?"

I nodded.

"Laying up in the barn rusting now, but when I was a boy, he run it with a mule. Made his own molasses. Well, all the time I was laying up in the hospital and dragging around on crutches, and after that, when I had to go back to the field and was waiting for the parole to come through, I kept thinking about that mule. How he would go around and 'round dragging the bar that turned the mill. I come to call myself a mule. 'Keep on going around, mule,' was what I said to myself. 'Don't raise your eyes. Don't wish for nothing. The time's coming when your strength will grow and you'll shake off the harness.' That's what I thought about. Nothing else. Not whiskey, not women, not money. Not even my daddy or any of my people."

"But you're out now," I said. "You can forget all that."

"It's not as easy to forget as you might think," he said, "not even when you want to. When the Lord gives me back my full strength, then maybe I can forget." He shrugged his heavy shoulders with the quick shucking-off gesture that he had acquired at Parchman. "I wait on the Lord," he said.

So he was sober that night. When he came in, Leila got up and stared at him for a minute and he stared at her and then her eyes filled with tears and she crossed the room and took his hand. She hadn't seen him, of course, since Parchman. "Sam!" she said. *"Sam!"*

"Yeah, it's me, believe it or not." The lid on the blind eye drooped. The damaged legs, buckling, as it appeared, under the weight of the shoulders and arms, bowed out like a cowboy's. "You see me," he said. A muscle quivered in his cheek below his good eye.

"Sam!" she said again.

"I heard you was coming," he said.

"How *are* you?"

"You see me, Leila," he said again. He looked her over with a sly sardonic smile. "You ain't lost no weight," he said. "Ain't lost a pound. "You looking *fine.*" And then, to me, "Wanted to tell you the road's washed out back there by the graveyard pond. Bad wash. Don't drive back there, OK? Liable to cave off in that gully."

"Sam, this is Miriam," I said. "You remember I told you she was coming down to see me?"

Although we invited him to sit and offered him a drink, he shook his head and stayed just inside the door, leaning heavily on his stick. "Tired," he said. "The old hip socket's giving me trouble." And to Leila, "We're going to have to get a back hoe in here to fix that washout. You want me to see if I can get one from the county?"

Leila seemed to collect herself and they talked earnestly for a few minutes about the wash and about culverts and fences and ditching, and then she saw him out and stood on the back porch still talking to him in a low, drunk, passionate voice. The wind blew through the open door and the fire flared up and I grabbed Miriam and pulled her down on the floor by me in front of the fire and put my hand between her legs and made noises about fucking.

When Leila came back into the house, what was left of a drink of bourbon in her hand, a drink that I knew from having seen her mix drinks in the past was strong enough to make an elephant crash, her cheeks were wet with tears and in the firelight her dark hair curled and glinted around her pale face. She stared through us as if we weren't there and said, "I can't *believe* it." She sat down heavily in the armchair by the fire and turned the glass slowly in her hands. "His legs . . ." she said, and then, "He was so *beautiful,* Alan. When he was a young man, not much older than you are now, and I came out here and saw him . . ."

Miriam sat up.

I said nothing.

"*You* know," she said.

"Yes," I said. "It's rough."

She turned to Miriam. "I suppose he's told you Sam and I had an affair years ago."

"No," Miriam said. "He didn't tell me."

And I hadn't, because I had never dreamed of such a thing, much less known it. I felt the lurching adrenaline thrill that signals desperate danger.

"Things like that never come to an end," she said. "Not really."

Christ! I thought. *What kind of shit is this?*

Now, looking back, I remember the sensation of wanting to cover my ears with my hands. *Wait! Wait! I'm too young to hear such things. And about my own aunt!*

FOURTEEN

SHE HAD come home, she said, after the end of her marriage, to begin to put her life together again. "I was thinking about childhood refuges," she said. "About getting as far away as I could from what I had had. Away from the queer young executives and their queer wives—the queerest people I had ever known, except that it turned out that *I* was queer and the world was entirely peopled with *them*. Well, if I was the last eccentric in the world, I would have to put up with myself—I couldn't put up with them. I hadn't bargained for it, I hated it, and I couldn't get Bill even to *want* to get out of it. Fortunately . . ." (she echoed my father's words) "we didn't have any children.

"The farthest place from *them* that I knew about was Homochitto —Chickasaw Ridge—with Mama and Daddy in town and Uncle D. out here. So I came. Within a month—even though my life was wrecked—I was going crazy—bored—roaming the county because I didn't have anything to do. It turned out that Homochitto was as up-to-date as the suburbs of Akron or St. Louis—Mrs. Stouffer's broccoli soufflé and Pepperidge Farm's rolls in every supermarket and the children at Halloween Trick-or-Treating for UNICEF instead of putting your porch rocker on the garage roof. I was queer everywhere. I came out here and tried to get Uncle D. to let me learn to farm the place. It would have made sense. Daddy was already too crippled and Uncle D. was getting older. Your father couldn't, and Lester . . . Lester was out of the question. I was the only person who might have taken over from Uncle D. and made a working farm of it. But Daddy was as bad as Uncle D. Neither of them wanted a working farm. If Daddy had had his way (if Mama hadn't kept him in line) he would have been out here with Uncle D. using the privy and cistern and catching typhoid. And, furthermore, they didn't want a woman meddling in their business, finding out they were hopeless incompetents. By the time I gave up trying to make them see the reasonableness of my proposition, I was in a rage that included all the family."

She shrugged. "I didn't have any money," she said. "Didn't ask for support from Bill. Daddy was willing enough to dole out what I needed until I could 'pull myself together and think straight,' as he put it. I was dependent on him." She took a long drink and smiled—that curly, scary, angelic smile. "Bastards," she said good-naturedly. "They're all bastards. Well . . . It was a hard winter. I got a part-time job. Doing what? It doesn't matter. Filing something. There's no way to make a man understand how I felt—not even you, Alan, with all your understanding ways."

"Alan tries," Miriam said seriously.

I looked compassionately and intelligently at the two of them. That was my way of trying.

"I began coming out here in the afternoons. What can you *do* in Homochitto? The white folks sit around and talk about the niggers and the niggers . . . I suppose they sit around and talk about the white folks. No sign of a change in that situation. So it was anything to get away. I found a couple of old chests in the attic and repaired and refinished them just for something to do. Then one day I found that old loom. I'd never seen it before. The way I happened on it, I knocked the staple out of the door to get into the back part of the attic—just out of curiosity. I suppose Uncle D. had a key, but I wouldn't have asked him for it—out of spite."

"Spite?"

"I told you you wouldn't understand."

"He wouldn't have wanted *me* to come out here and farm the place, either," I said. "Or *anybody*. Now, would he?"

"Alan! You don't believe that. It's just comfortable to pretend you do."

"And interfere? And try to change the way he did things?"

"A *man*? He would have welcomed a young man."

I shook my head.

"Well, anyhow, the loom," she said. "It needed hardly any work to be usable. And I knew how to weave—had taken courses, first at camp and then at school." Her eyes opened wide and she seemed for a few minutes to be sober, as she talked of the loom—of her excitement at finding it, of how she immediately knew that here was the way out, a new life. How forgotten skills came back. "I worked out my future in a day," she said, "and was sure I could make a go of it.

"Of course, *that* was acceptable. Designing. Weaving. Women's work. No threat. They probably thought I would fail—wouldn't be able to support myself—which would have been even more satisfactory to Daddy and Uncle D."

Miriam was listening, bemused, believing every word of it. She tends to believe people and to think that she, too, can be believed.

"I ordered yarn and thread and went to work," Leila said, "relearning the weaving skills, trying some designs, and experimenting with dyes.

"It was then that Sam came back from the war. What year was it? God, I've forgotten when the Korean War ended. And it was before the end, anyhow. He got a discharge before it was over. You know about that, don't you, Alan?"

I did, of course. Sam had come home from the war under unusual circumstances. I reckon you can't give a man a dishonorable or undesirable discharge or throw him in the stockade after he's won the Congressional Medal of Honor. I don't know whether or not you can take it away from him, but I wouldn't think so. Anyhow, he won it. Killed a thousand Philistines with the jawbone of an ass, so to speak. His company got stranded during some retreat or other and he was holed up in a slit trench with North Koreans all around him. Company commander wounded and unconscious, top sergeant dead, company demoralized. He shot his way out of the hole, put an enemy machine-gun nest out of action, and, with the captain slung over his shoulder and the body of the dead sergeant under the other arm, led what was left of the company through the break he had made in the line. He had told me a little bit about it when I was a child. It was a kind of joke to him. "They couldn't kill me," he said. "I *knew* they couldn't kill me, so there wasn't nothing very brave about it. Those other guys, they felt just the opposite. They were sure every bullet had their name on it. . . . And some of them were right," he added somberly. "I've seen days when we were shaking the trees for dogtags."

They gave him the medal, but he didn't give a damn about it. They were getting ready to fly him back to the States for the president to present it to him, when he went AWOL. There was a woman in Seoul he wanted to see. They found him and explained to him about going to get the medal from the president, but he just went off again. And again. There was *always* a woman he wanted to see. It got to be an embarrassment. They told him he had done more than any one man could be expected to do and gave him the medal right there with as little publicity as possible— and a discharge along with it.

"I was working in the attic," Leila said, "standing at the window, looking out at the light on the new leaves unfurling in the crape myrtle trees, like little green shells with a cast to the edges and the stems like the rosy inside of a seashell. I was thinking of a design—using the green and rosy leaves against the bone-colored twisted branches—when I saw him. You can see the horse lot from that window, you know, and he was in the lot working a colt. I knew what Noah's sons looked like—the Indian cheekbones and nose, the black skin—and I knew this must be the youngest of them, although I hadn't seen him since we were children. I stood a long time watching him work. He had the colt—a beautiful palomino two-year-old—tied with a halter and head stall to the post in the pen and he stood close beside him talking into his ear and stroking his flanks and back, and I watched. It was a hot May morning. He had taken off his shirt and hung it on the fence and I watched the muscles in his back and shoulders move as he stroked the colt and talked to him. Then he pressed his hands on the colt's back and bent down, slowly and easily, and picked up a blanket from the ground and laid it over the colt's back. It was all in slow motion, like a dream. (That's the way you begin to break a horse, Miriam, every move deliberate, so as not to frighten him.) He kept at it a long time, laying the blanket over the colt's back and lifting it off again and again until the colt stopped trembling and shying and began to relax and look interested. I stood and watched: the skittish movements of the colt, his mane flicking and shining under the morning sun, and Sam's slow work, in and out and around and around with the blanket, like a toreador, in slow motion, watched as if I were in a trance, feeling the heat of the sun on my arms and face and the movement of the air, like breath, heavy with the smell of the chinaberry blooms that hung everywhere in the woods like a sweet lavender mist.

"I hadn't thought of a man for almost a year—hadn't thought of wanting sex. It was as if I had been frozen, as if sex had gotten tangled in my mind with the mean commonplace life I had led, with all those men and women in their ranch-style houses. Sometimes at night when I walked the streets of the suburb where we lived (nobody walked but me; and Bill didn't like me to walk, because it "looked queer," so I would wait until night for my walks), I would pass by the rows of houses with their flimsy walls (even the brick veneer was flimsy) and think about houses like that, thousands of them, stretching out, side by side, through miles and miles of identical streets, and I would wonder what would happen if everybody started fucking simultaneously one night, in time with one another, so to speak. After all, everybody went to bed at the same time. It didn't do to go to bed or get up at a *different* time. All the thousands of houses would begin to vibrate and sway, and then they would fall in on all the queen-sized Hollywood beds, like the paper houses of a movie set." She grinned at us. "A housequake!" Then she went on. "It was as if, too, my quarrels with Uncle D. and with Daddy and Mama, their refusal to let me do what had been so obviously the best thing for everybody, had shriveled up what was left, the last twinge of feeling.

"It was noon when Sam quit working the colt and I came out of my trance—felt the glacier in my veins begin to melt and let go. I went downstairs and out to the horse lot where he was rubbing him down and said that I was Leila, and he told me that he was Sam, back from the army.

"Who made the first unmistakable gesture? I did, of course. I had already made up my mind before I was out of the house. Besides, he wouldn't have—inconvenienced himself. He had women enough without setting out to get entangled with a white woman.

"We never wanted to bother anybody," she said.

I must have looked astonished, because she said, "I suppose *bother* is a mild word for what I mean, although I swear to God I wasn't *afraid*. Those years in the suburbs, sneaking my walks at night, watching people spend their lives doing what was expected —those years had made me determined not to be afraid, not to stoop to fear. And Sam, of course, wasn't afraid of the Devil when he was young. But I was sensible. I planned things for us so that we wouldn't get caught—Sam wouldn't get lynched and the family wouldn't be forced to disown me. I wasn't angry enough with them to want that."

She stopped talking and looked at me expectantly. I didn't know what she expected and hadn't the least intention of saying anything. I remember feeling a draft from the open bedroom door. You have to keep that door cracked or the fireplace in the dining room won't draw.

I'd like to be able to put down what I thought at that moment— when I was called upon to respond. Instead, I dredge up this: I am eight or nine years old, walking home from school, and I get a terrible bellyache—so painful that I can't walk anymore. I see— feel—myself squatting on the sidewalk, doubled up, squeezing my knees to my chest. My nose is six inches from the sidewalk and I see the gray color of the concrete, small pebbles embedded in the slab, grass sprouting out of a crack. No one passes, no other children, no adults. End of memory. It's hard to extract the significance from a solitary bellyache with no pre-bellyache memory, no post-bellyache memory, and no other people present.

Why do I remember the bellyache in connection with Leila's confession?

It was not that I gave a shit who she slept with. I was a liberated young man.

It was not, I hastened to congratulate myself at the time, that I was a racist.

But *they* were—Uncle D. and the rest of them: kindly, quiet, unostentatious, God-fearing racists on whom a romance between Leila and Sam would have (no shit) breathed the fetid breath of Hell. For her to have begun that love affair . . . The virulence of her hatred of them was unthinkable from the ground on which I had been standing. And when she began that quiet drunk tearful sentence—"I suppose he's told you that Sam and I . . ." etc.— she handed me with it the job of finding someplace to put it down

137

where the weight of it wouldn't tilt Chickasaw so steeply that we would all slide right off the ridge into the ravine.

So perhaps when I ask what I thought, the answer is that I did not, I could not think. *Now* . . . Now I recall the bellyache.

"Sometimes I can't believe everybody in the family doesn't know all about it, hasn't always known," she said. "I suppose that's why I said to begin with that you probably knew about Sam and me. I halfway believe that they kept silent about it as you might keep silent skiing on a steep mountainside in late winter—for fear a shout would start an avalanche. But your generation is different, Alan." She was beginning to sound drunk again, the words coming out as if her tongue were asleep. "Aren't you? You keep saying you are. Free spirits. And your difference gives me room, gives me the luxury of *honesty*. Finally . . . *someone*—someone in the *family* who may eventually have all the data and be able to understand as much about me as anyone can understand, is able to hear me out. I can speak to you, shout, even, without starting any snow slides."

Still I said nothing.

"Well," she went on, "we were careful. I already had a reason to come to Chickasaw every day and I had set up years earlier the pattern of disappearing and reappearing, of fishing alone on the ponds at the back of the place or walking in the woods looking for mushrooms and wild flowers and ferns—of not being accountable to anybody. We had no problems. *There,* in his house that Uncle D. had helped him build, in his bedroom that looked out across the horse lot and the driveway toward the dam . . . I would leave my weaving and go out the side gate and turn off into the woods and circle around and come through his garden and in at his back door, and he would be waiting. That's all there was to it." Again she smiled. "Sometimes we would look out the window and see Uncle D. sitting on his porch," she said. "Once we heard a car drive up and we got out of bed, naked, and stood there together and looked out and it was Daddy."

Melodrama is distasteful to me, but it was not to Leila.

"I sank into a dream of sex," she said. "Even when I was at work at the loom, it was as if it were a sexual act."

Like Mehitabel, a lady in spite of Hell, she drew a cloak of reticence over the actual lovemaking. Instead she fell silent again, staring at the door as if she could still see Sam leaning on the twisted hickory limb he uses for a cane, rolling to the right to favor his bad hip, turning at the door with the one-eyed grin that seemed in the shadowy doorway more a leer than a smile. Tears welled up in her loving blue eyes.

After a few minutes she went on: "I would have gone anywhere with him. I had dreams of vanishing into Harlem, of going to Paris to live. I believed then that he didn't belong here any more than I did. He was too strong, too intelligent to waste himself here. I suppose at the beginning I must have thought about him as I did about other blacks—that he was ground down by the circumstances of his life—that if he had a chance to go someplace else and do something better, he would go there and do it. That he might not even *want* to go never occurred to me.

"But I wasn't thinking. I *loved* him.

"We talked of leaving," she said. "I thought that we were beginning to make plans. And then Daddy died. I didn't care. I went through the motions of grief, the proprieties of burial, mainly thinking that his death gave me some money. Not a lot, but enough to leave with Sam as soon as the probate period was over.

"But he wouldn't go. I couldn't believe it! I still can't believe it, even now when it hasn't made any difference to me for years. We quarreled. Mostly he talked and I listened. He kept repeating over and over, 'I got to swing free, Leila, got to swing free.' And 'Can't stand cities. Can't stand a street the sun don't strike except at noon.' He didn't listen when I said we wouldn't have to stay in a city. 'Like a yo-yo swinging on a string, and right here at Chickasaw's the finger holding the string.' That wasn't swinging free, I said, that was slavery and cowardice. None of it made any sense to me." Abruptly she got up, jerked the fire screen aside, poked at the dying fire, threw on a log. She turned around and glared at us. *"Now* I know that what he meant by swinging free was to have the room, the territory, to have other women. Not to be tied to me. The rest was double-talk. At the time I never thought of that. It didn't cross my mind that I wouldn't be more than enough for him. I thought he didn't want to go with me because he believed he would be my captive if we went someplace on my terms and my money—that it was a commonplace, respectable, bourgeois *man's* fear."

"Maybe he really didn't want to go," I said. "Didn't want to leave Chickasaw. I can't imagine Sam as a young man thinking of . . . of anyone as a threat." I had started to say, "of you," and then, "any woman," but I said "anyone."

"Not even me?" she said.

Wasn't he already courting Timmie by then? I thought of what he had said the night I arrived at Chickasaw: "I wanted the skin for Timmie." What year had that been? Nineteen fifty-six, maybe? I would have been eight.

As if I had spoken aloud, she said, "I was probably already interfering with his other romances. Although, from his point of view, our arrangement was convenient enough. He had me in the daytime; then I went to town where I couldn't possibly cross his path— an unexpected marginal benefit of segregation. And he had— whoever.

"And while *I* was thinking only of what I would be willing to abandon for him—friends, family, my country, the world— *he . . .*" She broke off, went to the kitchen, and poured some more bourbon into her glass.

Miriam said, "Weren't you, no matter what happened, an enemy? I mean, *white?* Wouldn't that enter into it?"

"Does anybody want a drink?" Leila said.

We shook our heads no.

She came back into the room and sat down again. "I don't think so," she said. "It's not easy to say who the enemy is to Sam. His enmities aren't—don't seem to me to be—personal. He killed all those Koreans, but I never thought from anything he said about them that he thought they were his own personal enemies."

"Maybe they weren't, but you—or Alan, or any white person around here—wouldn't that be another matter?"

"If you knew him," Leila said, "you'd know what I'm talking about. There's something so random about him, it makes you hate him. At least it made me hate him. He didn't want to kill Koreans. He would just as soon have killed Americans. He didn't want me. He would just as soon have loved—have abandoned—another woman, black or white. The enemy, or the beloved, is whoever is in his path." She lapsed here, allowed herself to lapse, or, to give herself cover, pretended to lapse into more drunken speech. "But he loved me," she said. "He *did.*" And then, ". . . would've murdered him, 'f I could've gotten away with it. Thought—about poison. Put something in his food. Or . . . or . . . his ear." She laughed. "Weave him a fiery mantle, hmm? Weave his hair into my loom."

"Last time that was tried, it didn't work," I said.

"Didn't work this time either." She shrugged. "But I forgot all that a long time ago. What happened—I came out here one night to our house—*his* house—and he wasn't expecting me. He was with another woman."

Timmie, I suppose.

I must have begun to try to think about them while she was talking, because I remember asking her: "How could you have been so different from what everyone thought you were, have been leading that life and not have a single soul even suspect there was something . . . ?"

"Didn't they?" she said. "Maybe." And then, "Afterwards I was gone—almost a stranger here. Besides" (she looked coldly at us) "if you don't know that people can conceal *everything* about themselves from each other, that other people embrace the deception, you haven't even begun to find out what happens to love." Her face shone pale in the reflected firelight, her breath clouded the cooling air.

Miriam, sitting on the floor now, cross-legged, the three of us facing one another in front of the fire, shivered. "All of us are not like that," she said.

"All of us don't know we're like that," Leila said.

FIFTEEN

HE AFFAIR ended. Either no one found out about it or, as used to be the practice among respectable people, no one admitted to what he knew. Leila went off to Memphis and became phenomenally successful at fabric designing. Sam got married and, until the family leased the last of his land to the SPASURSTA, went right on raising cattle. In the loss of his land lay the real sequel to the affair. But more of that in its proper place.

After we were in bed the night of Leila's confession and Lorene's dance, Miriam and I quarreled—briefly and, as I thought, not very seriously. Miriam claimed that I was like a snail drawn back into its shell, the entrance blocked off by my big snail foot. This because I professed no interest in analyzing either the confession or the dance.

"Are you *afraid* to talk about them?" she said, and, without waiting for an answer, "Why?" and again without waiting for an answer, "You feel threatened, don't you? Women's troubles, women's *energy* threatens you."

Shit.

I claimed in reply that I was as simple as a running brook. All I wanted was to fuck.

"Like Leila said about Sam," Miriam said. "Anybody. Just fuck. You don't care who."

"No," I said. "That's nonsense. I want *you*." (I did! I did!) Also, I said, I was sick of all the confusion and hassle these people had added to our country romance and I didn't want to spend our brief hours alone together analyzing their behavior.

We were lying naked in the big bed under the down comforter, her nipples against my chest, her long legs entwined with mine, the skin of her back smooth and warm under my hand, and I meant exactly what I said. Leila and her loves and hates, Lorene and her nuttiness—the hell with both of them.

"You see," she said. "You can't resist undercutting us, even to get your way. *Country romance*. What does that mean?"

"It means I love you and we're out in the country," I said and fluttered my fingers as lightly as a butterfly's wings down her silky bottom and along the insides of her thighs and then pulled her over on top of me.

We effected a compromise—fuck first and talk afterwards. But afterwards I was too sleepy to talk. As I drifted off to sleep, I had a vague sense of her frustration—felt her turn away from me with a flounce, a hitch of her shoulder and a twitch of the comforter. By the time I woke up the next morning, she was gone.

Where had she gone to at nine o'clock in the morning? Leila (singing "Love, oh, love, oh, cärless love") was already in the attic at her loom and didn't know. The coffee pot was still warm. I fed my cat, poured myself a cup of coffee, poked up the fire, and sat down with a happy sense of lust satisfied and love in bloom that turned out to be premature.

As I discovered shortly, Miriam had gone off with Lee who, with his salesman's pertinacity, had appeared at eight thirty, ready to take her (us, he *said*) on a tour of Chickasaw Ridge—before I had had so much as a chance to show her my favorite tree or even my house. They came in, rosy-cheeked and enthusiastic, while I was still staring contentedly into the fire and drinking my second cup of coffee. Lee had a project for the three of us. Miriam was full of approval.

Everything about Miriam's and my sudden deepening involvement with Lee, murky at the time, seems sadly obvious to me now. To begin with I didn't want her to think I would stoop to jealousy, that surely was a part of the reason for it. Another part was, as Noah and Dallas would have said, the Devil's work. Lee led me up into the top of the tallest parent pine in the Chickasaw pine plantation and spread out his arms toward the horizons and said, "Lo, the *New York Times* will give you money and fame and power, if you will deliver over to them the secrets of this land. It doesn't matter in the least that this isn't what you believe you should be doing. Just get to work. And if we can't sell to the *Times,* we can find a market elsewhere. You start taping and editing. I'll work up a spec and market it and start taking pictures. Miriam can type. Have you got a typewriter?" Miriam wasn't in the room to hear herself assigned the role of stenographer. When she was around, he talked about focus and ideological framework and other such matters.

From the beginning we disagreed about what we were looking for in our oral history. Lee wanted to do a story on the organization and collapse of the pulpwood cutters' union in the county. Miriam was interested in the Klan and the civil rights movement. I wanted to talk about old times with people like Noah. I kept thinking of his version of the Slaughter of the Innocents (the one, circa 1863, that included his grandmother and my great-grandfather) and of his Guinea grandfather who could dance on his belly like a toadfrog and of other tales—of buried treasure and runaway slaves and vengeful Indians and miraculous cures. That was the kind of thing I cared about—a mythology of Homochitto County. To tell the truth, I didn't care a shit about pulpwood cutters' unions or Klansmen unless they proved to be picturesque or lent themselves to mythological treatment.

But Lee said we should "keep our options open"—should develop all three. "After all," he said, "we haven't placed anything yet. We can change the focus, depending on what'll sell. If we get three stories going, so much the better. Isn't there a trashy mag called *Southern Life* or some such thing? The old-times story might sell to that. And besides, we'll need human interest stuff, regardless of how we develop the other two."

I gave him a withering look. "I'm not talking about trash," I said.

"I didn't mean it that way," he said. "Listen, let's just begin taping and photographing and, most important, looking for money, and decide later how to structure the pieces."

"Alan, the politics and economics—and morality—of what's going on in the South *now*—that's what is important," Miriam said.

"I've done my time," I said. "I'm on vacation."

"But . . ." She was wearing her solemn Friends Service Committee face.

"OK." I said. "I'll go along with y'all."

In the long run our differences of opinion did not matter. None of us carried the project through. We made two tapes (the transcriptions of which I intend to include in this account), the first of Noah and the second of Calhoun Levitt. And I learned far more than I wanted to know of the life of one family of pulpwood cutters—the Boykins. None of these stories lent themselves to the needs of the *New York Times*—or *The Speckled Bird*. I doubt they would have borne out anybody's theories—economic, political, moral—or mythological. The light they shed on the past was too specific, too personal, too eccentric.

In any case, Lee and Miriam and I worked out our plans that day, most of which Lee spent with us. He made a few phone calls and produced a nibble—"So-and-so says get him some pictures and a sample tape. He's interested in both stories" (the union and the Movement). We decided that we would try to get acquainted with the Levitts, who, as Mrs. Calloway had told us, had cut pulpwood in the past. We would talk with one or both of them, if we could persuade them to talk, and with Noah.

Two other things happened that day: Lorene called and invited us to go to church with her and Dallas Sunday night and we accepted. (Miriam jumped at the chance. We needed white subjects for our project, she said, and we might get acquainted with some at church.) And in the afternoon, just after Lee left, my grandmother and Denny and Lester came to call.

SIXTEEN

LESTER HAS always been a restless man, I suppose, although I don't remember noticing it as a child. Now that I think back about him, though, I have a sense of him as someone who always stood or walked up and down the house. I see him, particularly at a picnic or a barbecue, standing at the edge of a group in which everyone else is seated—on the ground or on blankets, maybe. I must have taken it for granted that he didn't want to get his clothes dirty. The other men would have on khakis and the women shorts and shirts, but Lester might be wearing a hat and a jacket (from which one sometimes saw him remove an invisible thread) and carrying a raincoat—as if he were getting ready to leave on a trip to the city.

Those picnics took place when we were too small to roam the woods or go back to the creek alone—long before Phoebe was killed. As we got older, the picnics got fewer and after her death they ceased. Even a self-absorbed adolescent like me recognized then that Lester hated Chickasaw, that he came only to be polite

and was always waiting for the moment when he could say to
Denny, "Let's go, dear. I have to . . ." whatever he had made
up to excuse himself and get away from all of us and the memories
of that awful night.

Today, while my grandmother and Denny tried to visit with
Leila and get acquainted with Miriam, he paced the porch and
house like a restless dog. I saw Denny's smile begin to congeal
and felt in the air the tension that makes your eyeballs ache—as
if you might be coming down with acute glaucoma.

"Lester!" my grandmother said. "For God's sake, quit pacing.
You're driving us crazy."

I got up from the hammock. (It was a balmy afternoon, the
sun pouring in from the southwest, and we were sitting on the
porch.) "Come on, Uncle Lester," I said. "Leave the women to
their talk." I made an ironic bow to Miriam. "There's a ditching
problem down by the front gate. I want to show you. . . ." Now
what do you suppose came over me to be such a shit? I suppose
I must have told myself that I was kidding and Miriam knew it
and would think it was funny. Besides, I was doing the right thing.
I knew everybody needed to get Lester off the porch for a while.

He followed me obediently and we walked along the road to the
gate and examined the beginnings of a new gully where the last
rain had sluiced down the ditches and washed out the makeshift
runoff. I talked about drainage and whether we might be able to
get the county to dump a load of gravel on the road and run the
grader over it.

"Who's the Supervisor for this beat?" I asked. "I don't even
know who to call."

"Melton McGee," he said. "I play golf with him. I'll speak to
him about it. No problem."

Instead of turning back toward the house, he looked around as
if searching out some other way to go.

"We could take a look at the trees," I said. "Something has
gotten into the pines over by the SPASURSTA."

We left the road and cut through a stand of young pines set so
close there was almost no underbrush. I glanced at him now and
then, trying to think of something to talk about. His clean, sharp,
1930s, movie-star profile, I observed, was getting sharper, the
neatly clipped sandy hair thinner, the skin, curiously, tight but
at the same time wrinkled, as if it had been crumpled and then

stretched. He adjusted his tie and cleared his throat and looked at me earnestly.

"I've never been one for small talk," he said. "Makes me restless. Gossip." He looked for agreement and I nodded, although in fact I've always liked to gossip.

"Not a reader, either," he said. Then, "Well, son, have you made any decisions about your future?"

"In a way, sir," I said. I had the notion that he would like to hear a deferential "sir" from a young man every now and then and I didn't mind obliging. "I'm writing. I haven't decided how I'll support myself while I'm doing it. I reckon that'll depend on what comes up from time to time."

"Ah," he said, and then, hopefully, "Some writers make a lot of money. Like, uh, the one who's related to Jackie Onassis. What's his name?"

"Gore Vidal? But he's not a poet."

"Who's this fellow I hear about on the TV every now and then? I understand he makes money writing poetry."

I thought. "Rod McKuen?"

"That's right. That's the one."

"I don't think I can do as well as he does, sir," I said. "Not many poets do."

"Money-wise, you mean?"

"Yes."

"I was afraid that was the case. Hmmmm," he said. Then, "Women. Women poets. They do better, don't they? There's a woman who writes these—I suppose you would call them love poems, I saw her on the 'Today Show.' *That's* not the kind of stuff you write, is it?"

"No," I said.

"Well," he said, "I didn't much like the ones she read." Then, "Denny and I worry about you, Alan."

I was surprised. It had never occurred to me that Lester might worry about me. "I worry some, too," I said. "But maybe I can figure out a way to make it."

"Poetry," he said. "Very long, the poems you write?"

"Oh, some of them run thirty or forty lines. Nothing much longer than that yet."

"Maybe you could write them in your spare time," he said, "at night and on weekends."

"I reckon when I run out of money I'll have to," I said, "unless I can find a part-time job."

"If you'd like me to, I could put you in touch with the right people at Penney's," he said. "I mean for a *serious* job—not part-time. They have an executive training program. . . . It's not a bad place to work, son. Steady advancement, if you apply yourself. And you've never been lazy. *That's* not your problem." He looked at me for a response. "Good retirement," he said.

"Thank you, sir," I said. "I . . ."

Abruptly we came out on the edge of the ravine through which Palestine Creek flows after it leaves the lake. Here the creek used to be a clear shallow stream running over white sand and clean gravel, but now the runoff is controlled. A huge culvert, connected on the north side of the dam to the concrete column of the spillway, takes in a small steady stream of lake water and empties it into a pool below the dam. The water spreads and oozes sluggishly along the ravine and the creek bed is a tangled brake of willows and young sycamores, disturbed only by an occasional deluge, when the lake (Chickasaw Ridge, rising in a long curve behind the lake, is a watershed for this part of the country) rises to within a few feet of the top of the dam, and the water gushes out of the spillway and goes roaring down the ravine for a few hours, six or eight or even ten feet deep.

"Where are we, anyhow?" Lester said. "Where are the trees you're talking about?"

"The pool below the spillway is down there. See? And there's the dam. We can follow the edge of the ravine this way and come out on top of it. The trees are on the other side."

We turned northward and picked our way through a brambly stretch of woods. This had used to be a cornfield and had not been replanted with pines—it was a tangle of trash trees and blackberry brambles. I picked up a stick and walked ahead, trampling and knocking down a pathway for Lester.

"I didn't mean to get you into this, sir," I said, "but it doesn't last long." I was hoping it would make him forget about Penney's.

We crossed the auxiliary runoff and climbed to the top of the dam. We were north of and above the house now, having made a half-circle around it from the gate. We could look out to the south from the top of the dam and see below us the pool and the ravine choked with young willows and sycamores and, on its west bank, a quarter of a mile away, a stand of pines growing right up to the picket fence that surrounded the house, and, scattered through the yard around the house, the wide-spreading live oaks and ancient twisted dying cedar trees. The late sun reflected dully from the earth-red roof and a faint wash of blue smoke rose from the chimney.

"In my opinion, this is a dangerous place for a dam," Lester said. "But nobody asked me what I thought about it."

"Dangerous?"

"Look there," he said. "If it washed out on this end (and who's to say it won't in one of those downpours like we have), just a little movement of the dirt over there and the ravine would channel the water right down through the horse lot toward the house."

I could think of nothing to say about this farfetched possibility. "Those trees I was talking about are beyond the dam," I said. "Between the lake and the SPASURSTA."

As we walked along the top of the dam, he began methodically to pick beggar lice from the sleeves of his jacket and flick them away.

"There they are," I said. "Look. Three dead ones over there and then, here, a ring of sickly-looking ones. What do you think?"

But he was no more interested in sick pine trees than I was. He picked another seedpod off his coat, muttered somthing about beetles and borers, and suggested that I should show them to the state forester. Then we walked down the fire lane a couple of hundred yards, with me following him, and stopped beside the SPASURSTA fence. "I like to stand here and look at this place," he said. "It's a marvel."

The air above the glistening black loops and coils of cable seemed to me, even in the late afternoon light, to shimmer and vibrate with energy like the air above a highway on a hot summer day. I stared at a cone-shaped web of steel wire. There had hung the broken body of a cattle egret. I said nothing.

"I brought a couple of my friends out here to see it a few months ago," he said, "and they couldn't believe their eyes. You think about the power, the complexity of it, Alan—all laid out for you, right where you can look at it. We got the fellow who runs the place to take us on a tour. Have you ever been inside?"

"Yes, sir. Leila and I went through it years ago."

"Now, you take Penney's," he said, "or any big corporation. The

150

complexity of an organization like that, the brains it takes to put it together, to keep it operating at peak efficiency, to make the decisions that keep you competitive, to place everybody where he makes his best contribution . . . Everything is connected to everything else, every part sensitive to signals from the outside world, alert to the changes that are always going on there (in the labor market, for instance, in the government, among the consumers). It's the same thing as this, only you don't see it all laid out for you like you do here. Do you see what I mean?"

"Yes, sir," I said.

"Son, I'm telling you, that's the real world," he said.

A face appeared at the window of the bleak little asbestos-shingled building. I recognized the thin pot-bellied TV watcher whom Sam and Eagle had run down. We waved and smiled reassuringly and he vanished. I heard a soft rustle behind me. A couple of Noah's cows moved slowly out of the fire lane, gazed inquiringly at us, mooed a soft greeting, drifted into the open space between fence and woods, and began to crop the frost-yellowed grass. Overhead an egret banked and swooped in to light beside them.

"Those damn cows," Lester said, "trampling the pines again. It's incredible what you people still let the Danielses get away with."

"The trees around here are big enough now so they can't damage them," I said.

He shrugged. "Anyhow," he said, "I'll have to hand it to Leila for this—the SPASURSTA, I mean. She did a good day's work when she got us this lease. For once in her life, she was practical."

"Leila?" I said. "I thought you were the one who handled the negotiations for the SPASURSTA."

He shook his head, "Leila lucked into it. But she could have missed. She was designing the fabrics for all the officers' clubs in the Eighth Naval District—one of the first big jobs she got, I believe; and at the time the navy was negotiating for these leases all over the South and Southwest. They've got a string of them, you know, to track their satellites—everybody's satellites. She happened to hear about it and think about the landing strip. A little push here and a nudge there—you understand. I think at the time she had a friend from Jackson who was on the Senate Armed Forces Committee staff."

"Oh," I said. I turned this information around like a piece from a jigsaw puzzle, trying to find someplace to fit it in. Then I repeated myself. "I thought it was you."

"I was for it, naturally. But she really knocked herself out to get it."

We stood in silence by the fence, looking down the long, clipped meadow. A few yards away one of the cows pulled at a mouthful of yellowed grass beside a metal fence post.

Finally I said, "What about Sam? How did he feel about it?"

"Sam?"

"It was his land, wasn't it?"

"You know how he felt. He tore the damn place apart."

"Well, it *was* his land, wasn't it?"

"Sam's? *Sam's?*"

"I mean, he'd been renting it for years. And before him, Noah. Why . . . ?" I broke off. I was sorry I had spoken. For Christ's sake it was over and done with.

"I wouldn't open that can of worms, if I were you, son," he said. "Leila had it in for Sam all through there, God knows why. (Although, if I were you people, I'd have it in for the Danielses permanently.) And she was right about this in the long run. The government pays us a helluva lot more money than Sam ever did."

He stretched out his left arm, examined the sleeve with close attention, pulled off the last tiny seedpod, looked down, and began to work on his trouser legs. "We really got into them, didn't we?" he said. Then, without looking up, "I want to talk to you about something else, Alan," he said. "All right?"

"Sure," I said unhappily.

"No one will tell you this except me," he said. "I don't suppose anyone can. No one is both inside and outside your family like I am, not your mother certainly. She's more like one of them than they are. Solitary. Headstrong. And besides, she doesn't live here and doesn't see this place as I do. The *place*. That may be what's given me some insight. . . ."

"Sir . . . " I began.

"Don't interrupt me, my boy. This is something I've been trying to make up my mind to say to you ever since I heard you were coming down here with this—this project." He paused. "It's hard for me," he said. There was an intent inward look on his face, the parchment skin dry as a mummy's, tight over his sharp straight nose, covered with minute wrinkles on his cheeks and brow. His eyes were cast down and his shoulders slightly hunched and tense, as if he examined, not the beggar lice on his legs, but some source of pain in the middle of his belly. "I may not get a chance for another talk with you any time soon," he said. And then, "I've given my own boys this warning, too. Not just you."

I nodded.

"I failed to give it to Phoebe," he said. "She was—so young—and besides, I didn't think it was necessary for a girl. I was wrong."

"But Phoebe . . ."

"You people . . ." He broke off and began again. "It's about eccentricity," he said. "Frivolity. The dangers of eccentricity and frivolity." He turned and made a sweeping gesture toward the landscape—the steely sparkling lake, the sailing clouds, the sky—as if the landscape itself were frivolous.

"They," he said, *"you*—all of you—think it's so beautiful out here. Sometimes I've thought that's the main part of the temptation—especially to you younger ones. You haven't learned that beauty isn't the least bit important. It's *exotic.* Yes, you revel in that, all of you. You feel almost like you own a foreign country, don't you? *Nobody* has an abandoned farm to play with—an eighteenth-century abandoned farm. But that *isn't* the main thing. The main thing is that you're all eccentric. Yes. And frivolous. You're all a little bit crazy—you and the whole kit and kaboodle of you, black and white. If you weren't, there wouldn't *be* an abandoned farm." He had forgotten the beggar lice and was looking earnestly into my eyes, intent on convincing me. "I feel I can speak to you, Alan, and you can be sure I want only the best for you. After all, I married your aunt. I joined your craziness. All right?"

Again I nodded.

"So that's what I want to warn you about. I want to explain to you that you have to try to combat this eccentricity with every tool you have.

"Look here, for example. If you were starting out in life and both your grandfathers and maybe a couple of uncles and assorted cousins had died or at the least wrecked their lives by drinking, common sense would tell you to stay away from liquor. Right? But it's hard to convince anyone that eccentricity can be just as dangerous as whiskey—that putting landscapes and queer old houses ahead of security can destroy you."

"Uncle Lester," I said, "the *world* is eccentric now. Everybody is off on some trip or other. What's not eccentric? Eccentricity is average." I would ignore the frivolity charge, I decided. Our notions of frivolity could not possibly agree.

"Penney's," he said. "Penney's is not. All right. Laugh, if you like. You're an intellectual. (Forgive me, my boy. I don't mean to offend you.) You think you're superior. But nobody's superior to disaster. And Penney's is the kind of shelter that can bring you through in disaster."

I was silent. I thought of Phoebe. I saw Lester again, as I remembered seeing him that night, sitting on the ground, his feet encased in their Penney's bedroom slippers, Phoebe's head on his thighs, her chin tucked down, her bone-white arm stretched out on the blood-soaked dirt.

"I have to tell Denny," he had said and looked down at his bloody hands. "I have to tell Denny."

"I don't talk much about Phoebe," he said in a low voice, "but I know that you cared for her, Alan. Maybe that's why Denny and I feel a special affection for you, why I feel obligated to warn you in this way."

I shivered.

"Phoebe's death was the result of the kind of pride in eccentricity, the . . . frivolity that I'm talking about."

For the second time I found myself saying automatically, "Phoebe's death was an accident. Nobody could have done anything. . . ."

"On the face of it," he said. "But if she had been behaving that summer like an ordinary, sensible, popular young girl should behave, the 'accident' wouldn't have happened."

"What do you mean?"

"What seventeen-year-old girl with a thought for her own future or the opinion of her friends and relatives—for her own safety and reputation—spends her days wandering around the woods *alone*—or with a child—you were still a child, Alan—instead of gossiping with her girl friends about clothes and schools and dances and going out with boys her own age? What was she doing here all day long day after day but rejecting—*shaming*—me and my values—the life I'd worked to give her?"

"No," I said. "I don't think it was like that." I was still thinking of the bloodless body, the head resting on his bloody thighs. Could he believe that what he was saying had anything to do with that?

"Did you know she'd already told us she wasn't going to college? And you know, Alan, that was long before it got so damn stylish not to go to college. That she wasn't even going to make her debut? She wanted to go to some weird school she'd found out about where you learn how to *train horses.*"

"I know," I said miserably. What I knew was that Phoebe hadn't had the least intention of going to horse school. She'd dreamed up that idea one boring day to torment her parents.

He went on. "I don't want to talk about Phoebe, Alan. I hate to talk about her. I wouldn't, except that I see you out here plunging into eccentricities of your own. . . . I'm fond of you. I remember the two of you together on horseback . . . canoeing . . ." I heard the break in his light, scratchy voice. He cleared his throat, looked furtively at me, and picked one more seedpod from his trouser leg.

My eyes filled with tears.

He began again. "I see that your father won't advise you. He doesn't, does he? Not sure enough, himself, of the difference between good and bad advice. Infected with the same virus. And your mother . . ." He shrugged.

"I probably wouldn't take their advice unless it was what I had already decided to do," I said.

"But surely *I* have some weight with you, Alan."

"Yes, sir," I said. What else could I say?

He sighed. "You're humoring me. But that's all right, as long as you listen and think seriously about what I say. That's all I'm asking of you. Here's a way to think about it: it's possible to keep everything quiet and orderly, to survive, but it takes constant serious effort—effort to hold off—*chaos.* Yes. That's not overstating it. You have to think of your life as a holding action, a drawing in, a defense. All my life has been a defense for Denny and Phoebe and the boys. . . ." He broke off.

The sun was going down. A light chilly wind had begun to blow. A long bank of low clouds burned in the western sky. Crows were flying and cawing in the cold burning air.

Not my life, I thought. My life won't be like that.

The sun dropped behind the pine plantation beyond the lake.

"Denny will be wondering where we are," he said. "We'd better start back." And then, as we walked toward the dam, he said abruptly, "I grew up in St. Louis in the thirties. Did you know my father deserted my mother and my brother and me?"

I shook my head. I had never thought about Lester's past. Vaguely he had seemed to me always to have worked at Penney's, to have been married to Denny, to be Phoebe's father.

"Nineteen thirty-two. Does that year mean anything to you? No, I don't suppose it does. Nineteen thirty-two is just another year before you were born. Well, in 1932 in St. Louis people like me— ordinary working people—starved to death. When I was younger, I used to *hate* my father, but now I believe he left because he couldn't bear to see us hungry. Maybe *he* starved to death or died of exposure or got hit on the head by someone as desperate as he was." He came to a halt, standing now at the end of the dam. Methodically, still talking, he removed his jacket, unbuttoned his left shirt-sleeve, and began to roll it up. "When *your* family talks about the Depression," he said, "it's like it was some huge, funny adventure. 'That was the winter old so-and-so moved into the commissary,' they say. 'You remember—they'd cut off the gas in the house.' Or (your grandmother), 'I made Leila a tailored suit out of that old brown pinstripe of her father's. My God, it was ugly! But she thought she was the cat's pajamas.' And the blacks do them the courtesy of bragging on them, knowing it's unseemly for them to brag on themselves. 'Boss Alan, he never turn *nobody* away hongry from his do'.' " He mimicked Noah's complicated mock-servile delivery. Then he held out his bare arm to me, palm down. A long jagged scar furrowed through the sparse hair from just above the knot of bone at his wrist almost to his elbow. "That happened to me the winter of 1932," he said evenly. "I was fighting with another boy over the contents of a garbage can."

Shit.

He turned his sleeve down, buttoned it, and put on his jacket.

"I never thought about 1932 or any of that in connection with us—or you," I said in a low voice. "Only as history."

"Penney's is like a fortress to me," he said. "A place where everything is safe and predictable." He put his hands in his pockets and walked slowly on. "People like Leila and your Uncle Dennison never see the threat of chaos until it destroys them. They spend their lives playing. Playing with Chickasaw or weaving or whatever strikes their fancy. I'm not talking about farming, you understand. Farming can be a business—as orderly, almost as safe as

Penney's. I'm talking about how the way you people deal with Chickasaw exposes the dangerous—*dangerous*—weakness in the family character. Leila, for example. She comes out here, thinks she can walk in the woods, work up her designs, stir up the people out here—Sam, Noah, whoever—and then leave and there will be no consequences for anybody. Consequences are something she never gives a thought to."

"Leila told me she would have farmed the place if Uncle D. and Grandfather had let her," I said. "I wonder she didn't come back and take over when Uncle D. died."

"She talked about it," he said. "Years ago. She never meant it seriously. Leila couldn't put up with a farmer's life. She's too much of a wanderer." He glanced at me and said cautiously, "But, as to that, it's just as well she's not right here under her mother's nose."

"I suppose so," I said.

With sudden irritation he added, "Besides, what the hell does she know about farming? She'd be up in the attic making wall hangings when it was time to defoliate. That's exactly what I'm talking about. That was a pose. *I* could have farmed. I would have hired a good manager to begin with (while I was learning) if they'd been willing to give me a free hand. We could have begun a cattle operation here twenty years ago that would be making money now for everybody. And if we had—look at Marathon, for instance. Same kind of land, in the same shape after the war (I do mean World War II—*not* the Civil War). And now it's a profitable business. Because the owners took it seriously. But nobody would hear of my taking over. I suppose they were afraid I would turn their *fossil* into a home—a money-maker. As your grandmother would put it, they took their talent and buried it."

I felt a constriction in my throat, a tightness in my chest. Penney's! Fossil! I realized that my right fist was clenched, that I wanted to hit him and at the same time I wanted to cry. What kind of confusion was this? I must say something wise and temperate, I decided. "I suppose we all have to be whatever it is we think we're meant to be, Uncle Lester," I said.

I shot back the bolt in the aluminum gate to the horse lot, stepped aside to let him pass through, and then followed him and refastened the gate. He shook his head, looked down, and saw that he had missed one last seedpod on his sleeve. He picked it off and smiled at me, a curious, closed-in, yet vulnerable smile. Suddenly his eyes were Phoebe's. She looked at me out of his prematurely wrinkled eunuch's face as if she were imprisoned in him—her eyes in his head all that was left of her life. I shuddered.

"Until the world teaches us we're something else, son," he said.

SEVENTEEN

SUNDAY NIGHT we went to church. The state campground and regional offices for Lorene and Dallas's church are outside Homochitto, and the local congregation turned out to be far larger and richer and more joyous—gayer—than I had expected it to be. I had thought we would go to some little hole-in-corner building with a prefab spire and sit in uneasy boredom while a few pitifully drab and unfortunate misfits induced in themselves the hysteria that provided the only excitement in their lives. Such was not the case.

"We did have a frame church," Lorene told us, "*big,* but not fancy. After it burned down a few years ago, it didn't take the congregation six months to raise the money for the new one."

The new brick church, set between a Gulf Service Station and a cornfield out on the edge of town, had a parking lot crowded with cars, new pickups and shining Buicks and Oldsmobiles and Lincolns. Banks of long narrow windows let into the walls were glazed, not with the usual cheap painted glass one finds in poor churches in the South, or even with the smarmy stained-glass scenes of Jesus and the children or Abraham and Isaac that one finds in rich churches, but with huge uninterrupted panes of a roiling, smoke-drifted red—as if there were a fire inside the church. (And then, when we got inside, the panes had somehow been lighted from without as well as within, so that the fiery light seemed to be outside—as if our music-filled, air-conditioned sanctuary were set down in the middle of Hell.)

When we got there, the choir milling around in the vestibule was forming up to march in—fifty or sixty strong, young and old, men and women. As we came through the door, there was a piercing fanfare on a trumpet. My eyes popped open and my back snapped straight, as if I'd gotten a direct message from the angel Gabriel. The inner doors to the sanctuary were thrown wide and two young girls with long straight hair hanging, brushed and shining, below their waists began to shake tambourines. A drummer, whom I couldn't see for the crowd, tossed off a roll, the organ music swelled, the trumpet picked up the melody, and everyone began to sing and march:

> "Holy Spirit, from on high,
> O'er us bend a pitying eye;
> Now refresh the drooping heart;
> Bid the pow'r of sin depart. . . ."

Lorene was standing alone against an inside wall of the vestibule waiting for us and when she saw us, beckoned us over, and we stood waiting for the choir to pass by. Then we followed her into an auditorium brilliantly lighted with tiers of wall sconces and three huge chandeliers glittering with crystal pendants; and filled with people rising, singing, raising their arms as Lorene had at Chickasaw, to receive the Spirit. We slipped into a pew next to Dallas, who was sitting down, hunched over, his forehead cupped in his hand, as if he were praying. The trumpet blared out and up in the pulpit the preacher raised his arms heavenward like the others and sang out very loud, and then, "Praise the Lord, brothers, sisters. *Praise* Him," he shouted above the music. "We're going to *sing* tonight. We're going to sing His praise."

A deep contralto voice that seemed to come from the organ loft and resounded like a trumpet through the church repeated, "Praise Him. Praise Him."

"Hallelujah," the preacher said. "Hallelujah, amen," and there was a chorus of *Hallelujahs* and *Praise Hims* from all around us and the hymn ended and there was a spattering of applause like rain and the organ music swelled out again and the choir immediately took up another hymn, "All Hail the Power of Jesus' Name," and Lorene, smiling that curious ecstatic smile, handed a hymnbook to me and one to Miriam and we began to sing. All around us faces and bodies were alert, intent, secret, like the faces and bodies of people at a rock concert, as if everyone there were absorbed in watching his own soul float free.

The singing lasted a long, long time, one song after another, with rhythmic hand-clapping ("Precious Saviour, take my hand / I need Thee every hour") and a gathering murmurous sound and movement through the church, as sometimes one and sometimes another would fall on his knees and whisper, as Lorene had done in the living room at Chickasaw, or speak out loud a long unintelligible chant with lots of *K* sounds in it like Greek, or step out into the aisle and dance and clap. Two or three pews down from us a middle-aged man, tall and narrow-shouldered with deep-set scornful eyes, a full passionate lower lip, and thin graying hair brushed back from his high forehead ("I'll fly away / Oh, glory, I'll fly away"), raised his arms, shook his shoulders convulsively inside a rumpled seersucker jacket, stretched his arms out stiffly to the sides, and began to spin and rock like an off-balance top. A little boy of seven or eight, sitting between his parents in the pew in front of the whirler, squirmed around, got up on his knees, and, holding onto the back of the pew, leaned back so as to avoid the flailing arms and stared first at the whirler and then at us and around the church, a calm bored smile on his round face. ("In the morning, when I die / I'll fly away.") The music swelled and sank, chorus after chorus.

I had my tonsils out when I was six, and I still remember the sensation of going under, a sweetish burning, suffocating smell, and then a long dream of being inside a turning, roaring drum—as if the pressure of air and sound on my ears were being rhythmically altered by a giant hand that stretched and slacked the drum head or squeezed a bellows.

The windows smoked and flamed.

"This is bad news, buddy," some reasonable guy seemed to be saying to me from far away, but the pressure of the music and the whispering voices and clapping hands continued to move me along.

Dallas sat impassive, unmoving, looking straight ahead of him, his shoulders hunched over, as if he shielded himself from the Spirit rather than inviting Him. But, as if it didn't belong to him, his hand beat the pew seat in time to the music. Beside me Miriam, her face quiet, questioning, turned the pages of the hymnbook and sang softly in her clear pure voice. The faces of the people around us, all but the children's, began to have the fixed ecstatic joyousness of trance. ("Just a few more weary days and then / I'll fly away . . .") The children moved restlessly in their places and here and there a mother would stop singing long enough to give one a shake or to rise and take out a crying baby. Directly in front of us a little girl of five or six knelt and, folding her arms on the back of the pew, pillowed her head on them and stared into my face out of small pale eyes, as if she were sure that in a moment I would do something interesting. Briefly, I wanted, like Dallas, to hunch forward and protect myself.

It passed through my mind that all this must be threatening to Miriam. I thought of the Friends meetings she had told me about, how everyone sat in Meeting, saying not a word, not for the whole hour, if no one was moved to speak. But maybe she didn't feel the power that I felt here; maybe it was so foreign that it passed her by, could not touch her.

I felt a curious drawing sensation in the bands of muscle across my chest and over my shoulders and back, as if those muscles were drawing my arms upward in supplication and invitation, whether I wanted to raise them or not. I put all my consciousness into the songs and it was a trip ("Like a bird from prison bars has flown / I'll fly away").

Dallas still had not stood up or looked up or opened his mouth, although now he was beating on the bench with both hands and pounding the floor with his heels, a jarring beat.

Again the singing died away in a rain of applause and scattered "Hallelujahs." I looked around the church. What next?

That was when I saw Lee for the first time. He was sitting far off to our left and toward the front of the church and I could see the camera strap cutting across his jacket collar. He had evidently dressed up in his middle-class disguise, a crinkly polyester suit with an iridescent thread in it, and he had cut his hair. I glanced uneasily at Dallas and Lorene, but they seemed unaware of his presence.

Goddamn, I thought. Do I want to be involved in this? With *him?*

A damn magazine story about middle-class Jesus freaks? It's not at all, not at *all* what I want to be thinking about. Then: But I'm as much a voyeur as he is. I do the same thing, I just don't take pictures and don't make any money.

Shit!

No! It's *not* the same thing. I'm a *poet.*

I looked away from him toward the preacher and put him out of my mind. I realized then that the music had never stopped, although the singing had, and that the preacher was talking—a curious-looking, cocky-looking, feisty-looking little man in his sixties, muscles like an aging acrobat, like old Picasso, iron-gray, coarse hair standing up wildly from half a dozen cowlicks and hot cinnamon-brown eyes darting over the congregation.

". . . a fanatic, brothers, sisters. I'm a fanatic for God and that's what I'm preaching about tonight. I'm going to tell you why."

The woman who had been playing the organ accompanying the choir stood up and stepped down behind him, tall, majestic, and thin, with great thyroidal eyes, a thin hooked nose, and narrow face, the reincarnation of Virginia Woolf.

". . . and the sea gave up the dead which were in it," the preacher said, "and Hell gave up the dead, and they were judged. I'm talking about the judgment day, about what's going to happen on the judgment day and why it makes me a fanatic," he said.

"The *sea*," the woman said, her resonant contralto voice echoing through the church. "The *sea—*gave—up—the—dead. . . ."

"And death and Hades were thrown into the lake of fire."

"And if anyone's name was not found written in the book of life, he was hurled, *hurled* into a lake of fire forever. . . ."

"Hurled," the woman said. "Hurled . . . into a lake of fire. Forever. For-e-v-er. Forever hurled into a lake of fire."

"Tormented."

"Forever."

"Tormented day and night forever and ever."

"Hurled . . ."

"How long is Hell, brothers?"

"Forever."

"Oh, sisters, brothers, the Devil hates this church. The Devil hates this preacher. The Devil *hates* this preacher. I'm asking you why? Why? Because he's a fanatic, brothers. Yes. The Devil says I'm a fanatic and the sinner says I'm a fanatic and I say, *Yes!"*

"Fanatic!" the woman said.

"Listen to *me*. Listen to *me*. I can save your soul from Hell."

"Yes."

"My wife knows it. She knows me. She knows how I spend my nights and days. I'm praying for *you*. I'm fanatic for *you*. I'm going to save your souls, brothers, sisters. Yes, I been wrestling with the Devil for your souls. Wrestling with him. Seems like along about last October he got stronger. And then *I* got stronger. I'm wrestling with him for you. The muscles of my soul are getting stronger and stronger.

"Because I *know* . . . I know about that lake of fire."

"Burning, burning, burning," the woman said.

"Oh, they're burning down there, brothers, sisters."

"Burning."

"I saw a man die burning once, friends. I received a call from a friend and there had been a wreck there on the highway just a few blocks from my house and I went out there and I saw him. Oh, he was pinned, friends, pinned in the cab of his truck, and I stood there on the highway and I heard him scream, brothers. I saw him writhe and I heard him howl. 'Oh, Father Abraham, have mercy on me and send Lazarus that he may dip the tip of his finger in water and cool off my tongue; for I am in agony in this flame.' Luke sixteen, twenty-four.

"And his brother was standing there beside me, friends, watching his own brother burn.

"Too late . . . too late . . . Will it be too late for you?"

"Howling . . ."

"And oh, my friends, when the fire was out, his brother took up that black, charred, dead, stinking body in his arms and lifted up his head to God and he *screamed*. . . . He cried out to God: 'Oh, my brother! Oh, I love him, God!' Too late. Too late. . . .'"

"Howling."

"Ten minutes? That's how long he suffered, that's how long that man screamed in his agony and then he bent down and breathed the flames into his lungs like the martyrs of old, so he would die. But Hell? Think about ten minutes in that fire, friends, and then think about *Hell*. How long is Hell? Hell is forever."

"Forever. For-e-v-er."

"Oh, my brother. Oh, I love him."

"Too late . . . too late."

"So, yes, friends, I'm a fanatic. I'll risk his foul stinking fiery

164

breath on my face, if I can snatch back one sinner from that lake of fire.

"Let me tell you, friends in Jesus, I saw a mother once and she was a fanatic. She loved her children. Oh, yes, she never had a thought that wasn't for them. And one day, friends, oh, the horror of it, one day her house caught on fire and I saw her there, yes, she was outside that burning house and two policemen were holding her and she was screaming, 'Let me go, oh, let me go! My child is in there! He's in there, *burning.*' And her strength was more than the strength of those two strong men and she broke away from them and ran toward the flames and, friends, they burned their hands and their arms and faces to run in after her and drag her out and she was fighting all the time. *'My child is in there!'*

"And I'm like that mother. Fanatic! Yes, brothers, sisters! To save your souls. To snatch you back! My hands are burned and my eyebrows are all singed off and the skin on my lips is parched and cracked with the fire."

"Fanatic . . ."

"Oh, I've gone down to the mat with him.

"And friends, when the fire was out in that house and the ashes were still smoking, they played the hoses on that black ruin and they went in and there, curled up under the stinking ruins, under the smoking soggy mattress and the twisted, melted bed frame, they found the little body. And its little fingers were burned stumps and its face was burned away and it was dead."

"Dead! Dead! Dead!" the woman chanted.

" 'I would have died to save my baby.' That's what the mother said. But it was too late."

"Too late . . . too late. . . ."

"I'm like a mother to you, children. I rush into the fire every day to save your souls. Yes. *Me.*" He snatched a chair forward from the back of the stage and jumped up on it and put up his fists like a boxer. "I'm here, fiend. I'm here, Beelzebub. Satan. Here I am. Burn *me*. I see you. I know you. You can't fool me. Come on in after me. Put on your disguises. I can smell your breath." He whirled around on the chair slashing the air with an imaginary sword, leaped down and began to dance a kind of stamping fox-trot while he talked. "Let me tell you, friends. I know him. I study him. Oh, there are plenty of people will tell you he's got horns and a tail, he wears a red suit. They think they'll see him a long way off, know he's coming, they'll run for it. It's not so, friends. You've got to wrestle with him to know him. He might come right up to you and take your arm and you would think he was a friend. He was going to *give* you something. I'm telling you he's handsome. He's smiling. He can sing. Friends, he's got a pipe organ inside of him, plays nothing but rock 'n' roll. He hands you a ticket. Says, the government's going to take care of you, says, you don't need to take care of your pore old mama, the government'll take care of her. Communist! He's a Communist. Says, go out on your husband. Ain't going to hurt him if he don't know about it. Cut your hair, ladies. Put on your tight pants and your lipstick, switch your hips. Open your legs. Oh, I know him!

"Burn *me*. That's what I tell him. Fight *me*. I'm going to keep him away from you. Ohhhh, *Jesus!*" He continued to dance and began a long unintelligible chant.

"Break us up, Lord!" the woman in front of me shouted, and across the church another, "Break us up!"

The music swelled and soared. The guitar sounded out louder and the guy on drums began to play a *barumm, brum, brum; barumm, brum, brum;* and a *barumm, brum, brum.* A man in the front pew stood up and began to dance before the pulpit. Two women fell on their knees in the pew behind him and all over the church the sound rose of rapid, sibilant whispering.

"Whoop sallillabee, whoop sallillabee," the preacher shouted. "Hulla, hulla, hulla, hulla."

I saw that Lee had stood up as if carried away like the others. With the Leica cradled low in one hand, he was snapping pictures. No one paid the least attention. Lorene stood up and stepped out into the aisle and began a dance, transformed, as she had been in our dining room, from a narrow-bodied, high-shouldered, puritan country girl to something else—sexy and flexible and glistening as a snake, pouring out her sex and herself before her God.

Dallas beat the pew seat and stamped his feet. Then he raised his arms as creakily as if they were doors whose hinges were frozen with rust. He held them above his head, palms cupped as if to catch the rain.

Lorene danced all the way down the aisle and across the front of the church and up the aisle on the other side and, circling around the back, returned to us and subsided into the pew, leaning forward, whispering, shaking her head from side to side and throwing it up like a nervous mare.

166

But Dallas's gesture had broken the trance I felt I had been in. I glanced surreptitiously at the watch on Miriam's wrist. More than two hours had gone by since we'd followed the choir singing and praising God into the church.

The preacher continued to dance, spiky hair standing up strongly from his temples, cinnamon eyes fixed straight ahead. He leaped up on the chair again, mimed another battle, and leaped down, chattering all the while. ("I'll fly away, I'll fly away, / Oh, Glory, I'll fly away / in the morning / When I die / I'll fly away.")

Miriam looked at me with soft bewildered eyes. "I don't think this is so good, Alan," she whispered.

I took her hand in mine and shook my head. "We *can't* leave," I said in her ear. "I think it must be almost over." I took up the hymnal (they had begun to sing again), found the page, and we sang, too, "What a beautiful thought I am thinking concerning the Great Speckled Bird / Remember her name is recorded on the pages of God's holy word / There are many who'd lower her standards. . . ."

A guttural shriek sounded at the rear of the church. I felt Miriam flinch and shrink against me, glanced over my shoulder. A man in one of the back pews stumbled out into the aisle, shouting, and made his way, staggering and dancing down one aisle and up the other, around the back and down to the pulpit again.

"Oh, He's with us, brothers, sisters. He's in our presence to-night!" the preacher shouted.

The man faced us, threw up his arms, and fell on his knees. Youngish (maybe thirty-five), with the heavy shoulders and thickening waist of an ex-athlete, his black hair slicked neatly down, his face contorted, he threw out his arms and began to chant in a hoarse unearthly voice. This had evidently not been expected. A murmur as of wonder and joy passed through the crowd.

"Another soul, God! Another soul!"

". . . He comes on a cloud in the morning / and His voice round the earth shall be heard . . ."

"Oh, I've fought the Devil for him. Oh, he's labored to come through."

The man began to weep, covered his face with his hands, and slumped to the floor. A woman slipped out of the pew where he had been sitting, hurried to the front of the church, and threw her arms about him.

Lorene got abruptly up from her knees, turned off her own chant as if it were a running hot-water faucet, put the ecstatic sweet smile back on her face, and leaned over to me. "He's come through," she said. "Look. The Spirit has come down on him. Praise God. Oh, he's been trying," she said. "He was already trying when we first came back to Homochitto. Brother Tidwell has been praying him through. And all of us! All of us! Dallas, you see that? You see?"

Three or four other men and an elderly woman had come down to the pulpit now. Someone helped him get to his feet. There were shy embraces and handshakes and tears. The old woman took the young man's head between her hands and kissed him.

Dallas nodded grimly without looking at Lorene and folded his arms across his chest. Lee, I saw, had slipped out of his pew and moved to a seat directly behind the convert and was continuing to take pictures. I could see this by the way he was holding his arms. His camera, still cradled in one hand, was not visible from where we sat.

Now the preacher and his wife came down and joined the group around the man and his wife. The drummer began to brush his drum softly with the whisk, the guitarist to play, and the choir, humming, "I'll Fly Away," to drift quietly out of the choir loft. The service, it appeared, was over. Here and there parents gathered sleeping children into their arms and, without waiting for a benediction, left the church. Teenagers clustered in chattering groups at the back of the church. The whirling man sat slumped in exhaustion in his pew and his wife tugged at his coat to rouse him.

Dallas stood up and, brushing past us, hurried out of the church.

"Oh, it hurts him so that he hasn't come through, yet," Lorene said. "Oh, it hurts us both. But we have faith. We know he will. In God's time."

"I want to tell you people," the preacher said, "I been carried away tonight, I missed the announcements, but God will forgive me when he smells the sweet perfume of this saved soul rising to heaven. I want to tell you, we got a missionary service next Wednesday night. We got a grand soul saver been doing the Lord's work in Ghana coming to tell us about it. And brothers, he can shout! He can dance! Don't fail to be here. And I want to tell you, too, friends, we got a fine young man taking pictures here tonight. Don't let his beard put you off. It's a neat beard. A clean beard.

The prophets had beards. *Jesus* had a beard. Not to mention my old granddaddy who preached the Holy Spirit for fifty years and died a saint. Now, let me tell you, this young man's gonna write an article about our church, about the work we been doing here. Be in the national media. Spread the Word. So welcome him to our church, friends, here he is right here in front of me and . . ."

"That's *Lee*," Lorene said.

"I think I'll go find Dallas," I said.

"God brought him here," Lorene said. "Look at him. He's cut his hair."

Miriam said nothing. She looked as if she'd been caught with her hand in the cookie jar.

I found Dallas leaning against the pickup, looking at the clear night sky, his hands in his pockets.

We were used to being silent together and so I did not feel uncomfortable, standing beside him for a few minutes gazing up at the stars. Perseus and Cassiopeia had heeled over westward and were only faintly visible through the lights that surrounded the service station next door. Overhead, Orion shone out and, beyond the cornfield to the east, the Twins.

Someone inside the church was playing chords softly on the organ. Figures moved back and forth behind the fiery windows. Three children were playing hopscotch on the expanse of concrete around the service station.

"I've decided I have to put some insulation in the attic of my house," I said finally. "That place is like the outdoors since I've pulled the newspapers off the walls and ceiling."

He did not answer for a while. Then, "Nothing to that," he said. "You can put it down in an hour or two."

"The walls are something else," I said. "I've got to find some more cypress siding. . . ." I could see his hands, knotted into fists inside the pockets of his Sunday suit pants. The muscles in his jaws were clenched. He turned away from me and gazed off across the rows of broken brownish stalks in the cornfield beyond the church.

"The Spirit came down early on my mother," he said. "When she was in her teens. Right in this church. She told me it was when she was fifteen. Far as I know, it hadn't ever come onto my daddy. Hadn't, anyway, last time I saw him. He might be an atheist, far as I know. He never said. I always thought it was because he didn't want to worry her. Not that being an atheist would keep the Spirit from moving in him. Miracles happen every day."

I said nothing.

"But I *believe*," he said. "I'm not any damn fool shit-ass, fake-smart atheist like Lee."

"All that in there . . . it scares me," I said. "How can anybody tell whether or not it—whether it comes from—God? And it scares me to think about giving up control. If . . . if He were to ask something of you, would it be to give up control?"

He turned back and looked at me as if I were feebleminded. "Of course you have to give yourself up," he said. "Any fool knows that. But how to do it?" Still he was rigid, the clenched fists in his pockets. *"How to do it? That's my problem."* He moved his shoulders restlessly. "As for the other, it comes from *Him,* all right. I know that. I hadn't lived all these years with my mother and then with Lorene for nothing. And it doesn't scare me—losing control, or dying or killing. It happens. Just dying *before* . . . But He won't come down to me. He *won't.* How can I make Him come down?"

"Maybe there are other ways God shows Himself," I said. "Maybe that's not the only way. Or maybe He won't show Himself at all. Maybe that's another kind of test. That you have to have faith whether He shows Himself or not. I would like to have that kind of faith."

"Why won't He? *Why?*" He took his hands out of his pockets and stood gazing, as I thought, at the facade of the church, the smoky flaming windows. His eyes narrowed and his face lost the uncharacteristically vulnerable look he had turned on me when he said, "Why won't He? Why?"

"Shit," he said. "That's my fucking brother over there shining his ass with that fucking camera. Where did he come from?"

"It's OK," I said. "The preacher said it was OK. He made an announcement after you left. Said Lee was doing a picture story on the church."

"He's cut his fucking hair," he said. A noise like a growl seemed caught in his throat.

"Wait," I said.

He turned his cold closed face to me. "I'm not going to make a scene here," he said. "If I decide to kill the bastard, it won't be in front of the church." He put his hands back in his pockets and walked over to Lee. I followed.

Lee was standing to the left of the entrance at the foot of the steps now, shooting up toward the open doors of the church as the crowd came out.

Dallas took hold of his shoulder and jerked him around. "Put the fucking camera away," he said. "Didn't I tell you there were some people in the world didn't want their pictures in the paper?"

"I'm through anyway," Lee said evenly. "All right? I got some good stuff. But if I wasn't through, it wouldn't be any of your business, see? This is not your church. It doesn't belong to you. You haven't got anything to say about whether I take pictures or don't take pictures. So let go of my fucking shoulder."

The children under the Gulf sign had stopped playing hopscotch and were staring at us. Out of the corner of my eye I saw Miriam and Lorene coming out of the church. "Dallas," I said, "you said you wouldn't make a scene in front of the church, didn't you? Let go of his shoulder. Your wife is looking at you. Do you want to upset her?"

"Let him," Lee said. He spoke a little louder. "I'm doing God's work here," he said. "I'm spreading the Gospel like the preacher said, in my own particular way. I'm witnessing."

Dallas let him go. "Yeah," he said.

"How many people are going to be touched by the Holy Spirit when they see my pictures in the *New York Times Sunday Magazine?*" Lee said. "Those atheists up there in New York are going to be doing God's work without having sense enough to know they're doing it."

"I could pulverize you if I wanted to," Dallas said. "I could destroy you. So be careful."

"What the hell does that mean?" Lee said, his voice lower now. "Listen to the crazy bastard, Alan. You hear that? And have you heard him talk about killing slopes yet?"

"I don't let other people do my killing for me," Dallas said. "I didn't fake a goddamn bleeding ulcer to stay out. Is that what you did? Or did you tell them you were a queer? Or had fits?"

"Get him to give you his whole fucking philosophy," Lee said. "That's what the war does to people. Drives 'em nuts."

The two women had joined us by now and Lorene took Dallas's hand and led him away, murmuring in his ear.

"For Christ's sake, Lee!" I said. I headed him toward his VW. "You might have known how he would react to your taking pictures. Come on, Miriam. Let's all get away from here."

He stared me down. "This is my church," he said. "I was raised in it. It doesn't belong to him. What I do here is none of his business." He opened his car door.

"You weren't talking about church," I said. "You were talking about the war, about killing people."

"And if it wasn't my church," he said, "you heard what the preacher said. They want me in there taking their pictures and putting them on the front page of the paper. That's what it's all about and they know it. Where do you think Jerry Rubin or Rap Brown or . . . or *Nixon* would be if they didn't know how to play the media like violins? Nowhere. *Nowhere.* So, as far as they're concerned, I'm an instrument of God to spread the word, and as far as they're concerned, they're right."

"But what about *you?*" Miriam said.

He looked at her meltingly. "All I want to do, *ever,* Miriam, is to tell the truth."

EIGHTEEN

MONDAY MORNING, Tuesday morning, Wednesday morning, Lee—that bastard, that shithead, that *salesman*—came by again and again, always with news or questions about our project, earnest talk about making money and offing the system at the same time.

Here he comes—gets out of his shiny, spotless VW. (He's probably still a car freak and, now that he's made it, spends Saturday afternoon washing and waxing and polishing his BMW and has an antique Chrysler or a reproduction Cord in the garage.) His hair is squeaky clean and his beard is combed and trimmed like General Grant's and his fringed jacket is just worn and dirty enough to be acceptable among his peers. He has that boyish, eager smile on his dish face. (I didn't notice the first couple of times I saw him that he was dish-faced. Or maybe the more he homed in on Miriam, the more he stuck out his chin and beetled his brow.)

Monday the three of us taped Noah. He was the obvious choice to start practicing on. More of that tape later. That afternoon I worked on my house. Miriam said she would like to walk over the place and then maybe visit with Leila and watch her work. The weather continued good. Wednesday Dallas called and said he could lend a hand with the house and I took him up on it. I thought Miriam would come and keep us company, maybe even knock a few nails out of boards; and she said that later she might, but that she wanted to take a nap. I left her lying on the bed asleep, smiling at her dreams like an angel, her fair hair drifted across the pillow. She didn't come by all afternoon. Dallas was touchy and preoccupied; when we were only three-quarters through insulating the attic, he dusted off his jeans, climbed down the ladder, and drove away without a word.

Miriam had been uncommonly quiet, I thought, ever since Friday night. Whatever had seemed important to say about Leila's confession or about church or about Noah's tape she had not said. She's looked at me now and then, it's true, with a speculative eye, but I'd made no inquiries as to what she was speculating about. I didn't want any deep talks.

Thinking back now as detachedly, as honestly as I can about Alan McLaurin—that faraway young man—I can't say that I feel any admiration for his behavior. He'd been acting like a shit, had been saying, to himself and to her, one thing about what he was doing, and feeling in his gut another.

You move along with a woman, side by side, wanting her, not wanting her. Sex, lust (the hopeful penis rising, questing like the snorkle of a nuclear sub and supplied like the sub with inexhaustible fuel), plays wild tricks on you. Was it Sophocles said at eighty-five, "At last I'm free of that. That beast is off my back"? No, it was Noah. But it's hard for me to imagine, no matter how much pain the beast inflicts, *ever,* even at eighty-five, wanting to be "free of that."

Anyhow, he, Alan, yearned for new excitement, as you do, as you get used to doing after a while. At twenty-two, though, he was pure and so he called it something else. And he initiated that series of small betrayals of her and of himself that were meant to drive her away without driving her away and without his having to admit to himself what he was doing.

First he wrote her about the girl with the silver and turquoise rings—a wry, sophisticated (as he thought, amusing) account of his expectations and his failure. (We were supposed to be honest

174

with each other.) Then he didn't hesitate, as soon as he was feeling so horny he couldn't stand it, to tell her to come down and interrupt the solitude that had been so important to him when he left her. And when she came, he continued with his mean little games: he put her down at Calloway's and on the front porch; he fucked and went to sleep instead of talking. There were more things than Leila's love life that he and she needed to talk about and he knew it well, but he turned his back.

What the hell did he expect—the dog, the buffoon, the ape who took over that young man for a while? One thing he did not expect was that she would respond to his signals as alertly as she did. *He* would doubtless have preferred to engineer a series of quarrels, a drifting apart, a period in which she gradually became more and more unattractive and he was importuned by beauties who needed not just his sexual services, but under*stand*ing, *love,* self-*sac*rifice. Also, he would have liked to see her go into a suitable period of mourning at being abandoned. After all, he was an attractive fellow. Any woman should mourn at least six months after being abandoned by him. (But no longer than that. He wasn't a sadist.)

He miscalculated. She proved far more acute and far readier to assume responsibility for her fate than he would have dreamed possible. She was unaware of the suitability of mourning after abandonment. Ah, sorrow! She didn't even give him time to abandon her properly! He'd barely got started.

～

She was inordinately cheerful when I got back to the house just at dark that afternoon. Lee had come by, she said, and they'd gone for a drive around the county.

It was that night in bed that she told me.

"I want to be honest with you," she said.

I heard a faint warning rumble of thunder. It seemed to come from my belly.

"We've always been honest with each other," she said. "I *think.*"

I drew her to me and we lay under the covers, nose to nose. I lifted a strand of her hair from her cheek, put it aside, and kissed her and told my belly to be quiet. "Of course," I said. I ran my hand down her back and over the curve of her ass.

"No," she said. "Listen."

175

"I'm listening."

"We said we would never try to possess each other, *control* each other," she said. She put her hands against my chest and gently pushed herself away from me. "That we wouldn't fall into that trap. Care and let go. Isn't that what love is all about?"

"Hmmmm. Sure." I burrowed into the covers and nuzzled her neck.

"Alan, I'm *talking* to you."

At last I heard her voice. It didn't sound good. Not good at all. I sat up in bed and turned on the light. I *looked* at her. I'd never seen her looking looser and more beautiful—like every joint had just been oiled. And there on her face was that fuzzy smile I knew only too well—postcoital satisfaction, the recollection in tranquillity of pleasures past. I'm doing that for you, I said to myself. (Was I so vain, so fond, as to believe she was still recollecting last night?)

"What's on your mind?" I said.

"I *have* to tell you this . . ." She broke off.

Again the deep seriousness of her voice penetrated my little self-congratulatory world. What was she going to say? That she'd ratted on me in Boston? I could live with that. I was ready. "Or," the ape whispered, "you can use it against her when you're ready, if you want to."

She took a deep breath. "Lee and I . . ." she continued, still solemn.

Lee? *Lee?*

"We've gotten to be good friends," she said. "It's amazing how —how in tune we seem to be."

"Good," I said. "That's great."

"And . . . it just happened," she said. "We were swept away." *Shit!*

"Are you telling me you've been fucking *Lee?* When?"

"Today," she said. "This afternoon. It wasn't his fault," she went on nobly. "It was me, really, more than it was him—if you want to think about it in terms of fault. But . . ."

"It's OK." I said. "It's OK. It can happen to anybody." I felt very noble, too. "Forget it," I said.

"I can't forget it," she said. "I like him a lot. I expect we're going to keep on doing it."

This, friends, as we all know, is one of the tests of love. Or is it? Can we care and let go?

I was genuinely interested. No, not interested, excited. Some people, and I am one of them, tend to yearn for, to thrive on crisis. I used to say to myself that the artist requires crisis—that he has to have his emotions screwed up every so often to a certain pitch or he won't receive those gifts from God, those precious insights so essential to his work. What did Faulkner say? "Between grief and nothing, I'll take grief."

But the thing about that fellow, that ape (is he still down here inside me? Yes, I am afraid he is) is that grief to him isn't *just* grief. It's exciting.

I don't know, I think that this character is probably simply corrupt, *evil*—the ape. How far would he take his need for another and another turn of the emotional screw? Would it be exciting, for example, to watch his fifteen-year-old son die of leukemia? Doubtless he will find out this kind of thing in the course of a lifetime. I know for a fact that he found his grandmother's death exciting—as well as grievously painful. It was, after all, his first opportunity to learn about, to observe the natural, leisurely, terrible approach of what old H.J. called "the distinguished thing." But his grandmother was *old*. So that was OK.

Anyhow, there I was, feeling what can only be described as excitement at this new turn to my—our—affairs, wondering how I'd take it, being able to afford, in the surge of adrenaline, the magnanimity, the generosity we had told each other we would use if an occasion like this arose.

"I really meant it," I said. "I love you for what you are—not for what I want you to be. I want you to be free. OK? I wasn't bullshitting you. But . . ." And the *but* that seemed close enough to the truth to be useful occurred to me instantly. "But Lee . . ." I hesitated. "I don't want you to be—*used*—hurt. Lee . . ."

I mustn't fall into the trap of calling the salesman a salesman, I suddenly realized. That would never do. It would only antagonize her and make the ape look like an ape. I shut up and gathered her into my arms and slid down in the bed and kissed her shoulder where the milk-white skin stretched over the clavicle and dropped into the blue shadow at the base of her throat. "I love you," I said again.

She sighed and kissed the top of my head. "Oh, Alan," she said, "I do love you, too. You're my *dear* friend."

I ran my free hand down her belly and between her legs and

stroked the skin at the back of her thigh exactly where I knew she liked to be stroked. The old nuclear sub shifted into high gear. I took a flaccid nipple between my teeth.

"No," she said. "I don't want to. Things are too . . . too confusing right now."

She kissed me again, reached over and turned off the light, gave me a couple of sisterly pats on the butt, turned over, and was asleep almost before I knew she was gone.

My magnanimity—only a moment ago as perfect and glitteringly beautiful as a snowflake under a microscope—went up in a sizzling puff, as if it had fallen on a hot skillet. She'd gone to sleep! She had no interest in making love with me. She'd already made love today—all afternoon, doubtless. She probably hadn't even been asleep when I'd left her smiling so angelically in her dreams. Just waiting for me to get out of the house, so she could call Lee. I—*I* —*me*—I was not enough for her. She preferred *that* to me. That dish-faced, self-righteous monster of treachery and ingratitude who had come into *my* house, eaten *my* food, drunk *my* brandy (well, Leila's brandy), and deliberately, cold-bloodedly, calculatingly seduced my girl.

And, as the preacher said when the elders were consoling him after his wife's funeral, "But what am I going to do *tonight?*"

You have never been jealous, friends? You are fortunate. But don't delude yourself. You may feel it tonight, or, if not tonight, next week. Contemptible emotion. Not *most* contemptible of emotions, but contemptible. And surely, most ignoble.

Suddenly, magically, she became, not the girl I'd been living with the last couple of years, the girl who looked like Phoebe, the girl toward whom I felt friendly and sexy but, at this point, a tiny bit bored, the girl who probably loved me more than I loved her. She became, instead, totally, excruciatingly desirable.

Who was the mysterious stranger inside her whom I had not taken into account? Who was capable of failing to love me single-mindedly and without reservation, capable of this monstrous betrayal? Where had she been all this time?

I lay there, eyes open, in the dark. I spread my hands out, palms down, on the sheet. Had they fucked *here*—in this bed? Surely not. She would at least have had the decency . . . Where had Leila been? I turned over and tried to think about . . . What did I try to think about? Everywhere I turned, it seemed, my mind entangled itself in a thicket of briars. Our project? *Lee's* project? Dallas and his crazy wife and his religious misery? Leila? Sam?

Unbidden, there came into my mind a picture of Leila standing naked at the window of Sam's house. My grandfather has just driven into the yard. He leans out the window of his old black Buick, talking to Uncle Dennison, who is sitting on the back steps. The dust stirred up on the road by his tires is settling on the cedar trees. Behind Leila in Sam's little house, Sam, his dark face still and without expression, lies on the bed, his head propped on his hand, and looks at her body, outlined against the light. Whoa!

My childhood, then. Summer joys.

Phoebe, leaning close to Bald Eagle's strong sweat-streaked neck, rides under a low-hanging branch of the live-oak tree by the gate. . . .

Maybe I could imagine myself to sleep with . . . horses . . . swimming . . . The lake shines under the quiet summer sky. Crows flying . . .

Phoebe's eyes look at me out of Lester's sad, tight face. She picks a seedpod from his sleeve.

I swung my feet to the cold floor and sat up. The fire had gone out. Miriam slept on. What the hell kind of vacation was this?

So there I was, friends, helpless, bewildered, suffering a pain between my ribs, as if she'd thrust an ice pick neatly in and probed at my heart. What is your advice to me? For that matter, what is my advice to myself, looking back now from seven years' distance at that unhappy and (deservedly?) unfortunate young man? *Tough it out, buddy,* I could tell him. *All things change in time. Try not to do anything mean or treacherous.*

And things were going to change shortly, but not for the better.

NINETEEN

MONDAY, as I said, we had taped Noah. Miriam didn't have time to type up the transcript, but I did, and here it is:

Alan: Hi, Noah. Here we are.

Noah: Yeah. Return, O Lord, how long? and let it repent Thee concerning Thy servants.

Lee: It's a privilege for us to be taping you, Mr. Daniels, sir. Alan says you know everything there is to know about this part of the world. What it was like living here sixty and seventy years ago; sharecropping and the Depression and all that. We want to put what you know on the record for people to hear a hundred years from now, so they won't forget what things were like. Let's start off with how old you are and what your name is. OK?

Noah: When was I born, boys? When was I born into this mysterious world? 'Twas in eighteen and eighty-five. Makes me eighty-five years old. I *heard* so much, I *know* so much, I done already forgot four times as many nights as you lived through. Far as I know, it's been forty-five years since I made a child. Not more'n two since I quit trying. Finally the Lord took that dog off my back.

Lee: We'd like to say to begin with, sir . . .

Noah: And my name is writ in stone, boys. Yeah, the grass withers, but you can look right yawnder and see my name in the concrete of that cistern. Me and the old man built it back in nineteen and thirty-seven. My mind told me where would be best to dig and I dug the hole. And *he* come, and the two of us laid the bricks and plastered it up and when we was finished, we put our names in: *Noah Daniels. Dennison McLaurin.* Right there. And along come your granddaddy about that time, Alan, and the concrete was setting up, but he scratched in his initials over yawnder. *A. McL.* But he didn't help us none building it.

Lee: You don't have to worry about getting into trouble talking with us, Mr. Daniels. You can be open—you know what I mean? Whatever we write down, we'll keep your name out of it. Alan and I won't tell anybody we're taping you and Miriam doesn't know anybody to tell. Right, Alan?

Noah: What you talking about? What's the use in putting me down if you ain't going to tell it?

Alan: Look, Noah, Lee thinks you might be afraid. See? That you might not want to talk to us if we were going to tell anybody.

Noah: Son, I'm eighty-five years old. I seen it all and heard it all. I been *there* and I'm still *here.* Anything going to happen to me would've already happened. More times than once I been passed over by the angel of death. My onliest fear is the fear of the Lord. And the secret of the Lord is with them that fear Him. He will show them His covenant. Yeah.

Alan: Yeah.

Noah: You tell um, Alan. Now what I was talking about was bricks. The cistern and how me and the old man built it. Because it says there: "Drink waters out of your own cistern and running water out of your own well." That's what it says. But his kilt him.

Lee: *Who?* Who killed who? That's the kind of thing we want to hear about, Mr. Daniels.

Noah: Ain't that right, Alan? Don't they say he was kilt by the waters of his own cistern?

Lee: It was *poisoned?* Who poisoned it?

Alan: Uncle D. That's right. He died of typhoid fever. They say it was from drinking cistern water.

Lee: Who did it?

Alan: Nobody, for crying out loud.

Noah: Yeah, I'm going to tell you how come him to be poison. Can't say it was nobody. And I'm the onliest one knows who did it. [Here the tape hisses along for a few moments, then Noah's voice begins again.] You might be surprise to hear it, but I can remember the old man's granddaddy, born long before the stars fell. I can see um now setting out on the gallery of an evening like we setting here. 'Twas always a breeze there on the hottest day. The sun go off yawnder behind that big walnut tree and a breeze come up. The people commence coming in from the field 'long the road over by Alan's house. Used to be fifteen or more houses over there—old slave houses. Yeah. And when I was a little bit of a skinny boy my grandmother live over there. House gone to earth now. Gone to earth. Every board eat up. The earth is strong, boys. Strong. Take us all back. Take our houses. Take our clothes. [He laughs here. Then . . .] Skunk spray you, take and bury your clothes seven days in the earth. All *right*. Dig 'em up and the earth has took the scent clean off. Not many know that.

Lee: Sir . . .

Noah: Yeah. And I can remember my granddaddies, too. 'Twas one Ibo and one Guinea. And my grandmama, sold down from West Virginia. She was a black Indian. Put up on the block and sold like a piece of horse meat. One hundred and fifty dollars. That's what they paid for her and she told me herself. Like a mule at auction. Oh, the bondage was cruel, miss. Ain't that right, Alan?

Alan: Yes. She was a slave.

Noah: Tell it like it is! Ain't we lucky it's over?

Miriam: I wish you'd call me Miriam, Mr. Daniels.

Lee: You were going to tell about who poisoned the cistern, sir.

Noah: But I'm going to commence by telling you about my granddaddy. The one was Ibo. All *right*. There's a time for everything.

Oh, he was *black*. Tall, like me and Sam, tall as a pine tree. And he was a slave, too. He stood up on the block before the peoples and they prod him with one them old ox-goads. Right, Alan? Turn him this way and that way. He told it. I *heard* him. Yeah, taken by the Ishmaelites and sold into Homochitto County.

And a little small man come along in a tailcoat, had a high hat on his head and a band around it, snakeskin—skin of a rattlesnake.

And long teethes up under his upper lip and little bitty eyes. And
he heist his tailcoat and pull out his money and bought him. My
granddaddy. That's how he told it to me when I was a little boy.
And hear this, boys, miss: they put him in a wagon and went a long
way through the wilderness. 'Twas along the old Trace and then
the Chickasaw road, but he didn't know it, because it was wilderness to him, a strange land and a strange tongue.

And the third night, when the sun was going down, a deep sleep
come on him and a horror of darkness fell on him. Visions come
to him in his sleep, he say, and he seen trees could walk like men
and monkeys stood on their hind legs and had feets like people.
And then he seen himself down a hole, a smoky hole, laid there so
long, the scabs come on his left side and the blue flies crawl over
him. The earth rock under his body like water under a boat. Then
it come to pass he was like in a field of grass and six dead trees
got faces on their trunks get up and walk off and pile theyselves
up and commence to burn. And a Voice say to him, "Ain't no dead
trees allowed here." And a lot more stuff like that, and say, "Ain't
I told you, as you a living man, to bow down on your knees and
worship *Me* and no other?" And he did. And the Voice say, "I'm
satisfied." And then say, "I'm telling you as you a living man, you
done come here for a *reason*." Say, "I'm working it all out." And
then say, "Regarding your seed, they shall be a stranger in a land
ain't theirs and shall serve them, yeah, wait on 'em, and they shall
afflict 'em four hundred years, and *that nation*" (talking about your
great-granddaddy and all, Alan) *"that nation, I'm gon' judge 'em.
And afterwards you gon' come out with great substance. Rich,"*
he say. *"Rich."* Talking about *us,* his children, his seed.

That's what it said, only the way he told it, the voice must've
spoke in the Ibo tongue, because that was the onliest tongue he
knew at the time. And later, he learned to say it like we do.

That was my grandpa. And when I was a little boy, he told me
that, and he could still speak the Ibo tongue and he spoke it to me,
but I never knew what he was saying.

Lee: Sir . . .

Noah: And when the darkness passed off'n his eyes, he seen a
smoking furnace and a burning lamp and it was a sign to him, he
say. Because he was a mason, and a brick man and a concrete
man, and when he woke up from his vision and come to himself,
that's where he was, he was at the kiln—over yawnder where the

brick kiln used to be. Smoke coming out and he was making bricks. Can you beat that? All *right*. He could make bricks. Best in the county.

And furthermore, the angel had done touched his tongue and he could speak good as you and me. And we all been good brick men, good concrete men, good Christians, ever since. And some of us preachers. I can *preach*.

Alan: Yeah.

Noah: You can have a *true dream,* miss, and it'll stay with you till you die.

Alan: Yeah.

Noah: I'm on my way. . . .

Alan: Yeah.

Noah: Lord, You kept watch over me all night. . . .

Alan: Amen.

Noah: Early this morning You touch me with Your finger and I rose up rejoicing. Yeah.

Lee: Mr. Daniels, sir, I want to ask you . . .

Noah: You want to ax me or you want me to tell you? Alan here, he say talk about old times. We got to commence at the beginning and come forward. I'm ready. I got it all right here in my head. [The tape hisses here for a few seconds, then:]

Miriam: Go on, Mr. Daniels. We're listening.

Noah: Let me ax you this. Who do you think 'twas, that little small man with the tailcoat and the rattlesnake skin around his hat and them long teethes? Who do *you* think 'twas, Alan? You might say it was the Devil, but that ain't so. 'Twas the old man's grandpa. Old man *Dennison's* grandpa, and *your* great-great, and that's who brung him into servitude. Yeah, I can remember him, and here's what I remember. Time I seen him, he done shriveled up until he wasn't much bigger than a possum. My daddy used to carry him out on the gallery, set him up in his chair, and wrap his blanket around him, because when he got old, he was *cold*. He never could get warm, no matter the weather. Not like me. I'm old, but my blood still thick. He could look out over his fields on a August afternoon (so hot and so still you could hear the cotton growing) and *shiver*. And my daddy would fix him a hot toddy and wrap him in a blanket on the hottest day and carry him around like a baby. For some years that was his job of work; spite of him being the best brick mason on Chickasaw Ridge, it come to pass that the old man wouldn't have nobody to carry him but my daddy and so they took him off bricks and put him to nursing.

He was a tough one, that old man (your great-great-grandpa). Lived to be most a hundred years old and his toenails was so thick, boys, you couldn't cut 'em with the scissors. Had to cut 'em with wire clippers.

All *right*. And he give up the ghost and they took and buried him in a cave way yawnder back to Chickasaw bluff, back by the Indian burying ground.

Alan: A *cave!* In a *cave,* Noah? I thought they buried him in town.

Noah: Might've put up a tombstone in town to satisfy the times. But I'm telling you, his bones in the earth of this place. He *here.* My grandpas both here and *he* here.

Alan: Hmmmm.

Noah: Well, that was long after the war, so there wasn't no building going on then. Times done change by the time he died. I'm talking about the Civil War, miss. No more building. No more making bricks. Them was rich could buy 'em. The rest done without—black and white. The mule was in the ditch, boys. So they put my daddy to cropping like the rest, and he *excelled.* He was a beekeeper, too, and knew well how to tame the bees and draw 'em down to the hive and take the honey, and taught me and I taught Sam: we was all of us more able than most. 'Twasn't long, as he told it, till he was renting instead of cropping. Oh, it's a wilderness until you make it bloom.

Well, at that time we lived down yawnder by the creek. Long way around by the road, but no distance across the ravine, if you know the way. Back behind Mercy Seat Church, Alan, that's where we lived. The church where Timmie and Phoebe died. Where the fire burnt Timmie and Phoebe. And now, miss, Alan done brought you down here and you look just like her.

Alan: What?

Noah: Yas, miss, you look like this boy's cousin died in a turrible car wreck and fire some yeahs ago. Ain't no missing it. I see what he seen in you, all right. You like one of his family. Ain't it so, Alan?

Miriam: Is that right, Alan?

Lee: Who's he talking about?

Alan: Phoebe, for Christ's sake. But you don't look like her,

Miriam, not really. Only for a minute or two from the back.

Lee: Phoebe?

Noah: You remember her, son. A year or two older than you. And Sam's wife, Timmie. She died, too.

[The tape hisses. There is an unintelligible sentence or two, low and mumbled, in Lee's voice.]

Noah: What you say?

Lee: I never knew her. I didn't hang out with Alan back then. Sam who?

Noah: My boy, Sam. But when we live over there behind the church, 'twas long before Sam was born. Mercy Seat was new. Because it didn't use to be there. Use to be lower down the creek up under a brush pile. Open to the sky. Vines for walls.

Lee: *What?*

Alan: When was that, Noah?

Noah: You know what I'm talking about, Alan. When they wouldn't let 'em have no church. So the peoples would sneak off, go around, 'long the bottom of the ravine, winding this way and that, gather together by the creek. Nobody seen 'em. Nobody knew. Patterrollers riding, but the peoples stay off the roads.

Lee: What's he talking about now?

Alan: Slavery times. When they had road patrols to see to it the slaves weren't out after curfew.

Noah: That's where the peoples went to church *then,* but I started out going to old Mercy Seat, the one burnt. 'Twas all right by then. I mean you could go. Nobody mess with you.

Miriam: I thought you were talking about some people killed in a wreck. Alan's cousin? The one you say looked like me.

Noah: I ain't confuse, miss. It's y'all. How come I'm talking about the church burning and the car wreck both is they happen along about the same time.

Turrible. Turrible. Oh, the fire, the stink of it. *You* know, Alan.

[The tape hisses briefly here, then Noah's voice again:] Can't never forget it. If He wasn't holding my hand every step, I couldn't never go back there.

Alan: Let's don't talk about it, Noah.

Noah: All the peoples was there when the wreck happen. Not only us, but them others. Like *you,* son. You, Boykin. All you young white peoples was there, some inside, some out. Organizing —that's what 'twas. For us to get the vote. And others spying out the land. Right? That's how come I thought you knew about Phoebe, because it all happen the same week. They burnt and then the church burnt.

Lee: Me? No, sir, I wasn't there. I was just a kid then, not old enough to be in on that. But that's one thing I want to talk about—organizing. Not only to vote, but the union. Do you remember when they tried to organize the sharecroppers' union back in the thirties? And then later the pulpwood cutters. I'd like to ask you, sir . . .

Noah: I got it all in my head and I can tell you without no asking. I could talk a year and not tell all I got in my head. But I ain't up to that time yet. I ain't told you my lives yet. Oh, I've lived and died three lives already. I'm in my fourth. You understand me? No. Ain't no way you could. [Here Noah begins to hum a hymn tune in a deep powerful voice and then:] "Got something to tell you, 'fore I leave you / Something to tell you, 'fore I leave you / Something to tell you, 'fore I leave-a this world. Yeah.

Alan: Amen.

Noah: All *right*. Let's start out talking about my second life. Because my first life I was a child. But the second commence when I'm a young man. Plowed every field on Chickasaw. Scattered my seed in every furrow. Yeah. From that time come Noah, my first-born. Be sixty-five years old if he was on this earth today. He's got living in the world twelve children and sixty grands. Boys, I could *dance* then! Nobody on Chickasaw could dance like me. Lord, don't wake that up, don't wake it *up*. When I was a tad, I used to put on them palmetta fans like a tail and dance the buzzard lope for the ladies. Come home with a hatful of nickels. And then with my first wife, when I was still no more than sixteen, seventeen, I used to put on my pajamas and dance before the glass—show her how I could kill it.

Miriam: What about music? What kind of music did you have?

Noah: Fiddles. Guitars. Banjos. Fifes. Old Henry Powell could play the *fife!* Yeah. Don't wake it up. *Whooo!* Don't say a word.

Well. Come nineteen and fifteen. That time of my youth had went by me. You carry 'em off like a flood, Lord. In the morning the grass flourish and in the evening come along a combine and cut it down. You ain't young long. So there commence my third life. Thirty years old and already I got seven kids. My mind tells me I got to settle down to raising children up to the Lord and I done it. Yeah, I have done raise the kids in my day. Children, grandchildren. I raised 'em. And ain't no winter when I didn't feed my own. But the world was different then, miss. Wasn't no disease like high blood, no operating. Nothing but yellow fever and small-pox. Wasn't no televisions. Seems like people done capsize since that time. World's all right, but the people done capsize. God has brought us a long way and I'm still holding His hand. Yeah. Rejoice.

Because at that time, nineteen and fifteen, I seen a vision. Like my grandpa. That's what I want to tell you. Seems like I was nekkid and I was running and it seems like they was ladies around and I took newspapers and covered up my nekkidness and the wind took and blew 'em away and I called on Him and said, "Lord, Lord, ain't this pitiful? Look at me down here nekkid." He says to me, "You nekkid be*fore* Me." He says, "Get down on your knees," and I did and, lo, raiment come on me and clothe me, also shoes and a hat, and I bow down before Him. A true dream, miss. The Lord gives us a true dream. That was the year and the month and the week I come to Him. Went down into the water and jumped up happy. Entered on my third life.

Alan: Yeah.

Noah: He step into my soul. Answer my lonely cries.

Alan: Amen.

Noah: For He heareth the poor and despiseth not prisoners. Amen.

Alan: Amen, Noah.

Noah: What man is he that lives and ain't *bound* to see death?

Alan: Yeah.

Noah: Still holding His hand. Put my foot in the road and I ain't drawed back.

Lee: Sir . . .

Noah: Well, I come now to my fourth life and that's what I'm living in now. Eighty-five years old and I can still plow a straight furrow and climb a fig tree. Almost there, I'm almost there. He give me beauty for ashes and the oil of joy for mourning. Amen.

Lee: You were going to tell us about poisoning the cistern, sir.

Noah: His will be done. 'Twas not so long ago, and this is how it went. Just shortly before the old man died, when him and me was both in our old age. (I mean now, Old Man Dennison.) And they brought in the first oil well. The oil men was traipsing over the county, looking here, looking there. Come to my house. The old man, he was down to Lafayette hunting with them Frenchmen he used to hang out with down there. Didn't mind how long he went off, he knew he could leave the place to me and wouldn't nothing happen. Back in the days when we was farming cotton out here, he'd go off, and his daddy before him, come time for the people to bring the crop in, who do you think run the gin, counted the bales, settled up? 'Twas me, and my daddy before me. We was stewards. Never buried our talents. And in the old days when we was cutting trees, who marked the trees? That was up until the time Old Man Boykin begun to tell lies on me. (*You*—talking about *your* daddy.) But the truth is the old man never mistrusted me, no matter for that. But that ain't what I aim to tell you about. I aim to tell you about the salt. Well, so they come, and I'm setting here and they says, "Say, old man, we looking for oil. We going to plant this land with derricks like fig trees and oil going to sprout up out the tops." Well, I already know we got oil. Ain't I seen the actual sand *burn* down yawnder by the creek where it seeps up through the ground? Strike a match and the ground burn. But all it done was to ruin the land for cotton, or anything else. So I took and showed 'em along the creek where 'twas seeping up through the sand and floating on the water—rainbows—and they put down a peg. Buzzard roost on the left and where that old Indian house used to be on the right, no more than a hundred yards from the Duck Pawnd line. And they drill. Oil wasn't no deeper in the ground than I am tall.

So it ain't long before the old man come on down to the house and set up on the porch here and took off his shoes and drunk a glass of root beer with me and eat a lemon snap (this was before he commence saying, "Eh? Eh?" everything you said to him— acting like he's deaf), and he say, "Well, Noah, looks to me like we going to be rich." And he gets out the map of the place and shows me on it where they going to build roads and drill wells here and there over it. "Oil," he says. "They say we sitting on top of a lake of it." And I say, "Ain't I the one showed it to 'em when you was down to Lafayette hunting deer and eating barbecue pig with them Frenchmen?"

But I mistrusted it from the beginning, miss. That ain't no way to farm. Will the Lord be please with thousands of rams or with ten thousand rivers of oil?

And he say, yeah, he knows I done showed it to 'em and say *(mark my words, Alan)* he say, *"Next one comes in is yours."* That's right. But didn't nobody hear him but me. 'Twasn't no light word he spoke, but solemn. Put me in mind of what my daddy told me about when the *old* man (his grandpa) was on his bed, ready to die. Done shrunk up until he wasn't no bigger than a rabbit. Doubled up like a baby just come out the womb. Back to the earth, that's where he was headed. And he called in my grandpa and my daddy. And all his generations was dead and 'twasn't but only his grandsons, that's your grandpa and Old Man Dennison, to listen to what he says and they was young men—boys. Nineteen and five, 'twas. I know, because I was twenty years old and 'twas the year I got my third boy, Ingle. And he's laying up there in a ball shivering and he say, "Dennison," say, "I wants you to move old Noah" (that's my daddy) "and all his peoples from down yawnder by the creek and build them a house up here by the road. And that's my dying wish." And your uncle, he took it serious and done it.

Well, and that wasn't all he said, neither. Because my daddy done carried him like a baby for twelve years and cut them horny toenails and wrop him in blankets and sometimes warm him with his actual body. This is what else he say, after he tells your uncle and your grandpa about taking and moving us from down yawnder by the creek to up by the road. He say, "And that land is *yours,"* he say this to the face of my daddy. He say, "Take a line on the corner fence by the creek and let it pass through the big pine tree" (use to stand on the bluff before the creek changed in its bed and washed it away) "and make you a square on that line, sixty acres, and all the money and crops from it is yours and your children's and won't no more rent be charge on it." And so we raise cattle on it all these years. (And more, too, but we paid rent on the rest of what we had.) But nobody change the deed on it like they was suppose to.

Lee: Mr. Daniels, you've got a legal case here. You know that? Who was paying taxes on it? Who was keeping the fences up? You need to get a lawyer.

Noah: Who *always* keep up the fences? I'm talking about all the fences on the *entire* place. We been keeping up the fences since I was a boy. You take a look at them fences along the top of the bluff over by the Chickasaw road. Me and one of my boy Ingle's

190

grandsons run that fence two years ago and ain't a better fence in Homochitto County. Cut the locust posts ourselves back yawnder in that locust thicket by the old spring. That's how come we don't pay no money rent on the rest of the land. Fences is rent.

Lee: But . . .

Noah: Wait on the Lord, son. Wait, I say, on the Lord. So I'm telling you about when the wells come in. You want to hear?

Alan: Yes.

Noah: Well, it come about when the first oil well come in, I say to myself, Look like the four hundred years is about up. And I spoke to him about it. Say, "Judgment time is come, boss man." He says, "Eh? Eh?" (I believe that's when he start that "Eh? Eh?" business.) I say, "Ain't this our land ever since your granddaddy told you to take a line on the corner fence and the big pine tree fell in the creek during of that storm in nineteen and thirty-seven and count off sixty acres?" And *he* says (talking about your uncle), "Noah, hit's all yours, *all* yours. Won't never be a day when you wants for nothing whatever, neither you nor Sarah. Nor I won't take this land from you." And after that another well come in.

[Here there is a pause. The tape hisses. A chair creaks. Then:]

Noah: Didn't it, Alan?

Alan: Shit, Noah, I wasn't but three years old when those wells came in. Didn't know what an oil well was.

Noah: Hmmm. Well, to continue on, he died. They say 'twas the typhoid. All I know is that cistern of his wasn't never the same after the wells commence to come in. He took to complaining about the water. Said 'twas salty, said it tasted like sulfur and iron. But he was hard-headed. He *would* drink it. Yeah, gall and vinegar the Lord give him to eat and drink. Except some days he'd bring his jug down to my house because my cistern wasn't never poison. The Lord never poison my well. But He pass His hand over his and lo, 'twas salt, and the little old gum seedlings crep' up through the pine trees like green ghosts, ain't good for nothing but goat food, and the pine trees got borers in 'em and got cancers on 'em. And *weak*. The least snowfall snap 'em off like sticks. Nettles and salt pits and desolation. That's the Lord's work—Amen.

[Again there is a pause on the tape.]

Lee: Mr. Daniels, there are some other areas we'd like to explore with you. For example . . .

Alan: We don't want to wear Noah out.

Lee: And we haven't really finished talking about *this* area. Maybe we can come back?

Noah: Sho', boys. Ax me. I'll tell you.

TWENTY

IT WAS Sunday again. Almost a week had gone by since Miriam's confession. We had been living side by side, uneasy, affectionate, sleeping like two lost children with our arms about each other, as if we would protect each other; open, yet secret, me trying to keep the ape under wraps, Miriam pursuing (quietly, so as to cause me as little pain as possible) her new, to me, inexplicable passion for the salesman.

What do they say you are? Hoist on your own petard? A phrase for a writer, even if he doesn't know what it means. I used to think vaguely that it meant hanging from your own flagpole or maybe yardarm, but it turns out that it means blown up with your own rocket. And mine was the rocket of sexual freedom that, instead (I had fondly believed), would blow open the prison men and women had been locked together in for a couple of thousand years; would give us a quick thrilling trip to a new Eden of love and trust.

One night Miriam had come out of her bemusement and made love, absentmindedly, accommodatingly. Afterwards I held her in my arms and murmured love words in her ear. "We'll make it," I said. "How can we not? I *love* you."

"Hmmmm," she said, and patted me on the head and ran her fingers through my hair.

At the time I paid no attention to the reservation in her voice, although *hmmmm* is a word I often use, myself.

Other nights, lying awake, I said over and over to myself things like, This is a Momentary Aberration. She'll be through with it as soon as . . . She'll come to her senses when . . . (*As soon as* what? *When* what?) Or, We're not just lovers, we're friends. I mean, I *really* love her. Or, Can I get along without her? No!

And then there would come without warning a shining, throbbing image of the two of them in bed together. She might be on her stomach with a couple of pillows under her belly and he would be humping her dog-fashion. She liked it that way. I would see her pale hair spread across her shoulders and his hands on her white swelling ass, lifting her, moving her in time to his thrusts. And I could see his face, intent, absorbed, the salesman's chin jutting, the salesman's glinty eyes taking her in as if she were a hot new line of women's wear. She moaned. I heard her moan. The ice pick probed at my guts and, picking up a loop, gave it a twist that made me think I had appendicitis.

In the daytime the three of us circled warily around one another. She'd told him after the first fuck that she had no intention of deceiving me; and he had assured her that he had nothing but admiration and respect for our "relationship." Maybe that's why he wanted in.

To myself I said things like, I *will* be civilized. I *will* be patient. I will wait it out.

He came by. We talked about our project. We smiled at one another. He explained to us the comparative virtues of Leicas and Rolleiflexes and mentioned Hasselblads.

They left. Through the front window I would watch them driving away together, talking animatedly, their heads turned toward each other, laughing, almost driving off the road in their absorption.

Miriam! Miriam! Here I am. It's me. *Me!* Are none of the things we believed about ourselves true? None?

Shit!

Noah had gotten us an invitation to Calhoun Levitt's house and a promise that he would listen to our questions. As for our taping him, he would see, he said, after he had talked with us. On Sunday morning, we drove a long way on a winding graveled road and, back toward the edge of Levitt's Bottom, at the entrance to a deep cleft in the shale bluffs that bordered the road, we came to his mailbox, turned in, and drove up the steep driveway onto a graveled parking ground in front of a neat white house surrounded by a picket fence. Walker hounds, beagles, a pointer, and a savage-looking German shepherd with only one eye swirled around the car barking frantically. A small, neatly lettered sign on the fence read BAD DOG. We sat there talking politely about whether or not the German shepherd would bite us. We were extraordinarily polite to one another, dancing around, as it seemed to me, on our tiptoes, bowing each other in and out of rooms like Victorian ladies and gentlemen. So now we sat in the car and talked politely, my thigh against Miriam's warm right flank, Lee's against her warm left flank. I smiled like a sick clown and tried to observe my surroundings as carefully as a poet should.

Inside the fence the small yard was crowded with shrubs and fruit trees—two figs against a south wall of the house; in a corner a peach and a couple of ancient pears ringed with the drillings of generations of sapsuckers; gardenias, mounds of lantana by the front porch; and, on either side of the gate, bare, bony old crape myrtle trees. The dark green jasmine vine on the fence was already heavy with swelling buds. In a couple of weeks it would be a mass of yellow trumpets.

While we were still sitting in the car, the old man, swarthy and heavy-shouldered, came out on the porch, shouted down the dogs, and scattered them. We got out as carelessly as if we'd not noticed them, shook hands, introduced ourselves, and thanked him for letting us come—all a bit stiff and formal; and he led us into his house.

"My wife died five years ago," he said. "The house isn't what it was when she was alive. I took the doilies off the tables—I can't starch and iron them and none of the grandchildren take to that kind of thing." He spoke carefully and precisely in a deep voice, educated, but still the unmistakably black voice that seems to come from a larger, more resonant voice box than ours.

"Sir . . ." Lee said. He always stuck in a "sir" as early as possible, to make clear his respect for black men.

"Sit down there on the sofa, young lady," the old man said to Miriam. "Now, let me look at you boys. Yes, I told Noah when he called, I've known your people all my life. Never crossed my mind who you were until *you*"—he gestured to me—"butt in on Henry's fight. That was a ruckus, eh? I usually manage to stay clear of Henry's fights." He laughed. Then, "Would you like a cup of coffee? I've got some on the stove." He stepped back into the kitchen, still talking. "You could see that my brother Henry was drunk when he jumped on you down there," he said. "He wouldn't have done it if he'd been sober. But drunk . . ." He grunted. "He likes to fight when he's drunk and he can't get used to the idea of being too old to win."

He must have had the cups ready and the coffee hot, for he came back into the room almost immediately with a tray and set it on a small sturdy oak table beside the sofa. "I'm not saying, you understand, that he's bent on suicide. (Sit down, boys, sit down.)"

While he went on talking, we sat, Miriam and Lee on the sofa and me in a cane-backed rocker. I glanced quickly around the small crowded room. There was a clutter of family photographs on the mantel, the young men in uniform or cap and gown, the girls in wedding or graduation dresses; in the place of honor was a portrait of a serious, pale-skinned young woman in a 1920s-style wedding dress. A butane heater hissed and glowed. Heavy over-stuffed chairs were crowded around a TV set. Against one wall a small bookcase held a few dog-eared hardbacks and stacks of paperbacks in various states of disintegration. I cocked my head sideways, as I always automatically do when I see books, to read the titles and authors, and saw W. E. B. Du Bois and Cash and Claude Williams on top of a pile of Nero Wolfes, thought, *Hmmm,* and put my attention back on him.

". . . steers clear of white men," he was saying. "But you two! You'll have to agree we had a new situation there. True, you're white. But the way you looked that day nobody could take you for a threat. There wasn't a kid here in 'sixty-four who would have come in Calloway's looking like you. And if Henry wanted to fight you, I doubt if there is a white man on Chickasaw Ridge who would take your part. Yeah, I know you're from around here; but who would stop to ask where you were from or believe you, if you told them?

"Or maybe they'd think you were even worse for being *from*

here, a disgrace to your families, hardly worth killing." He nodded at me. "Old Man Dennison would rise straight up out of his coffin if he could see you with that terrible-looking hairdo and beard. And a *poet*. Isn't that what Noah says you are?

"And as for you," he said to Lee, "I see you've cut your hair, but looking at you down there at the store, listening to you, I might have thought *you* were the one bent on suicide."

"Mr. Levitt," Lee said, "Sam Daniels told Alan you've been involved in the civil rights movement from the beginning. You ought to be used to beards and beads."

"Mistah Levitt. Ah cain't help laughin' when I heah that *mistah,"* the old man said.

I pricked up my ears. He had lapsed, as I had so often heard my grandfather do, into country black.

"Oh, yas, it's fine. It's all right. Ah've heard it befo' and Ah don't mean to make you feel bad. But it don't make me no more than Ah already was and it don't get you out from under, does it?"

If we're going to get him to let us tape him, I thought, we can't rub him the wrong way; so we may as well not get irritated with him. But I was feeling irritated. "Lee's just trying to be polite," I said. "There's nothing wrong with being polite."

"And I'm not?" He laughed again. "Son, I'm the man who can give you a lecture on manners, black, white, and integrated." He had switched back to standard English without batting an eye. "You're right. There's nothing wrong with being polite most of the time. But I've lived by myself so long, I may have fallen out of the habit."

I said nothing.

"Besides," he went on, "if I tell you you look terrible, it may not be polite, but on the other hand, out here in the country, it might save you some trouble. You both ought to know that."

"Sam said the same thing to me when I first got here," I said. "I wear my hat."

"The Klan is a power around here," he said, "and it's stupid to try to get yourself killed. *Stupid."*

"I know."

"All right. We've got that out of the way, then. And I think I'm going to talk to you young people." He was leaning against the mantelpiece, looking down at us as he spoke, a heavy, solid presence above us, while we sat, uncomfortably balancing our coffee cups, looking up at him. Now he crossed the room, put his own cup on the tray, sat down, and looked at Lee. "The truth is," he said, "I had already just about made up my mind to talk to you before you got here. I spent some time thinking about you after I heard your names down at Calloway's the other day. Mainly you," he said to Lee. "Up until then I had thought there were no more Boykins left in the county. But I heard your name and I said to myself, Well, look who's back. He doesn't know a damn thing about his family and it's not likely he ever will, unless I tell him. Maybe he's better off that way. And then Noah came around saying that you're Alan McLaurin's friend and the young lady is his girl friend; and he is Old Man McLaurin's great-nephew; and all of you say you're look-ing for the truth about Homochitto County. Well, I said to myself, it's very seldom outside of church you hear anyone in Homochitto County say they're looking for the truth about anything. So I gave the matter a little more thought. It seems to me, I said to myself, if you come and ask questions, you deserve to get answers. So I made up my mind to give you the answers I know. To tell you about your people. The problem is, my answers may not be the answers to your questions." He put his hands on his knees and looked from one to another of us in a schoolteacherish way. "But that's their problem, I said to myself. Maybe they can think up some questions to fit my answers. So get out your recording ma-chine and show me how it works."

"But, Mr. Levitt, we want to hear about you, about *your* life," Lee said, "and the people who worked with you and *your* family, and what it's been like for you to live here. Of course, I'd like to hear about my people, too. My daddy and all. But I did work for him some when I was a kid, and I heard him talk, and I can go out to Texas and get him to talk some more. On the other hand, nobody can tell us about you except you and your brother." He laughed. "And your brother doesn't seem to be all that sociable," he said.

"Son, there are very few people besides me—maybe not any—who can tell you some things about your daddy. And your mama, too."

"We'd like to hear whatever you want to tell us, Mr. Levitt," Miriam said. "Maybe if we don't ask the right questions, you can tell us what questions to ask. Come on, Lee, let's get started."

We set up the tape deck and explained to him how it worked, showed him the on-off button, so that he could cut it off if he wanted to say something off the record, and handed him a mike. What follows is a transcript of the tape we made that day.

Lee: I'm going to start, sir, by saying that there are three of us here interviewing you today, February 28, 1971: Me, Lee Boykin, Miriam West, and Alan McLaurin. Would you tell us first what your name is and where and when you were born? Get that out of the way.

Levitt: I am Calhoun Levitt, born right here on the edge of Levitt's Bottom in 1907. I'm sixty-four years old and you might expect me to start by saying, "I don't know what the world is coming to," or something like that. Isn't that what old people are supposed to say? Especially when they meet young men with beards and [He hesitated an instant.] young ladies in blue jeans and T-shirts.

And that's indirectly what we were talking about when you first came in, before you turned the machine on, isn't it? I mentioned to you, Alan, what your great-uncle might think if he saw you in here today in your hippie outfit, and I might have added, socializing with me. But, to continue on that subject, I'm going to take back what I said. As for the socializing, your uncle sat down with Edna and me often enough, although he never brought any ladies with him. And he might not think anything at all about the beard. After all, his father had a beard and he was used to those long-haired portraits he had hanging around his house. Besides, he never was much concerned with conforming. But you can be sure he'd wonder about you being a poet. *"Poet?"* he'd say. "Eh? Eh? But do you know how to train a bird dog? Can you tell a good mule from a bad one? Or a skunk from a possum?"

Alan: I haven't gotten around to mules and bird dogs yet, but I can tell a skunk from a possum. Noah says Uncle D. found out the difference the hard way.

Levitt: That's right. That's right. [He laughs here.] I remember that hunt. Noah says the earth took the stink right off his clothes. But if it'd been me, I wouldn't have dug them up to find out.

Lee: Would you like to tell us about your family, Mr. Levitt? Your childhood?

Levitt: Son, you're looking at the color of my skin, which is not much darker than yours, and so you know I've got white blood. I reckon you want me to tell you where it came from. Young white people like you are always curious about that. The old ones don't ask. They don't want to know. Well, I'm going to tell you, because in a way it's part of how I got myself tangled up with your family.

To begin with, the first of it came from my grandfather Calhoun, from whose people I also get my name. My grandmother called herself Lilian Calhoun, even before she lived with him and had his children. She got that from her *mother,* who was a Calhoun slave and took the name. Years ago, the family lived on Duck Pond, over there southeast of Chickasaw. Old Man Calhoun was living out there when my grandmother was a young woman. He ran the place. The rest of the family lived in town. All gone, they're all gone now—the white branch of the family, that is, although the descendants still own the land. There are still plenty of *us* in the county, my brother's children and grandchildren and mine, and our cousins and their children—because my grandmother Lilian had two daughters by Old Man Calhoun.

She and he [There is a pause here. The tape hisses by with the sound of escaping gas. He must have forgotten to click his on-off button. Then:] cohabited is the legal term, I suppose, although they didn't live in the same house, for a number of years, up until her death, in fact. [Another hissing silence, then abruptly:] How to make all that blood flow peaceably together in your veins? That's a problem you young people wouldn't know much about yet. Oh, I'm not talking just about black and white. I'm talking about *all* blood—all those warring people behind us. There's a war going on in every man's blood. [Another pause.] I see those who live by ignorance. I knew a family—wife and children and grandchildren —who lived out their whole lives on the man's Civil War pension. I'm talking about a black man. A *federal* pension. And they never asked him where he fought or why, or why he came back to the South—*not one of them asked.* They're not stupid, either. Passed their days talking about the fishing and the weather and who had died and what to plant on the back forty. The past was swallowed up, just swallowed up. . . . Well, I could never live like that. Cause and effect, even if they get complicated, I think about them. I ask questions and I read books and when there is no one to ask and there are no books on the subject, I speculate.

Well, to go on, as to my grandmother and grandfather, they

lived together a long time. He was better than most white men who took a black woman in those days. He was in his forties, a bachelor, when she went to work for him and live with him and, according to my mother, he never had another woman as long as she lived. I call that passing strange. His fidelity. A strange kind of fidelity.

Because, although they had that "stable relationship," as the books would call it now, he was as distant from my mother and from me, his grandson, as any other white man would have been.

Miriam: You knew him, then?

Levitt: Yes, I knew him when he was an old man. My grandmother was younger than he was and she died when she was in her fifties—before I was born. He must have been sixty when I was born. My mother used to go over there to Duck Pond and clean up his house for him and look after him. Henry and I would go with her—play out in the yard under the chinaberry tree while my mother tended to him.

[The tape clicks off here. I remember he sat with the mike in his hand, as if he were considering what to say, and then clicked it back on.]

Levitt: He never said to me, "Come here, boy, I'm your grandpa." He never paid the least attention to Henry or me. Or to her, either, for that matter, to say, Daughter, this, or Daughter, that. Let her wait on him, that's all. He paid her to wait on him. He paid my grandmother to wait on him, too. My mother remembered how that was, of course. She remembered hearing him come into their little house in his backyard at night after she was in bed, remembered seeing him in the kitchen drinking his coffee in the morning, remembered how he would put on his coat and step out the front door and look around and sniff like he was testing the air. (He was a great one for recording the weather, she said, and knew what the temperature had been and whether it had rained or snowed every day since 1867.) And then he'd step across the yard to his own house—not saying good-bye, because in a little while my grandmother would put on her clean apron and go after him to tend to his house and fix his lunch.

My mother said he lived all his life out in the country, isolated most of the time from his people. He had plenty of family in Homochitto and he would go in every week, regular as clockwork, on Saturday afternoon and stay until after dinner on Sunday, paying his respects, so my mother said, doing like he was supposed to with his mother and daddy and brothers and sisters. He kept up appearances. He even went to church up until his mother died.

That was the way they lived.

When I was ten and Henry was nine, he bought us each a good rifle and a twelve-gauge shotgun. Gave them to us out in the yard under the chinaberry tree one day and said, "Learn to shoot, Calhoun, Henry. Nobody can stand up for himself and look after his people if he can't shoot a gun." He hired a black man from Chickasaw Ridge, the best hunter and bird-dog handler in the neighborhood, to teach us to shoot straight and train a dog and hunt. By that time he had quit hunting himself, maybe that was why he hired it done.

When he died, he left most of the land (all of Duck Pond) to his nieces and nephews, but he left my mother and her sister six hundred acres of good bottomland and that's what we're on right now. Three hundred of it went to my cousins and three hundred to me and my brother. He left a little money to me and Henry, too. 'Twasn't much. He was land poor by the time he died, like most white people around here before the oil came in. According to my mother, he'd never said a word to her about the will. (Maybe my grandmother knew he was going to do it, but I doubt it. Surely if she had, she would have told my mother. Although she died like people did in those days—in a hurry, of diphtheria or pneumonia or scarlet fever or something like that.)

He took trouble with it, too. Set it up with a lawyer he trusted, so that it would be hard for anybody to beat her out of it—to her and her heirs and assigns, forever—that kind of arrangement. The white family took it ill, my mother said. According to kitchen gossip in Homochitto, his sister never spoke his name again. They were all strict Presbyterians, women kind to the servants, men Sunday school teachers. Their reputation was never for putting on a big show, as it was with some, but for piety.

Well, now, next, boys, young lady (or maybe it was *first,* before I began to think about my grandfather, but more than likely it was all mixed up together). Anyhow, I began to speculate about my father whom I never remember seeing in my life.

Look at me. I'm too white to be just half white. You can see that. The case, as I figured it out, was that my mother knew how to get along in the world as well as my grandmother did, and in her view one way to get along (besides looking after your white daddy) was to have children whiter than you. Plenty of Negroes used to think that way in her time.

But my daddy was not so conscientious as my grandfather. He went his way. That is, he killed himself. When we were little tads —two and three. Not over her or over the evils of racial hatred. Nothing so romantic as that. Over money. He didn't mention us in his will. Not that it mattered. He didn't have anything to leave us.

I abandoned my inquiries and speculations about him when she told me that. (It had been difficult enough in any case to get her to talk about him.) There wasn't much he could teach me, I decided. He was a weak man. He's no more than a name and a white ghost in my life, and maybe he was hardly more real in hers. All I have of his is this skin that is white enough so that I could *pass,* if I wanted to.

But my grandfather . . . He was a country man like me. He lived his own life and he acknowledged us in the end, in spite of his people. That was interesting and useful.

And my grandmother. I thought about her. But who ever knows what goes on behind the bedroom door . . . ?

I asked my mother once how come she went on waiting on the old man all those years when he never even called her *Daughter,* and she didn't know he was going to name us in the will. "We're supposed to live like civilized people," she said, "and don't you forget it. Living like civilized people means looking after your own."

So that's all there is left to speculate on in those lives. No. Not all. Or maybe all that's left to speculate on, but not all I know. Because, of course, I know a lot about my mother. [Here he gave a dry, rueful laugh.] Yeah. Like Henry said down at Calloway's, she spent forty years trying to organize us and never had any luck at all. She was . . . I suppose you would say she was an irritable woman. If we didn't hop when she said frog, she let us know about it. She knew she was superior to just about everybody she'd met, and she was bent on our being superior, too. Yeah, my mother looked down on *everybody.* Looked down on Jews. Looked down on dagos. Looked down on poor white trash—what *she* called poor white trash. Taught us to keep ourselves apart like she had done and her mother before her. (Maybe—for all I know—they both looked down on the white men they slept with, too.) And of course they looked down on niggers. That goes without saying.

But she didn't have much luck with us. Henry quit school in the eighth grade and he's spent the rest of his life showing the world, one, that he's a nigger; two, that he ain't afraid of the Devil; and three, that he's just as superior as she was, but damn it, in his own way. As for me, when the land and the money came, I did what she wanted me to do, went to college and learned to talk like a Yankee. But past that she had to give up on me. I suppose she had visions of me being a college professor or a lawyer in some ideal world where everybody knows who the superior people are and pays them the homage due them. . . . But I was a country man and I knew it. I hated those cold cities. And when the money was used up, I came on home and went to farming.

Lee: That would have been . . . when, sir? The twenties?

Levitt: That's right, the late twenties. 'Twenty-seven, 'twenty-eight. And the Depression was already on as far as I was concerned—as far as the *South* was concerned. Poor people in the South never did much good in my lifetime. Even rich people weren't all *that* rich. So I came back here and farmed. Cut pulpwood. Did daywork when I could get it. Turned my hand to anything I could get. It was *root, hog, or die.* I knew that from the start. But different for us than for most people. *We had land.* That's what my mind was on, mine and Henry's, too: we meant to keep the land and make it pay. The other—cutting pulpwood and so forth—served to keep us going through that bad time.

Lee: That's one of the things we want you to tell us about. Pulpwood cutting. The I.P. and the Georgia Pacific. The unions. But that would be later, wouldn't it? In the fifties? The sixties?

Levitt: What you can say about pulpwood cutting in general is that it's a rough way to make a living. The middleman is a crook, the hauler is illiterate, and the I.P. and the Georgia Pacific—well, I could write a book about all that. I didn't do it any longer than I had to. Got in it to begin with to cut some of my own wood— you can make a little money on it if it belongs to you. I soon found out, first, that most people who cut pulpwood are drunks: it's the only way you can endure the life. Second, they're cripples: eventually you're bound to get hurt—ruptured, a leg torn off, your chest crushed in; and third, they're stupid. If they weren't they'd get into something else.

No, son. Maybe stupid is wrong. More like they hate themselves. Want to destroy themselves. God knows, there are enough niggers around who want to destroy themselves to cut down all the woods between here and McComb. And that's a good way to do it.

But you know all that, or ought to. Your daddy cut pulpwood until he left town. He was smarter than most—and better. He paid as well as he could and still make it, and he managed to keep his head above water for a long time—until he fortunately came into some money.

Oh, there's a lot to talk about, a lot to talk about. But not about pulpwood or unions or the I.P. No, that's not important. We need to start way back during the Depression, because the truth is that your family is involved from then on. Everything that happened in my life after—let's see: 1933, I reckon—involved your family in a distant kind of way. That is, not that they were around or that I saw them, but that certain things happened in connection with them that influenced the way my life went after that.

Lee: But my father would still have been a kid, barely in his teens, in 1933, my mother even younger than that.

Levitt: Yes, that's true. I wasn't talking so much about them—but a generation back.

[Perhaps I should say that, when he heard this, Lee seemed immediately to relax. I sensed it because I knew the feeling myself. Nineteen thirty-three? OK. That was *years* before I was even born. Can't have anything to do with me. And I can listen to tales about my parents' parents without a twinge of feeling. *Nobody* is supposed to feel responsible for what his grandparents did or didn't do. Anyhow, Lee sat back with a glance that seemed to say, We're going to have to indulge this crazy old man's garrulity and maybe we'll finally get what we want.]

Lee: Well, to begin with, sir, why don't you just tell us in your own way how you happened to get involved with the Boykin family and how they influenced your life.

TWENTY-ONE

LEVITT: *To begin with,* it wasn't the Boykins I got involved with. It was your mother's family. You know your mother was adopted (taken in—I don't know if they ever adopted her) by Mac Boykin's uncle, don't you?

Lee: Yes, sir. She never talked much about her early childhood. Said she couldn't remember it. But she told us that the Boykins took her in after her mama and daddy both died and that they, her parents, weren't either one from around here. I don't think she knew where they were from or what they were doing here or re-membered much of anything about them. She was too young when they died. Let's see, I reckon maybe they were just passing through or something. Nobody in the family knew anything about them. I think they died of pneumonia or something that people used to die of in those days. So, if you're talking about what she considered her family, you're still talking about the Boykins.

Levitt: Yes, I know that. But I knew her people before they died.

[Lee gave him an incredulous look and shook his head. I could see what he was thinking: if she couldn't even remember them and if the Boykins didn't know anything about them, how come this old man had known them?]

Levitt: Yes, I did. I never will forget the first time I saw your grandmother. Strange. She was older than me by ten years, but I still think of her as a young woman—because she died young, I reckon. And because of her hair. Her hair!

This is how it happened. It was the winter of 'thirty-three and 'thirty-four, sometime early in December. My wife Edna was teaching school—making twenty-five dollars a month, which was twenty-five more cash dollars than most people had; but even so, it didn't go far. We already had two boys old enough to need shoes and winter clothes. We ate well, I'll say that, between the garden and Edna's canning and my hunting and fishing. And we kept a milk cow and raised our own pigs and, naturally, chickens. My mother was still alive, lived in a little house next to us, and she saw to all of that. But *taxes*. That twenty-five dollars went for taxes. Not to lose our land for taxes, that was what we thought most about in those days.

It was when I was out hunting one day that I met your people. When I say we made every nickel count, I can give you an example of it. We hadn't killed a pig yet that year because it had been too warm. 'Twas an exceptionally warm winter up until February. So we were low on meat. But tax time was coming and every penny of Edna's was going into the tax fund. And wasn't that the year they didn't pay the teachers but six months? I think it was. Anyhow, I had taken out a dollar for hunting money in November. Shells were three for a dime down at Calloway's. They'd break the boxes, because most people never had enough cash at one time to buy a whole box. It was early December and I was down to my last dime. I bought my three shells and put 'em in my pocket and set off for that part of the bottom back behind where we own, where is was still wild, uncutover land. Left my horse with some people I knew on the edge of the bottom and walked in.

You would see back there, naturally, plenty of squirrels and coons and so forth, and in those days you might even see panthers. Deer were all killed out in the county. Didn't begin to come back until up in the fifties. But you might get a turkey if you were lucky. That day I had no luck. (I wouldn't waste a shell on a squirrel. I was looking for a turkey.) Decided late in the afternoon that I would stay on until after dark. I'd brought my carbide light and I had a good coon dog. So I was thinking I would build a little fire and sit there by it until dark rather than go any farther back in the bottom, when I smelled smoke. Somebody's already in here, I said to myself, and I thought it might be one of my cousins. They were the only ones I knew who hunted much in the bottom. I didn't want to join up with any of them: I had a good dog and I'd rather hunt by myself, get one coon if I was lucky or maybe a possum, and go on home. Save my last two shells for another day, if I could.

But I'm always curious about who's hanging around, so I climbed up the nearest tree, located the direction the smoke was coming from, and eased on over to see who it could be. I came out all at once on a little clearing with a fallen-down house on one side and, on the other, a camp, a tent. Somebody was living there. An old wagon track came in from the other side of the clearing and whoever lived in the tent had driven an old piece of Chevy in on that wagon track. It was parked next to the tent.

I can't say I was surprised. All kinds passed through the county in those days. People were wandering, riding the rails, driving old T-Model Fords, walking. Looking for work, for food, for a barn to sleep in. The country was disrupted. But then, deep in the bottom, in a tent?

I thought I was safe, that nobody'd heard me or seen me, and I stood there just inside the woods, looking, speculating.

But *she* had a sense about presences. I saw the tent flap move and squatted down behind some briars. She stepped out of the tent like she'd been expecting somebody and looked straight toward me. She was a sight to see in the middle of the woods at four o'clock on a winter afternoon. Her hair! The sun struck down into the clearing from just over the tops of the trees, lighted up her face and her hair. It hung down below her waist, threads of gold, ropes of gold, falling all down her bosom and her back, thick enough to keep her warm like a shawl. She was a little bit of a thing, slender, and she had on, I reckon, a pair of boy's coveralls, because a man's, even a small man's, would have been way too big for her.

She leaned back into the tent and said something, and then she continued to stand there, and pulled her hair over her shoulder and began to plait it.

I knew she couldn't have seen me. Yes, she'd looked right toward me, but I was back in the woods and there was a thicket of briars between us. I was squatting down, my dog by me, and neither one of us had moved a muscle. Best not to move in a situation like that. But I was alarmed. A *white* woman. And somebody in the tent. I tensed up, ready to slip back without making a sound or shaking the briars. And then *he* came out of the tent, and with him a child. (That was your mama. About ten or eleven years old at the time.) She had on coveralls like her mama and she was a tough, wiry little thing, not an ounce of fat on her, with her hair in a rough bob. She already had a watchful face, like she knew the world was dangerous. The woman pointed and he looked my way. Didn't have a gun, just holding the little girl by the hand.

"Who's there?" he says.

Well, I could have just faded on back and left. But I was curious and instead of a gun he was holding a child by the hand. I put my gun against the tree behind me (didn't want to alarm *him*) and stepped on out into the clearing.

"Good evening," I say.

And he said, "Good evening."

"Just hunting," I say. I pulled the two shells out of my pocket and showed them to him. "I didn't know anybody lived back in here," I say.

"Am I on your land, sir?" he says.

Well, that "sir" brought me up short. Of course he thought I was a white man. I'd run into that mistake more than once with strangers.

"No, sir," I say back to him. "You're not. All this bottom in here belongs to some white people who live off in Kentucky someplace, New York, some of them." (That's my cousins, the great-nephews and nieces of my grandfather.)

"Well, come in, come in," he says. "We don't get company coming by very often." He looks around him at the bare trees stretching off in every direction and then smiles at his wife. "She gets lonesome," he says.

So I tell my dog to lie down, step back and pick up my gun (holding it by the barrel), and he lifts up the tent flap and we all go inside. He's got the tent floored with beams and boards he must have pulled out of the old house, and he's got a little hearth of dirt and brickbats with a fire burning on it and a hole above to let out the smoke, and a couple of mattresses against the back wall, and boxes and a stool or two.

To begin with, we stood around the fire and talked about hunting, and it was plain he'd been raised in the country. Then she pulled forward a box and invited me to sit down.

"We haven't introduced ourselves," he said. "I'm Gene Hamm and this is my wife, Frances, and my little girl."

"My name is Calhoun, Mr. Hamm," I said. Sometimes, if you call yourself by your first name only, it will locate you for the other person. But of course my first name is a last name.

He pulled up a stool for himself. "Sit down, Mr. Calhoun," he said.

"Calhoun is my first name," I said.

"Calhoun what?" he said.

So I said Levitt and sat. The little girl got her baby doll and a box made to look like a bed and sat down on the floor by him, and the wife began to fool around the fire, getting out a skillet and some meal and this and that. I tried not to look at her. What kind of white people are these? I said to myself, because I had never seen anyone like either one of them before.

In a minute she asked me if I would eat supper with them and I said, "No, ma'am, I better get on my way shortly if I expect to kill a coon and get home before my wife begins to worry about me." I still didn't look at her.

"You might as well eat," she said. "You can't hunt until dark."

"You can look at her," he said to me. "You're not going to turn her to stone."

"Sir?" I said.

"My wife."

I made my face as blank as I could. "Mr. Hamm," I said, "I'm colored. I don't look it, but I am." I could have added, "And even if I wasn't, I'm a young man and she's a beautiful woman."

"I know," he said. "I knew you must be colored as soon as you spoke outside about the white people who own the land."

These are crazy people, I thought, and I've got a family to raise. I better get out of here. I continued to look at the floor and began to gather my feet under me to get up.

"Hadn't she got the most beautiful hair you ever saw?" he said.

I didn't raise my eyes. "Yes, sir."

She had her back to us, cooking something on a little Coleman stove that was sitting on the bricks next to the fire. She spoke out in a low voice—the softest, sweetest voice I had almost ever heard. "Don't pay any attention to him," she said. "He's just trying to be friendly."

"Come over here, darlin'," he says to her and she comes over to where we're sitting and he pulls her down between us, picks up a strand of her hair, and passes it through his fingers. "You want to touch it?" he says.

"Mister," I said, "I wouldn't touch her hair unless you picked my hand up and laid it on her head."

"Do you mind, Frances?" he said.

And she said, "Of course not."

And he did. Picked up my hand and laid it on her head.

I felt like my hand was on fire. I held it there on her head a minute, looking at him, not her, and then drew it back.

She got up and went back to the stove and in a few minutes she brought plates for all of us. The little girl put her baby doll to bed and we all sat there around the fire and ate supper.

While we ate he began to talk to me as openly, as trusting, as if he'd known me all his life. Have you seen people like that? It's like they've made up their minds to float—maybe they can't swim even, but they trust themselves to the water. . . .

Alan: "To the destructive element . . ."

Levitt: Mostly he talked about the times—how people were starving to death in the cities, how the banks were getting the land from the little farmers—that kind of thing—and he asked me about myself and my work and how Edna and I managed. Before I left, he gave me a book to read. And she told me to come back and bring Edna. "I get lonesome for another woman," she said, "and my little girl gets lonesome for somebody to play with."

"My boys are too young for her," I said. They were only three and four at the time.

"Never mind that. She would love to nurse them."

So that was how we got acquainted and after that, the next two or three months, Edna and I and the children used to ride back there to see them every now and then. And sometimes I would go alone on horseback, because it was a long slow ride in the wagon or because he and I had fixed it up to hunt coon together, and we would sit around the fire late, talking about all the things he knew.

TWENTY-TWO

LEVITT: He was the first man I'd been around since I got out of college who liked to sit by the fire and talk about why things are like they are and that they might be some other way—that maybe he or I could begin to make them some other way. Always before I had not thought much about things being some other way.

Oh, I knew I could go up to New York and eat in the same automat as a white man. But I didn't want to eat in an automat. The way my mind worked was the same way my mother's and grandmother's minds had worked before me. They had said to themselves, We're different. We're smarter, a *lot* smarter, and stronger, and the women better-looking. We have to keep ourselves apart and we have to be tougher than anybody else and we can do it. So all our energy was taken up with holding ourselves apart and *making it* for ourselves and our children where almost nobody else could. *We had three hundred acres of bottomland in Homochitto County, and nobody had gotten it away from us.* Goddamn, we *were* different. We *were* smarter.

Well, that white preacher—yes, he was a preacher, along with everything else, a crazy preacher graduated from Vanderbilt Divinity School back when they were graduating crazy radical preachers up there by the dozens—kept giving me books to read and I began to read them. As he explained it to me, they were teaching socialism —communism—up at Vanderbilt.

"What else can you call Christianity?" he said to me. "What else? Jesus said it and all you got to do is follow His instructions." And he gave me chapter and verse about the rich man and the camel and the needle; and about leaving all that you hath and following Him and so forth.

He and she had bought the whole thing. We never left that ragged tent that she didn't find something to share with us—even if it was no more than a handful of sassafras roots or half a bucket of pecans.

What about him? What was he doing back in the woods? Well, he'd been down in Louisiana working for some pitiful little church outfit trying to get justice (postmortem—all the good it did him) for a man who had been lynched down there; and in the process he had got beat up and his ribs cracked and barely missed getting lynched himself. (Oh, yes, he was for what your grandpa would probably call the mongrelization of the races, too, and all that went with it. One of his favorite quotes—Edna wrote it down and I came across it marking the place in her Bible after she died—was along the lines of that God made of *one blood* all the nations of men to dwell on the face of the earth. . . . That's out of Acts.)

I can hear him say it now, see him sitting there by the fire looking so earnest. . . . He was a small man, but stocky, like you, son, with thick brown hair like yours, but cut short and standing up in cowlicks all over his head as if somebody had just given him a jolt of electric shock. He had a wide sad mouth like he'd seen too much and wanted to smile but couldn't, and a voice and delivery not like a preacher's but light and full of life. When he quoted the Bible it was like he was making it up, *thinking* it as he went along.

But there's a tail end to that verse about our being of one blood that he didn't read: "and hath determined the times before appointed and the *bounds of their habitations*." [He turned to me.] What are you? A Presbyterian?

Alan: No. Nothing.

Levitt: Well, your people are Presbyterians and that's the kind of verse your old-fashioned southern Presbyterian (or Methodist or anything else) can turn into a biblical precedent for segregated housing.

But I was talking about him—them. He was a country boy. Plenty of those radical Methodist preachers out of Vanderbilt in those days were country boys. Some of them ended up in the Movement later. The old professors gave them scholarships for piety and brains and then began hiring them to teach in the seminary and before the professors knew it, they had turned it (the school) into something else. He thought it was funny.

And his wife, with all that gold hair, knowing where to dig sassafras roots and when you could eat poke salad and so forth, she was a country girl, a mountain girl.

After he got beat up in New Orleans, they'd left Louisiana. (He needed a few weeks to get over the beating, he said, and they both needed to get their minds straight and get right with the Lord.) They were burned out with cities. Nashville, and then they'd been in Miami about some other lynching, and then New Orleans, and it seemed to both of them that they heard a Voice saying they should go out into the wilderness and pray. So they started east and north from New Orleans, and when they got to Homochitto County it was November, the woods were coppery and the weather fine and the sun shining and the creeks sparkling; and it seemed like exactly the place the Lord had in mind for them. That's what she told me.

It didn't seem strange to them at all, I don't think, to be living in a tent back in the bottom for a winter while they made up their minds—or rather, while they waited for the *Lord* to make up their minds—what they were supposed to do next. Yes, they were crazy.

They must've had a little bit of money. Once or twice in the three months I knew them, they went to town or to Calloway's in that old piece of a car and bought supplies—cornmeal and side meat and so forth. And they bought greens and eggs and milk from a family that farmed on the edge of the deep bottom. He got around pretty soon to telling me he was a union organizer—some half-assed union that paid him about like the school board paid Edna. So they weren't just waiting on the Lord, they were waiting on the union, too.

Well, Edna and I read all those books he gave us and the truth is they didn't make a socialist out of either one of us or a Christian out of me, or even a good man. As for the Christianity, he never gave me a book that convinced me his religion was enough like what he said it was *supposed* to be for me to take it up. What church would I have gone to? There wasn't even one *he* could go to around Chickasaw then, much less one he could have preached his gospel in. Niggers would have been scared of him and the whites would've killed him. And as for the socialism: my land—mine and Henry's—that our grandmother had bought with her entire life and that the old white man, my grandfather, had thrown away his reputation to leave to us—I couldn't see dividing it up in forty-acre plots and handing it out to those miserable drunks and incompetents who cut pulpwood for me from time to time—no matter whose fault it was they were drunks and incompetents. Oh, I knew how they tried to destroy themselves and all that went into the way they hated themselves. But it didn't change my conviction about what *I* ought to do when he would argue, one night that it was the system made them do it and that we had to start changing the system by changing ourselves; and the next night that it was *God* more than Karl Marx who told him this was the case.

I explained to him that in his view I would probably classify as one of those rich men who were unacceptable to either Jesus or Marx, and he said he knew what I was, but he also knew what I could become.

I couldn't see it. I meant to live my life on my own land and make it produce, by God, and raise my kids on it and leave it to them in better shape than it was when I got it—if they wanted it. (Or even if they didn't want it, because the old man's will had fixed it so we couldn't leave it away from them.)

I'm not a saint or a hero. No, I'm a farmer and a family man.

I felt bad about that. Bad to begin with, when he was trying to convert me and worse afterwards when he was dead.

But two things he did convince me of—one, that there was such a thing in the world as a good white man—him—and, two, that I might not be a Christian, or a Communist either, but that neither was I a superman (my mother's view) or a dog (the sheriff's view). I was a *man*, like other men, white and black. And that's what I mean when I say that everything that has happened to me in my life since I knew him, he has influenced.

Because later, when it came time to stand up and register to vote and take a risk or two, to march and picket, when you began to see that . . . not that it was the dream of some visionary like him that could never come true, but that it was possible and practical and we could do it, I never had to think a minute to decide to stand up, and that was because of him. And in town the summer of 'sixty-four, when the college kids came down to help us and when the Klan burned the churches and when the police would be on either side of the street where we'd be marching, with their pistols in their holsters, while *we*, we wouldn't have so much as a stickpin to protect ourselves with, and later when the Klan would put its mark in the road in front of your house, Edna and I would think about them and mention their names.

So that was your grandfather, son, and your grandmother, and they died back there in the swamp that winter.

What happened, as far as I could make it out from what she said before she died:

We had one of those bitter cold spells in February that winter. They said there was ice in the river, and that only happens once every ten years or so. I don't know, I couldn't afford to waste my energy going down to the river to look at the ice.

One day, she said, a couple of white men out turkey hunting stumbled on the tent like I had and he invited them in, just like he had invited me in. They were father and son, they said, pulpwood cutters. (He'd had a bee in his bonnet about the pulpwood people from the time I'd begun to tell him what a rough life that was.) They were poor men, she said, and he always preached his particular sermon to poor men, black or white. He was convinced right down to the soles of his shoes that we could get together and make things better for ourselves. "Not only that," he'd say, "but it'll take all that worrisome guilt off other people."

On their way home that day—they hadn't killed a thing—they stopped by again—came back to hear more and egged him on.

"I knew something was wrong with it from the beginning," she said. "I can almost always tell about things like that. But he said we had to treat them like men." She wasn't crying when she told me about it, but talking in a dead voice, like she was in shock and hardly knew what she was saying, which she undoubtedly was. "Besides," she said, "I was sick, feverish, getting the flu. I thought maybe my judgment was affected."

The third time they came by—it was the middle of the afternoon the next day—they'd been drinking. They'd been polite from the beginning—too polite, maybe—and, drunk or sober, they stayed that way. Sat around the fire on their boxes and nodded their heads. Now and then the young one smiled and said, "Yeah, preacher."

Her husband had progressed to talking about what had happened in New Orleans and why it had happened and of course that involved mixing niggers and whites.

Still they were quiet. Only the older one, who said he was sometimes a preacher, too, in his spare time, told about how Ham looked on his daddy's nakedness and that afterwards he was cursed and a servant of servants.

The son, she said, looked at her long and hard, made her uneasy. Her husband didn't ask him if he would like to touch her hair. Finally, though, the young man said, "Well, you might think the race mixing is all right, but you shore picked you a towhead."

"And Gene said that he was lucky, that I had picked him, or something like that. He always joked about how I was so smart and good and beautiful he would never have had the nerve to come courting, that I was the one who came courting him, and I did."

Well, they had a camp farther back in the bottom, they said, a cabin. "Come on over and preach to us some more, preacher," the old man said. "We're interested." And he went with them.

She never saw him alive again or knew what happened. The cold began to come down even harder shortly after they left. It hadn't been much above freezing for days, but a north wind set in and by dark the temperature was down to fifteen, something that never happens around here, never.

She had thought, if she thought at all, that he would be home by dark. When dark came and he wasn't there, with the wind blowing so hard the tent was almost like outdoors, she knew something was bad wrong. He would not stay away and leave her and the child alone after dark, and especially not in this weather. She was afraid, frantic. They had done something to him, she was sure of it. He was out there in the woods in the cold somewhere, wherever they had left him, hurt, unconscious, maybe, and now, probably, she thought (remembering the way the young one had looked at her) at least one of them was on his way back. She couldn't leave the child, so she got them both into as many layers of clothes as they could load on and started out in the direction the men had gone. She had a compass and a flashlight. She was a country girl and in the three months they'd been camping there she had gotten to know the terrain for a couple of miles around—which way the ravines ran, where the log crossings were, and where the woods were briar-free and easy to walk through. And the little girl—your mother—was tough, too. I suppose, if she wasn't grown up already, she grew up some that night.

They cast back and forth in a pattern through the woods, using the compass, flashing the light for an instant to read it, and before an hour had gone by, she smelled wood smoke and followed her nose and found, not a cabin, but a dying fire smoldering beside a fallen tree in the lea of a low bluff. She and the child stood behind a briar thicket for a while, listening and waiting, afraid to go close to the fire; but they saw no one, heard nothing. Then, she said, she left the child and circled all the way around the fire, looking, sniffing (*praying*, for all I know—whatever she did with that sixth sense of hers), trying to pick up a trail. And then, she said, when she was sure what direction they had taken, she got the child and went that way, and it was back toward the tent, only three or four hundred yards to the north of the segment of the circle she had been searching. Very shortly they found him.

Nobody ever found out what happened. Nobody except me, I don't suppose, and maybe Selman Boykin, spent much time wondering about it.

She said she knew when she got near him, she *knew;* and she sat the child down on a log and said, "Wait here, I've got to climb down this ravine." And she climbed down and he was lying at the bottom. He was still warm, the sleet that was beginning to fall melting on his face. He must have just died. She, of course, to begin with, was hoping he was alive, she felt for his pulse, but there wasn't any, she didn't see any marks on his body, but he was dead. She lifted up his head, still thinking, maybe, maybe, and the back of it was bashed in, a mush of blood and brains.

No time now to grieve for him. She had to think about the child.

She got herself together and climbed up the side of the ravine. The two men, she was thinking, or one of them, might be at the tent waiting. She explained in a whisper to the child that they needed to go for help to find her daddy, that those men he'd gone off with she was afraid were bad men. She outlined the plan she had made, climbing up the ravine with his blood freezing on her mittens. They would go to the clearing, she said, as quietly as possible, and see if the men were there. If they were, she and the child would have to walk to the nearest house; if not, they would get the keys and drive the car out. Edna and I were the only people she knew except the old couple she had bought eggs and milk from. They would come to our house.

The cold was on her side. If that man, whoever he was, had rape on his mind, the cold must have driven it out. Again she left the child and slipped up to the tent. No one was there. She got the car keys and went back to the woods and got the child and they came to our house.

So she knocked on our door that freezing night, burning with fever, half out of her head. I suppose, climbing up the side of that ravine with the blood freezing on her mittens, she caught despair, although the doctor Selman Boykin took her to called it pneumonia.

By the time she finished telling us what had happened, she was delirious or crazy with grief or both. We didn't know what to believe. While she talked and rambled, the child sat in a corner and stared at her and said not a word. Edna and I listened and we didn't say much, either. After a while she passed out.

Maybe they were fragile people, I don't know. I've often thought about it—if it had been Edna, would she have allowed herself to take sick? There were the boys to look out for. She couldn't afford to get pneumonia. And then I thought about them being fragile in another way—that they were people who were not able to live in this evil world, who felt other people's suffering like their own. An ordinarily weak person can't do that. It'll give him pneumonia in nothing flat—or drive him to drink or suicide.

I took your mama up on my lap and held her and she put her head on my shoulder and was so quiet, I thought she was going to sleep, but after a while she reached up and pulled my head down and said in my ear, "Is my daddy dead?" and I said, yes. I kept running my hand over her rough bobbed hair and saying, "It'll be all right, sister. It'll be all right." And then Edna took her and held her and she cried and after a while she went to sleep.

Well, there we were, in a predicament. The middle of the night. A white woman and a child on our hands, the woman burning up with fever. A man's body back in the woods and two white loonies out somewhere, maybe looking for the woman. All the time I was patting your mama and saying, "It'll be all right," I was staring at Edna and casting around in my mind. What to do? What to do? What was going to become of them, miserable creatures? Suppose I were to go for the sheriff? For all we knew it could have been one of his deputies or his brother that did the murder.

"Honey," I said, after a while, "where does your grandma live? Your mama's mama or your daddy's mama?"

She had begun to get herself together by now. "I hadn't got any," she said. "They're all dead. Me and my mama and daddy are the only ones in my family."

"How about aunts and uncles?" I said. "Cousins?" But she shook her head, no.

It was Edna who came up with the idea of going to Selman Boykin. She knew him and his wife because he was Supervisor for our beat and had been on the county school board, and she had respect for him. He was the only Supervisor (or school board member, either) as far as she knew from talking to the other teachers, *in the entire county,* who had ever visited a nigger school. He saw to it that they got a load of wood at the school when they needed it, instead of having to chop their own. He and his wife belonged to a shouting church, she said, and Selman would bring testaments around to the school every year and pass them out to the children. He was a good man, the man to go to.

I got on my horse that night. (It was already getting toward eleven.) I wouldn't have driven that car. Might've run into those white loonies and had to explain what I was doing with it. I rode the five miles to his house and told him what had happened. "I can't keep them at my house," I said, "It's too dangerous—for them as much as for us." (The truth is, as I thought afterwards, after she died, Edna and I would have liked to raise the little girl ourselves. She could have passed for ours.) [He gestured to the photograph in the center of the mantelpiece.] Edna was light as me. But of course that was out of the question.

Well, Selman Boykin got in his car, middle of the night or not, and went on back, with me following on horseback. Took your grandma into town and put her in the hospital where she died. Left your mama that night with Edna and me. "I'll come get her tomorrow," he said. "My wife and me will keep her a few days."

While he was in town, he called the sheriff and he left us out of it. "No use you and Edna getting mixed up in it," he said when he came back the next day with his brother to get the child and the car. "You got yourselves and your children to think about. Nothing anybody can do for him now except get him buried and I'll see to that when they find him."

"He's a preacher," I said. "He's a Christian."

"I'll see to it that he gets a Christian burial," he said.

"Who killed him?" I said. "Who killed him?"

"That's the sheriff's business," he said.

I never knew. There are certain white men in the county to this day, I look into their faces and say to myself, Was it you? But I never knew.

Oh, the sheriff sent a couple of deputies out there and they found the body and I suppose they made a show of trying to find out who did it. There was a line or two about it in the paper a couple of times. The people down at Calloway's who'd seen him said he was a vagrant, or crazy—those who didn't know. Those who did kept their mouths shut.

The woman died. There were no relatives. Selman Boykin kept his mouth shut, too. By that time he and his wife had decided to keep your mother and so, I suppose, in his view, the less said about what had happened to her mama and daddy, the better. People, black and white, didn't talk any more than they had to in those days about things like that.

We were silent, too. We wanted the child to have as good a chance as she could; and having a murdered Communist labor organizer for a daddy hung around her neck wouldn't improve her situation.

She was lucky. Do you know what happened to orphan children in the thirties, children of poor wanderers, children who nobody knew where they belonged? They ended up in orphan asylums or in foster homes with people who had taken them for the miserable ten or twenty dollars a month the welfare paid to feed and clothe and house them. No, I didn't want to do anything to queer her chances with the Boykins.

TWENTY-THREE

LEVITT: So that was your mama and she never was like the people around her, not at the beginning when she was already quiet and independent, solitary, and not later, after she married Mac Boykin. She always kept to herself and, if I knew her at all, it's because we had that secret together of what her mama and daddy had been, and that Edna and I were the ones who had set her on the path she had to take. We might see each other at Calloway's or even sometimes in town at the post office or the A & P, and she would stop and speak and look at me with that deep look she had, and I knew she hadn't forgotten any of it. Once, long after she was grown, after you boys were born, I met her one day back in the woods by herself, where she'd gone, she said, to dig sassafras roots, and we talked awhile, as naturally as if we talked intimately every day. She had done all right, she said. Your daddy was good to her, a good man. And then she looked at me and said, "It's like that time, that winter when I was a little girl and we lived in the tent and you used to come back to see us, it's like it was a dream. It's back there in my mind—I see you and my daddy and mama sitting around the fire talking. And my mama's long hair, sometimes I dream about her holding me in her lap and her hair is like a tent around me. Do you remember her hair? And then, *this*." She held out the knotty rusty-looking sassafras root she had dug up. "All she taught me, I remember. And that night my daddy died and we came to you. But it's like I learned it all in a dream. And I never did even say thank you for what you did for me. What would have become of me if it hadn't been for you and Edna? I reckon you hardly ever do say thank you in a dream, do you? But now, awake, out here in the woods, I'll say it."

Afterwards, when we saw each other, we would talk about our gardens and the weather and so forth in an easy friendly way, but we never either one said any more about that time we'd met in the woods or about the rest of it, not until she was sick the last time and sent for me.

Lee had been listening without a word to all this, only shaking his head and frowning every now and then. Now the tape was ready to run out and he interrupted so that he could change reels. He was more subdued than I had ever seen him. Switching the reels, he said to Levitt, "It doesn't seem possible all that could have happened and that she could have kept it to herself for her entire life. It just doesn't seem possible. I can't believe it."

"Your grandfather was *murdered*," Miriam said. "And you were not much more than a child when your mother died. Maybe she meant to tell you when you were grown."

"Yes," he said, "that must be it. She would have told us about it later."

"No," Calhoun said. "She would never have told you. Never. I thought about that when I was deciding if *I* would tell you. She thought she could keep you out of all that, protect you from it, and she would never have told you. That's my opinion. And at the last, when she saw she was wrong, that there's no way to stay out of anything, it was too late. She was as good as dead.

"It's too late for her to speak, is what I said to myself. But it's not too late for me. Let's open it up. Keeping it shut in the closet all these years hasn't been any use to anybody. So let's go on."

223

"But there's nothing else to say about any of that, is there?" Lee said in a low voice. "She died. They're all dead—and that's the end of it. Nothing came of any of it. But . . ." He hesitated. "But anyhow, *he*—my grandfather—he would think I'm doing the right thing now—with the Movement and all."

He had the reel in place now and Calhoun reached over and clicked the switch to turn on the machine. Then he pressed down on his mike button.

❧

Levitt: This is the second reel of Lee Boykin's interview with Calhoun Levitt. February 28, 1971. Yes, there is more to say, son. There is more to talk about concerning the summer your mama died, for you to take with you on this record. So, to go on, the rest of what I want to tell you happened in the summer of 1964.

By that time Edna and I were deep in the Movement. We'd felt the force of it growing stronger all summer. They would put a few of us in jail and the next time we marched, there would be twice as many marching. They never seemed to grasp what they were doing when they put us in jail. And, at the churches, we were meeting, night after night; night after night the preachers would recite the law—most who were there had never dreamed the law could be for them. In the daytime we were filling the courthouse halls, waiting to register. Nothing could stop us. That was all Edna and I thought about, and our boys, too, who were grown and gone, but would write or call and tell us what *they* were doing. We put the Movement first, always, and had no time for anything or anybody else. It's surprising on that account that when I saw her down at Calloway's one day in June, I even noticed she was sick. But I did. She was yellow as a gourd.

I knew, because we made it our business to know those things, that Mac Boykin was going to Klan meetings. What could I say to her? We looked at each other across the store. The whites of her eyes were the color of greasy dishwater. She nodded to me and turned away. I thought about her daddy. I often thought of him that year.

Late in July, after Mercy Seat burned, she sent for me. Sent the little girl who was waiting on her. (She couldn't get out of bed without help by then. They said afterwards that she had gone down in a hurry. Cooking supper one night, vomited blood, and three weeks later she was dead.) Anyway, she sent the little girl with a note. She wanted to see me. I should come when Mac Boykin and you two boys were out of the house; and you would be gone to town, she said, the next afternoon. Don't fail me, the letter said. So I went, and she told me what she had done. This was just a couple of weeks after the church burned and she was dead within another week after that.

It hadn't been hard to do or to get away with, she said. She'd always been a churchgoing Christian. Standoffish with her neighbors, maybe, but prayer meeting on Wednesday nights and Sunday services, morning and night, she was there, shouting. The Spirit had come down on her when she was young and He hadn't deserted her. It was the Spirit who told her what she had to do. If He told her, she said, it was bound to be right. And so it was also bound to be right for her to have used the church to begin doing it, to find out what she needed to know.

[Here Levitt paused and cocked his eye at Lee as if to assess his reaction. Then:]

Levitt: Don't make the mistake of thinking your mama was dumb.

Lee: I never thought she was dumb.

Levitt: At the age you were when she died, you probably never thought about her at all, if you're like every other boy in his teens. I mean, *now*. Thinking back on her because of what I'm saying. I see you're a city boy, working for a newspaper. I mean, don't think, because she had the Spirit, that she was no better than a dumb nigger.

Lee: Jesus *Christ!* I don't think niggers are dumb.

Levitt: Well, plenty of 'em *are*. Make no mistake about that. Whether they shout or not. But there is such a thing as a person the Spirit descends on who is neither dumb nor crazy. I find that hard to believe, but my observations tell me it's true. And your mother was one of those.

So: She'd been going to church as usual all that year and the year before and she'd heard the women talking at the ladies' aid meetings or whatever they call them, and she had cooked for the men's suppers and she thought about all she had heard.

And of course that spring and summer at church, they'd mainly been talking about the college students—the Yankee Communist college students—coming, and about the meetings that were going on in the nigger churches, the registration drive. . . .

[Here Levitt clicked off the tape deck and sat thinking for a minute. Then he clicked it back on and continued.]

Levitt: It's a funny thing to me, this church business. It reminded me—and still does, because it's still going on—of some of the things I read in those books on southern history that your grandpa gave me years ago. One thing I especially remember was about the Methodists up in the border states before the Civil War. The Civil War started in church, you know. Those old abolitionists, the most of them were preachers and big Christians. And the see-sesh, they used the churches to organize themselves and preach the truth about how God had ordained slavery. So up in Tennessee, Kentucky, the circuit riders on one side were fighting to carry the border states with the Union, and on the other, they were fighting to get out. So I read how sometimes the radicals on one side or the other would set up a bushwhacking or a murder of *one of their own preachers,* and then rig the evidence so it would look like the other side did it. Just trying to get everybody fired up.

And what about the Irish—the Catholics and Protestants killing each other for three hundred years or more? My God, churches! Stay away from churches!

But I'm getting off the subject of your mama. What I meant to say was that the white church is the home of the Klan, just like the black church is the home of the Movement. So she had listened to the men talking. (What *I* don't understand is how she could be moved by the *Spirit* in a church where all that was going on. Well, I don't have to understand it. I suppose some psychologist could give a name to it, but then he probably wouldn't understand it, either.) To go on, she knew what was happening.

And here's what she saw, *early,* that a lot of men still haven't seen. She saw how quick the whole thing began to wear thin with the women. The meetings and the agitating had already been going on a couple of years by then. Some of the women already didn't believe their husbands even *went* to the meetings. Or if they went, they would go someplace else afterwards, because they would come home drunk or smelling like another woman or both or not come home at all until the next day, and it was always for the Cause.

I heard the same thing last year from that crazy skinny little Jew lawyer over in Buchanan County—the niggers' Jew, they call him

—when he was down here from the Justice Department looking into a boycott case. He had got run out of his county for registering niggers. He said to me, The way they'll break the back of the Klan all over the state—all over the *country*—is through the women. The women get sick of the men staying out all night, and already, he said, they're writing in to the FBI and the Justice Department to tell 'em where the guns and the dynamite and so forth are hidden; and they'll name so-and-so and so-and-so who did this and that (not their own men, usually, but sometimes, if they're mad enough, their own) and before you know it, that Klavern is busted up and their men are staying home nights.

So that was what she wanted to tell me. She had learned plenty at the church suppers and the all-day singing on the grounds and she had done exactly that. She'd written to the FBI and what she knew, she told me, was enough to tie three men in this Klavern to every church-burning in three counties besides Homochitto, and not only that, to the fire-bombing of a Jew lawyer's house in Port Simpson.

"Not Mac," she said. "I was sure of that. He hasn't brought a thing into this house that isn't his own or handled any gun but his."

As to that, who knows? I said to myself. We knew at Mercy Seat that the Homochitto Klavern had been watching us, taking our license numbers. Some had lost their jobs. I, myself, had seen the very place up over the parking area by the church where somebody had watched us. The evidence was there—trampled weeds, burned matches, cigarette butts, a crumpled pack. Somebody had sat up there for quite a while and I doubt that he was on a picnic. Not that year.

[The crowded little room where we sat seemed to grow closer, the butane heater sucking the moisture from the air, so that it was like breathing in a desert. Lee was sweating.]

Lee: No. Absolutely not.

Levitt: That's what *she* said: "Not Mac. I know he wouldn't do anything like burn a church. I know it." She was weak and sick, her voice faint. She rambled a bit, I think, and then, "He takes the boys to the meetings," she said. "The boys . . . And Lindsay Lee, especially, came home so upset one night, and he was sick, although we didn't realize it at the time and he's been half-sick ever since. And Dallas . . . even Dallas, who is always steady, always the same . . ." That's what I remember her saying about you two.

227

"It's bad for them," she said. "He shouldn't take them. And then, the church . . . Mercy Seat . . . right here in our own neighborhood. They burned a *church,* Edna's church. . . . And, *you* know, Calhoun . . . I thought about my mother . . . my father. What would they say? I thought about them, even though, like I told you, it seems as if their lives were only a dream I had when I was a little girl, still, I kept seeing them and seeing you and Edna sitting by the fire with them . . . and I couldn't suffer it anymore. That's all, I said, after the church burned. No more."

So that was what she wanted to tell me. She had written to the FBI. And especially she wanted to tell me that she was going to get the reward. Somebody, the Anti-Defamation League, I think, had posted a five-thousand-dollar reward for blowing the whistle on the fire-bombing in Port Simpson. She was going to get it, she said, and she intended for it to go to rebuild Mercy Seat.

"Yes," I said to all that. "Yes, ma'am, yes, ma'am." I looked at her, her hair falling out in patches, all the flesh fallen away under her skin, her yellow face and skinny arms and the mound of her belly under the sheet, and I knew she was going to die *soon.* So I said, "Yes, ma'am, yes."

She calmed down and looked straight at me and said, "Don't say *ma'am* to me."

"I didn't mean to," I said. "I was upset. I'm sorry."

"It's in my will," she said. She was whispering now. I could hardly hear her. "I made a will. Mac . . . Mac . . . He'll honor my will. Won't he?"

"Yes," I said. "Of course."

Why had she called me? Why didn't she call a lawyer? That was what she needed. She needed that Jew lawyer from over at Port Simpson. But he was already gone. There wasn't a lawyer in Homochitto she could trust and she knew it. There wasn't a person besides me she could call to keep her will for her and put it in probate. Well, I was ready to do it.

"I thought about mailing it in," she said.

"Where is it?" I said. "I'll take it."

"But I didn't mail it," she said. "I got to worrying about . . . about Mac and the boys. Because . . . because I'm afraid if anybody finds out I did it, the boys will suffer. Mac will suffer."

Well, she was right. They would.

"So a will won't do," she said. The sweat was running down her face. I could see every bone in her chest and shoulders. "I have to live," she said. "I have to live until the check gets here."

I said nothing. It had been only three weeks since the church burned, only two weeks since she mailed her letter. The reward money probably wouldn't come for months, if she actually got it at all.

"I'm going to call you," she said. "That's what I want to tell you. As soon as it comes, I'll call you, send the little girl for you, and you must come as quick as you can. I want you to promise me that you will come and take the money and put it in the bank for Mercy Seat."

"Yes," I said. "I'll do that for you. You can trust me."

A week later she died. They hadn't expected it to be so soon, the little girl told me afterwards. As to when the check came or *if* it came, or if she had torn up the will, I never heard. All I know is that some months after she died, your daddy bought a big new truck with one of those wood eaters on it that can take a tree and turn it into sawdust, and a cherry picker—and moved away. And pretty soon he had another wife and he was getting rich. You can't blame him for that.

And so it turned out that her calling me in and telling me what she had done was very much like you calling me *mister*. It didn't have any significant results—just served to ease her mind.

As we walked toward the car after the taping, Lee handed me the keys. "You drive," he said.

Again Miriam sat between us.

"It's all a lie," he said, when we were out of the driveway and on the road again. He did not look at either of us.

I was silent. I had not the least doubt that every word Levitt had said was the truth. How can I use it? I was thinking. And then, Not a poem. A story, or part of a story.

"You're not responsible for the behavior of your father," Miriam said, "and your mother was trying to do the right thing."

"I was *there*. I would have known. You can't *not know* something like that."

"Lee, your mother was dying. You were probably too upset to think about the Klan or church-burnings or anything else."

"It's a lie," he said. "We might as well throw away the whole damn tape. If he lied about my mother and father, he was probably lying about the rest of it, too." His voice was trembling.

Miriam turned toward him, took his hand in hers.

"Why would he lie?" I said coldly. "He didn't seem the kind of man who would make up a complicated story like that."

"Alan, hush," Miriam said, and then, to Lee, quietly, "You're probably right, but even if you're not, it doesn't matter anymore. It was all a long time ago. You were a child. If it happened, it happened to people who are dead."

"Do you know what it's like to hear something like that?" he said. "Something about your family that turns them into strangers? It's like being in an earthquake. You feel the ground slide away under your feet."

Miriam put her arm around him.

My heart began to jump. My chest felt as if it were filled up to the throat with rocks, the sharp edges of the rocks cutting into my ribs and into my heart when it jumped, and squeezing my lungs so that I couldn't breathe. "I know it's bound to be upsetting," I said in what sounded to me like a suitably detached way. "But it's pretty interesting stuff."

"If my father went to those meetings, he went to make people see . . ."

"Of course," Miriam said. She glared at me.

"He has prejudices, just like everybody. We're red-necks. But he would *never* . . ."

"Come *on*, Lee," I said.

He reached across Miriam, gripped my leg, and said, "What does that mean, '*Come on, Lee*'?"

My heart thudded against the rocks. "I've heard elsewhere that your daddy was in the Klan," I said. "Besides, *didn't* he take you and Dallas to the meetings, like your mother said?" (The ape speaking.)

"My mother never said that. Never. That's why I know it's a lie. And . . . all that crazy stuff about the two men murdering my grandfather. I don't even believe *that*. Why did he say he doesn't know who they are? Pulpwood cutters? Father and son? If there were any such people, he'd be bound to know them."

"He said there were people he suspected, didn't he? And suppose he knew? What could he have done about it?"

"Hush, Alan," Miriam said again. "Shut up."

Lee let go of my leg and sat back. I glanced in their direction. He was staring at the road, tears rolling down his cheeks. Miriam put both arms around him. Under her sweater I could see the shape of her shoulders, a trifle wide for a woman, one raised and hunched forward as if to protect him, her arms cradling him.

Phoebe.

I looked at the road and gripped the steering wheel.

I saw them fucking again.

Uncivilized, damn it! Uncivilized to be made the victim of these visions. I pressed the accelerator to the floorboards. The car fishtailed in the gravel.

"Alan!" Miriam said.

I eased off. I would get us back to Chickasaw and they could play out their big scene in private.

At the turnoff I got out of the car. "I'll open the gate," I said. "Good-bye, I'm going." And I opened it and then cut off through the woods, running.

"Alan, wait," she called. "Where are you going?"

"Back later. Good-bye."

Miserable boy. I still feel the ice pick probing at his gut, still remember, as if it were mine, his grief and rage.

Miriam! I can't, after all, love and let go. I want you for *my own.* I want you to admire, to desire, to love me—only me. He pushed on, walking and running, stumbling and cursing.

Deep in the woods he came again on the spring he had found weeks earlier—shadowy now in its hollow, the sunlight that had glinted from its moving sands curtained away behind dark cedar trees.

He stood staring down into the hollow, shivering, feeling the sweat cold and sticky under his shirt. A dead limb as thick as his arm had fallen from one of the over-arching trees and lay half in, half out of the water. He put his foot on it, heaved it toward him, broke off a length, and began to beat the post by the spring where the dipper hung. Mud and bark spattered his face and hair. The blows jarred his arms and shoulders. Splinters from the broken limb dug into his palms. He beat and beat until the limb splintered in his hand; and then he threw it down and started home.

Somewhere along the walk through the stirring woods, he said,

Very well, I will go all the way with it, because that is absolutely what one has to do.

Then he said, Goddamn it, I'll kill the fucking bastard. That'll show him.

Then he said, Poor me. Nobody, *nobody* really loves me.

Rain clouds were gathering as he walked and thunder rolled faintly out of the west.

TWENTY-FOUR

THE WIND had begun to blow. Under a sky alternately overcast and blue, I came out of the woods to the east of the horse lot. Far away I heard a calf bawling—that hollow country cry of loss. I gave an experimental bawl myself; I could have used a warm titty and a comfortable flank to lean against.

Behind the house I saw the salesman's VW parked. I didn't think I could look at him or listen to him. I circled around through the woods, along the edge of the horse lot and the garden back of Sam's house, past the abandoned well site, the waste pit gleaming like polished onyx in its setting of broken concrete and dead thistles; climbed the ridge; and came out in the backyard of my cabin.

From this angle, leaning slightly toward the pole that the REA had put up to carry the power line, my house looked as if it were ready to collapse—as if the weight of the line attached at the corner of the porch had pulled it out of plumb. I began to drag stacks of ship lap from under the house; I had measured and sawed the boards and they were ready to replace the rotten ones I had ripped out of the porch floor. I kept pulling out boards and stacking them within easy reach.

The calf was still bawling. The sound in my ears might have been my own voice. Where was Mama?

I saw now that the calf, still spindly-legged and frail, had blundered into an old fence, a few sections of which were standing along the back of my yard. He was leaning against the wire, crying his heart out. Then I saw Sam and Leila coming along the top of the ridge beyond the fence, driving Mama ahead of them, Sam listing into his sailor's gait, waving his stick and saying, "Sooo, soo-o-o, darling," to the cow, Leila carrying a handful of ferns and a branch of blooming dogwood and walking a few yards forward and to the left to keep the cow from breaking and running away. They coaxed her around the fence toward her baby and Sam stood watching until the calf found the teat. Leila crossed the yard and held out her ferns. "Look at these little furled ones, like scrolls . . ." Then, "And look at *you*. Where have you been?"

"Got into some mud," I said. I laid a board in place, fitted the lap into its groove, and banged in a nail.

Sam joined us. "Damn fool cows. Not much more sense than chickens. We been looking for this mama an hour. Supposed to be a storm tonight, TV says. Storm. Hurricane in the Gulf. Did you hear that?"

I shook my head no and picked up another board. I didn't care if the whole state of Mississippi blew away.

"What are you doing?" Leila said.

"Flooring the porch."

She looked at me curiously and then laid out the ferns and dogwood on the cistern cover. "Sam and I were down by the creek and I was thinking how I'd like to fill a canvas with the way the water looks running over sand and rocks. The *light*. The water is blue sky over the brown gravel. And the green light in the dogwood petals. That should go in."

I thought of Miriam's changing eyes, her white skin.

"The bass are spawning," Sam said. "Rolling around in the shallows over there at the north end of the lake where the creek comes in. Don't care if you walk right up to them. Yesterday I dropped a minnow in front of . . ."

"We ought to go fishing," Leila said. She touched him on the arm and looked at him in a proprietary way.

For a minute I stopped thinking about myself: Jesus Christ! *Again?* In the state he's in?

But then I looked at him. He was standing straighter. I could swear he looked taller. The skin on his cheekbones and over the delicate flaring nostrils shone with a dark light and a patch over his bad eye set off the hawkish Indian profile and the heavy passionate mouth.

"You look like the Hathaway Shirt Man, Sam. I mean like maybe for *Ebony.*"

He touched the patch and gave me a look. "Leila got it for me." He grinned.

"Sharp," I said.

"Legs ain't everything," Sam said.

"We ought to go fishing," Leila said again dreamily.

"Look at the wind," Sam said. "You think a fish would bite in that? And besides, bass won't bite when they're spawning. But we might gig one. Hey, I remember one year when they were spawning, I saw the grandma of 'em all up in the shallows; fixed up a frog gig, and—you won't believe it, but it's true—she weighed twelve pounds. Gig broke off in her back and she commenced to swim off with it. *I'm going to get you, Grandma!* Dived in after her. Smack *into* her. Knocked her out. Floated up. . . . Floated right up, both of us. . . ."

"It's getting warmer," Leila said. "The sun feels good on my back. I don't care if we catch anything."

"I floated up after her. She knocked *me* out. Would you believe it?"

I laid another board across the porch beams. "Sam!" I said. "You're kidding. Twelve pounds?" I was thinking, I'm going to stay with her. I'm going all the way, as far as she wants to take us, because that's what you have to do. ("And you can make her suffer, too," the ape said in such a low voice I barely heard him. "She *deserves* to suffer.")

"Daddy fished me out. Grabbed me by the leg. . . ."

. . . pain is supposed to make poets, isn't it?

"He can't swim, but he grabbed me by the leg with one hand, grabbed that grandma with the other and . . ."

"Can't swim? Noah?" Leila said. "Baptizings, I've seen him wade in chest deep, put his stick down to mark off . . ."

. . . with *her.* I can go all the way with her. But with him? The

235

salesman? The ice pick pierced a loop of my gut. I'm not going to think any more about this. Noah. Think about Noah.

I'd seen him, too, like a prophet out of the wilderness, like John the Baptist, wade in, him and another elder, that's the way they do it, wading in on either side of the preacher and setting their long sticks in the mud as supports and markers, two more elders standing at the water's edge to make a square, and two bringing out the candidates, the preacher preaching, the congregation singing all along the curve of the lake bank.

I've seen him preach, chest deep in water, when the Spirit moved in him. Lying in bed in the house on a Sunday morning, I've waked up to that carrying voice: "Something to tell you 'fore I leave you / Something to tell you 'fore I leave-a this world. . . ."

"Well, he can't. Fished me out and . . ."

"My God, your daddy, Sam," I said. I had thought of something else. "He likes to make me feel as bad as possible."

Sam sat down on the cistern cover, his stick between his knees, both hands resting on the gnarled head, the dark arms smooth and powerful below his T-shirt sleeves. "Yeah, he plays that game," he said. "Gives him some kind of satisfaction." He laughed. "What's he been telling you?"

"Did my great-grandfather . . . great-great, or whoever it was, give him—his daddy—that land? Did Uncle D. give him an oil well?"

"An *oil well!*" Leila said. "An oil well?"

"I never paid any attention to all that foolishness," Sam said. "Foolishness. It's not the kind of thing I pay attention to. They probably said something of the kind. How can you tell about what Daddy says? Or the old man, either?"

"Uncle D. never gave away a broken rocking chair, much less an oil well," Leila said.

"That kind of giving away wouldn't be no problem to a miser," Sam said. Then: "I *had* the land. Fences were rent—you know. That suited me. It wasn't until your *auntee* here got them to put in the SPASURSTA that I cared about any of it. That was what frustrated me. First, the wells: OK. I see if you got oil, you're gonna have wells. Then the pine trees: well, now, wait a *minute*. But your *auntee's* SPASURSTA was the last straw."

"I never . . ." Leila said.

"She was going to have her revenge on me. Wasn't you, Leila?

236

Waited and waited, looking for what you could do to get back at me."

I banged in another nail.

"She says she told you all about her and me, Alan," Sam said.

"Yeah."

"It wasn't revenge," she said. "I loved you, damn it." She took up the dogwood branch, blew gently on the flowers, and smiled her deep curly smile.

"How come you to worry Alan with it, that's what I want to know?" Sam said good-naturedly. "And his girl friend? You got something against him, too?"

"I was drunk," she said. She fanned him with the branch. "Besides, he was interested. Weren't you, Alan?"

"Sure." I drew a deep breath. Again I saw them at the window of Sam's house, naked, looking out at Uncle D. and my grandfather. But that was long before the SPASURSTA, wasn't it?

"What did the SPASURSTA . . . ?" I began, but I broke off. The ice pick was exploring my liver.

"Never stop trying to seine me out of the creek, do you, Leila? Like I'm a big old catfish. And the SPASURSTA was her biggest seine." He did not seem to be waiting for an answer.

Leila continued to sit on the cistern and watch him. " 'Love, oh, love, oh, careless love,' " she sang softly and smiled. " 'You see what careless love has done.' Come on, Sam, I think there's a patch of trillium there on the edge of the ravine. I need it in my work."

Sam got up from the cistern, dragged a few boards from under the house, picked up a wrecking bar from the porch floor, and began to pry out nails. "Go ahead," he said. "I'm coming."

"We could go bream fishing over by the spillway one day this week," she said. "Let's do that. You want to, Alan?"

"Sure."

"They'll bite good after a rain," Sam said. "If it rains tonight."

Leila laid down her dogwood branch and headed for the ravine.

I saw Miriam and Lee approaching along the top of the ridge. "I feel bad, Sam," I said. "Like my head is full of acid and my belly's full of rocks."

"Because of Leila and me?"

"No! Christ, no. I think my girl's getting ready to leave me."

He looked at me a long time and then said in Noah's deep

church voice, " 'The Lord giveth. The Lord taketh away. Blessed be the name of the Lord.' "

I had to laugh. "Shit, you're not much help," I said.

"You know that woman I told you I busted out of the Homochitto County jail?"

"Yeah."

" 'Twasn't two months before she run off with my brother-in-law, Freddie."

"Well?" I said. *"Well?"*

He shrugged. "It's always worth it," he said. "You can get as low as I got at Parchman, but if you tough it out, you'll find you can take hold again."

Miriam had come through the cabin from the back and now her shadow moved across my work. She put her hand on my shoulder and spoke in a low voice in my ear. "Are you all right? Are you OK, Alan?"

"No," I said. "I'm not OK. But it can't be helped, can it?"

Lee took Leila's place on the cistern cover and stared at us in a distracted way, while Sam glanced curiously from one to another of us and then went back to pulling nails.

It seemed to me that a change had come over Lee, as if his weight, his stockiness, were air, as if he were one of those inflatable plastic toys that children play with in a swimming pool, and someone had squeezed the stem of his valve and let out a quart or so of air. His face sagged slightly and his shoulders slumped. Even his hair and beard were flat.

Miriam seemed not to see Sam. "Lee is *sick* over that interview," she said. "Sick. It upset him terribly."

"I'm sorry," I said. I was conscious of the creaking sound of nails being drawn, the rattle of boards.

"I hear you and Alan been letting my daddy entertain you with his tales," Sam said politely to Lee.

"Yes, sir," Lee said. "He talked to us."

"Hey, man—*sir?*" Sam said. "What's this with the *sir?*"

"He says he's going back to New Orleans, that he can't stick around here any longer," Miriam said, still speaking in a low voice, her hand on my shoulder.

What could I say? Was she going with him? She *couldn't* be going with him, could she? I didn't know whether to vomit or whistle a happy tune.

"Hmmm," I said.

"Sam," Leila called, "bring me a spade, will you? I want to dig these up."

Sam put down the wrecking bar. "I don't need all that respect," he said to Lee. "Just *Sam* will do."

"He needs our help, our support," Miriam said. "That crazy story . . ."

"Look, man, I'll call you any goddamn thing I want to," Lee said to Sam. "If you don't appreciate respect, you can shove it. OK?" He got up and walked across the yard toward the fence where the cow stood nuzzling her baby. When he got there, he leaned blindly against the fence as the calf had, as if there were no way to get around it.

"Lee's upset, too," I said to Sam.

". . . a world of objective reality for his work." (I realized Miriam was still talking.) "Everyone around here seems to have a stake in lies. Even you."

"Fuck objective reality," I said.

"*Sam.*"

"Leila's calling me," Sam said. "That white boy can say *sir* till the cows come home. Or not say it. I don't care. Where's your spade?"

"Over by the privy," I said.

"I'm not going to get mad with you, Alan," Miriam said.

"I don't *care* about Lee's problems," I said. "How can I care?"

◥≋

Here they came, two by two. The next pair arrived by truck: Dallas and Lorene. Were we going to have another party? Dancing and shouting around my house to drive out the Devil and bless the porch floor?

Maybe this time I can get the Spirit, I thought. Jesus knows I need it.

But I had forgotten it was Sunday. They had come by to invite us to church again. The baby sat in Lorene's lap, round-eyed and solemn. Dallas nodded at us and then stared straight ahead and gripped the steering wheel, while Lorene extended her invitation and I, mindful of my manners, asked them to get out and stay awhile.

"We tried to call you folks earlier," Lorene said, "but the phone didn't answer."

"We were over at Calhoun Levitt's place interviewing him," I said.

"Interviewing?" Lorene smoothed the top of the baby's head. She had on the wide-eyed, expectant, loving, intensely Christian look that scared the shit out of me.

"Look," I heard Leila saying to Sam. *"Look."* And Sam, "Nothing but a big old king snake. And Leila: "I know, but look, red rings . . . yellow . . . Oh, she moves those rings along." "She?" Sam said. "Is it a *she?*" Leila laughed. "Leila, you're crazy," Sam said. "You know it?" "It's spring," Leila said. "She just waked up."

"We've been getting some material for articles," I said. "Picture stories."

Dallas reached down and turned the switch on the CB radio. We heard the intermittent rasp of the open channel and faint voices in the background. ". . . south on Sixty-one," somebody said. "Come in, buddy."

"Lee says the rest of the country doesn't realize how complex the situation is down here," Miriam said. "Don't you think that's true? The problems of the lower-middle-class whites, you know, nobody gives them any coverage. Everything is presented as so . . . black and white."

"Look at me and Sam, for instance," I said. "He's black and I'm white. On the other hand, the Levitts . . ."

"Alan never takes anything seriously," Miriam said to Lorene.

I was looking at Dallas. His face was haggard, his eyes opaque. He had his head bent down to the radio now, as if he might be expecting a message. He, too, looked thinner, not deflated, but as if his body were a rope that had been twisted and stretched taut. He's been fasting, I thought.

"We're doing a kind of sociological study," I said. "Investigating human relations. Miriam thinks I don't take it seriously, but I do."

Lorene looked deeply, deeply into my eyes. My ears popped. I might have been in a climbing airplane at twenty thousand feet. "I know you're interested in our church," she said. "I certainly think if you're going to write about anything that's important around here, human relations or anything, you should study our church. Why don't you talk to Brother Snyder? And Sister, too.

Sister is a powerful woman, Alan. She has the gift of interpreta-
tion—and the gift of prophecy. And they've both been sinners.
They were *lost*. Brother Snyder . . ." She hesitated. "He had this
terrible problem—he says it himself—that he was tempted by evil
women and . . ."

My ears popped.

"Do you mean that he had *sex* with women he wasn't *married*
to?" Miriam said. "How *awful*."

"Oh, Miriam, I didn't mean to offend you. That's not what I
meant at *all*. I . . . There's Lee," she said. "What's he doing over
there?"

"Miriam," I said. "I . . ."

"Is something the matter with him? Is he sick?" Lorene called
to him: "Lee? Lee, honey?"

Lee turned and stared distractedly at her, then he crossed the
yard. His shoulders were still slumped and he raised his feet and
put them down as if they were asleep, as if he couldn't feel where
the ground was.

"Where have you been? We haven't seen you all week, Lee,
honey. I thought you'd gone back to New Orleans without even
telling us."

That was the first I knew that he wasn't staying with them anymore.

"I rented a room in town," he said. "I thought I was going to
be here awhile. But . . ." He broke off and his face puckered as if
he might cry. "It probably won't work out, after all," he said.

What wasn't going to work out?

"I thought you were mad with us," she said. "About last Sunday.
We don't want you to be mad with us."

"Is that right, Dallas?" he said. "You don't want me to be
mad?"

Dallas did not look up. "No," he said. "I don't."

"We're going to church tonight," Lorene said. "Why don't you
come with us? Now, don't say you can't. Alan says you're interviewing people, and you should interview some of the ones you
took pictures of last week. And our preacher." She smiled en-
couragingly at him. "Miriam says you're trying to understand
what's going on around here and he would be an important person to help you. And Sister. His wife. I was telling them, Lee, she's
a powerful woman. The Spirit is a power in her."

He shook his head. With a visible effort, puffing up his chest, raising his shoulders, he said, "Well, really, Lorene, the subjects we're interested in were voter registration and union organization. Not . . . not . . ."

"But the pictures you took. Last week . . ."

"I need to get back to New Orleans."

"You could go out to Texas and interview your daddy," Dallas said. "Or me. You could interview me."

"I'm not interviewing any-fucking-body else," Lee said. "Not around here. Everybody lies too fucking much."

"You don't want to talk like that in front of my wife and baby," Dallas said in his flat country voice. "OK?"

"It's all right, Dallas," Lorene said. "The Spirit is leading us, *all* of us, in His own way, His own time."

Again on the CB radio I heard the static of opening and closing channels. A faint distant voice said, "Where are you, buddy? You're fading out."

"I'm sorry," Lee said. "OK?" A tear rolled down his face.

"Sister Snyder . . ." Lorene began.

"Look, Lorene, there's a boycott planned in New Orleans, see? And I have a commitment to cover it. Besides, this isn't the place for me to be right now. In my business you get where you can sense something like that." As he talked, his voice gathered strength and he filled out, blew himself up with another breath. "You get a sixth sense. And in New Orleans a key issue is involved. The Klan . . ."

"Yeah, go on back to New Or*leans,*" Dallas said. "Join the revolution. A revolution in New Or*leans.*" He laughed. "That ought to be your kind of revolution."

"Where do you get off, for Christ's sake?" Lee said. "I'm trying to . . . trying with you to . . . at least to touch base. There are things I could tell you, things I've heard that would . . . but they're all lies and why should I make you miserable with a lot of lies? I don't hate you. But *you.* What is it with you? You *hate* me. Why? I never did a goddamn thing to you. *She* talks all week to me about God, but does she talk to you about hating me? Do you, Lorene? Do you?"

"Yes," Dallas said. "She talks to me about that."

"You haven't got anything to worry about with me," Lee said. "I'm not coming back to your church. I'm not interviewing anybody else. You don't have to worry about me making fun of your church or your God or your wife or your preacher. I never *was* going to do that, *never*. It's in your *head* that they're vulnerable, that they're easy to make fun of, and so you hate me because you think I can do it. But I don't want to. I care about them. About *you*." He was weeping openly, tears running down his face. He seemed not to be aware that his face was wet with tears. "We're brothers. We're all the family we have."

"You've got Daddy," Dallas said, still in his flat country voice.

"Dallas," Lorene said. "Dallas, don't *do* that. You're wrong to do that."

"Never mind Daddy," Lee said. "Never mind all the insinuations, the innuendos, whatever they mean. Peace, brother." His voice broke. "That's all I'm saying. Peace."

I suppose he meant it. Yes, however hard it is for me to believe, he meant it. Even then I knew it.

"And *you* need to come away, too," he said. "You'll get so tangled up here, you'll . . ."

"We've got to go," Dallas said. "I've got to go home and dress for church." He started the truck and put his hand on the stick to shift. He looked at Lorene, at me, at Miriam, at Lee. "I got to stay here," he said. His face was stiff, every word coming out of his mouth as if he willed himself not to hold it back. "I don't see no place else to go. Whatever comes of it, I'm staying."

Lorene gave Miriam her look. "It's God's will that you're here," she said. "The Spirit is leading us *all*."

They drove away.

"What did all that mean?" Miriam said when they were gone.

"I don't know," I said.

"I'm going to town to pack, Miriam," Lee said. "I'll see you later. OK?"

"Yes," she said.

By the fence the cow lowed a quiet evening message to her calf. A few drops of rain spattered the roof. From the other side of the ravine now, I could hear Sam's and Leila's voices, laughing first, then in unintelligible murmured conversation.

"We need to talk, Alan," Miriam said.

I put down the hammer and dropped the nails into the pocket of my apron. "Don't go," I said. "I *love* you, Miriam. Don't go."

TWENTY-FIVE

IT BEGAN to rain while Miriam and I were talking and it rained all night—one of those rains that ride in on the leading edge of a Gulf storm, so hard and steady that within a few hours every gully and ravine and creek and bayou is filling its banks. Gusts of wind drove hailstones clattering against the tin roof.

I didn't sleep much. I remember getting up and going out on the long gallery where the hammock flapped and knocked against the side of the house in the wind. I took it off its hooks and rolled it up and brought it in. The wind blew in the cedar trees and gusted through the Spanish moss and the rain fell in sheets. The rainspouts at the corners of the house poured and the gutters over-flowed.

My grandfather once told me of coming home from town in a rain like that, a boy in his teens driving a horse and buggy. At that time the gully that runs under the road by Mercy Seat was an open creek bed, usually dry, worn down on either side by years of foot and horse traffic. In ordinary weather you drove the buggy through and in storms you stayed home.

That night he had set out (it took a couple of hours to make the trip in a buggy) under a shifting sky and was deep in the country when the storm began. He drove on, thinking he'd make it before the water rose, but by the time he got to Mercy Seat, the creek bed was filling fast. He urged the mare in, but halfway across, the water sucking around her hocks, she panicked and froze. Knee-deep in a strong current, he waded to her head and tried first to coax her forward, then to back her out. She reared and whinnied.

In a space of minutes, while he struggled with her, the water rose above his knees. The buggy tipped and shivered. He hadn't time to unhitch the mare, but jerked out his pocketknife and cut the traces. By the time he finished, the water was thigh-deep, the current so strong he could hardly keep his footing. He pulled at the reins again. The water was under her belly, tree limbs and trash pouring down around them.

The buggy moved and leaned in the current. He had no decision to make: before he could make one, he lost his footing, went under, fought the current, grabbed a jutting log a few yards downstream, and dragged himself out. He stood and watched the mare until she was swept down, beyond his reach, and after her the buggy.

He followed along the top of the ravine, but the mare was swept out of sight and drowned.

Miriam was gone.

Toward five in the morning the rain stopped. By the time it was daylight, the sky had cleared. I stood on the porch and stared at the dripping trees. She was gone.

"What's going on with you?" she had said, standing on the porch of my cabin while I put away my tools. "How can you stay here? Come away with us."

Us?

"Do you think there's someplace in the world that's different from here?" I said. I hadn't known I was going to say that, but saying it, I meant what I hadn't known.

"Yes," she said. *"Yes!* I hate your picturesque darkies and your seafood gumbo. Ugh. And that madwoman and her church. And Dallas. Christ! And Noah and his 'Yas, miss,' and his 'Boss man.' And that crazy self-satisfied old man with his lies about Lee's mother. And this ridiculous cabin you keep puttering around in and *that* house. Oh, it's all awful."

"Miriam . . ." My chest was full of rocks.

"You wallow in it. You love it. You're like that horrible pig behind Sam's house—eating garbage and wallowing in mud and loving it. And *me*. You don't even see me. You don't know I'm here. Who do you think I am? I'm not your dead cousin. I'm *me*."

"Why didn't you tell me what you were thinking?" I said.

"Why didn't you ask me?"

"I'm sorry," I said.

"You've never seen me or said a true word to me in my life and I didn't know it until I came down here."

But I did see her then, standing in the rainy dusk on my porch, her blue-green eyes full of tears and earnestness. "It hasn't been much of a vacation, has it?" I said.

"I don't want a vacation. I want to live in the real world where people know where I stand and what I say makes sense and what I do has some effect."

"I love you," I said again.

"You! You'll stand by and let these people crucify Lee. That's his *mother* the old man was telling lies about. His *mother*."

"Fuck Lee. Fuck the goddamn salesman."

"And why should you hate him? Wasn't all that part of our agreement from the beginning? Freedom? I *believe* in that. I don't believe in *this*."

"Are you going to share him with the woman he's already living with in New Orleans?"

"The old ways of living together don't work," she said. "You know that. Haven't we talked all that out?"

"I don't know anything, Miriam. Everything is awful with me. I love you and I'm jealous and I can't help that it wasn't in the agreement to be jealous. I think Lee is running away from the truth, whatever it is, and taking you with him and I see that he's a creepy, treacherous, self-righteous little bastard and you're far too good for him, and I can't help hating him."

"What about you and your teeny-bopper at the library? And as for the *truth*, the truth is that you ought to give Noah and Sam your damn oil wells and get out of here for good."

"How can I give away what doesn't even belong to me?"

"It *will* belong to you, and wait, you won't give it away then. *Will you?*"

"For Christ's sake, Miriam, I can see Sam at seventy, still creeping around waiting for my father to die, so he can get my third of a third of an eighth of thirty barrels of oil a day."

"*Will* you? Even then?"

"Yes," I said, "I'll give my oil away to anybody you want me to."

"And the land? The whole place? The trees and the lake and the house and the cabin?"

"No," I said. "I wouldn't if I could and there will never be any way I can. But I'll forget it all and come with you now, if you want me to. With *you*. Not him."

I was doing whatever I was doing, I can't even remember what, and she came over and pulled me down and sat facing me and we were sitting cross-legged on the floor of my porch in the sawdust, looking at each other and the rain was beginning to come harder, although not yet pouring, as it would later.

"I don't mean to be hateful," she said. "I'm sorry." She took my hand in hers and kissed it and looked at me as tenderly as she ever had in her life. "Lee," she said. "That's not the way he is. He's a wonderful, generous-hearted, open-hearted guy. He wants to be your friend. *Listen* to me." Her hair fell forward over her cheek and she pushed it back with a gesture so much her own I almost began to cry. *"Listen* to me. He believes in all the things we believe in. He wants to help make the world better."

"Oh, Miriam," I said, "here you are and here I am. I believe in you—in us."

Ah, love, let us be true to one another . . .

She was still intent on trying to persuade me, intent on Lee, smiling at her thoughts of him. "He's *grand,*" she said. "Alan, give him a chance. Give us all a chance together."

I remember her smile, when she spoke of him. She was happy. He made her happy and she wanted me to be happy, too. I remember that for an instant, for no longer, perhaps, than ten seconds, even in my misery, I saw her smile and felt my heart lift with joy at her happiness. *For that ten seconds,* I loved her.

So it was the middle of the morning on Monday. The Gulf storm had veered off toward the Mexican coast and the day was clearing. Noah had called to say that the pond behind his house had overflowed his road and the hail had damaged his roof. Sam

247

and Leila had just left the house together to go over and check his roof and then, they said, they would see how high the lake was and how the dam looked. Sam's radio had advised him that ten inches of rain had fallen in the night, the heaviest rain we'd had in years. The water in some of the ponds around Chickasaw was flowing over the tops of the dams.

I was alone in the house when the telephone rang, sitting in the parlor staring at my ancestress on the wall—the lady that my mother says looks like a preacher with a wig on and Leila says looks like me. She stared back at me from under her long blond ringlets, stared at me out of deep-set light blue eyes. It was the two dots of kremnitz white next to the pupils, I decided, that gave her the gleaming fanatic look.

Miriam was gone.

If I could put my hands around the salesman's throat, I thought, I would strangle him.

Could I?

Yes, she said.

I would like him to be dead. Could I shoot him, if he were here and I had a loaded gun?

Yes, she said.

I stood up and turned my back on her. No, I couldn't kill him. Why the hell should I kill him? She *wanted* to go with him.

I would like to kill him, sanctimonious shit.

I'm not going to kill him—or anybody. But I'll *tell* him . . . What can I say to him that will *destroy* him, make him knock off the sanctimonious shit? In front of her I'll tell him . . . and I don't care if she hears it. . . . It'll make her *see.* . . .

"I'm *open* to human experience." Was that what he had said that first night? And what was it he said about "focus" and "ideological framework"? That *she* had the mind for it? And afterwards, when she wasn't in the room, "Can she type?" But shittiest of all, that night at the church, "All I'm looking for, *ever,* Miriam, is the truth."

So you're running, coward, phony, fucker, and taking her along to protect and comfort you. To . . .

Hell, they're gone, you stupid jackass. You're not going to say *anything* to him—to them. They're gone.

I saw them again, as I had the first days, when she would go off with him—saw them driving away together, laughing, their heads close, almost going off the road in their absorption. Ugh.

To *me!* She prefers him—*that*—to me. That's the worst of it, isn't it, you vain, self-absorbed bastard? It's enough to make you doubt your own worth.

I felt so awful, so sick, so pitifully sorry for myself, so full of rage and hatred, I stood in the middle of the parlor and bellowed like a frustrated bull shut off in his pasture from a field of heifers in heat.

The telephone rang. *They're coming back. She changed her mind.*

But when I answered, Lorene's voice came over the wire, light and hurried, with an edge of hysteria. My impulse was to hang up. No Boykins today, please.

"Alan?" she said. "Alan? Something bad has happened to Dallas. Something . . . Alan?"

"Yes?" I said.

"I've been praying and praying, but . . . I'm afraid, Alan, *scared*. I had to call somebody. He . . ." Her voice broke. Then, "I'm here at the house with the baby, listening to the base and he's got the truck and . . . Are you there, Alan?"

"Yes," I said. You can't hang up on a woman who is telling you that something has happened to her husband. "What's the trouble, Lorene?"

"I'm on the base and . . ." Her voice quavered.

"Base? What are you talking about? Calm down."

"He . . . He left in the truck this morning," she said. "Last night at church he *couldn't* . . . And then the rain: like a message, like God was showing us He could wash the world clean, that only *He* could do it. But Dallas—like always, he couldn't let go. He can't understand that you don't *try*. No use to try. You have to give up. After we went to bed, it was worse. He was up and down, praying and pacing the house, and Alan, oh, I was like the disciples in the Garden. I couldn't watch and pray one hour with him and it's my fault. . . . And when I woke up, he was gone."

"What's the matter? Where is he?"

She was silent a few seconds and when she spoke her voice was quieter, less hysterical. "He said that God had told him what to do. He told me *that* before I fell asleep and explained it to me and I knew he was right, that he had to follow God's will and I said, yes, go ahead. But that's not what he's doing, I don't think that's what he's doing *at all.*"

Silence.

"Lorene?"

"I'm going to stay calm. Wait. Let me tell you. There's a CB radio in his pickup. You've seen it?"

"Yes."

"The base is here at the house, so I can always get him and he can get me when he's on the job. And the other truck, the pulpwood truck, you know, there's one in it, too, so he and Dwayne (you know, his partner), they use it when they're working different stands, to keep in touch. But Dwayne is out of town. I would have called him. . . . I shouldn't be calling you. But he's out of town and . . ."

"It's OK," I said. "But you still haven't told me what's going on."

"He left in the pickup this morning and now . . . I switched it on as soon as I got up and I've been listening for him and for a while I didn't hear him at all. And then he began to come in—not talking to *me:* he won't answer me. It sounds like . . . He's muttering and talking to himself and it sounds like he's riding around, because he fades out and then fades back in when he gets closer to home and I hear other people, too, not with him, but trying to talk to him, like . . . A few minutes ago . . . I don't want you to think I'm hysterical, but a minute ago he must have been coming toward the house, the signal—his voice—kept getting stronger, and then Mrs. Wills—she has a base in her house, just south of Mercy Seat Church—she was trying to talk to him, and then she called me and said that he had passed their house, she'd seen him out the window, doing eighty up the hill, by that deep curve. 'I don't know how he stayed on the road,' she said, 'and he was talking crazy into the CB, shouting. I think he's trying to kill himself, Lorene.' That's what she said."

"Where's the other truck?" I said. "Did his partner take it?"

"It's here—at Dwayne's trailer. They went in their car. It's the—the power of evil, Alan. Not God. He's tried to overcome it. . . ." Her voice faded as she spoke, then she came back. "Hold on. Listen." Her voice went away.

I heard the rasp of the CB channel through the phone as if she were holding the telephone receiver and the headset together and then, far away, a strange strained voice. ". . . hear me? *Jesus Christ,* buddy! What are you doing there?"

A blast of static, then Dallas's voice. "If He wants me to die, then let Him kill me."

". . . *shoulder. Take the shoulder.*"

"I'm ready."

"KRV-400. This is KRV-400 calling anybody. Maniac! There's a maniac out here. Tried to run me off the road. Somebody call the highway patrol. I'm on the Chickasaw road, north of Homochitto. Somebody . . ."

Faintly I heard Lorene's voice talking into the base sender. "KVX-219. Base to mobile. Dallas? *Come home!* He can't want you to take somebody with you, to kill somebody. . . . A stranger? A child?"

". . . not trying to run you off." (Dallas's voice.) "Nobody in this but me, friend. You were just *there.* I didn't see you, friend. I'm not . . ." Abruptly his voice went out.

"Base to mobile. Dallas?" I heard Lorene say. Then she came back on the phone. "He won't answer me. See? He's riding up and down the highway trying to get himself killed. God couldn't . . . Wait."

"Listen," I yelled. "Find out from that guy exactly where they are."

Silence. Then again I heard Lorene talking into the sender. "This is base KVX-219 to KRV-400 . . . Where are you? Out."

And then, faintly, a hollow staticky voice, getting fainter: "Seven miles north of Homochitto on the Chickasaw road. Just passed a little country store—says *Calloway's.* This guy's ahead of me now, driving a blue Chevrolet pickup, 'sixty-two, 'sixty-three model. Weaving . . . Passed me doing eighty in that old piece of truck, almost crowded me into a ravine. If anybody'd been coming over the hill . . . Wait! He just turned off. *Left* on a blacktop road, first blacktop after *Calloway's.* Call the highway patrol. He's got to be drunk—or crazy. Do you read me on that? Out."

Static.

"Yes," I heard Lorene say. "I read you. Out."

"Lorene?" I said.

"Somebody has to find him before . . ."

"Listen, I'm coming to get the other truck with the CB. It's there?"

"Yes," she said. "Their trailer is just down from us."

"That's the only way I know to get on his trail. You keep talking to him and try to get him to listen, to talk to you. OK? I'll be there in five minutes."

As soon as she heard me drive up in the pickup, Lorene came

out of her trailer with the keys to the truck in her hand. A two-ton Dodge, modified to haul pulpwood, superstructure like a gallows with a winch and chain attached onto the back. She didn't waste any time. "Get in," she said. "Hurry. Have you driven one of these?"

"I can drive it," I said.

"Are you sure? The brakes could be better, but they'll do. Just be careful. You may have to pump them a little. You know about the dog?"

"Dog?"

"Hurry. Hurry. Let me show you. This is the dog here on the stick. See? Eight gears. Four in low and then you shift the dog into high and you've got four more. It's in high now. You only use low when it's loaded. OK? Let it alone."

How the fuck . . . ? Well, I said to myself, It'll be interesting. Take my mind off my troubles.

"Now, the CB."

I gazed at her, amazed. Transformed from the pale-faced country virgin to the hysterical Christian mystic and now to this: pioneer woman, ready to drive an oil rig down the Alcan highway in midwinter.

Without wasting a word she explained how to work the CB. Then, "I've been trying to get him," she said, "but he's got his mike keyed. He's talking, talking, not listening to me or anybody. For a while he was going away, fading, but then he started to come back stronger. He's still driving around. And he can't be more than five or six miles from here or I wouldn't hear him so well. Maybe he hasn't gotten back on the highway. I haven't heard anybody else trying to talk to him. Keep listening to him and calling me, checking back with me. OK? When you get closer to him, the signal gets stronger . . ."

"Yeah, I know. Where's he most likely to go? Do you know?"

"Chickasaw. He's always wandered Chickasaw," she said. "And you know those roads after a rain. Be careful."

TWENTY-SIX

HERE'S A maze of oil field roads and old county roads and turn rows and fire lanes on Chickasaw. I know them like the back of my hand, rode them with Phoebe every summer of my childhood, on horseback to begin with, and then, as soon as she got a driver's license, in her mother's car.

Late at night all through the summers when she was sixteen and seventeen, we'd play a wild game we called Foxhunt, chasing each other, doubling back and forth, cutting from one road to another on the fire lanes. She'd be driving her car and I would have waited until everyone was asleep and sneaked away in the pickup, or whatever car I could find the keys to. On the ridge one or the other of us would stop, jump out, climb up on the hood of the car or the truck, and locate the headlights of the other tunneling through the pine plantations or under the live oaks and gum and pecan trees; jump down and take off, along some fire lane or turn row, cut the lights, stop at an intersection, and lie in wait, heart pounding, fingers on the light switch, for the other to approach. If the hunter's headlights picked up the fox as he passed, the fox was caught. Then we'd leave one car, drive to town together, and stop at Salvo's drive-in, where we could get the confection we favored at the time—a pink Italian ice.

Like most of the drive-ins where kids hung out in the fifties and early sixties, Salvo's is as empty now as an old railroad depot; but then it was swarming with cars from three or four in the afternoon until it closed at two in the morning, patronized mostly by a rougher crowd than its competitor on the other side of town—by the local hoods and red-necks. I preferred it to the place where the hip crowd—Phoebe's friends—hung out. I didn't want any competition for her attention from smooth-talking eighteen-year-old high school seniors and college freshmen leaning in the car window, flirting with her, condescending to me. As for Phoebe, I suppose she liked it because it was different—not the place to go. Besides, both of us were looking for excitement—crisis—always had been, from the days when we were eight and ten and used to dare each other to step in the quicksand.

I remember one night just a month or so before she died. I was driving—we were in Leila's GTO with its Tennessee license plates. Turned in and drove the wrong way around the parking area. There was a right way and a wrong way to turn in at Salvo's and although there were no "one-way" signs, everybody knew it. Everybody just *knew,* like you do in a small town. So I turned in going the wrong way.

Probably I did it deliberately. It was exciting to go the wrong way around at Salvo's drive-in in Homochitto in 1964. At that time in that place there were all kinds of thrills to be had in cars, if one invited them, or even if one didn't, driving in the wrong ways to the wrong places, or maybe with the wrong bumper stickers. Cars were weapons, political posters, social statements. There were parts of the state where it was dangerous to drive a car if you had a New York or a California license, where even a Tennessee license was suspect. If you were black, it was dangerous to drive any half-way decent-looking car with an out-of-state license. It was dangerous to have an LBJ or a Kennedy sticker on your bumper. Favored bumper stickers read:

PUT YOUR ♥ IN MISSISSIPPI OR GET YOUR 🐴 OUT.

So there we were in the GTO, four on the floor, three-fifty horsepower, three-eighty-nine cc's, going the wrong way around at Salvo's at one thirty in the morning, feeling courageous, powerful, invulnerable. I was still crazy with the chase, with having Phoebe out in the middle of the night, with my own adrenaline.

Somebody in a '61 Chevy, the usual Confederate flag on the windshield, leaned out to see who was violating Salvo's law of car circulation. I remember his face, round and innocent under a shock of black hair almost as curly as mine.

". . . going the wrong way!"

I tried to make myself taller and the pitch of my voice lower. "So?"

". . . understand you being so stupid if you was niggers."

We exchanged insults. I forget what I said. Something about red-necks probably.

"Goddamn hillbillies." They must have seen Leila's Tennessee license tag.

And then Phoebe, who'd seen a Louisiana license on their car: "At least we're not Coonies. Y'all just come up out of the swamp?"

I remember she leaned across me to holler out the window. I felt her breast against my arm. She was giggling.

There were four of them—sixteen-, seventeen-year-olds. The driver started their car. One of the guys in the backseat leaned out. "Fuckin Commonist nigger-lovers!"

"Come on, Alan. Let's go. We can lose them easy."

And then we were on the street again, humming along toward Chickasaw road, taking our time, waiting for them. They had to get rid of the window tray and back out of their slot. On the road, outside the city limits, with the Chevy a few blocks behind us, I felt the power of the GTO jumping under my foot. I could judge the curves like a pro. I was on the track at Indy, the last lap. The crowd roared.

"Go," Phoebe said. "Go."

We got so far ahead we had to slow down and wait for their lights to bear down on us or we would have lost them too soon. When we were sure they saw us, we speeded up, pulled away, and turned in by Mercy Seat. I spun the wheels on the gravel and raised a cloud of dust, drove on, spun the wheels again to mask the point where I planned to turn off, passed the dead-end road that led in to one of the oil well sites, McLaurin Heirs Number One, cut my lights, passed a fork in the main road, and took the first turn to the right. Beyond me, I knew, another right turn led down to a pond that had been an abandoned oil well site before we dug it out and dammed it, and beyond that the road went meandering across the place and came out on Duck Pond, with half a dozen turnoffs and double-backs before you got there.

The road I took ran out at an old barn, but on the other side of the barn there was a fire lane leading back to the house and lake. We eased along the fire lane with the lights off, stopped on top of the ridge behind the house, got out of the car, and climbed up on the hood. We could see the lights of our pursuers tunneling through the trees, blundering this way and that. They would never find their way to us, hidden now in the end of the fire lane, high above them.

Phoebe jumped off the hood of the car and lay down on the pine needles and I lay beside her and we rolled over and over, giggling and moaning with joy at the success of our adventure.

I looked up at the deep sky, pure and black, and picked out the two or three constellations I knew and showed them to Phoebe— Cassiopeia, the Pleiades, and, on the southern horizon, Pisces Austrinus.

We heard the drone of a motor and the spurt of gravel and, climbing back on the hood, saw the lights of the other car moving down the road that ended at the pond, then heard it turning and saw the lights coming back. After a while, when everything was still and dark and we knew our pursuers must be gone for good, Phoebe climbed down and turned on the car radio and kicked off her shoes and began to dance by herself in the pine needles and I lay on the ground with my head propped on my elbow and watched her until she cut off the radio and threw herself down by me and grabbed my hand in both of hers.

"Oh, Alan, I want to *do* something," she said. "Something grand. Something big. I don't want just to outwit red-necks and dance in the pine needles and play Foxhunt. Oh, it doesn't matter how beautiful everything is, it doesn't matter how happy we are. . . . I want to *do* something."

Lust! Christ, that poor miserable boy! But she was unconscious of his feelings, full of vague yearnings and sisterly love.

What I started to say was that, because of our fox-hunting game, I knew the back roads on Chickasaw better than anyone except maybe Noah and Sam; and so, in the pulpwood truck, with the CB on, listening for Dallas, I began to cast back and forth across the place.

For a little while he was silent. I'd hear Lorene calling him: *Come home*. But I said nothing. I didn't want him to know I was looking for him. Then all at once, while I was cruising along on the north end of the place, his voice came in, faraway and weak.

"I tried to tell them, Lorene," he said. "I tried. They wouldn't listen."

He was silent again for maybe a minute or two and then he began to talk, and once he had begun he didn't shut up.

TWENTY-SEVEN

TO BEGIN with, listening to Dallas, trying to use his voice and Lorene's on the base to triangulate, I only halfway paid attention to what he was saying. I drove, the tearing sound of gravel raveling out behind me, the gallows shadow of the winch rushing along the ground beside me. I concentrated on bucking that stiff two-ton over ruts and washouts and wondered why the hell it was me who had to be out chasing a lunatic around the county because the Holy Ghost wouldn't visit him. But afterwards I remembered most of what he said as I remember what I have said myself.

He began with some crazy talk about the law and amnesia:

"I don't care about the law. There's nothing in it about the law. It's God's law that matters, not the U.S. government or the state of Mississippi. Like the lawyer said about that guy they had on trial for murder over in Buchanan County last year. The law gave him a gun, taught him how to use it, told him killing was the thing to do, sent him out there and had him killing slopes for a year, and then brought him home and said, Now, son, it ain't right anymore. You done all the killing we need, so quit. He got off. He had a smart lawyer, but he was meant to get off. The lawyer wasn't just smart. He was right. Well, I went through all that. I killed slopes like they told me to and it wasn't so bad. You get so you like doing it, or I did, because every one I killed was one couldn't kill me and I can't stand to think anybody is going to fuck over me, much less kill me.

("Lorene, you have to listen to this like I'm telling it, dirty words and all, because I'm going to lay it out not just to you but to whoever wants to listen exactly like I think it and say it to myself. That's the *only way*.)

"I could always take care of myself and I didn't want to die. (Not that I cared so much whether I died or not. It wasn't that. It was knowing some slope even shorter than me living on a bowl of rice a day, or maybe even some slope *kid* had fucked over me.)

"That's not the main thing I mean to talk about, but it's part of it. I never had trouble confessing to God or anybody else about killing slopes. I would have confessed it to *them,* if I could've gone back over there and if the Lord led me to it. And they would've said, OK, they were supposed to kill me, too, and it was all right. It was an open book. Well, the law said I could be proud of it and I suppose I was, until Lorene showed me that was no way for a man to live and took all that meanness out of me and begun to lead me to the Spirit. And even then, I knew and she knew I'd done what I had to. But when we begun to talk that out, all the *other*—the old business—came up and begun to get to me.

"Not that I'd *forgotten.* I'm not like Lindsay Lee. I don't understand him and never did. What do you think goes on inside a man's head can make him *forget*—forget what he saw, what he said and did?

"Like in some old movie on TV where the guy leaves home and goes to war and a shell explodes in his ear and he wakes up in the hospital and can't remember who he is and he goes off and finds a new wife (rich) and starts all over again. I know it happens. They didn't make those movies out of nothing. But it could never happen to me. I never in my life woke up in the morning and didn't remember what I did the day before. I can remember seeing my mama change Lindsay Lee's diaper when I was two years old. Oh, I might forget who Truman's vice-president was.

But I'm talking about what counts for me—or for Lorene and me and my boy.

"I never was able, either, to kid myself like he did and does, and I reckon kidding yourself is training for amnesia.

"When did he forget?

"Right off, I think. Immediately.

"We looked at each other that night, after it was over, when we were still on top of the hill where we could see everything, and he pointed his finger at me—still not dark, the moon coming up, and I could see him pretty good, and he said, '*You.*' Like, *You did it.* And I looked back at him and didn't say anything and he turned and run off down the hill and when I got home a couple of hours later (I stayed and watched a long time, the whole thing, until the fire went out) he was asleep. He slept all the next morning. Then he woke up with a high fever and was out of his head.

"So he was sick a few days.

"And I was sick, too, holed up in the woods mostly, couldn't stand to see a human face, thinking about it, thinking about it. I got so I wished I could take a saw and saw the top off my head and reach in with a spoon and scrape my brains out and throw them away. That would be the only way I could stop thinking about it.

"Well, we never have been a family that talked. Alan, people like him, talk, talk, talk. It's like talking is what people are supposed to do. To me it's weakness. I hate it. And now I'm talking for the first time, saying all this—but I wouldn't be, if . . . if Sam or Chipman would've listened to what I want to say *to them only.* They didn't need explanations. All I would have said to them was: I'm sorry. Forgive me or kill me or whatever you have to do. It's OK."

It was when he said, "if Sam or Chipman would have listened . . ." that the rocks in my chest began to shift and grind against each other and I began to listen with more attention and to feel myself press my foot down on the accelerator and then to ease off and say to myself, *Hey, what's going on here?*

And he went on talking and I went on tracking, listening, beginning to know that what he was saying didn't concern just him and the Holy Ghost.

"So we none of us talked about what happened that night," he said. "Daddy knew we'd been up there. He never said a word. As for Lindsay Lee, as soon as the fever left him, it seemed like he begun talking and he hasn't stopped yet. Like his nature changed. But he never talked about what had happened. And after I begun to come out of myself, I knew that either he had forgot or he was pretending he had forgot. I didn't care. If he wanted to spend his time on earth kidding himself, that was his business. After a while, I decided he wasn't pretending. Some way he would've given himself away to me.

("I won't die, Lorene. I won't ask Him anymore to kill me. I see the sin in it. I'll do *this* and then I'll go where the Spirit leads me.)

"It seems as if I could just *say*—just confess in about three sentences to anybody that wants to listen—and then shut up and be through with talking. But I don't want to make any mistakes. I want to be sure He sees that I've looked at every corner of my soul and said what's in it, at every rotten termite-eaten board and every choked-up drain spout and broken shingle and even every spiderweb that might not bother me, but that Lorene would take a broom to before she could move in. I want everything out in the open, and then . . . then the Spirit will come, and the fruit. . . . Yes, the fruit of the Spirit, like you said, Lorene, love and joy and *peace*. . . .

"So I'm going to go on, one step and one sentence at a time, and cover the whole thing. I can ride around this county all day. . . .

"What time is it?

"Is anybody listening?"

Yes.

"All right. Lindsay Lee took sick, got a fever, and begun talking. All that has happened in his life since then, I think, come out of that night. He run off, of course, the next year, soon after our daddy remarried. He wasn't but fifteen. Maybe it was looking at Daddy and me every day and having to keep on forgetting what he knew and what he knew we knew. Daddy went after him and brought him back but he run off again.

"Started hanging out with hippies and then with niggers. By the time he was sixteen he was out on his own, become a crusader or so he would want you to believe. No, that's not the way to say it.

I'm not saying he's a fake—or a coward. Not about the world—only about the inside of his own soul. He and those people he hung out with would get on a bus with niggers in Birmingham or Yazoo City or Philadelphia, Miss. (if there was such a thing as a bus in those towns), sit on the front seat with them, and stare down any red-neck that got on. And not only in the daytime, either.

"As for my mother, that's the part *I* would forget, if I could. I would forget she died. I would forget . . . what? Lorene says she was a good Christian and that I don't have to even think about what a hard life she had, how my daddy and Lindsay Lee and me were a cross to her, that she's with God.

"I *know* the Spirit come down on her. I've seen it happen more than once. And God took her, Lorene says, in His own time and for His own reasons.

"But I would forget what she suffered, with none of us paying attention. I would forget her face, how she looked at me like she had *something*—something she needed to say. . . .

"And then the money came. I never knew the straight of *that*. The money made it worse.

"He—my daddy—must have turned in *somebody*. Why? For the money? That's bound to be why. And after all he preached to us about principles and responsibility.

"But I didn't care about that, either. All that was *nothing* to me.

"The way it all happened, the reason we got mixed up in it to begin with, was because of him. He was going to the meetings and sometimes he took me and Lindsay Lee with him. I didn't have my mind on it, to tell the truth. I wasn't but fifteen, after all. I went because he took us, and it made kids like us feel like men to go off with the men in the pickup trucks and go to somebody's house where there were nothing but men and a few older boys and talk about men's business. Especially since there seemed to be some danger in it and it was a secret from everybody. But once we got there, I would be thinking mostly about . . . well, maybe I'd be thinking about what I'd been doing that day, or what I'd be doing tomorrow, about fishing or hunting, or . . .

"I'm lying. I'd be thinking about fucking. (All right, Lorene. It has to be. I have to tell it. You say to confess, to right wrongs. You say I've got to be sure to tell the straight truth, but I know you don't want to hear about my lusts, my carnal thoughts. I can't help it. It has to be. I know *you*. You'd say, 'You don't have to confess *that*. That's *nothing*, Dallas. You were just a little kid and you didn't have any understanding. God wouldn't hold those lusts against you.' But thinking about fucking was what started the whole thing, so it has to go in, the way it was.)

"Lorene says she used to kiss the bedpost when she was thirteen, fourteen, dreaming it was some boy she loved. She knew she had to get married quick or sin and that God would forgive all that when she was married. (That's the way you would think Lorene, not me. That would've been sin to your mind, when you were that age. And even now.)

"But it was more than that with me. My lusts were too strong for me—all my lusts, even when I was that young. I wasn't even *thinking* about sin—in spite of all my mother tried to teach me about pure thoughts and clean lives. I was thinking about fucking. It was too strong for me to let the thought of sin get in my way. I took out after every little girl that looked halfway interested and I got some—not enough to suit me, but some.

"That's the way it was with me then. And *now* . . . Now it's just as bad in other ways. I told Lorene (I never thought I could confess *this* to anyone, Lorene, but you) sometimes I feel so full of rage—the lust of rage (at what? I don't even know at what) that I know I might kill my boy. I *know* it's possible I could do that. It was when I told her *that* (mind you, I hadn't laid a finger on him. I might whale him when he's older, if he needs it, but she knew I wasn't talking about anything like that), it was when I said *that* to her that she said I didn't need her to tell me nothing could save me from that—nothing but the Holy Spirit.

"So I understand how bad a man could need to have amnesia.

"But it's all in me and I can't ever forget it or lie to myself about it.

"There was something else in it, too, that spring and summer of 'sixty-four, when I was fifteen. I was already looking for love and I didn't have sense enough to know how or where to look, didn't know what I was looking for.

"And then in May . . .

"I saw her the first time one afternoon in May.

"Oh, I'd *seen* her. I knew her. By that time I'd been coming around to get Alan to go fishing with me for three or four years. He admired me, more like a younger kid than one my own age;

and who doesn't like to have somebody hanging around that you always know more than, that you can be superior to? (That's the truth, too, one more thing I never lied to myself about.) So I'd seen her and I recognized her. But the year before, the last time I'd seen her, we'd both been different. I hadn't been thinking about fucking twenty-four hours a day, and she hadn't got to be what she was that summer.

"She used to ride the big bay stallion that belongs to the niggers and that was the way I saw her. I was walking along the road toward the graveyard pond, had come in the back way across the cattle gap that marks the line between Chickasaw and the Shields place, and here she came flying down the road. She'd let her hair grow since the summer before and it hung down below her waist, thick and coarse and blond, flying out now, as she rode, so that the first thing you thought of if you were a kid like me, raised night after night on Bible-reading, was how Absalom died. But I only thought about Absalom for about five seconds. After that I thought about Phoebe."

Phoebe? Phoebe?

"She pulled up when she saw me and said hello to me like we'd just seen each other last week and I must've stared at her, I suppose, because then she said something like, 'Hey, Dallas! *Dallas!* Aren't you going to speak to me?' And she took one foot out of the stirrup and cocked it up across the front of the saddle (she had one of those fancy pancake saddles like you see in the movies) and lifted that long heavy hair off her neck and stretched her neck up and arched her back and I could see the little blond shiny hairs glittering on the insides of her thighs, and her nipples under the T-shirt she had on. 'It's hot already, isn't it?' she said, and she pulled the hair over one shoulder and separated it into strands and begun to braid it, sitting on the horse in the middle of the road, me standing below her gaping up like a scared kid, and I *was* a kid, but not scared, just feeling like I must be dreaming.

"*Now* it seems to me I stayed in a dream all the rest of that spring and summer. I quit thinking about other girls. I even quit jerking off. I was like a monk or a bridegroom.

"I'd been fishing around here and there and, at night, frog-grabbing—everybody knew me and nobody cared if I fished their ponds —but after that I stuck to Chickasaw, wandered Chickasaw night and day. I'd come out every afternoon soon as I got off the school bus, make a beeline for Chickasaw, in hopes I might see her. I give up all thoughts of everybody else. Or don't call it thoughts. I wasn't thinking. I just come and waited and watched her.

"What the hell is in a kid's mind when something like that happens to him? She was two years older than me, remember that. I figured I couldn't possibly have a chance with her. I dreamed about growing up and going off and getting as tall as John Wayne and making a million dollars and coming back and she wouldn't even know me and I would introduce myself to her one day. Maybe I'd be riding my palomino that I had bought someplace out West where they raise the best palominos, and I'd be riding along the road, along the cut there on the way to the graveyard pond. I'd have a big creaky saddle, all tooled leather and silver fittings, and she would come along, like the day I first saw her on the big stallion, and just when she'd come even with me, the stallion would bolt and I would take out after her and catch up and grab the reins, because she would've lost her head and would be screaming for help. And she wouldn't even recognize me at first. That's the kind of kid fantasies I would have, watching her every afternoon that spring.

"She was a strange one and nobody knew her but me. That was what I thought. She was *my* secret. Because how many girls like that—seventeen years old, getting sexy and just beginning to know it, girls whose families are rich, who can go to the dances and belong to the clubs and so on, how many of them would want to spend their afternoons bucking around a place like Chickasaw on an old stallion? They're in town, fixing their fingernails, listening to the Beatles on their hi-fi, figuring out how to keep this or that guy on their string without giving him any pussy, talking to their girl friends about who's making out and who isn't, sneaking off with their boy friends and drinking beer and thinking it's a big deal. But not her. There she was, out there all by herself, just about every afternoon in the week. I got so I knew what wagon tracks and roads she'd take and, where the tracks doubled around the ravines and ridges, I could cut across and lie down on a bluff above the track and wait for her. I'd hear her, or rather, hear her horse a long way off, if I put my ear to the ground like in the old cowboy movies, and then here she'd come and I would watch her ride by. And I would know why she did it, because that was the way I wanted to spend my time, too.

"And I knew that all those woods and flowers and the creek belonged to her and me, because nobody else cared about them but us.

"There was a bayou emptied into the creek and the source of it was an old spring that all those town people on Chickasaw and even the niggers had long since forgotten, and she would tie her horse by the spring and climb down into the ravine and follow the bayou, going along the bottom, and I would follow, up above her head on the bluff. I could hear her, when I lost sight of her, but she never knew I was there. The ferns grew out of the banks and dripped water, sometimes on her face and hair, and the hydrangeas were all covered with pale flowers, and the branches of the oak trees met across the top of the ravine, and it was like the beginning of the world; and I would see her walking along, climbing over a log, and the sun shining in the drops of water in her hair.

"Sometimes, all of a sudden, she would stop and look up like she expected to see something, and I would wonder if she knew I was watching her.

"We'd had heavy rains in April. For a couple of days the water was as high on the dam as it is now and the spillway was under ten feet or more. The fall of the land, see, from where the bayou empties into the creek all the way down to the lake, is steep, and big rains like that scour the creek out and the logs wash down and hang up and change the course, so that every year, sometimes oftener, there will be a new swimming hole.

"The bluffs along the creek are thirty, forty feet high, and the wild purple mulberry bushes and hydrangeas and wax myrtles grow out of the banks and hang down toward the water. And the pine trees and oaks lean out over the edge of the bluff and grow up out of its sides and down below, the water is cold and clear as glass running over the sand, and you see the little striped bass holding themselves against the current and the blue kingfishers sitting on snags cocking their heads and watching the water, and the herons wading.

"I used to go back there with my mother when I was a little kid, and she would dig herbs and wood ferns and flowers and take them home and plant them around the house and tell me the names of all of them. Oh, it's better than anything I ever saw when I was in the army and went to Colorado and saw all those big mountains.

"Well. . . . So Phoebe would leave her horse by the spring

and go along and sometimes she would find a path the cattle had made when they went down to drink, where she could take the horse down to the creek bed and walk him along in the water; and I wanted to tell her not to, because there is quicksand, but I never did find any deep enough to be all that dangerous (I'd wish it *would* be dangerous, so I could save her) and so I never said anything, I just went along on the bluff and watched. And at one place just before the creek opened out into the lake a big log had washed down and lodged so that a new swimming hole had been made beyond where the log and the trash piled up behind it blocked the main channel. The water was deep and green, *still,* the current rippling over the sand and around the end of the log and then pouring into the hole and spreading and getting quiet as the lake.

"And the third time I followed her, she rode the horse all the way down the creek bed and when she came to the swimming hole, she tied him to a tree root sticking out of the bluff and . . .

"Is there anybody listening to me? You might think . . ."

God knows I was listening and it was like listening to my own voice.

". . . might think I'm gonna say she got naked and went swimming and . . . what? I raped her, maybe? But she was two inches taller than me and two years older—a grown woman to me, and I knew she thought I was a kid. I'd've played hell raping her. What went on in my mind was, I was afraid she would laugh at me or feel sorry for me if she even dreamed of the way I felt. And at the same time I was sure that she was . . . was *like* me, that if she knew me, she would love me. And so, all that happened was that she walked out on the log and sat down and took off her shoes and socks and threw them over onto the little strip of gravelly beach at the edge of the pool and put her feet in the water and sat there a long time while I lay in the grass up over her head and looked down at her sitting there.

"That's the way it went for two months, until Alan and his family came.

"Are you listening? Is anybody listening but you, Lorene? Maybe I started out talking without explaining why I'm doing it this way. I *know* the ones who count aren't listening. Sam's not listening. What's it to him? He didn't care and he still doesn't. That's what it looks like to me. I went and tried to tell him first. Lorene said, Yes, you're right. Go and tell him and tell Mr. Chipman, and then you can get right. It's no use worrying about going to jail or none of that. And I don't. Jail is all the same to me now, I'm in some kind of jail already and I've got to get out of it even if it means getting sent to another one. But I know you, Lorene. You've thought about it every way, from every angle, and you don't think I'll go to jail. Who would want to spend money on sending me to jail? Who would want to drag up all that old business? Nobody wants to think about those days anymore, if they can help it. *Nobody.* Something might come out that would be an embarrassment. But you didn't think that even *Sam,* even Chipman, wouldn't care, wouldn't want to hear it, that I'd be left with what happened, that I couldn't hand it to anybody. That nobody would kill me, or hit me, or even curse me. And that the Spirit would still draw back from me."

Tell *what?* They wouldn't want to hear *what?* Damn crazy man! Whatever the sin he thought he'd committed against Phoebe—dead Phoebe—the world didn't need to hear about it. I drove more and more carefully, followed him, as I thought, more and more craftily. I would not skid off the road. I would not get mired down in a washout. I would grip the steering wheel and watch the road and I would find him.

"But that's the way it was. I left you asleep, Lorene, early this morning soon after the rain let up, and went to tell them. I stood in the door of Sam's house and looked at him and he looked over my shoulder and didn't say, Come in, and so I had to tell him, standing in the door of his house, who I was and what I wanted and after I had begun to tell him, he passed his eye over me and I felt it like fire, like he could turn me to ashes if he wanted to, and then he looked way beyond me again and said, 'I've moved on from that night, white boy. I know all I need to know about it. I don't want to hear nothing you've got to say,' and he shut the door in my face."

Sam? *Sam?*

"And Chipman, when I tried to tell him: I drove straight from

Sam's to his house, because I wanted to see him at home, not down where he works and where his office has glass all around it and people can see him; because that might keep him from doing whatever he had to do to me. But even though I thought about *that,* in some ways I was still a coward. I couldn't have told *her*—the mother. Because what could she do to me? How could she punish me? She would just have to hear it and suffer. So I had thought ahead of time that I would ask him to come outside. But I didn't have to. He was coming out of the house when I got there, dressed up like he always is, with his shoes polished and his hair clipped, and I stopped him when he was laying his hands on the car door. He stood there with the keys in one hand and the other on the door and never moved toward me or away. Only his face looked like it begun to shrivel—it puckered in on itself like an apple drying up. And he said, 'I already know it was you—or somebody like you. Do you think it matters? All that matters is for things to stay like they are. For Denny and me not to have to think about it. So keep your secrets to yourself. I'm going to forget I ever heard of you, much less saw you.' And he got in the car and started it up and then he said, 'Besides, I don't believe you. Do you understand? You must be crazy. You probably need to see a doctor.'

"*I already knew it was you or somebody like you.* And at the same time, *I don't believe you.*

" 'Go on away,' he said. 'Go away.' And he rolled his window up and I saw him push down the button to lock his car door like I might be going to try to get in with him and attack him and he sat and waited until I got in my truck and drove off.

"I felt like my head was going to explode, Lorene. What am I going to do now? I said. Where am I going to take myself? And the Spirit drew back from me. I felt the drawing off. Outside the ditches were running and the streets flooded, but inside I felt the Spirit drawing off like the world was dried out, like what was in my head making it want to explode was a whirlwind of dust, a dust devil like you see in the fields in August. At first I couldn't think of anything to do but drive up and down and I didn't know what I was doing it for, but then I looked at the CB. *He* guided me to the CB and said, '*Speak.*'

"So here I am. I'm talking to whoever wants to or needs to listen. That's what I have to do. And I've got the mike keyed, see,

269

so nobody can stop me, nobody can break in until I've finished. And then let them come, whoever they are, and do whatever they have to do. I'm in His hands."

TWENTY-EIGHT

"ALL RIGHT. I'm going on with it.

"Alan and his family come on down to Chickasaw like they did every summer and she—Phoebe—began to go out on the lake with him. I wasn't jealous. Alan didn't seem like much to me then. Him being there was like you might be listening to a beautiful piece of music and begun to hear static in the background. And so I wouldn't follow them when they went off together, only her when she went alone. But she wasn't alone all that much anymore.

"And some days I would come around and get Alan to go fishing with me, like I always had. And I wished he would mention her or that I could talk to him about her. All the time we would be out together fishing (like a kid out on a date who, all the time he's chattering to the girl he's with, saying things that don't even make sense, all that time he's saying over and over to himself, Now in a minute I'm going to brush against her arm, now in a minute I'm going to kiss her, I'm going to put my hand on her leg, and so forth and so forth), all the time we'd be fishing and I would be saying nothing except about where we were going to find the next bass or what was wrong with the way he was casting, I'd be thinking the things I wanted to say about her. Not because I wanted to *confide* in him. I didn't care a shit about confiding in anybody. I just wanted to hear myself talking out loud about her to *anybody* —to hear anybody say her name to me.

"Ah, I was crazy, crazy. For her, at fifteen, I give up fucking. Can you believe it?

"At the same time, everything at home was boiling like a pot of dirty clothes. Mama was looking thinner and sadder every day. She was sick already that spring and early summer, although she never went to the doctor, so far as I know. She went to church a lot and she prayed a lot, and I didn't think about it, the way you don't think about your mother if you can help it when you're fifteen.

"Lorene says the cancer begun in her soul, not her liver like the doctor told us afterwards. This is what she thinks: that evil—the Devil—attacks in different ways and one way people have of fighting him off is cancer. And there are people like this and you can tell it by looking at them—dark, nervous, silent people like my mother. So when temptation comes, when the evil in the world weighs down on them, instead of sinning, these people keep their souls pure and then the evil takes over the cells in their bodies. And if they are strong enough in their faith or if the evil is weaker than they are, sometimes they can fight it off, but more often it kills them. She says my mother was a cancer person like that and she must've had some terrible thing eating at her soul and her soul was steadfast, so it attacked her body. She says so from what I tell her and from looking at pictures of my mother, because she never knew her.

"I know my mother was strong in her faith, but there was something else she had, *Grace*, that's what I have to call it, and oh, it should have been—it was—strong enough to stand up against the Devil no matter where he attacked.

"I look at her face in the pictures and what I see is that it looks a lot like me. I know I keep my face *still* like she did and when I talk I practice keeping my voice level, *plain*. I'd just as soon nobody knew from my face or voice what I was thinking or feeling, like it's weakness to spread out your life on your face and in your voice. But I haven't got her faith. And the Grace won't come down on me. So there will be nothing to keep the cancer from taking my soul instead of my body.

"And if I'm talking, talking today, it may not be just to confess, but because I have to go down in weakness to come through, to give up not just the worst in me, but the best, my will, my pride, to kill the cancer in my soul or let it have my body, if that's God's will.

"Anyhow, at home that spring and summer she was weakening, and my daddy was gone all the time—gone to work in the daytime, gone to the meetings at night, taking me and Lindsay Lee with him sometimes, but not all the time. And then summer come on and the college kids we'd been hearing about begun to come down and spread through the state and we heard at the meetings there were three or four of them in Homochitto County, going around picking up niggers, taking 'em to register, holding meetings at the churches and all that. I don't have to fill anybody in on that—everybody knows. But I didn't care. I didn't care then and I don't care now. Who gives a damn if the niggers vote? They're welcome to do what they want to as far as I'm concerned. Anybody is. All I want is to go my own way—God's way. But at the same time, I liked to go to the meetings and I would say to myself when we got in the truck to go: *If she could see me now, she'd know I was a man.* We would come out of the house and we'd be carrying our guns. I had a bolt-action Springfield thirty-aught-six that I'd got from the army surplus. I'd saved my money two years to buy it, working for my daddy Saturdays and some in the summers. (I'll say this for him. He would pay us fair wages when we worked for him and he paid the niggers better than us.) And Lindsay Lee had a little no-'count twenty-two. And we'd put them up in the gun rack and start out and there would be some low-voiced double-talk on the CB's and we might ride around awhile to make sure nobody was following us and then we'd pull up at some dark house where men were gathering—coming across backyards and out of shadows and all I would think to myself would be, *She'd know I was a man if she could see me now,* and I would decide to borrow the twenty-two from Lindsay Lee and ask her if she'd like to go target shooting with me some afternoon, because I knew she'd like that, and I would figure on how I could manage it so Alan wouldn't tag along.

"That's what I would be thinking about.

"And I didn't pay attention to anything my mother said during that time, not anything at all, because that wasn't what I was thinking about.

"But even so I remember being impatient with her and brushing her off sometimes when we would be leaving and she would want to touch me, kiss me. A fifteen-year-old kid *hates* for his mother to touch him. And I didn't understand what she was in such a sweat about, why she didn't want me to go and she didn't want Lindsay Lee to go and she didn't even want the old man to go.

"One night especially I remember because they had an actual fight about it. I hung my head and was ashamed for them. They were decent people, my mother and daddy, and they didn't fight before the kids and he never hit her in his life, so far as I know. But that night she had Lindsay Lee locked up in his room and she said I could go, I was old enough to be responsible for my own soul, but Lindsay Lee wasn't going, and my daddy was saying things like, 'Now, Sally, it ain't right for you to cross me with the boys,' and things like that, and she run at him and begun to hit him. And he said, 'Sally, you're sick. Ain't no explanation I can think of other than that for you to hit me.' And she said, 'You know why I'm hitting you.' And he said, 'You need to see a doctor,' and he took her under one arm because he was strong even if he wasn't any bigger than me and held her there and reached in her pocket and got the key out of it and let Lindsay Lee out of his room and said, 'Come on, son.' And all the time she was batting at him and he didn't pay the least bit of attention. 'I'm doing what's right, that's all,' he said. And 'Somebody's got to keep things under control,' and 'Do you want people to think you got a coward for a husband, Sally?' And I especially remember as we were going out the door, in that quiet voice, 'Do you want some nigger to take the bread out of your children's mouths? Do you?' And she said, 'I'm going to stop you. I'm going to find some way to stop you. You wait.'

"I was embarrassed for them, trying not to watch them. Lindsay Lee had run out of the house when Daddy opened the door and he was sitting in the truck already with his fingers in his ears and I went on ahead of Daddy and left him there to calm my mother down and when I got to the truck, I gave Lindsay Lee a shove and said, 'Dummy! Baby! Take your fingers out of your ears,' and climbed in by him.

"But even while I said it, even while I was embarrassed for my mother and father in one part of my mind, I was still thinking, If she could see me now, she'd know I was a man, and looking around at the thirty-aught-six up in the gun rack; and after I batted Lindsay Lee's hands away from his ears I reached back and rubbed my thumb over the plate and along the curve of the stock.

"That must have been in June after Alan and his family come. It may have been the same night the men got to talking about the church meetings and begun to organize to put a stop to them. I don't know, I never paid all that much attention.

"Then, not so long afterwards, there come a night when they said there was going to be a meeting the following Monday night at Mercy Seat Church. And of course that was our part of the county, so my daddy was put in charge of it.

"What they had been doing at the other church meetings: they'd station somebody to take license numbers of all the cars were there and of course, too, if it was your part of the county, you'd recognize some of the niggers—and then, the ones you didn't know, they would have somebody to go the next day and look up the license numbers at the courthouse and read out the lists at the meetings. Anybody who knew a nigger who'd been at a church meeting would say what he knew about him. And there were different ways of dealing with him. Like somebody might say a word to the guy he worked for: This nigger is going to Communist meetings, and so forth. Or, if somebody felt like he had a good relationship with the nigger, he might volunteer to go and talk to him and explain to him that he was making a mistake, headed for trouble. And we had a couple of preachers would go talk to the nigger preachers and the board of deacons and some of the big church mothers, explaining to them how these college kids from the North, kids that didn't know nothing about the circumstances of their lives, were going to get them in trouble and how their church was going to get a bad reputation and so forth.

"One or two of these preachers were *out of it*. The things they said—not even halfway paying attention, I heard craziness like I hadn't heard before or since, like if you married into the line of Cain you had to be degenerate and your children would be degenerate, and that was where niggers come from; and that if you consorted with niggers you'd get something wrong with your liver and this was why it was bad to sit next to one. According to them that was the main meaning of the sins of the fathers being visited on the children.

"But my daddy didn't talk that stuff. He didn't say much of anything at the meetings except that we had to persuade the niggers of what was best for them and us both. It was all going to be persuasion, according to him.

"And I reckon at the beginning most everybody thought that would work and the niggers would see reason and the kids would go home—they were mostly rich college kids, after all, and who would have expected them to stick it out the way they did? But they turned out to be crazy, and the niggers were crazy, too. Everybody down here was crazy that summer, one way or another. And so it all got out of hand, as everybody knows.

"So my daddy said everybody had to learn to be responsible and that he was teaching Lindsay Lee and me to be responsible and we couldn't go and not do our part, and so when they were going to have the meeting at Mercy Seat, he told us that it would be our job to watch and take down the license numbers, and that he would go with us and help us and be there. And one day we walked over the area and he picked out a spot for us up on top of the bluff where we could look down on the road where it turned in to Mercy Seat and also down on the parking area in front of the church. And he got us pads and pencils to write down names and numbers and we took our guns because we both had telescopic sights on them, so we could see the faces and the plates, but he told us to unload them, because he didn't want us getting in any kind of trouble. And he picked out another spot for himself back behind the church and on up the road a little piece, so we wouldn't miss anybody might be coming in from the Duck Pond side and might park in the back.

"I was listening to what he told us in an absentminded way when he took us over there. I could see it would be fun to train the sights of my thirty-aught-six on the license plates and the faces and see who I knew and write everything down. I wanted to do it, I was excited about it, but at the same time it wasn't important to me. . . .

"I wanted to see her that afternoon—the afternoon of the meeting—and so I told Lindsay Lee I had some things to see to and he should meet me on the bluff where the road divides where we were supposed to be, that I would come around through the woods and he could go with my father. I went like I always did to watch the road by the lake and the creek to see if she would be riding that day. But she was already gone. I could look over the whole lake from the high point above the ravine at the south end and I saw her and Alan out in the canoe together and then they paddled up toward the cove where the creek opens out into the lake. I was carrying my gun and I could see them through the sights, as plain as if I was sitting in the canoe with them. They looked so friendly and easy with each other, it made the muscles in my arms ache to watch them, and for the first time that day I envied Alan, little pipsqueak, curly-headed, tow-headed, blue-eyed virgin kid, because he was so easy with her. Watching them, I ached, my arms ached and the back of my shoulder on one side, like it had a knot in it. I could hear their voices echoing across the lake like you can some days in some spots. It's strange how voices carry across water that way and you can hear someone far off when maybe somebody just a couple of hundred yards away will wave and yell and you can barely hear them at all. And they were singing—or she was mostly and sometimes he would join in, but his voice was changing and would break and he was so easy and at home with her that they would both laugh when that happened. He must have known she cared about him to let her laugh at him like that.

"And when they come in off the lake . . ."

It was right about here that I got stuck. Somewhere in here. I remember his talking about Mercy Seat, and then there was a low place covered with water that I thought I could get through easily enough; but the briars and dead horse fennel were thick in the ditches and leaning over the edges of the road and I didn't see that at one side there was a cave-off. Before I knew what had happened, the front axle was resting on the road and the right front wheel was spinning in the air over the cave-off.

I turned up the volume on the CB so I wouldn't miss a word he said and got out to look. I wanted to hear him and I wanted to shut him up both at once, but most to *shut him up*. All the time I was looking for the quickest way to get out of there, he kept talking, talking, his voice all around me, staticky and loud, but plodding and expressionless as if he were proceeding from one point to the next in a checklist. I thought for a minute that I would have to leave the truck and start out after him running; I didn't think I could stand to keep on listening. But I still wasn't sure where he was or how far away—not more than a mile, I guessed, because his voice was coming in strong, but I wasn't sure from what direction.

I got the jack out and jacked up the front axle and then, working as if I might die if I didn't get finished and get moving again, I shoved everything I could find under the wheel, kicked in gravel that just skittered off into the ditch, and then threw in sticks and branches and even found myself pulling weeds and briars to throw under there, and my hands and arms were scratched and bleeding. Then I saw a length of tree limb as thick as my trunk lying half in the ditch and half in the road and I dragged it to the hole and shoved it under the wheel and then I got back in the truck and backed off the jack and out of the hole and started after him again, leaving the jack lying in the middle of the road.

But I stopped and backed up and got it, because I thought I might get stuck again and I meant to get to him.

And all the time he had been going on, talking, talking.

"And when they come in off the lake, I followed them up to the edge of the stand of pines that stops just on the northeast side of the horse lot and I saw Alan go on into the house and she went across the back and headed for Sam's house and I circled around behind the garden watching, because the woods come almost up to the yard all around the house and there are horse and cow paths you can follow easy without being seen.

"I circled around, looking into the yard while she was walking across, and I still ached all over thinking about her out in the canoe with him and how I would like to paddle her up the creek and show her the things I knew—things he never could see or wouldn't know about that I had learned for myself or that my mother had showed me in the woods, because she knew all kinds of stuff that her mother, who'd been an herb doctor, had taught her. I would show her the maypop flowers that some people call passion flowers and those orange mushrooms like little fans that look so poisonous and taste so good and puff balls as big as round loaves of brown bread in the pastures. . . . And then I wondered if she would care about things like that, but I was sure she would, because if she didn't she would never be riding the woods alone and sitting by the creek with her feet in the water watching the bass fingerlings and not even fishing.

"So I was jealous and envious and that was my first sin. But it wasn't much of a sin. I was a kid, remember—a kid in love and no place to put it. But feeling so raw and aching like that, I got

278

around to the side of the yard where the woods push in toward Sam's house and she was already there sitting on his porch talking to him.

"He was tall then and instead of thick through the waist like he is now from not being able to get out and exercise, he was strong— tough and long in the leg and thigh and just beginning to get heavy.

"I never told myself the lies people tell themselves about niggers —not even when I was a kid. Oh, I see well enough how it happens. Any kid listens to what his mother says or what his daddy says and takes it in and believes it and that's all there is to it. Why not? Almost everything your daddy or your mother tells you is true and most of it is useful. Like, Don't touch that, it's hot. Look both ways before you cross the street and don't stick your finger in that socket, you'll get a shock, and so forth. And when they say niggers are ugly because their skin is dark and because they have thick lips and flat noses, you believe it the same way you believe the other. And I suppose that's the way you get all your opinions about everything—although nobody wants to admit it. Everybody wants to believe that what *he* thinks is right and true. Lorene says about things like that that if it's important enough, God will come to you some way and tell you whatever you need to know—count on Him and forget your mother and daddy. And that's what I mean to do, if He will just come and tell me. But the truth is I believe the reason I never thought niggers were ugly was because my mother and father disagreed about niggers and, that way, I had a choice about what I would think. And although I went to the meetings, it was a game to me, like something you were expected to do when you were grown—like sitting in front of a TV set watching football games and drinking beer. Men just *did* it.

"And that's another thing. I think it was a game to some of them, too. They did it like they did the football and baseball, because it was what they were expected to do. And then it turned into something else and some of them were bewildered and ashamed. But their daddies had said: This is true. Do this. And how could they turn their backs and shame their daddies and call them sinners and criminals? They had to go on.

"So, anyhow, what I thought about Sam was that he was tall and strong and he knew everything about the woods, just like my mother did, and he made a kid like me look like *nothing*. And how well he could ride a horse and he had been in the army and I had heard about him winning the medal and all—everybody had. And I knew he had plenty of cows and knew more about raising cows than anybody, because people would ask his advice and quote him. And the color of his skin was nothing to me and I believed that *she* thought the same way I did, so I must have thought it would be nothing to her, too.

"I watched them on his porch together. I was too far off to hear anything they said, just their voices talking to each other in an easy quiet way about something. She would talk awhile and he would answer and shake his head and smile and you could tell he was saying, *No,* and then she got up and leaned over him and pointed her finger at him like she was lecturing him and put her finger on his chest, and he kept on shaking his head and laughed. She frowned and you could tell she was playing like she was mad— *flirting*—and she turned her back on him and I had the sights on her, her long legs with the fine blond hairs glittering against her tan skin, and her shoulders—oh, I liked the way she carried one shoulder a little bit forward, like she would fight anybody. And then she turned around and raised her voice and I could hear her say, 'But I *want* to, Sam. And you ought to want to. And tonight. . . .' That was all I heard.

"Want to *what?* Tonight *what?* That was what I wanted to know.

"All afternoon she'd been with Alan and now here she was arranging something or other with Sam. I knew there wasn't but one thing made a woman flirt with a man. I felt my throat dry up so that I was almost suffocating. I hadn't had a drink of water all afternoon following her around the lake. And now dusk would be coming on soon and the mosquitoes and gnats had already begun to come down like they do that time of day and I was hot and dry; and while I was watching, miserable, a woman (his wife, she was, although I didn't know it at the time. I'd never paid any attention before—didn't even know if he lived by himself or with a woman or what), anyhow she came out with two glasses in her hands and so they were sitting there drinking something—Cokes or lemonade, I suppose—and laughing and arguing and the woman went back in the house and maybe she didn't even notice what seemed too obvious to me.

"One thing that made me feel so awful was that she was flirting with him. She never did that with Alan. But she was wheedling something out of him, I could tell it.

"I couldn't look at them anymore. I dropped back into the woods and cut out for the church, slapping mosquitoes, hot, aching. And when I got there, Lindsay Lee was already there and my daddy was mad at me because I was late and he couldn't yell at me because people were walking around below us on the parking lot and the meeting was about to start. The cars were mostly already there. Lindsay Lee and him had written the licenses down. And he knocked the shit out of me, gave me a slap on the side of the head that laid me flat for not doing what I was supposed to do; and then he went on off, circling around, to the back of the church to watch from the Duck Pond side and pick up the numbers on the back lot. My head was ringing and my eyeballs hot.

"I'm almost through. Come on. Come on and get me."

I felt as if his voice were inside the grinding engine of the pulpwood truck. I wanted to stop the truck and open the hood and rip out the wires and smash the connections that kept his voice going on and on.

As if he knew what I was thinking, he was silent for a minute. Static roared in my ears.

"I'm here where I watched her and Alan that day," he said.

"I know where you are now," I said. "I know. I'm coming."

"Here they came down the road.

"I had my sights trained on Mercy Seat Road where it veered off from the road into Homochitto. The light was treacherous, like it is that time of evening, after the sun is down and before dark, so I was concentrating on what I was doing. My head hurt, but I wasn't mad with *him*. I'd been late, so it wasn't surprising he hit me. I meant to put the afternoon out of my mind and get a good look at whoever was in every car that come toward the church and then, after they turned in, to try to see the license.

"And here they come. I could see them already a long way off. She was riding in the front seat by him. I saw him and then her through the sights of the gun and I didn't even see the wife in the back. To me it was the two of them alone together.

"Lindsay Lee was crouched down by me looking through the sights of his twenty-two and he said, 'That's Sam Daniels.'

"I didn't answer.

" 'Look at that, will you? He's got a white girl riding in the front seat right by him.'

"Riding in the front seat together was a big thing, a sign you believed in race-mixing and all.

"I didn't say anything. I had the sights first on him and then on her. They were still a quarter of a mile away.

" 'What do you reckon they're doing out riding together like that?' Lindsay Lee said. 'Ain't that one of them Chipmans?' "

"They were coming closer fast.

"What I'm doing now is telling the world what I did when I was a fifteen-year-old kid. Exactly what I did.

"While I was looking, shifting the sights back and forth from him to her, she leaned over toward him, flirting still, it looked like, and laid her hand on his arm.

" 'Look at that,' Lindsay Lee said, whispering right in my ear. 'She *touched* him. Look!'

"I squeezed down.

"I must have meant to do it. I didn't mean to do it.

"I remember now how when you put the cross hairs on a slope and squeeze down, you forget for a minute it's a man. And you know it isn't a mistake, that if you don't do it first, he will.

"Why had I left the gun loaded? When did I take the safety off?

"The windshield exploded, glass flashing in the air, and it was like looking at a flock of birds through the scope, very close and very far away. You see every detail for one second, better than if you were three feet off, and then a blur—it's gone. I felt like every piece of flying glass was coming straight at me, but as far away as shooting stars.

"I heard Lindsay Lee saying, 'Jesus Christ, Dallas. Jesus *Christ*.'

"In the church the people were singing.

"Everything was over before I knew what I had done. The car was at the bottom of the ravine and we were up there on the bluff and Lindsay Lee was staring at me and pointing and saying, 'You!'

"We could see down into the ravine, we could see it all. We saw him jerk the door off the car and pull her out and when the car begun to burn, we could smell meat cooking and I didn't know what it was until afterwards, because I never realized she—his wife —was in the backseat.

"That was when Lindsay Lee left, when we begun to smell that.

"By that time Daddy had left where he was and circled around and come up on us from behind. He walked right up on me and leaned down and picked up the gun and ejected the shell casing and sniffed at the barrel, and then he looked at me and didn't say a word. He'd heard the shot, of course, had heard the car crashing down into the ravine. He looked at me and I looked at him and the tires had begun to burn now and the stink was everywhere and people were coming out of the church, running around yelling like niggers do.

"Finally he said, 'Where's your brother?'

" 'Took off. Probably home by now.'

" 'Go home,' he said. 'And don't say nothing about this. You understand? You been fishing today. You hadn't been with me and Lindsay Lee. I'm going to move my car farther off and then I'm going after Lindsay Lee.' And he left. But it's my opinion he never caught up with Lindsay Lee or said a word to him, that night or later.

"I didn't go home. I stayed and watched it all.

"That was the way it happened. And I carried it with me ever since, carried it by myself, because Lindsay Lee forgot and I never told my mother and my daddy never said a word and I could look at him and see he never meant to say a word, and my mother died and the next year he married and went off and I joined the army and I carried it to Basic and to AIT and then I carried it to Nam and brought it home and then I give it to Lorene to help me carry because we were married and I give her all I had which included that.

"And after more than a year went by and I couldn't . . . At first I could and she got pregnant, but then, later, no, I couldn't. It was like a curse on me, my manhood left me.

"And I had thought, to begin with, that it would be enough to confess it to her and to God and to pray over it, but still the Spirit wouldn't come down.

"And during that time—it was after the kid was born—I told her that I knew what I was like, that I knew my soul was treacherous and full of rage and hate, that I could do terrible things—even to my own boy or maybe to her—and it was then that we decided I would have to go and make it right with the people I had wronged, or I would never come through. And so I'm telling, everything, everything, because that's the only way."

TWENTY-NINE

HIS VOICE stopped. He had finished. He was waiting and I knew where he was. There was only one place where you could look out over the dam and lake, turn and look the other way over the horse lot and the roofs of the house and outbuildings, turn again and look down on the pool below the spillway and the ravine that wound away to the south.

When he stopped talking, I was driving toward his voice along an oil field road on the east side of the lake. A quarter of a mile from the lake, where the road intersected the fire lane, I left the truck; ran down the fire lane, jumping puddles and mud holes; climbed the SPASURSTA fence, dodging through fields of antennae, stooping to go under the trestles that supported the SPASURSTA cables, shining and coiling blackly around their uprights; climbed the fence on the other side, ran on along the fire lane where Lester and I had walked and talked about the wonders and dangers of the modern world; and came out on the dam.

The lake spread away in its valley, bigger than I'd ever seen it, lapping within a foot of the dam's top. The wind was out of the north now and choppy waves struck again and again at the dam, leaching the mud from the grass roots all along the slope.

I saw Sam and Leila standing on the dam. If I had thought about it, I would have known they might be there—they'd said they were going first to see how much damage the hail had done to Noah's roof and to check the pond behind his house; and that then they would go to look at the lake.

But I had not thought about them or Noah's pond or his roof. I had not thought about anything since I had begun to listen to Dallas's voice on the CB. I had fought the truck and looked for Dallas and I had not thought anything, except that I would find him and shut him up.

On the point of land that jutted up to the southwest of the lake I saw a huge old beech tree, its crown chestnut-brown among the green pines. Dallas stood, his back against its mottled bole, waiting.

I ran toward him, not even glancing at Sam and Leila as I ran, hearing their voices, snatches of words that I paid no attention to.

". . . spillway . . ."

"Wait! Alan!"

And then: ". . . rain. If the wind . . ."

Sam grabbed my arm as I came even with them and stopped me short. "The berm's washed out," he said. "Look! Give us a hand with the gate valve. Frozen."

The dam that makes our lake lies across the mouth of a small valley, with the curve of Chickasaw Ridge enclosing it on three sides. Like most of the small earth dams constructed by the U.S. engineers during the fifties, it has a berm running along its downstream face at a gradual slope from the top at one side to the bottom at the other, its purpose to lead off the rain that would otherwise erode the dam face. Sometime that winter, long before the storm, the low wall of the berm must have given way; and for months rain had been coursing through the break, straight down the slope, eating out and enlarging a channel and, where the spillway culvert jutted out, a hole in the dam's side. Masked by tall grass and briars, the channel and the hole had been invisible from above. But last night's storm had widened and deepened the breach, uprooted and swept away the briars, and exposed the gaping hole just above the spillway, big enough to drop a couple of cars into.

This is what Leila and Sam had found when they had come to look at the lake after their visit to Noah.

When Leila saw that huge hole (she told me afterwards), she began to feel as if the dam were made of jelly. It quaked underfoot.

On the upstream side the mud slipped away from the grass roots and the water continued to rise. The wind was blowing, cold and damp. The sun shone; the sky above the lake was clear; but there were clouds piled up in the southwest. Was it going to rain again? If the dam broke with the water at this level, the house would go. Calloway's store, the Calloway house, and all the houses along the creek below Calloway's would go, too. She and Sam had not said much to each other before they decided to open the gate valve on the spillway and lower the level of the lake as fast as possible to take the pressure off the dam.

The gate valve hadn't been opened in years. I remember once, when I was a kid, Sam had opened it and lowered the water to kill out the water hyacinths that were beginning to grow around the edges and interfere with the bass fishing. But no one I'd ever talked with except Lester had given a thought to the possibility that the dam might *break*.

So, when I came out on the dam, Sam and Leila had been struggling with the wheel that raised the gate in the spillway. But the gate was frozen, rusted tight to the culvert.

I didn't give a shit what they were doing. I hardly saw them. All I wanted was to get my hands on Dallas Boykin's throat. I could feel the emptiness aching in the palms of my hands where I wanted his throat to be.

Sam was holding me, shaking me, but I gave him a kick in the shins, broke loose, ran on, and scrambled across the briary ground where the dam joined the upward sloping area below the point. Leila was still yelling, something about a crowbar.

Dallas was above me. He had not moved. When he heard me crashing through the briars, he turned and looked down to see who was coming and then was still again. He did not speak. I stumbled over a fallen limb and sprawled headlong on the flat ground at his feet, my face in the wet pine needles and brown beech leaves and the wet pine-smelling dirt. I got up and stood, breathing heavily, facing him.

He was wearing a worn army issue windbreaker, his hands in the pockets, and faded khaki pants as mottled as the bole of the tree. He looked at me out of alert brown fox eyes and leaned against the tree under the arch of a cave of dead beech leaves, like a brown den in the stirring March woods; and he was as still as a squirrel watching a hunter pass by. Then he drew a deep sighing breath and took his hands out of his pockets.

"I've got a crowbar in the pickup," he said. "That's what they're yelling about. They need a crowbar. Maybe we ought to go help them first."

"First?" I said. *"First?"* My face was wet with mud and tears. I saw Phoebe, dancing barefoot under the black starry sky. "Oh, Alan," she said, "I want to do something *grand."*

"First I'll kill you," I said.

"Lead me in a plain path, O Lord," he said.

"Shut up," I said.

I don't remember throwing myself at him, just the jar of our bodies when I hit him and he hit the tree. Then we were on the ground and he was lying under me, lying still. I thought I'd knocked him out.

We were almost nose to nose, lying there, and he was perfectly still and I reached for his throat like I had been wanting to do and he didn't raise his hands, but he looked at me and I saw that he was not knocked out and then he said, "Forgive . . ." That was all he said. Then he closed his mouth and his eyes and was silent.

We were at the edge of the bluff and I could feel us beginning to slide. My left foot struck a root and I jammed my heel against it and gave myself a shove to get more purchase on him, got to my knees, grabbed the front of his jacket, shook him as hard as I could, and slammed him against the ground. I would make him knock off that shit.

He opened his eyes. "Forgive . . ."

"Shut up, shut up, shut up, *shut up."*

I threw myself on him again and got my hands around his neck and started to drag him back, but he hooked his foot under a root and said in a strangled voice, "This is where the Spirit brought me and this is where I stay."

The ground, heavy with the night's rain, began to shift. I tried again to drag him back, and while we were scrabbling and struggling in the mud and pine needles, the bluff caved away under us and we fell five or six feet to a shelf supported by the network of beech tree roots. Mud and gravel rolled down around us and down the bluff below us to the floor of the ravine.

He was on top of me now, but I was holding him by the throat and we were nose to nose and he was still passive.

I squeezed as hard as I could and his eyes bugged out at me and his legs began to thrash and he made a terrible gargling noise. He reached between my arms with both his hands and jerked outward and at the same time one of his thrashing legs caught me in the groin and I let out a scream and let go of his neck and grabbed my balls. Pain, like fire, burned through my belly and legs and I doubled up and moaned and thought I would vomit, but I didn't.

He rolled off of me and hitched himself to the back of the shelf beside me. " 'Thy will be done,' " he said, " 'on earth as it is in heaven.' I didn't mean to do that."

I couldn't move. If I could have moved, I would have kicked him off the shelf and jumped on top of him. All I could think was: *Shut up, shut up, shut up.* And then, *Wait a minute. I can move in a minute. In a minute I can kill you.*

Below us the bluff dropped six or eight feet to the next narrow shelf, held in place by twisting tree roots, ferns, hydrangeas, and moss, the old foliage earth-colored, streaked with yellow clay, dripping with rain, the pale scrolls of new fern fronds rising from black rosettes of last year's leaves. A third drop sloped to the pool where the spillway, day in, day out, delivered its trickle of water. The pool now was deeper than usual, the flooded spillway delivering its maximum flow; and the water coursing along the creek bed was thigh-deep instead of ankle-deep, the runoff from the night's rain still draining into it all along the channel.

My mouth was against the piny mud, my teeth and tongue gritty with raw fungus-tasting earth. I saw the pool and the creek through a yellowish haze, as if my liver had burst and spilled its bile all through my body.

From far away I heard Sam's voice: "Alan? What the *hell* . . . ? What the *hell* you doing? Dallas, where is your pickup?"

I felt the cramps ease in my legs and belly. I sat up and then stood up and looked at Dallas, and he was as yellow as Noah's eyeballs. My hands, as if they had their own will, grabbed him by the throat again and he put his arms around me, as if he were embracing me. The muscles in his arms and shoulders had been made by ten years of operating a chain saw and a winch and lifting and stacking the sawed wood to load onto a truck and when he squeezed my arms, my hands had to relax. As he held me, he began to talk into my ear.

"I'm holding you," he said. "You might not *want* to kill me. The Spirit tells me that you might not want to kill me. Think about it while I'm holding you. You might be sorry afterwards."

"A *crowbar* . . ." Sam yelled. *"Goddamn . . . !"*

Dallas continued to hold onto me, but I was beginning to feel the strength come back into my legs.

As if we were engaged in the most ordinary casual conversation there on the ledge, he raised his voice and called to Sam, "I got a crowbar in the toolbox in the back of my truck. Yonder, on the other side of the point."

"What's going on? Get *over* here, Alan! We *need* you, damn it."

"He thinks he wants to kill me," Dallas said. "But maybe . . ."

I shifted all my weight to my left leg, kneed him in the belly, and broke loose and we were teetering and staggering on the ledge, green new moss spongy underfoot, and then we were slipping down the muddy incline, checked for a moment by the next shelf, but then sliding into the pool.

(He and I had made a mud slide one year when we were kids—had it been here or farther up the creek?—that we'd lined with clay and made slippery with water and hurled ourselves down again and again on hot summer afternoons, into the lake, a breathless slide and then, under the burning sky, the water, warm at the surface, and below, mild and cool against our bodies; and we were as native to it as tadpoles.)

We were in the pool, in the icy water, and my legs and thighs and balls shriveled and the cold rose up through my belly toward my head and my head was ice, my brain a labyrinth of ice, and I was killing him again.

"I'm not going to stop you anymore," he said.

I had him by the throat and we were sinking deeper into the pool, thigh-deep and belly-deep on me and almost shoulder-deep on him, sliding through the mud, as fine and soupy as the finest clay slip; and he was passive, looking at me and then closing his eyes and saying no more. I pushed him under and held him and he didn't struggle against me. I held him away from me, so that he couldn't get his arms around me, but he didn't try.

I thought a long time had passed and I pulled him up, but he hadn't breathed in any water. He took a deep gasping breath.

"I'm going to drown you," I said. "You won't go to Heaven. You'll be dead."

His brown eyes were as steady, as secret, as fearless as the eyes of a trapped fox waiting for you to club him. I pushed him under again.

My hands held him and were not part of me and I was like an icicle with hands and ears and eyes. Hands not part of me, but bands of burning ice, frozen, sealed to his throat. Ears that heard the faintest crackle in the feathers of the red-tailed hawk that tilted away against the wind high above the dam, heard Sam's voice amplified and echoing from the hills like a blast: Ha! Ha! among the trumpets, he was laughing; heard the gate valve inside the culvert shriek with the thin sound of the highest note on a violin. And eyes as clear and cold and fiery as a laser of ice penetrating the water, seeing Dallas under my hands: he looked at me through the black moving water, looked at me with his dumb fox eyes and gave himself to me.

Leila was crashing through the briars on the side of the dam, yelling, "Alan! Stop!"

I heard everything, saw everything, as Dallas had said he saw the glass in the shattered windshield, clear and close, and at the same time infinitely far away.

Now Sam was back at the wheel that opened the gate valve, bending to it, and I could see the hunch of his back and he was yelling again, "Let 'em fight. Hadn't got time for *them*. We got to get this spillway *open*."

And Leila: "Knock it off and get *out* of there."

And then Sam: "Look out! It's *moving*."

And Leila! "He's *killing* . . ."

And Sam: "Get on up here, Leila, if you don't want to go for a swim. It's *moving*."

Leila was screaming again and Sam was laughing, "Ha! Ha!" and "This'll cool 'em off. Let 'em try to drown each other and swim at the same time."

The gate valve moved, the metal screamed, we slipped deeper into the pool, and under my hands in the water Dallas shifted and sank lower, and he must have doubled up and gotten a purchase on the bottom of the pool, because he came surging up out of the water like a hooked bass trying to throw the hook and grabbed

290

me again around the arms and I felt my hold giving way, my hands loosening, and concentrated all my strength on holding him and pushing him down again.

"No!" he said. And then, "Lorene!" in a gargling yell, and then, "*I* say, *No!*" and we were nose to nose once more and my hands slipped, no matter how hard I tried to hold him and push him down, and he said, hoarse and strangled, "I got to raise my kid."

The water hit us like a wall falling on us and tore us apart.

Took us both in the chest and knocked us down and sent us crashing and tumbling across the pool into the ravine. No way to swim in that. I went with the water, not resisting, taking a breath as I went. I could still hear Sam laughing. Submerged, battered, scraped along the bottom, I used my foot to shove myself up for a breath, popped out in a thrashing flood of water and tree limbs, and was pulled under again as if a huge hand had grabbed both my feet.

The next time I popped up, Dallas was washing along next to me, floating face-up, eyes closed, a gaping cut open to the bone above his left eye.

I knew he was dead. A horrible pain, unassuageable grief, seized me, worse than any kick in the balls, worse than any ice pick in my liver. I had killed him.

I grabbed him, embraced him with both arms, kicked out as hard as I could, shifted, got one arm across his chest, let go with the other, and took a strong stroke. Then we were rolling and tumbling in the current. I thought my face was in air, took a gasping breath, but the last half was water and I was choking and retching and still holding him against me, filled with a grief so deep that I knew it would never leave me. I had killed him.

I was still holding him against me when we came up with a crash against a log in the ravine below the pool, a log that had been entirely out of water a few minutes earlier and now was half submerged, one end floating low in the water, one still resting on the steep bank. The log trembled and held and the current held us against it. I grabbed a jutting stub of a limb with my free hand and pulled us along toward the bank, the current dragging at my feet and legs. The log trembled. Dallas was limp against my side, a dead weight. I held him locked against me. I pulled us along again and then I saw Sam crashing down the bank toward us.

"Hang on! Wait . . ."

He was reaching out toward us, the log shifted, and we were torn loose and rolling in the water again, but only for a minute or two. Around the next bend Leila was waiting for us. The ravine widened slightly here, and the water spread and moved more steadily along. I kicked out, trying to head us for the bank, and saw her. She had slid down the side of the ravine below the point where Sam had reached out to us, and now she was lying on another log, this one still just above water level and spanning the creek from bank to bank. She was straddling it, heavy and solid as a man, her legs wrapped around it, her feet locked together, reaching toward us as we swept down.

I gave a kick and reached toward her with my free hand and we seized each other, hand to wrist in the childhood basket carry. Again I gave a kick, feeling her strength and the power in my legs surge together.

"Take him!"

I let go of her and she let go of me and at the same time she grabbed him with both arms and pulled him across the log. The current, the water rising, the log beginning now to submerge, held us pinned.

"Go back. I can make it. Drag him back."

She started working herself backwards off the log, dragging him, his face in the water on one side and his body on the other, the water now lapping at the top of the log. I swung myself astraddle the log and gave his limp body a shove and humped along behind them. The log shifted and trembled in the current.

And then Sam was behind her and he had jerked her back and picked Dallas up as easily as if he were a small forked branch and reached out to me, and I was off the log and we were scrambling up the bank.

Behind us the water was tumbling and roaring like a shallow river in the mountains and the log we'd been on rose and swung and the bank crumbled and the log was out in the current bucking and plunging, and then it was gone.

Dallas lay on the ground, the blood welling out of the cut on his forehead, and when I saw the blood flow, I knew he might not be dead. The blood poured down his face. Sam knelt beside him and put him straight and began to breathe into his mouth. I tore off the tail of my shirt and folded it and squatted down and held it against the cut and Leila tore off a piece of her shirt and we put together a pressure bandage for his head and while we were doing that, he choked and retched and began to breathe for himself.

Sam wrapped him in his coat and picked him up and we started toward Leila's car and he opened his eyes and looked at us.

"I can't do that, Lorene," he said. "Oh, I wish I could." And then he said again, as he had in the pool, "I got to raise my kid."

THIRTY

FINISHING my cabin that spring, I spent some time thinking about the future. I knew I would never go back to shoveling sugar and shit and, despite Uncle Lester's recommendation, Penney's stores were no more to my taste than the caverns of Israel Putnam's sugar refinery. I decided to acquire a skill.

I persuaded my father to finance me in a course in welding at the local "industrial college" and to lend me five thousand dollars to buy a used Lincoln welding machine, a used truck, a cutting torch, and some tools. I made myself—I was going to write "a free man," but that, of course, is not true. I made it possible to spend considerable time writing.

As soon as I could make a respectable weld, I quit the course, went down to Morgan City, Louisiana, and spent four months in the yards there fabricating an offshore oil rig. At ten dollars an hour, ten hours a day, I could gross twenty-five hundred a month; and I could live on four hundred. I paid my debt to my father, traded my truck for a better one, bought some more tools, and came back to Homochitto. Here I can earn enough in four or five months, working on pulpwood trucks and oil field equipment, to do as I like (if I'm reasonably frugal) for the rest of the year. Occasionally, for extra capital, I go down to New Orleans and sign on as a welder on the offshore rigs for a month. Sometimes I wander for a month or two. One spring and summer I spent in Italy, mostly looking at churches. I thought a lot about Noah. There is a church in San Gemignano I would like to show him, with tales of the Old Testament laid out on the walls like an immense comic strip. He would especially like the panel of the crossing of the Red Sea—all those Egyptians drowning in droves. *The four hundred years is up, boss man.*

But except for an occasional trip out into the world, I stay here. This is where I live. My family likes having me here—my presence discourages poachers and wandering kids who might set fire to the woods. And, as I said, there is more than enough welding to keep me busy.

So I've joined the human race in its despoliation of the earth. Because, although the pulpwood trucks I work on belong mostly to poor men, ultimately, like them, I'm working for the International Paper Company and the Georgia Pacific. Or, if I'm in the oil fields, for Exxon and Cities Service.

No occupation for a poet? For a man who likes to sit on the ground and observe the chipmunks? Who hates compromise and wants to keep his purity?

But I knocked off being pure the day I strangled Dallas.

My hero—the *boy*—Alan—still dreams of solutions to moral problems, of doing time and being free. Who doesn't?

But free of using paper and gasoline?

Writing this, I've asked myself over and over what I should have him *do*—my hero. It's clear he's not ready for the crystal bed of perfect love. He has yet to earn it. Shall I send him in search of clear choices and heroic deeds? To Chile to rescue political dissidents? To Israel to join a kibbutz? To Jordan to join the PLO? Should I have him starve to death like Simone Weil? Give ten dollars to the Southern Poverty Law Center? Volunteer to work for the United Givers?

It is only in certain kinds of stories that you can pull off the kind of sacrifice Faulkner used in *The Bear* when he had Ike McCaslin give away his tainted inheritance and become a humble carpenter. Noah might put that in one of his stories, but I can't put it in mine.

Besides, my hero and I *like* to weld. It's pleasant work in the winter when the weather is cold. In the spring and summer and early fall we can throw off the asbestos gloves and heavy protective gear and spend our time gardening and fishing and writing.

And, as it has turned out, surprisingly perhaps, we not only like welding, we're good at it.

It's a solitary craft. Cut off from the outside world by the roar of the engine, the enclosing blindness of the helmet, we start up the machine and lose ourselves in the work, watching the miniature sun at the tip of the rod send tiny planets of glowing metal ricocheting in every direction through the vaporizing slag, the cosmic dust cloud.

Like knitting, welding is a soothing, repetitive occupation. Like drawing, it requires the kind of hand-eye coordination and manual dexterity that one develops and refines with practice; like painting watercolors, it requires a confident, decisive hand: you can't very easily go back and repair an error; you must be in control of every subtle change in the angle of the electrode and of that blinding six thousand degrees of heat and the stunning amperage and voltage of your machine.

The way time and space work in welding is interesting, too. You move the rod along and lay a bead at precisely the right speed and arc length. Getting more skillful doesn't make it possible to move faster. If you slow down or shorten the arc, like Phaeton driving Apollo's chariot, you may burn up the work; and if you move too fast or lengthen the arc, the weld doesn't make. Everything depends on a steady, timed, accurate sweep.

So we weld and write—not poems anymore, but stories and this record. We think about inching into a situation that might be a tad more comfortable for the moralist. Instead of welding for Exxon and Georgia Pacific, maybe we will design and build things like wood-burning heaters that people can use to warm their houses. Because that's what we like best of all about welding—making a design and taking a pile of scraps and making of it something useful and clean and pleasing to look at.

There were other questions besides what I was to do about earning a living and making a life that I asked that spring after Leila and Sam pulled Dallas and me out of the creek—some that I asked of myself and a few that I asked of other people.

Leila, for instance.

"Where do you *think* they were going?" she said, when I asked her. "To the meeting at Mercy Seat, of course. And of *course* Lester knew about it—afterwards. Everybody eventually knows everything around here. You can count on that."

Everybody but me, I said to myself. Sometimes it seemed to me as if I'd closed myself into a space as blind as the space inside my helmet before the rod begins to glow.

And then I went to see Noah and told him all that Dallas had said. He was the one who told me how Lester knew.

"I told him," he said. "Ain't he suppose to know the truth about how his own daughter die? I didn't say Dallas Boykin done it. Far as that goes, I didn't know 'twas him. I just knew they was *up* there. Anybody walked around in the woods the next day knew Ku Kluxers was up there. And strictly speaking, Alan, 'twasn't Dallas done it. Not by himself, anyhow. 'Twas all them Ku Kluxers together put him up on that hill."

"Why were you walking around in the woods the next day?" I said.

"The shot," he said. "I thought I heard a shot. Where'd it come from? We knew some of them Holy Rollers had been watching us. Who was it aimed at? But I didn't ask myself that. I knew it must've been aimed at Sam, if they seen him and Phoebe riding together in the front seat."

"Nobody else heard a shot," I said.

"*Maybe* nobody else heard it. They was singing and all. Or maybe nobody else wanted to hear it. Far as we knew, it could've been the sheriff himself up there.

"But let me tell you, Alan, my ears as sharp as they was fifty years ago. Don't much pass me by. And I want to know what's going on. So I went up there and looked and I saw where they'd been. And I went to town and told Lester Chipman my knowledge before they buried her and Timmie.

"He didn't want to hear it. 'Let it lay,' he says. 'You think I can take on the Klan? I got Denny and my boys to think about. Let it lay.' That's what he says, 'And besides,' he says, 'you ain't nothing but a crazy old man. A crazy old nigger.' That's what he told me. 'And furthermore, don't tell Sam, neither. He don't need to go running around the county killing Ku Kluxers and getting himself killed.'

"That's how come Lester Chipman feels so bad toward us," Noah said. "That's how come he's always talking about us being worthless and treacherous and all." He looked at me, his eyes, his face cold and detached, but at the same time full of the interested concern of the surgeon in the operating room.

"Well," he went on, "I thought about it and I says to myself, What about Sam? Am I going to tell Sam?"

"Did you?" I said.

He shook his head. "Sam was buried in grief," he said. "I saw he was sunk into a black grief. I was afraid to rouse him up." He shrugged. "Lester Chipman was right, for once," he said. "Sam woulda been raging over the county, killing Kluxers, getting himself and God knows who else killed. You seen for yourself what happen later when your *auntee* and Lester Chipman checked his will regarding that SPASURSTA."

"It seems like you or somebody might've told *me* about all that, Noah," I said. "All the time hinting at this and that and giving me looks and making me feel bad. Why not talk straight out about it?"

"You're still thinking only about yourself, ain't you, son?" Noah said. "Stop and consider. When you come down here this winter, what I actually *know* about you—now you're a man? If you expect somebody to talk to you, you got to tell them who you is. Teach 'em to trust you. All you ever done with me was throw me a bone every now and then—show me off to your girl friend."

It was later, much later, that I talked with Sam about that time, although questions I *wanted* to ask him stayed constantly on my mind. Like Noah, I feared the consequences of his wrath—even this late in the day. I still did not tell him Dallas's story.

But I was sitting by his fire one winter night a couple of years ago talking about fences and washouts and cattle and pigs (with his advice to help me, I was raising a pig for meat that winter) when I saw a thirty-aught-six shell casing on his mantelpiece and, beside it, a little lump of lead very much like a leaden mushroom with the brass jacket of the bullet for a stem.

I had gotten up from my chair to poke his fire and put on a

fresh log when I saw them. (I can build as good a fire as Sam now and split wood *almost* as fast, and he watches me with pride and no longer advises me about not letting the cedar pop.) I turned the back log and raked in the unburned ends of kindling that had fallen on either side of the dogs and laid on a piece of oak. Then I put down the poker and picked up the shell casing and the spent bullet and turned them over in my hands and stared at them. I knew Sam didn't have a thirty-aught-six.

I thought about Dallas's gun and about the spot on the bluff where Dallas and Lee had lain to shoot. I thought about the ejected shell casing and about the bullet burying itself in the up-holstered seat of the car, maybe striking against the steel frame, about the car burning and the bullet dropping through to the ground. I held the mushroom of lead and brass in my hand and looked at it and saw that the creases in the lead were lined with black.

I looked at Sam and he cocked his good eye at me, the lid drooping over the bad one (he only wears his Hathaway-Shirt-Man eye patch when Leila comes down) and for a moment said nothing. Then he reached out to me and I handed him the bullet and the casing.

"A thirty-aught-six is a good gun for shooting varmints and wild dogs," he said, "but I never have had one. I like my old seven-millimeter Mauser."

"Yeah," I said.

"I don't know why I've kept these so long," he said. "I haven't got any use for them."

So long?

"Since the summer of 'sixty-four," he said.

"Sam," I said, "I *know.*"

"Yeah?" he said.

The fire snapped and glowed and the back log broke and collapsed inward.

"Summer of 'sixty-four it wasn't only black churches like Mercy Seat got burned up," he said.

Sam! I did not say it.

"That shouting church there on the edge of town, you know the one I'm talking about? Between Old Man Griffin's cornfield and that Gulf station?"

"Yeah," I said. "I know that church."

"Used to be frame," he said. "They built the brick one in 'sixty-six. The old one burned."

"I reckon Noah would say it was the vengeance of the Lord," I said.

He rolled the shell casing once between his thumb and fore-finger and threw it in the fire. Then he threw the mushroomed bullet after it. "I thought I'd cleared all the junk off the mantel awhile back," he said.

I came into Homochitto a few days ago, after a month out in the Gulf working on an offshore rig. Before I came home, I'd spent a week in New Orleans with a friend and lover, a woman I met down there a couple of years ago. Her name is Rosa. Yes, in a way she too reminds me of Phoebe. She has that marvelous tall spare graceful body. . . . Hell, she reminds me of all the things I love in all women. She has short curly dark hair like my grandmother's and Leila's and a face as round and pure and lovely as the moon. And like my mother, she's always busy shaping, shaping, molding me and her flower beds and the kids in the community college where she teaches Shakespeare and the two fast-track freshman English classes. Like Miriam, she looks at me with a quizzical eye and smiles, as if to say, Can I help it if I'm smarter than you? With her, I pay attention.

We talk about getting married. I think now that I might be able to love a child, a woman. I can, anyhow, answer one question I asked myself in the course of putting all this down: *No!* I would not be "interested" in watching my fifteen-year-old son or anyone's fifteen-year-old son die of leukemia. But . . . I would use it.

So here I am again. It's the fourth of April today, the most beautiful time of the year. Or is it? May is nice. And June. And October. And November. And then, in January, when it's cold as a witch's tit outdoors, it's nice to hole up here after working all night on an oil rig somewhere nearby. There will be a steady slow fire in my new wood-burning heater, the icy rain sluicing down my gutters. I sleep off the night's work and then I sit at my work-table. (I have made one of cherry cut in my own woods, but I profited from looking at Uncle D.'s over in the big house and did not put the screws in on the top side.) I sit and think and write and look out at the wintry woods, the smilax and jasmine twisting dark green up into the bare trees, the wrens and towhees calling through the rain.

But it's early April now. The dogwood trees are in full bloom; the green light that glows in those pure white petals must be the kind of light that shines in the eyes of God. The yellow jasmine vines and redbud trees flicker with the fire of spring. And down in the bottoms of the deep ravines the swamp maples are flaming, the oak trees tasseling gold. The woods are burning with life.

I went (as I always do when I come back to the cabin) to see Noah yesterday. I think it is more important every year to go to see Noah, to talk with him. He'll be gone—soon. I want to hear everything he has to say before he dies. And he wants to tell me all he knows. Yes, he wants to tell me, so that I will *remember*. He tells me most things over and over to impress them on me, because he is the onliest one left, the onliest one who can tell me.

He's ninety-four now, but he's still spry. Last summer when we were picking plums in the thicket over by the edge of the horse lot (I'd told Denny I'd bring her a bucketful for jelly), he climbed up on the fence to reach the ripe ones on the high branches; straddling the top wire, one leg wrapped around the fence post, he was reaching out for plums with one hand, holding his hat to drop them in with the other, when the post gave way, cracked, and then broke under his weight just below the ground. The fence went down slowly. I was across the thicket, facing him. He didn't exactly fall, but went down as the wire gave with the breaking post, bent his long thin body, and rolled to the ground, holding his hat steady. He didn't spill a plum. Got up and went on picking.

"That post ain't locust," he said. "Sam's boy, son, must've put it in. He don't know locust from chinaberry."

"Are you OK?" I said.

"Ain't I standing here picking plums?"

He had a heart attack last year and while he was in the hospital, he had a vision.

" 'Twas like they didn't know I was alive," he said. "Standing around talking about me and moving me here and yawnder. Seemed like they put me in a box and hook these wires to my ears, sent a shock, like lightning, all through me, and I hear a Voice say, 'Noah. Noah.' And I say, 'Lord, here am I, a *old* man. Ain't it late in the day for You to be speaking to me?"

"But He says, 'Noah, child, I ain't letting one word of yours fall to the ground and that's my promise to you. And I want you to tell that boy of yourn, Alan, all you know. . . .' "

He gave me a sly look.

"Noah!"

"I ain't even hardly *started* telling you all I know," he said.

He was out of the hospital and home in two weeks, plowing his corn in two months.

So I went by to see him yesterday. He told me one story I'd heard and began a new one.

We were talking about Sam, who says he's just about made up his mind that he wants to go to Jackson to the bone doctor and get his hip socket replaced. "Tired of hobbling around on this old cane," he told me. "I'm ready to get a new leg."

"You see how it is," Noah told me. "He's got to do what he does in his own time. He's ready now, so now must be the time. Oh, he's *willful*." And then he told me again about how Sam was Sarah's latest-born child, and how she loved him above all the others and gave him his way. "Don't cross him," he said. "Don't bring his wrath down on you."

He looked at me with a calculating eye, as if to assess whether or not I was ready for the tale he meant to tell me and then he said, "He took it out on them Kluxers, you know. At the time I didn't know it, but it come to me in a vision not so long ago how he took it out on them. In a dream."

"Hmmm," I said.

"Yeah, he tied the torches to the foxes' tails and turned 'em loose in the cornfield. Burnt up the Philistines."

"Hmmm," I said.

"There's a lot more to that story," he said. "One these days I'll tell it to you."

My papers now are spread around me in neat stacks and I am adding a sentence here, a paragraph there, trying to put in everything, to ask and answer as many questions as I can. I can't help feeling the urge of the storyteller to tie up loose ends, to write, "And everybody lived happily (or unhappily) ever after." Plus the urge of the moralist to make his point, of both to give the tale a shape.

But the shape is still changing. Only the finished—the dead—
have a finished shape. Not even the dead, crumbling to earth. As
Noah says, "The earth is strong, boys."

Next year the dead will be flaming in the April trees.